ORIGINAL SINS

ALSO BY PEG KINGMAN

Not Yet Drown'd

W. W. NORTON & COMPANY

NEW YORK · LONDON

ORIGINAL SINS

A NOVEL

PEG
KINGMAN

For information about permission to reproduce selections from this book,
write to Permissions, W. W. Norton & Company, Inc.,
500 Fifth Avenue, New York, NY 10110

For information about special discounts for bulk purchases, please contact
W. W. Norton Special Sales at specialsales@wwnorton.com or 800-233-4830

Manufacturing by Courier Westford
Book design by Barbara M. Bachman
Production manager: Devon Zahn

Library of Congress Cataloging-in-Publication Data

Kingman, Peg.
Original sins : a novel of slavery and freedom / Peg Kingman. — 1st ed.
p. cm.
ISBN 978-0-393-06547-3 (hardcover)
1. Fugitive slaves—Fiction. 2. Missing children—Fiction.
3. Southern States—Fiction. 4. United States—
Social conditions—19th century—Fiction. I. Title.
PS3611.I62O75 2010
813'.6—dc22

                                                    2010006318

W. W. Norton & Company, Inc.
500 Fifth Avenue, New York, N.Y. 10110
www.wwnorton.com

W. W. Norton & Company Ltd.
Castle House, 75/76 Wells Street, London W1T 3QT

1 2 3 4 5 6 7 8 9 0

For my grandfathers:

Kenneth Edward Kingman, 1908–1995, chemical engineer

Frank Wilson Hays, 1910–1989, photographer

ORIGINAL SINS

CHAPTER

1

G RACE HAD IMAGINED DANIEL'S HOMECOMING HUNDREDS
of times; repeatedly she had painted the scene in her mind's eye. It was
one of her favorite thoughts, to be dwelt upon when she could not
sleep; or when she was sad and discouraged; or when some particular
delight befell her which would have been more delightful still if only
Dan had been present to share it.

Always, in her fancy, she had a few delicious hours of anticipation,
for Dan's ship *Rebecca Rolfe* would first be sighted rising imperceptibly
from the flat blue horizon as she entered the broad funnel that was the
mouth of Delaware Bay. She would have been identified by the time she
made the river channel, but her ascent, upon even a flood tide, would
be infuriatingly deliberate; maddeningly stately. And well before she
could anchor off the lazaretto station for her quarantine inspection, a
fast pilot boat would bring the news of her arrival up to Philadelphia.
Grace had been watching the shipping news for long months now,
knowing that Daniel might arrive at any time; he might well even
outpace his final letter from China, the letter that would announce his
embarkation. One day, she fancied, the longed-for words would leap to
her glad thirsty eye from the Arrivals column in the shipping news:
"REBECCA ROLFE, from Canton, 149 days, anchored Lazaretto."

And upon seeing that, in these delightful scenes of her own contriving, Grace would launch her preparations: bath, hair, dress. After
her baby had been born, fifteen months ago, the fantasy had expanded
to accommodate him too: washing his drooly chin and grubby fat
hands, smoothing his downy hair, making sure he was dry and clean,
and telling him once more that Dad, Papa, the father he had never seen
nor imagined nor missed, was coming.

And the house: flowers in a jug (lilacs or roses, lilies or chrysanthemums, depending on the season); floors swept, ashes cleaned out of the fireplace, and a fresh fire laid ready to the spill; a couple of the best cutlets brought in by the butcher's boy. Clean fresh linens on the bed upstairs, where she had been sleeping alone for far too long.

Then her warm fancy would conjure the meeting itself: Oh!—the exquisite instant of the first sight of him, the *darshan*, the actual sensation of himself imprinting on her eyes, filling all her field of vision! At the docks. Then home, inside, door closed, his hands spanning her waist; his arms around her; the pressure of his embrace on her breathless ribs. His neck, the smell of his own hair, the roughness of his shaved-hours-ago cheek. His mouth, lips, breath.

And so on, all of it.

But it happened nothing like that.

AFTER BREAKFAST, AS ALWAYS, Grace Pollocke sat at her desk under the drafty window and attended to the letters and accounts. The collier's account was an unpleasant shock. The spring had been bitterly cold, but had he really delivered so much coal as that? She set it aside, to consider his honesty. Last of all, she replied to her mother-in-law's invitation. Dipping her pen, she scratched out this note:

LOMBARD STREET, PHILADELPHIA
APRIL 22ND, 1840

Dear Mrs Pollocke,

Alas, that I cannot accept your kind invitation!—but a lady is coming to sit to me, whom I may not put off, and so I must decline the pleasure of your Work party this afternoon. Jamie has got a new tooth, and sends his best (and nearly complete) smile to his grandmamma.

Yrs Affctly,
G.P.

The elder Mrs Pollocke's work parties met twice or thrice each week. Occasionally they convened at her house in Race Street; but more often they were hosted by one or another of her circle of elderly female friends, pious stout widows living in well-furnished narrow brick houses. The declared purpose of these work parties was to produce garments for the benefit of that class of people invariably referred to by the elder Mrs Pollocke and her circle as the deserving poor, or—as Grace soon came to think of them (so glib and invariable was the work party's phrase)—the Deserving Poor. A certain quantity of plain needlework was indeed accomplished upon these occasions, but the garments produced were generally of such coarseness, of such unbecoming stuffs and cuts and workmanship, as probably to discourage the Deserving Poor from remaining poor any longer than they could help it. While they sewed, the benevolent ladies drank tea, ate cakes, and exchanged quantities of uncharitable gossip and misinformation upon subjects of no interest to Grace. Grace had attended enough of these tedious parties early in her marriage, when she was a new daughter-in-law, as to have arrived at a firm resolution of declining all further such invitations. Still, the invitations did not abate.

She blotted her note (poor thin brownish stuff, this ink, and excessively diluted); folded it (thick coarse rough paper, this; and unevenly sized, so that the ink often pooled or bled; she was unimpressed with American ink and paper, in general); sealed it; wrote the direction on the outside.

For comfort, she let her hand fall over the little red morocco case lying next to the inkwell. It was smooth, and very familiar to her hand, fitting intimately under her domed palm. She opened it, and there he was, gazing back at her from his golden oval: Daniel, her Dan.

To Grace, *Dàn* was Gaelic, her cradle language, embedded deepest in her Scottish childhood. There it meant Song; Poem; Fate; Destiny.

It was not a bad likeness, this portrait miniature which she had painted more than two years ago, just before he had sailed for Canton once more—sailed without her. It need not have taken long to paint this little portrait, for she could work quickly, when she liked. But on that occasion she had drawn out the pleasure of looking at him, of drinking up the sight of him, for as long as he would tolerate—or perhaps just a little longer. She had got his clear green eyes, the stiff unruly black hair, the level American gaze under straight brows, the sweet amused twist at one corner of his mouth. She'd had a bit of trouble with the folds of his stock. It was not perfectly satisfactory; it still disturbed her, though no eye but her own would have noticed.

Then, with the aid of a looking glass, she had painted a matching portrait miniature of herself, for him to take with him. She'd been pale, then, with the nausea of early pregnancy, freckles standing out and hair undeniably red. She might have corrected these shortcomings easily, and for another sitter, or another recipient, she might have done so. But for Dan she scorned such vanities. He loved even her red hair, even her pale freckled skin. When she gave him the finished miniature (and it had turned out well, even to her critical eye), he had kissed it, promising to carry it next to his heart forever. He meant it too; but Grace knew he was apt to lose things.

She replaced his miniature atop the thick stack of his letters from Canton: her treasures. He was a steady and faithful correspondent, for each evening he added at least a few sentences (and sometimes several pages) to a running letter, which he would fold, seal, and send—a fat packet—whenever an opportunity offered; whenever an America-bound ship left Canton. He numbered each letter, so that she would know if any were missing, and urged her to do the same.

Her letters to him were written on Sunday mornings, while everyone else in Philadelphia was at church. Daniel had given her a supply of black paper for making simultaneous copies of each letter she wrote. The black paper—coated with lampblack, or something equally smudgy, and laid between two sheets of writing paper—was messy to use, but saved considerable time. The supply he had left with her was now nearly exhausted, and the carbon copies of the letters she had written to him made a stack nearly as thick as his, to her.

DOWNSTAIRS, GRACE FOUND Rawley and Jamie in the warm kitchen. Jamie was in his little chair across from the stove, toying with his breakfast of bread and butter. The floor around his chair was littered with crumbs and worse, for he was old enough now to insist upon feeding himself, and to be fascinated by the tendency of things to fall downward, a phenomenon whose reliability he had been testing with diligence.

Rawley, who had just finished filling the boiler for the washing, said,

"And I hope it don't rain, missus, but seem like every Monday, it rain for sure. And if laundry day get changed to Tuesday—why, then I guess it commence to rain every Tuesday instead!" Rawley was only sixteen or seventeen years old, and very talkative, but she had abundant energy, and a surprising quantity of good practical sense for one so young. She was an adventurous cook too, with enthusiasm even for the spicy Oriental dishes Grace favored. She was willing to live in, not away, for she seemed to have no kin in the world. Most important of all, she was unfailingly patient and cheerful with Jamie, who could be trying.

"Oh, it's warm in here," said Grace, and held her hands close to the stove. "But that reminds me, Rawley: no more fires in my bedroom this season, not unless it absolutely snows. I have no sitter until one o'clock today, so between the two of us we ought to be able to get the washing done while the weather holds—if our wee man, here, does not get up to too much mischief."

"Mamma, mischief!" said Jamie, pointing at her.

WHEN GRACE'S SITTER finally arrived—at twenty minutes past one—for her second sitting, she brought another lady with her. "Allow me to present my sister Mrs MacFarlane, up from Virginia," said Mrs Ambler to Grace. Mrs Ambler and her sister were a little breathless from following Rawley up the three flights of stairs to Grace's studio at the top of the house. "She's paying me a visit for a few weeks. We'll need another chair, I guess. Oh la, Mrs Pollocke! I didn't mean you should fetch it yourself! But there, your negro girl has run downstairs again already. Well, Clara will sit with her book while you paint me. We've just been to see Mr Dunn's Chinese Collection, and Clara bought the little book that explains all about it. What's the book called, Clara?"

" 'A Peep at China in Mr Dunn's Chinese Collection, Ten Thousand Chinese Things,' " read out Mrs MacFarlane laboriously. "Well, there was plenty of things, that's for sure. Have you been and seen the Chinese Collection, Mrs Pollocke?"

Yes, she had.

"And was there really ten thousand things, do you reckon?"

"I daresay there might," said Grace. "But *wan*, in the Chinese numbering system, means—well, not just the actual number 'ten thousand,' but also 'a great many'—'a large number'—in the same way that when Hindus speak of a *lakh* or a *crore* of something or other, they may mean literally 'a hundred thousand' or 'ten million'—or they may only mean a certain large quantity, a complete lot."

"Well, I swan! You talk like you've been abroad yourself. You're not from here, I guess," said Mrs MacFarlane.

"No, I was born in Scotland," said Grace, "and brought up in the East Indies and the China coast. It was there I learned to paint; and there I met and married Mr Pollocke."

"And so—so there is a Mr Pollocke—I mean—is he—is your husband abroad, I guess?" said Mrs Ambler.

"He has been at Canton for these two years," said Grace.

"Oh la! That's a long time. But he don't mind you—you painting heads, even married?"

"No," said Grace.

"Imagine that! My husband would never stand for it," said Mrs MacFarlane.

"Mine either; just think, all and sundry in the house, coming and going all the time. Now, don't you go and make me laugh, Clara, that would be just too bad of you," Mrs Ambler said as she settled herself in the sitter's chair on its raised platform. "Or I'm sure Mrs Pollocke will scold me. She's mighty particular about my pose. Now, is this right, Mrs Pollocke?"

It was not: "The chin down just a little, please, Mrs Ambler," said Grace. "A little more. The shoulders lower and the neck longer, if you can manage it. Let us see the spine of the book under your left hand; that is better. And now, the jaw soft, the lips only gently touching, please." Grace moved Mrs Ambler's right shoulder down and back just a little. "Excellent," she said; and drew back the thin muslin curtain from the large north-facing dormers, to let in a little more light, for the day had darkened.

"What do you reckon it'll have cost Mr Dunn to buy up all those things, Anne, and ship it all here from China?" said Mrs MacFarlane.

"Plenty, I'm sure. Thousands and thousands," said Mrs Ambler. "I don't see how he can hope to recover his outlay, not even if ever so many folks go and see the collection."

"Well now, at twenty-five cents per head for admission," said Mrs MacFarlane, "let's see, that would be, oh . . ."

"Well, twenty-five cents is one-fourth of a dollar, so . . . so for every thousand people that pay up, that makes, ah, four hundred dollars," declared Mrs Ambler.

"Not forty?" suggested Mrs MacFarlane.

Grace held her tongue. She knew herself to be no great mathematician, particularly in comparison to the prodigies of Calcutta and Allahabad whose marvelous feats of mental calculation won them steady employment as clerks in the British and American merchant establishments of the Orient. But she had been astounded, upon coming to Philadelphia as a bride three years ago, to find that her own small proficiency set her well in advance of most American women.

Nor, it seemed, did American women study politics or letters. Resolving to read the documents which Americans so proudly cited in their incessant boastings about their superior political arrangements, Grace had called at four booksellers in vain before finding, at the fifth, an inexpensive and poorly printed edition of the Americans' Constitution, and their Declaration of Independence. She had read these closely; and had then attempted to discuss certain points—the self-evidence of truths; suffrage of the unpropertied—over needle and thread when her mother-in-law's sewing circle gathered for the benefit of the Deserving Poor. How astonished she had been, to find those ladies unable to discuss these points! How appalled, to realise that they had never actually quite read the documents in question! American men, she found (when accompanying her husband to the rare dinner which included wives) were slightly better informed; most of them had indeed read the documents—once—as schoolboys—years ago—and could sometimes even cite a clause, or two, in support of some cherished political theory of their own. And this was the City of Brotherly Love itself, the city where these famous beacons of liberty, these light-shedding treatises, had actually come into existence.

Mrs Ambler rolled her eyes across at her sister—and burst into laughter. "Oh, Mrs Pollocke, don't scold me, I couldn't help it! It wasn't my fault. You didn't see the look she gave me!"

Grace was twenty-six years old, and Mrs Ambler and Mrs MacFarlane were grown women too, Grace's age or somewhat older, but their company was as tiresome as the company of children. Little won-der, then, that the dinners and evening parties given by Philadelphia gentlemen seldom included wives. Rumor had it that the ladies of Bos-ton were better educated and more capable of rational talk; but Boston, alas, was a great distance from Philadelphia. Grace had not succeeded in finding friends among American women, and she was lonely.

"Oh la, Clara; don't! I won't have it, I tell you. I'll be good now, I promise, Mrs Pollocke," said Mrs Ambler, composing herself once more.

The portrait would be half-sized, half-length, with one hand show-ing, twenty-four inches by thirty, on a standard canvas ready-stretched and ready-primed by the supplier. Grace had always found it easier to draw left hands than right, so it was Mrs Ambler's left hand which rested on the book on the little table beside the chair; her right hand rested hidden behind her left forearm. Mrs Ambler would pay five dol-lars extra to have her hand portrayed.

At Mrs Ambler's first sitting two days earlier, Grace had begun (as always, as she had been taught) with her drawing, an oil sketch *en grisaille*. A likeness, Grace knew, could be obtained only by reproduc-ing with an exquisite nicety the precise relationship between the fea-tures. Even a scant hair's-breadth error of placement could diminish the likeness; could result in a fault in the finished portrait. Grace would search—with a frightening intensity, her sitters sometimes complained—for the length and shape of the face; for the breadth of forehead, cheekbones, jaw; the shape of the chin. Where is the center-line? How high in the head are the eyes placed? What is the distance between the eyes? At what altitude hover the brows above the eyes? Where falls the shadow under the nose? How far thence to the peak of the upper lip? What distinctive asymmetries are evident? These are the monuments, the corners to be surveyed and recorded first. Now Grace examined what she had done, and saw that it was good. There on canvas was Mrs Ambler as seen in a colorless dusk, in bright and shadowy tones of grey and sepia, like an engraved version of herself.

Now, color and surface. Mrs Ambler's flesh had a pillowy quality; her skin was pinkish, with some red rimming the eyes and, Grace saw, some yellow tones, especially about the mouth and at the sides of the nose. Her upper lip bore a faint shadow, a nearly invisible feathery

moustache. Her hair, fashionably arranged with smooth tubular ringlets at her temples, had the color and gloss of fresh chestnuts. She had
chosen to be painted in a low-necked evening dress the color of spring
ferns, a dress which showed her admirable well-fleshed shoulders to
advantage.

Taking up her palette, the colors on it ranged in order—lead white,
orpiment, vermilion, the ochres and umbers, ultramarine, and ivory
black—according to her invariable practice, Grace set to work.

Likeness was all this—outline, feature, color, texture—all recorded
with painstaking accuracy; but something more was required too.
The characteristic appearance of every living person, Grace had been
taught, derived from some air, some spirit, which animated the features from within. It derived from certain fleeting but habitual expressions, thoughts, feelings, and fears. Some painters—notably her teacher
Mr Chinnery, and the late Mr Gilbert Stuart, of whom Americans
boasted—were endowed with an easy clever torrent of patter and gossip which they let flow to put their sitters at ease, and thus elicit in
them these animating airs. For Grace, hindered by a reserved temper,
this was the most difficult part of her work. She was aware of this
deficiency in herself, and was glad even for a Mrs MacFarlane to chat
with her sister and make her look like herself.

But handsome as Mrs Ambler was—undeniably handsome in
feature—Grace found her repulsive. She was repelled by Mrs Ambler's
vulgar complacency, disgusted by her unwarranted assurance and self-
satisfaction. Perhaps this was only envy?

Grace had painted other sitters she'd disliked. It was not impossible. And usually—oddly!—the sitters were pleased by the result,
delighted by the excellent likeness Grace was always able to capture—
and blind, apparently, to precisely those qualities embodied in their
own faces and expressions.

Mrs MacFarlane was reading choice bits aloud from her book: "It
says here that Chinese women's tiny bound feet are called Golden
Lilies. . . . That lacquered-ware writing slope—now, that was pretty,
wasn't it, Anne? I wouldn't mind having that. . . . Well, I swan! Listen,
it says here the poorer people will even eat the flesh of dogs, cats, rats,
and mice! Imagine! Oh, and listen: 'The larvae of the sphinx-moth and
a grub bred in the sugar cane are much relished, as also sharks' fins,

the flesh of wild horses, the sea-slug, and a soup made of a species of birds'-nests.' I swow! Don't it make your stomach turn over, just to hear it?"

"La, Clara, do stop!" begged Mrs Ambler; indeed, the revulsion on her face, while lively, was not just what Grace wished to record.

Setting down her book, Mrs MacFarlane came to look over Grace's shoulder at the likeness of her sister. "Well, I declare," she said. "If you haven't got her, to the life! Her very spit!" Grace supposed this was meant as a compliment.

After watching for a few moments, Mrs MacFarlane sauntered about Grace's studio to look at the other canvases leaning against the walls or on stands: paintings in various states of completion. Presently Mrs MacFarlane asked her sister, "Are you going to have a real background to your picture, Anne? Or will it just be one of those dark skies?"

"Oh, I can't decide," said Mrs Ambler. "Mrs Pollocke says she does that part last, and I don't even have to sit for it, she can do that without me. Do you think I should, Clara?"

"It's nice to have a background, I guess, if it don't cost extra."

"A sky or landscape background costs five dollars more than a plain dark background," said Grace smoothly.

"I guess I could have it if I want. Mr Ambler won't object to five dollars more," said Mrs Ambler, with deepest satisfaction.

"This one has a column, and a red velvet curtain with tassels," said Mrs MacFarlane. She was standing before a nearly finished portrait of a local shipbuilder and packet operator. "It's prodigious genteel. And then the harbor, with ships, and those hills behind." The shipbuilder had chosen to be painted at half length, seated in a substantial chair before a marble column and a crimson velvet drape pulled back to overlook the ever-popular Merchants' Daydream, as Grace thought of this ideal harbor scene: a sunny calm, ships anchored on smooth water, heavily laden with valuable goods to be sold at tremendous profit.

It was a daydream she knew how to cherish. If not for the troubles which had broken out at Canton over the smuggling of opium, Daniel would have returned home a year ago. Yet Grace was not to repine; for, as Dan had explained in his letters, when the British agents withdrew from Canton—to express their outrage at the confiscation and destruction by the mandarin of more than two million pounds' worth of contraband opium—an unprecedented monopoly of the trade fell into the hands of the American agents. British merchant ships continued to arrive, but their business could now be conducted only through the agency of American traders; and there were generous commissions to be garnered on each transaction. This could not last long; indeed, British warships bent upon teaching the Chinese a lesson were expected at any moment; and whenever they should arrive, all trade would be at an end. While it lasted, though, Daniel remained at Canton, determined to profit by this singular opportunity.

"I wouldn't want a harbor; nothing with ships in it," said Mrs Ambler. "I might get seasick just looking at it."

"How about a landskip background, then? That's a handsome one, that big white house under the avenue of trees, there. Why, it looks just like home, don't it, Anne? Makes me homesick all over!"

"Better homesick than seasick," declared Mrs Ambler.

"Ha! Better homesick than seasick! That's a neat one! I swan, you're good as a picnic all by yourself," said Mrs MacFarlane, laughing.

"It does look like home, though," said Mrs Ambler seriously. "What house is that, Mrs Pollocke?"

"That is Butler Place, on the road to Germantown."

"Oh la, Mr Pierce Butler's house! I knew it must belong to a southern gentleman, because it looks so elegant and handsome, just like home. We're Virginians, you know, actually. By birth."

"Indeed," said Grace respectfully, as though being Virginian were a great accomplishment.

A LITTLE AFTER three o'clock, the sisters went away, having made a return appointment two days hence. Then Grace returned to her canvas to consider Mrs Ambler's hand. The fingers did not splay quite convincingly around the book, and she wished to correct them while the light still streamed strongly through the three big dormers which made up most of the north wall of this attic room at the top of house, just two blocks west of the Delaware River. The nearness of the river affected the quality of the light here, Grace believed; made it more liquid than it would have been further from the waterfront.

She worked until she was satisfied with Mrs Ambler's hand; until she had made the plump fingers curl quite naturally over the edge of the book, and made the fingernails just the size and shape of Mrs Ambler's. It was a much better hand than those small tapered paws generally depicted by the famous Mr Gilbert Stuart. Setting down her palette, Grace wiped her own smudged hands on the sides of her smock as she stepped back to judge. Not bad. Her stomach growled, a reminder that she was hungry—and that there was no meat for dinner. The light was failing already, and she had best hurry if she meant to get anything worth eating at the butcher's.

She set her brushes in a small tumbler of turpentine, promising herself to clean them later. As she hung up her smock, she heard the knocker at the street door below—and Rawley opening it—then a man's voice and Rawley's voice. Rawley's footsteps clattered up the stairs, three winding uncarpeted flights.

"It's a gentleman, here's his card," panted Rawley as she breasted the final landing. "He want to come up and see the studio, even though he don't have no appointment."

The caller was Mr Robert Cornelius, whose foundry had occasionally supplied Grace with copperplates suitable for engraving. "You may as well show him up, Rawley," she said. "Where is Jamie?"

"Just a-settin' in his little chair in the kitchen with me, and got his applesauce all over his face," said Rawley. "I bring that gentleman right on up, then." And she went clattering back down the stairwell again.

Alas for butcher's meat, alas for supper! It was a very inconvenient moment, but commissions, even possibilities of eventual commissions, were to be welcomed. Ever since the Panic in '37, the whole world had fallen into poverty. Portraits—luxuries much indulged in during fat times—had been in small demand. Grace was aware that the Cornelius metalworks was a prosperous exception, engaged in supplying light fixtures for the new gaslight which was spreading rapidly now through Philadelphia, even into the outlying corners of the city. If Mr Cornelius were thinking of sitting for his likeness, he might wish to see her studio and some examples of her work.

What a din he and Rawley made, coming up the stairs! A carpet would be worth having, Grace thought, at the cost of a portrait or two; or grass mats, for rather less. Mr Cornelius made his bow, a little breathless. "I must beg your pardon for intruding upon you without an appointment, Mrs Pollocke, but I wanted to see how a portrait studio is set up, and I remembered that you had mentioned your own studio."

"You are quite welcome to see it," she said.

"So that's the chair for your sitters, I guess," said Mr Cornelius. "Why is it on a raised platform?"

"As I prefer to paint standing," said Grace, "my sitters must be elevated, to bring their faces upon a level with mine. Otherwise I should be looking downward at them and they upward at me, quite unsuitable for gentleman sitters in particular, and likely to produce an unflattering distortion."

"Ah," he said. "And the light from your windows falls on the right side of the sitter's face, I see."

"Yes; though sometimes I get a sitter for whom I must reverse the entire *mise-en-scène*—a sitter whose left side is best."

"Mm-hm. And do you get enough light from your windows? North-facing, aren't they?"

"Ample light; sometimes too strong in summer. That is why I have had them fitted with muslin curtains."

"Too strong! And the little table, there, flanking the chair?"

"For props: books, maps, flowers, fruits, music, instruments—depending on the sitter."

"Ah—to express the sitter's interests, accomplishments, character, that sort of thing?"

"Just so," said Grace. She thought of these props as the sitter's attributes or properties—brandished as the gods and goddesses of the Hindu pantheon brandished in their various hands their particular attributes: Shiva his crescent moon, his trident, his tiger skin; Saraswati her book and her lute; Lakshmi her lotus and elephants. Through their choice of props, sitters laid claim—sometimes, as in Mrs Ambler's case, ill-founded—to certain virtues or qualities of mind and character.

"And the crimson velvet curtain, and the short Grecian column, there?"

"Some sitters want a classical background."

"Ah, backgrounds! Do people generally want backgrounds? Is it all the romantic sunset sky nowadays, or do people still want landscapes and harbor scenes, and that sort of thing?"

"I still do some scenic backgrounds," said Grace. "But they are far less in demand than formerly. I daresay that three-quarters of my portraits have a plain background now, either darkness, or else an expressive sky."

"Miniatures, though—do those commonly have scenic backgrounds?"

"Very seldom," said Grace. "Not since I have been in Philadelphia."

"And as for frames and cases—for miniatures, I mean—those are standard items sold by art suppliers, I believe?"

"Yes; from the same suppliers who furnish ivory blanks, and pigments, and brushes and stretched primed canvases, and all that sort of thing. Now, Mr Cornelius, I beg you will be so good as to tell me the reason for all your questions. Do you mean to set up a portrait studio of your own?"

"Well, Mrs Pollocke—indeed, you've hit the nail on the head," said Mr Cornelius. "Let me show you something." From inside his coat he brought out a small cloth-wrapped object. Tenderly laying back its coverings, he passed it to her.

"Ah!" sighed Grace, surprised—for here was a little portrait of himself, dazzling in its accuracy and perfection, the image both bright and shadowy, leaping up from a silvery plate in all vivid life when turned just so across the light. "A daguerreotype—surely?"

"Well, yes; it is a sort of daguerreotype," said Mr Cornelius. "Though we've made an important improvement over Mr Daguerre's process, my partner and I, using a—a proprietary and superior technique, which produces a quicker action than Mr Daguerre's process, so sitters don't have to remain motionless for so long."

"I have never seen one; only heard of them," said Grace. It was somewhat larger than an ivory portrait miniature, nearly five inches high, and three or four inches wide. She studied the image, turning it this way and that, so that the light falling across it brought up different tones and shadows, all in silvers, greys, and blacks, like grisaille; like someone seen in full moonlight. In the picture, Mr Cornelius's hair was unruly, sticking up at one side; and there was a fierce investigative light in his pale eyes. He looked as though he had been caught

dashing from here to there, pausing for an instant only to understand
one quick thing. The minute detail of the image transfixed her: each
freckle, each hair stood distinct. She turned it over; the reverse was a
copperplate.

"On silver over copper?" she asked.

"Yes, a Sheffield-rolled plate."

"Oh, aye," breathed Grace, and brushed knowing fingertips lightly
against the copper backplate. It was a good plate. She had mastered the
art of engraving years ago, as a girl, in India and China. She under-

stood copperplates. She knew a good polish when she felt it; knew about drawing the image in reverse; knew the metallurgy of the etching process; how to ink a plate and pull a faultless print. But although she had heard of the new process announced by M. Daguerre and M. Niepce in Paris during the previous autumn, she had never yet seen a daguerreotype. She turned it over to study the image again. "Uncanny," she said. "Very beautiful." It was far more beautiful than she had imagined, when she had heard of these new pictures; and not at all like an engraving, as she had supposed. It was more like a tiny looking glass which had captured and retained the image of him who had gazed into it. "I see that it is in fact a mirror image," she remarked, for she had noticed that the mark on Mr Cornelius's right cheek was on the image's left cheek. "A reverse image, just as one sees in a mirror."

"Yes; unfortunate, but not insurmountable. In theory it would be possible to use a mirror or a prism to reverse the image yet again inside the camera, correcting it before it falls upon the plate," he said.

"Oh, but to the sitter, this mirror image will look perfectly familiar," Grace said. "The only image one ever sees of oneself is the image in the looking glass. It is only to others, who are accustomed to gazing upon our actual flesh-and-blood faces, that the mirror image never looks quite right."

"Well, there's that to be considered too, I guess," said Mr Cornelius, putting away the exquisite little picture. "But I do intend to open a portrait studio, and I wanted to see about backgrounds and that sort of thing. I'd thought of a column; and I've got a velvet drape. I'd thought of asking you to paint some backgrounds of cloudy skies—or even something like this"—he pointed to the Merchants' Daydream— "to be hung up behind the sitters. But maybe there won't be much call for those after all."

"I will paint them for you, if you want them," said Grace. "If you find that your sitters want them."

"Another thing," he said. "What would you advise as to applying a color tint to the skin and hair, say—or to the sitter's dress? Like hand-tinting an engraving?"

"I daresay it might be done," said Grace after a moment. "Opaque colors would never do, lest they obscure the exquisite details of the image; and making colors stick to silver is not so easy. Watercolors, I should think, for their transparency—and I should recommend mixing in a little gum arabic, just as one does for watercolor miniatures on ivory."

"Ah! Would you be willing to make the attempt, by way of experiment," he asked, "if I left one of my plates with you?"

"Surely I will," said Grace. "But leave me a plate whose loss you will not mind, in case it is spoilt."

"Here's one you can spoil of—well, my partner, in fact," said Mr Cornelius, passing her another little picture. "It's a little blurred around the eyes because he blinked, but it'll do for painting on." Here, all black, grey, and silver, was a perfect little man in spectacles: serious, unimpressed, in a high-collared coat and patterned waistcoat. "His coat's brown," said Mr Cornelius, "and the stripes of his waistcoat should be green and yellow."

Grace attended him downstairs. An important question remained unasked, and as he stepped out onto her scrubbed doorstep, she asked it: "But tell me, Mr Cornelius; have you determined what price you will charge for making a likeness, at your studio?"

"Oh, price," said Mr Cornelius, donning his hat. "For an image four inches high, including an embossed brass frame, and ready the same day, five dollars. More with a fancy gilt frame, of course. Or with hand-tinting."

Five dollars. Five dollars, for a perfect scientific likeness, on silver, complete in one day's time! Who, then, would prefer to pay thirty-five dollars for a quite skillful likeness on ivory, painted by herself, and requiring several sittings over a period of days or weeks? Grace felt the approach of another financial collapse.

AND STILL NO MEAT in the house! She called to Rawley in the kitchen that she was going out to the butcher's, put on her cloak, and went out. The old butcher who had formerly had her custom knew how to deliver what she liked, two or three mornings each week. But he had gone bankrupt, so Grace had been cultivating a new butcher, six blocks away. She walked fast, noticing that the trees along the streets and squares were beginning to leaf out, just they ought by now, the week after Easter. The ice on the river had broken up long ago, but the wind was still cold, and she saw that dark clouds were piling up to the north. She stepped into the nearest newsstand for the paper which usually carried the most current shipping news, but it was nowhere in evidence. Late? Sold out? Presses broken down? When she asked, the proprietor only shrugged, and she left empty-handed, to hurry the four blocks to the butcher shop before the rain. She could try another news seller on her way home.

The handle of the butcher's heavy door had on it something sticky, disgusting. In a gesture that was automatic to her, she wiped her hand across her hip as she stepped inside. Now there was a black streak across the grey cloth of her skirt; and her hand was still smeared too, with pitch or tar or black grease. She asked the surly butcher behind his counter for a duster, trying to keep the exasperation out of her voice: "That is tar, I'm afraid, on your door handle."

He did not apologise; only handed Grace a bloodstained rag. "Now what'll it be, Mrs Pollocke? You're pretty late. There ain't much left at this hour of the day. Some nice juicy lamb kidneys for your supper? It's that or calves' liver, if you get here this late."

Juicy lamb kidneys, leaking and reeking of urine? Or calves' liver, which would leave a smell in the kitchen—in the whole house? Could Jamie be induced to eat either of these? He was like his father in his fastidious palate. Dan would touch neither kidneys nor liver, and referred to steak-and-kidney pie as a steak-and-urine pie.

But Dan was not here; and it was late—and beginning now to rain. How discouraging to walk four more blocks in a cold April rain to the next butcher, and that shop no better! "Oh—a half pound of each, then, if you please," said Grace. There were some potatoes, still, at home in the basement, and the last of the cabbages remained in the vegetable patch in the backyard. Everyone was tired of cabbage. The butcher weighed out the organs, wrapped them in paper, tied the parcel in string, and handed it over the counter to her. Grace turned to go; she eyed the door handle suspiciously. "Perhaps you will be so good as to come and open this door for me?" she asked. And he did, but would not meet her eyes nor smile nor say good evening.

It was frankly raining. She drew her shawl up over her head, knowing it would do little good. Her hair—in addition to being disgracefully red—had a knack of going wild whenever the slightest dampness got to it. The parcel containing the kidneys and the liver had a string loop at the top for carrying, but the butcher had made a poor job of his knot, and before she had gone half a block, the loop came untied. She nearly dropped the parcel, but bobbled it awkwardly and managed to catch it before it hit the brick sidewalk. Someone laughed—an old woman's witchy cackle—and, looking about, Grace saw that it was the ragpicker, a old negro scarecrow who generally loitered about this neighborhood. She owned only her wheelbarrow, it seemed, and probably slept in it of nights, among her begged rags. Grace tucked her wayward parcel within her arm, hugging it against her side under her shawl, and hurried homeward. Never mind the shipping news; she would get that tomorrow.

The rain suddenly redoubled its force, and redoubled again. Within a few moments Grace was drenched. It was heavy as a monsoon rain, an India or a China rain—but much colder. Two more long blocks to go. The gutters flooded almost immediately. All this city's sanitary arrangements left a great deal to be desired, and when Grace arrived at the next curb, the water was running a good four inches deep in the muddy street. Was there a better place to cross? While she paused to look up and down the street, a wagon came around the corner, the horses at a lumbering trot—and though Grace shrank back against the storefront behind her, the wheels threw up a plume of muddy spray and splashed her skirt heavily. *"Dūdhon nahāo pūton phaliyo!"* Grace shouted after the driver, the sarcasm arising unbidden from her Indian childhood: May you bathe in milk and be fruitful in children! The driver drove on, oblivious, hunched against the rain—but she felt the small satisfaction of having had the last word.

There was no help for it; she lifted her skirt and, stepping into the flooded street, made her way across. Her boots leaked. Upon reaching the far sidewalk, she abandoned what little dignity remained to her and ran for home.

She let herself in and bolted the door behind her. She took off her boots and soggy stockings and left them upon the mat just inside the door, not liking to leave water stains upon the waxed wooden floor or her parlor rug. Barefoot, she took the butcher's parcel to the kitchen at the back of the house, and laid it on the table. It had leaked through its paper, leaked disgustingly. Now she could smell where it had soaked her dress too; she could smell herself, reeking of lamb's urine.

She went up the steep stairs to her bedroom at the top of the house, to take off her cloak and see about dry stockings. Without a fire, her bedroom was cold. Where were Jamie and Rawley? She laid the heavy wet cloak across the back of a chair, and glanced at herself in the little looking glass over the clothespress. Her appalling hair was like a misty halo, though she was dripping wet. Her nose was red, and her freckles stood out like measles. Her toes were cold. And what was that doomful sound, that soggy muffled dripping? She spun about to look; and aye, there it was: a leak, a wet place on the slanting underside of the unceiled roof boards, dripping quietly onto her bed. Grace seized the basin from her washstand and set it under the drip, but she felt the dampness spreading all around it, into her coverlets, her woolen blanket, her sheets, her mattress. Ochone, ochone, the waywardness of everything! The discomfort of everything!

Then a voice reached her ears, a familiar voice, shouting. Was it Rawley, in the backyard? Grace peered down from her rain-streaked dormer window—and saw Rawley, holding Jamie under one arm, while shouting and beating a pig with a stick of firewood. The pig, oblivious to this abuse, was regaling itself on the late cabbages. Still barefoot, Grace leapt down the narrow turning stairs and, snatching up another faggot of firewood from the kitchen fire, its end aflame, ran out the back door, brandishing it.

The pig took notice when Grace thrust the glowing orange end against its flank. It squealed, and spun about angrily; and for a bad moment, Grace thought it would charge. Grace feared and loathed pigs, even such moderate-sized pigs as this one. It gave her the same feeling as she'd once had, years and long years ago, in the jungly grassy uplands of Assam, when a rhinoceros had contemplated charging.

But the pig, like the rhinoceros, decided upon mature consideration to retreat instead. It screeched again, and blinked, and then made for the opening where it had broken down the fence separating this back-yard from its own. It squeezed through the opening, fat obscene bare hams last, and Rawley, setting down Jamie, examined the shattered lathes. They would no longer do. "I think there are a few boards behind the wee house," said Grace. "Get those; and the hammer. There might be nails too." Rawley went to fetch what she could find, while Grace tried to wrestle the flimsy fence boards back into position. She glanced at Jamie; he'd made his staggering way among the ruined cabbages, now churned to mud. There was nothing like a pig for wanton destruction. Rawley came running back with a couple of boards, a hammer, and a half dozen nails. "This all I can find, missus," she said. "Maybe we can pull out some of these ol' rusty nails from these broken boards, and get them pounded straight again, straight enough to use."

But Jamie lifted up his voice in lusty complaint, a howl. Grace craned around, trying to see what was the matter, while holding a board in place as Rawley pounded a nail home. Jamie's face was screwed up in disgusted rage, red and distorted; for he had just fed himself a large handful of pig dung, and found it not to his liking. Grace dropped the board and ran to snatch him up, prying the rest of the stinking pig dung out of his tight grip. He howled, and Grace used her cleanest finger to scoop out his wide-open mouth as well as she could. "Oh! Rawley, I'm taking him in to wash out his mouth. Do you close up that gap, as best you can!" she cried, and picked her way barefoot across the muddy yard to the back door.

Inside the kitchen, Jamie's howls of rage resonated unchecked, as Grace dipped water from the bucket into a basin—but where were all the clean dusters? Of course; it was laundry day, so all the dishcloths and dusters, every dingy one, hung on the drying lines in the backyard, drooping now, soaked anew by the downpour. She could go get one. Instead, she dipped the hem of her bedraggled dress into the water, and used it to clean Jamie's mouth, and face, and hands. As his howls gradually abated, she heard a new sound, a thundering, from the front of the house. What was that? With the now-hiccuping Jamie on her hip, she went forward to find out. Someone was hammering at the front door, with great determination.

Oh, do go away! she thought. There was no one on earth she was willing to see just now; nor anyone she would willingly allow to see her. Go away. She had bolted the door when she'd come in; not even her mother-in-law, who had a key, could enter with the bolt home.

But the thundering only redoubled. And the someone shouted now, in the street. Called her name.

That voice!

She flew to the door, and with her free hand wrenched back the bolt, threw open the door.

He filled the doorway, filled all her field of vision, dark. Her breath caught in a sob as Daniel's arms went around her; around her and Jamie, the two of them dripping and stinking of turpentine, tar, liver, blood, lamb urine, mud, and pig dung.

CHAPTER
2

DANIEL SLIPPED AWAY BEFORE DAWN TO MAKE HIS CLANDES-
tine return to his ship, which lay at anchor off the lazaretto, below the
city. To land, as he had done, before the ship had received her health
certificate was expressly forbidden, and the transgression punishable
by fines of five hundred dollars—to be levied upon him, and upon the
captain who permitted it. Daniel had promised *Rebecca Rolfe*'s captain
that he would return without fail before the quarantine master should
come aboard at first light; had promised even to indemnify the captain
to the amount of any fine, if his crime should somehow be detected.
And, as Daniel owned a majority share in *Rebecca Rolfe*, the poor captain had not attempted to assert his scant authority.

Grace slept again after Daniel had gone, and did not awaken until
full daylight some hours later. She lay a few minutes to savor the full
ripeness of her joy; and then reluctantly arose, feeling as tossed and
tumbled as the bed—whose damp mattress they had hastily turned
last night. When she had dressed, she went to prepare the spare room
for the visitor he'd advised her to expect as soon as *Rebecca Rolfe* should
make her way up to the city, probably on the midday flood behind a
steam tug.

AT NOON, ACCORDINGLY, Grace was at the docks awaiting the ship.
The waterfront generally smelled of river mud and sewage, but for the
past three weeks a ship from California had been unloading its cargo
of forty thousand ill-cured hides. The district reeked of slaughter-
house, of shambles, of abattoir. Forty thousand hides! How much har-
ness could Philadelphians require? How many saddles, and shoes? Or

was it the mills, running day and night, which required these hides; the never-tiring mills that nevertheless wore out innumerable leather belts in the driving of their machinery? Grace shook her head and blinked, to banish from her mind's eye the horrid vision of forty thousand carcasses, red raw lumps left to rot, littering the hillscapes of faraway California, where even the vultures must be sated.

Probably, Grace assured herself as she paced the length of the waterfront, scanning the river for *Rebecca Rolfe*, the arriving visitor would be very much changed. No one here would recognise her, after eighteen years, after so full and trying a life, lived so far away. There could be little cause for concern, after so long.

But in fact Grace recognised her from a great distance: her height, her regal posture; the elegant angle at which her head rested atop her long neck; the unmistakable dip of her shoulder and arm, curved around the thinnest of the three figures at her side, in the little skiff which threaded between the several ships at anchor in the broad river. Grace could not take her eyes off the so-familiar, so-well-loved figure, now drawing in nearer, nearer, coming in to the dock.

HERE IS AN ODD SIGHT! passersby must think. Look at this neatly dressed red-haired lady, of genteel enough appearance, and very fair complexion—in the embrace of that tall thin negress! A negress of quite exceptional color, in fact; of extraordinary shiny blackness! And look, the white lady returns the embrace, with what appears to be equal affection, a matching enthusiasm! The negress's half-grown boys stand by in idle embarrassment, their thin wrists protruding awkwardly from their too-short sleeves. There is another white girl with them too, a young woman standing to one side, who does not smile.

Grace knew they were conspicious. "Come, let us get out of the street," she said, taking Anibaddh's heavy satchel from her. "Have you nothing else to bring? Your trunks?"

"They've promised to send them later," said Anibaddh; and she introduced her sons, which embarrassed them extremely. The elder, already as tall as his mother, was called Jeebon; and the younger, who might have looked Grace straight in the eye had he not been so bashful, was called Bajubon. Both of them were of an age characterised by the extreme awkwardness of being visible, of being caught in the act of growing tall. Grace did not wish to add to their confusion by gazing frankly at them; but oh! she longed to search their faces, to search for the look of their Asiatic father, mingled with that of their mother. High cheekbones; oblique black eyes, deeply lashed; and complexions quite a full shade lighter than their mother's.

"And Prince Teerut . . . ?" asked Grace of Anibaddh, though she felt shy about inquiring, afraid of what the answer might be; for Rajah Teerut Sing, Anibaddh's husband, the Khasi father of these boys, had been a state prisoner of the British ever since surrendering to the East India Company's Assam agents in '33.

"Still at Dacca, of course. As well as could be expected, when I sailed," said Anibaddh. "And here—can you guess? Do you recognise Miss Constantia Babcock, all grown up? Seventeen, this summer."

"Of course," said Grace to the girl. "You have a great look of your mother. You were six years old when I saw you last, in Calcutta; and I was fourteen. Do you remember me, at all?"

Miss Babcock gazed frankly before replying, "No. I think not, Mrs Pollocke."

"I was just little Grace MacDonald, then." Grace curbed her impulse to touch the girl's smooth cheek. Miss Babcock resembled her mother, whom Grace remembered well. There were the same round blue eyes, the curling light hair, the dimpled chin—but an entirely different person lived behind this face, she could see. There was a well-guarded presence behind those eyes, and no particular desire to please.

"Come now, and see my own little boy," Grace said, and led the way. The sooner they were out of the street, the better; for Grace's dear friend the Rani Anibaddh Lyngdoh had once been Annie, a runaway slave from Virginia.

SHE INTENDED TO STOP in America only long enough to throw a golden apple of discord among the American sericulturists, and to sell her cargo of silk, and of mulberry trees, the Rani explained; then she and her family would sail once more, for London and Glasgow.

"Mulberry trees! Not *multicaulis?*" said Grace.

"Yes, alas," said Anibaddh. "Well-rooted young *Morus multicaulis,* ready to burst into leaf as soon as they see sunlight."

"Oh, but the market has utterly collapsed!"

"So I learned, when we put in at Cape Town," said Anibaddh. "Too late. Nobody wanted them in Cape Town either. Seven thousand of them."

"What a fortune should have been yours, a year ago!" said Grace. "They were selling for prodigious sums, those *multicaulis* mulberries. Everyone who lost everything in the Panic had hoped to recover, it seems, by speculating in *multicaulis.* But now—now . . . Oh, my dear! What will you do?"

"Give them away as pea stakes, I suppose," said Anibaddh. "They are not the only string to my bow. I have sixty picul bales of silks, the very best and cleanest quality, some of it reeled, and some spun; the remainder re-reeled or ready-thrown to American specifications; and all of it ready for American throwsters, dyers, and looms. And I have a great many samples of Bengal and Turkish silks, raw and spun, and dyed, and woven. Some novelties too: even the beautiful Muga, the royal golden silk from Assam."

How oddly practiced—even rehearsed—this all sounded! Did the Rani always sound like this, Grace wondered, when speaking of her mercantile concerns? In the long years since the two had met, Anibaddh's speech had changed a great deal. Her English—originally the patois of an ignorant American slave girl—was now, after eighteen years of rubbing up against British traders in the Indies, quite correct, and quite unplaceable. She had also become something of a linguist; had picked up Khasi, Assamese, Bengali, Hindi, and some Cantonese, to Grace's knowledge—and perhaps more. But as for this practiced, this rehearsed style of speaking, so devoid of spirit, so controlled—did it not conceal something else? Grace made herself listen again.

"Most interesting of all," Anibaddh was saying blandly, "I have eight lakh of Eri silkworm eggs packed on ice in darkness, to prevent their hatching out too soon; and dozens of bushels of errindy beans, to grow their fodder. I am convinced that Eri silkworms are much better suited to the American climate than mulberry silkworms. And errindy thrives everywhere. It is an exceedingly eligible and useful plant in many respects, far superior to mulberry—and then too, castor oil is such a valuable commodity."

"Ah! That's it; I was trying to remember. Errindy is castor bean."

"Castor-oil plant," said Anibaddh. "Palma Christi; dog-tick plant; *Ricinus.*"

"Aye; I do remember it. In India it grows like a weed."

"And so it does here too. That is just what makes it so useful. It ought to become an important article of cultivation and commerce, particularly in the milder climate of the southern states," Anibaddh said. "I have already composed my advertisement, to be printed in the next issues of all the agricultural papers, to announce the introduction of these superior silkworms and eggs, and the plants they feed upon."

"How eminent you have become, Rani, and how useful in the world! I cannot help feeling quite provincial by comparison," said Grace. "But do you not mean to remain here, in America?"

"No; as soon as I have set the American silk growers to rights, I shall sail once more, for London," said Anibaddh, "where I mean to hunt up Lord Holland, and make him help us."

"Ought I to know who Lord Holland is? And what he is to do for you?"

"He is only the Chancellor of the Duchy of Lancaster now, and an old man—but I have got a letter of introduction to him. It was he who made Parliament relax the meanness, the severity, of Napoleon Bonaparte's last exile, on Saint Helena. Oh, Miss Grace, have you never read Sir Walter Scott's *Life of Napoleon*? Look, it is all here, a most complete account. I will lend it to you, if you like." From her satchel Anibaddh extracted a much-handled volume, of so daunting a thickness that Grace was not eager to take it. "Lord Holland was a compassionate friend to Napoleon, and I hope he will be a friend to us as well."

"Prince Teerut is petitioning for—"

"Nothing, not he; my husband will petition for nothing. He does not know of this particular errand; and he would not approve it, if he knew," admitted Anibaddh, turning her tremendous emerald ring around and around on her finger. "He is far too stoic ever to complain of his treatment, but I—I am not so patient on his behalf. General Bonaparte was treated with far greater consideration than has been shown my husband. *He* was permitted to live like a gentleman, in a commodious house, and was made a noble allowance for his maintenance and that of his household and servants. *He* was permitted to take exercise unaccompanied within a circuit of eight miles—or, if accompanied by an orderly officer, might range over the entire island, if he wished. Any books for which *he* expressed a desire were furnished to him, without charge. It is true that all his correspondence was opened and read by the governor, which is indignity enough—but my husband is not permitted to receive any letter of mine, neither sealed nor open! In vain have I petitioned the jailer for the privilege of sending food and clothing to him; and I am permitted to visit him only once each month, for two hours. He is confined to a single room except for one hour each day, when he is permitted to walk up and down a bare dirt yard under the eye of a casteless guard. Such harshness is unworthy of the Queen and her government. I am certain that upon this disgraceful state of affairs becoming known—with Lord Holland's aid—my husband's situation must improve."

"I wish you may meet with success," said Grace, "and with a gracious reception from Lord Holland, and the Lords and the Commons—and from the Queen herself, if you should find it necessary to pursue the matter so far."

"Oh, the Queen! Well; perhaps she may be too much occupied with her new husband, and I have heard that there may be a baby before long," said Anibaddh.

"Husbands and babies are exceedingly distracting," said Grace. "Especially when they are new."

"Even when they are old, I assure you. But I am prepared to exercise endless patience and persistence. I have learnt that success is almost always maddeningly elusive—but it can sometimes be seized at last, by dint of perseverance. In any case, from London I shall be able also to send Jeebon off to Glasgow, where he is to matriculate at the university to study—medicine."

"Medicine! He means to make a doctor of himself, then?"

"Yes; and Bajubon to read his Blackstone at Lincoln's Inn."

"Oh, Rani! How splendid it is, to have sons! And Miss Babcock?"

"She means to look up her people in England, if they are still to be found after so many years."

"And what news of your little girl?" inquired Grace carefully, for the daughter born to Anibaddh and her husband seven years ago had been taken by her Khasi great-aunts at a very tender age, to be reared and groomed for the powerful position she was destined to occupy in the celebrated Khasi lineage from which she was sprung. Not until the birth of that infant girl—the long-awaited, the all-important heir— had the Rajah surrendered himself at last.

There was an instant's hesitation before Anibaddh replied, "Oh— she does very well, and resembles my husband more each day."

"GRACE, MY DARLING," said Dan, "I have invited my mother to dine here."

"Today?" said Grace.

"Yes. She hinted very hard—and her old cook has been sick, you know—"

"Has she? I did not know that. It is biryani, however, for this festive occasion," Grace said. "And your mother has made it quite clear that she does not approve of spiced dishes."

"Oh, but biryani; what could be milder than biryani?" said Dan.

"And . . . do you think it quite prudent, to seat your mother at the same table with the Rani and her sons?"

"I've told her that they are a noble family from the Orient," said Dan. "She'll be on her best behavior."

"It's not that," said Grace, though she thought that even Mrs Pollocke's best behavior might offend. "It is only that I do not feel quite— quite easy, about the safety of Anibaddh and her sons here—and I am not entirely certain what your mother's views may be, as to negroes; she has dropped a remark or two from time to time which have led me to suppose that—that—oh, Dan! But I am so uneasy! Why did you let her come?"

"We must just make the best of it and get it over, Gracie. She is a lonely old woman—"

"No, no, my dear! Of course I mean the Rani. Why did you let her come here, to America? And with her sons? It is so exceedingly dangerous for them here!"

"I daresay she is well aware of the risks. And she does not mean to stop for long; only long enough to sell her goods—if anyone will have them now—and then she means to proceed to London, and to Glasgow."

"I do not think that you—nor she—can have realised how much worse it has become here, these last two or three years, during your absence. Aye, but it is, Dan; much worse now for colored people. The temper of the times—and of the white people—grows meaner each day, I think. When people are feeling poor or frightened, they become very mean. Do you know that the Pennsylvania legislature have taken away the right to vote from the free blacks? Aye, but so they have, for they assert that negroes cannot be citizens. And the school board has just announced that the black children's middle school is to be closed—the board having determined that three years' schooling is sufficient to meet all the rightful ambitions and requirements of any colored person. 'Philadelphia,' indeed! It is shameful. I wish you had dissuaded her from coming here."

"Nothing I could have said would have dissuaded her. She was determined to come."

"The city is infested with slave-catchers and kidnappers, the most vile beasts of prey. And if fugitive slaves are hard to get, then free colored people will do, to be kidnapped and sold at their market value."

"I daresay that none of them is hunting the Rani of Nungklow, however. Come, Gracie, it has been—what—twenty years? No one is looking for her, after all this time."

"Eighteen," said Grace. Probably Dan was correct in supposing that no one would be looking for her. Perhaps any legal claim to her had expired by now; was there a statute of limitations, even? American law was a puzzle to Grace, especially as the statutes differed greatly from one state to the next. What might be Anibaddh's legal standing here, after all these years? Grace wished she knew whom to ask. How might a sympathetic and trustworthy lawyer be found? Where did one begin to look for a good sound man, whose views and discretion and advice on such a matter could be trusted?

"WHY, THEY LOOK just like negroes!" cried the elder Mrs Pollocke, upon being introduced to the Rani and her sons. "I expected they'd look like Indians, or Chinese! I never was so surprised in my life! Do they understand any English?"

Grace saw Dan's flush.

"I was born in America," said Anibaddh, "and lived here till I was fifteen years old."

"The Rani grew up in Boston," put in Grace quickly, catching Anibaddh's eye. "Then she sailed to—to India as a young woman, where she met and married the Rajah of Nungklow, in Meghalaya."

"I'm afraid I didn't quite catch the name," said Mrs Pollocke. "My hearing's not what it used to be."

"I am Anibaddh Lyngdoh, Rani of Nungklow. Here is my card," said Anibaddh, taking one from a little silver case.

"Now, I always thought that 'Ronnie' was a man's name, short for Ronald," said Mrs Pollocke, taking the card and fishing for the spectacles she wore on a chain around her neck.

"No, it is 'Rani,' " explained Grace, pronouncing carefully. "It means 'queen.' "

"A queen! So I guess her husband would be a king?"

"My husband is Teerut Sing, Rajah of Nungklow," said Anibaddh politely.

"And 'rajah' means 'king,' " explained Grace to her mother-in-law.

"You don't say! Now, where might Nungklow be? I don't believe I've ever heard of it."

"It lies in the highlands of Meghalaya, between Assam and Burma—to the east of India," said Anibaddh.

Still not quite trusting the Rani to understand English, Mrs Pollocke said to Grace, "My, my! And those boys—her sons—I guess they'd be princes, then?"

"Yes," said Grace, unwilling to enter into the nuances of polity and inheritance among the Khasi.

"And where is the—the Rajah? Did he come too, or is he at home, ruling over his kingdom?"

"My husband the Rajah has been a state prisoner of the British at Dacca for the past seven years," said Anibaddh.

"A prisoner! Why, what has he done?"

"Only what the prince of any sovereign state may, and must, do," said Anibaddh, drawing herself up, "to rebuff aggression, to repulse the haughty encroachments and trespasses of interlopers bent upon subjugating a free and independent people."

"My, my!" said the widow Pollocke. "Don't it just go to show the—the danger of having kingdoms, and empires, and all that dangerous popishness. A republic is what we have here in America, which is how it should be everywhere, and I hope and pray that enlightenment may soon spread over all the nations of the earth. We don't have queens and suchlike in this country, you see, because this is a republic, with liberty and justice for all, so I'll just call you Mrs Lyngdoh, if I may. Now, who is this young lady, carrying my grandson?" she inquired, catching sight of Miss Babcock, with Jamie on her hip.

The introductions were made.

Grace did not yet know what to make of Miss Babcock, who was civil though reserved. But Jamie, still stricken with shyness by the advent of his tall deep-voiced stranger of a father, was smitten with Miss Babcock; and Grace trusted that his infant instincts with regard to her might prove well founded.

SEATED AT TABLE, Mrs Pollocke said, "Won't you say the blessing for us, Danny? Always supposing dear Grace don't mind. I know she don't hold with saying grace herself, though I always think it's curious, considering her name."

"You might say one for us if you like, Mamma," said Dan.

"It would be more proper coming from you, Danny," said his mother. "But if you won't, I will." And she bowed her head, put her hands together in prayer, closed her eyes, and intoned, "We give Thee thanks, O Lord, for these Thy gifts, that we're about to receive from Thy bounty. And also for the safe return of Thy traveler across Thy broad oceans, from distant pagan lands. Consecrate us unto Thy service. Permit us to dedicate our hands unto Thy holy work. And help us to keep humble and grateful hearts. Through Christ our Lord, Amen."

A silence ensued. "We Christians make it a practice to thank our Maker before every meal, Mrs Lyngdoh," explained Mrs Pollocke, speaking with unusual distinctness. "But there I go, forgetting already! I guess you must know all about it, if you lived in Boston. I guess you must have felt pretty homesick for America, all that time on the far side of the world? Is that what made you come back here? Or what?"

"No, Mamma," said Daniel. "I explained, you remember, that the Rani is a great authority on silk production and manufacture; and she is importing some of her superior breed of silkworms, and eggs, and the plants they feed upon. And she has a very considerable cargo of India and China silks of every description; and she means to advise our American silk manufacturers while she is here."

"We have splendid silk being produced here in America now, Mrs Lyngdoh," said the elder Mrs Pollocke. "Maybe you've heard of Mr Horstmann's silk mill, here in Philadelphia?"

"Yes, ma'am," replied Anibaddh. "I have been supplying Mr Horstmann with various reeled and thrown silks, some thousand pounds probably, for the past dozen years; and I look forward now to the pleasure of meeting him at last."

"Fancy your knowing Mr Horstmann! Well, it's a small world, I guess. I've never met him myself," said Mrs Pollocke. "But I have a footstool trimmed with silk fringe from Mr Horstmann's mill. Just imagine! Maybe it was made from the silk you sold him! Oh, now— what have we here?" she interrupted herself, for Rawley had just carried in a large heavy dish whose top edge was encrusted with a seal of baked bread, surrounding a volcano of glistening white rice striped with gold, flecked with scarlet; and the scent of saffron and spiced lamb suffused the room. "Well, I call that a pity. I can't digest curries. I'd be up all night. No curry for me, Rawley."

"No, ma'am," said Rawley, and she set the dish before Daniel to serve.

Turning to Anibaddh again, Mrs Pollocke said, "Now, these likely-looking boys of yours, here; I guess they'll be learning the silk trade too?" Jeebon and Bajubon had nothing at all to say for themselves, and did not look up from their plates.

"No, ma'am," said Anibaddh. "My eldest is to study medicine—"

"Oh, no, Mrs Lyngdoh—altogether too bad! Not a colored person! No college would let him, I'm very sorry to tell you," declared Mrs Pollocke.

"—at the University of Glasgow," said Anibaddh.

"Glasgow? In Scotland? Do they let colored boys there—? Are you certain? Well, I hope he don't meet with disappointment, when he gets there. When they see him. I guess he aims to be a pharmacist, or a barber?"

"No, ma'am; he is to be a doctor."

"Ha ha!" laughed Mrs Pollocke. "Altogether too much! A colored doctor! Ha ha! and Rawley, there, will be his first patient! Won't you, Rawley?"

"I hope I never need no doctor, ma'am," said Rawley, who had brought in a platter of chicken in a red sauce. "I never did yet."

"Nor none of us won't, if we only eat what's wholesome," said Mrs Pollocke. "Some folks hanker after spices and the like, but I never allow my cook to use anything but salt, or sometimes a dash of pepper. There's not a speck of nourishment in spices, and what's not nourishing isn't fit to eat, as any doctor will tell you, because it only clogs and burdens the—the digestion—if it don't do worse! Besides, it's well known that spices have a heating effect—so deplorable—and all too likely to inflame a thirst that can't be satisfied by wholesome water, nor even by good ale, but only by wine and the stronger liquors. Not to mention that spices are known to inflame the, ah, baser passions. Well! But I guess Danny already knows my views upon the subject; I guess I might as well save my breath."

"I think you might, on this occasion at least, Mamma," said Dan, and refilled the three wineglasses upon the table for the Rani, Grace, and himself.

"Is that a chicken, in that bright red gravy?" said Mrs Pollocke suspiciously.

"Yes, Mamma, very mild and sweet; you will like it, I'm sure," said Dan, and helped her to it. "You can scrape off the sauce if you like."

Rawley brought in a platter of asparagus.

"And sparrow grass!" exclaimed Mrs Pollocke. "Well! I call that extravagant! Not but what I wouldn't have got some too, for such a homecoming as this." And she demonstrated her appreciation of this delicacy by transferring a majority of the pale asparagus spears onto her own plate, before passing the platter. "You won't mind, Grace, dear," she said, "as you know I can't stomach your curries." There was a moment's silence; and then Mrs Pollocke fondly said, "My grandson!" as her eye fell upon Jamie, across the table, beside Miss Babcock. "What a fine boy!"

There was general agreement that he was.

"And they do grow up so fast. Especially when I only get to see him seldomer than I'd like," said Mrs Pollocke. "I declare, I think he grows from one week to the next! Do you think it has been every week or so, Grace, dear, that you've been able to spare me an hour's visit?"

"Mamma," said Daniel.

"I don't complain of it. Have you any grandchildren yourself, Mrs Lyngdoh? No? Dear Grace is kept dreadfully busy with her painting. And what with keeping a separate house of her own, and now the baby to look after, there's not much time for old ladies."

"Mamma," said Daniel again, more sternly. "Won't you have some relish?"

"Grace could have come to live with me, while Danny was in the Orient, and the darling baby could have been born at my house," continued Mrs Pollocke, still to Anibaddh. "There would have been plenty of room—oh, yes, very comfortable, up on Race Street—and a great savings, which is something to be taken into account, these days. There is quite a good pianoforte too, and I'd have been glad to hear it played again. If only it weren't for this painting business! Turpentine and whatnot; so bad-smelling! And the people—the 'sitters,' I believe they're called—of any station in life; one never knows! Coming and going at all hours, walking into one's house and parlor; and upstairs, even! It's worse than keeping shop. In America, Mrs Lyngdoh, respectable wives make themselves content to live upon whatever means their husbands are able to provide for them; one never hears of American wives carrying on with their paying work, if they have any, not after marrying. They don't go on spinning—or playacting, singing, painting, whatever it may be—not unless they're widowed and left without means. Oh, well, yes: tavern keepers' wives and that sort have to, I guess; and women with drunken or shiftless husbands, poor souls—but never among the better sort of families. Well, it's not quite decent, is it? And it looks like such a reproach to the husband. It may be different among foreigners, I guess—and of course for you too, Mrs Lyngdoh, with these boys to bring up, and your poor husband in prison. But dear Grace didn't see her way to giving up her painting—

and it's not something I could undertake to tolerate, not in my own house. I don't complain of it, not at all; but it is a pity, isn't it? And so awkward to explain to my circle of acquaintance."

Daniel said, "You will be glad to hear, Mamma, that I have succeeded in getting the japanned workbox you wanted from Canton, and you may expect to have it tomorrow or the day after—just as soon as the weighers and the gaugers at the Custom House have finished despoiling us."

"Oh—that reminds me: I meant to bring the newspaper," said Mrs Pollocke. "It had the announcement of your arrival, Danny—your ship's arrival, that is. I thought you might like to keep that, so I put it on the hall table to make sure to bring it, but then I forgot, and came away without it after all. There was a most complete account about that gang of runaways too, the ones from Leesburg that were taken up a few weeks ago from their hiding place in the cellar of that Quaker chair maker. Probably you've been following all that in the papers, Grace, dear?"

"I'm afraid I have not, Mrs Pollocke," said Grace, who generally tried to avert her glance from the more sensational newspaper accounts of human suffering, just as she did from martyr paintings and crucifixion scenes.

"No? What a pity that you're kept so much occupied. Well! It seems that one of the runaways was trained to do mason's work, you see, and he'd bricked up the opening at the back of the cellar, under the Quaker's house. But some observing person—the collier, I think it was—noticed the fresh mortar, and tipped off the police—and so they were captured, after a desperate fight. You might think that'd be the end of it; but no, that's just the beginning! The masters ain't permitted nowadays to just run them back where they came from; no, there has to be hearings, before judges, and that always means delays, don't it? The master's witnesses, and a lawyer, all had to come up from Virginia, to identify them. But those abolitionist Quakers hired a lawyer too—that Mr Brown, Mr David Paul Brown, with all his hairsplitting and objecting. I'm surprised you haven't been following, Grace, dear, it's been all over the newspapers, and the courtroom's been filled with spectators every day. Seems like that hearing might just go on till Judgment Day, at this rate—ha ha, Judgment Day! I guess it will! Meanwhile, the whole lot of them is lodged at the jail, four strapping negroes lounging about and eating up one meal after another, all provided at public expense. It's no wonder we're all so poor nowadays. I hope you get a good price for your goods, Danny, but it seems like most folks don't have much money to spend, these days, and no notion of any more turning up either."

. . .

"No, sir, she won't give her name," said Mr David Paul Brown's head clerk. "But she says it's important. She sounds foreign; English, maybe."

"Tell her I can spare her ten minutes, no more," said Mr Brown, for he was due at the courthouse by half-past nine. A moment later, the clerk ushered in a pale young woman with distinctly red hair. Explaining that she sought advice on behalf of a friend, she related a series of events that was far more interesting than he had expected; and she put her question.

Mr Brown leaned back in his chair and pushed his spectacles up onto his head while he considered. Not English; Scottish, certainly. "A remarkable story," he said. "But before I can advise you as to your friend's present situation, I must know a little more. Never fear, I will ask you no names; you are quite right not to divulge those lightly"— for the lady had told her story with great discretion—"but certain dates and other facts will be of material importance. First of all, what year was it, when your friend took her freedom in Scotland?"

"In 1822," replied the caller promptly. "Eighteen years ago."

"And your friend was brought to Scotland by her mistress?"

"Yes."

"That is an essential point. You are asserting that your friend did not enter Scotland as a fugitive; but rather that her owner brought her to Scotland. Is that correct?"

"Yes, sir," she replied, after a moment's hesitation.

"Now, these two sons of your friend's; what are their ages, and where were they born?"

"They are fifteen and fourteen years old now; and they were born in—in the Orient."

"And where has your friend been living, since she took her freedom?"

"In certain—in various countries of the Orient, sir, until her return to America, with her sons."

"Ah; and when precisely did she and these sons of hers return to America?"

"Within the present week."

"I will not ask the name of the ship; but tell me, from what port had their ship sailed?"

"From Canton . . . ," replied the lady, with some hesitation.

Clearly she feared to give away too much. Anyone might easily find out what ship had just arrived from Canton—and what passengers had been aboard it. "And did this ship touch at any American port before coming into Philadelphia?" he asked.

"No, sir."

"Did not call at Charleston? Norfolk? Wilmington?"

"No, sir."

"Or any other American port? Did not pay duty at any custom house before arriving in Philadelphia?"

"No, sir; that is correct."

"Then allow me to congratulate your friend, ma'am. She is in law most likely a free woman, as free as President Van Buren; and furthermore, so are any and all children born to her subsequent to the taking of her freedom. Oh, it is quite clear on the Scottish end; the Scottish Court of Session has held that the condition of slavery is not recognised by the laws of that kingdom; that was *Knight vs Wedderburn*, 1778, so very notable and, by now, thoroughly established. In taking your friend to Scotland, the owner gave up any right to compel any further service from her, or to remove her again from that country without her consent. In Scotland, your friend undoubtedly became free; and, as she is no fugitive, she is not liable to be returned to compulsory labor. You may congratulate her; but as a true friend, you will caution her too, now that she has returned to America. Juries—and even judges—are always unpredictable, and sometimes downright ignorant. Your friend must never set foot upon the soil of any state whose laws assert a right to hold human property; no, not so much as one toe! 'Once free, always free' makes a pretty slogan, but it would be of little solace to her if she were taken up in Virginia, for example. No, she must steer clear of the slave states, at all costs. Furthermore, this is not a thing she would like to have to prove in a courtroom—if she were lucky enough to get to a courtroom—because, of course, her own testimony on this matter would be worth very little in any court of law." Something then made him toss out a tempting morsel, for this lady to take up, if she would: "And it is too much to hope that any white witness could be found, after so many years, and at such a distance from Scotland, and brought here to testify as to how and when and where your friend took her freedom there, all those years ago. . . ."

The lady rose to his fly, sweet as a trout: "I beg your pardon, Mr Brown," said she. "But as it happens, there is such a witness. I myself was that small Scottish lass with whom . . . my friend . . . ran away, all those years ago. I was only eight years old then, but my memory of that day remains indelible, and complete in every detail. And," she added, "I am, as you see, quite as white as any judge could require."

Mr Brown allowed himself a smile, saying, "Ah! Imagine the look on opposing counsel's face, when I produced such an unlikely witness as you! That would be worth a good deal, to a vainer man than I am. Still—still, I'd advise your friend to avoid coming to the notice of the courts, eh? Or of her former mistress. And now, madam, I must beg you will excuse me; for I was due at the courthouse a quarter of an hour ago. Your question so interested me that I lost track of the time. Good morning."

As he hastened to court, Mr Brown mentally marshaled once more the arguments he would use on behalf of the fugitives from Leesburg; but even during the strenuous course of the day his thoughts reverted more than once to the discreet red-haired Scotswoman and her story.

"I KNEW THAT ALREADY, Miss Grace," said Anibaddh. "I could have told you that. I am not so foolhardy as to have failed to consult a lawyer before risking the liberty of my sons and myself here."

"I beg you will not call me Miss Grace," said Grace peevishly. "I do not like it. I never have liked it. It sounds like misgrace. Disgrace."

"I beg your pardon," said Anibaddh.

Grace wanted to say, But why did you come back to America, Rani?

Why did you and your sons not sail directly for London? You might have sold your silks to the weavers of Spitalfields—or Northampton— or wherever the English silk weavers may be settled, nowadays. You might have bestowed your errindy seeds upon the yeomen of Kent and Dorset, and your Eri silkworm eggs upon their wives. Why did you stop here? The truth, please.

But Grace was too polite to ask. She reminded herself that Anibaddh had a right to keep her own counsel; to conduct herself in accordance with her own judgment.

Was it indeed politeness which prevented the asking of these questions? Grace could not help doubting herself; perhaps instead she was merely not bold enough.

CHAPTER
3

Two Grunting Porters heaved the wooden crate up three marble steps, through the narrow doorway—marring the paint-work, alas—and onto the rug in Grace's front parlor.

Oh, the smell of those unvarnished rough boards, cut from some Oriental tree! Of that hemp cordage! And of the rice straw packing which poked from between the imperfect joins of the boards! Here in her parlor was the very smell of Macao itself, where she and Dan had met, courted, and married.

Some hours passed before Daniel came home. "It's not all from me," he declared as he pried off the top of the crate with a crowbar. "Old friends asked to me carry some things home too." He threw aside the dunnage, several armfuls of straw, onto the parlor rug. Grace drew breath to object, but stopped her words in her throat; this litter might all be swept up later. He was illuminated by the joy of presenting his gifts; of anticipating her happiness.

The top layer of presents in the crate were for others, not for Grace, and Dan lifted them out and set them aside. For his mother, there was a caddy of Hyson tea; a long box containing three thick bolts of fig-ured silk; and a japanned workbox, completely fitted out with needles, scissors, ivory thimbles, and ivory spools wound with silk sewing thread.

To Jamie, Dan presented a silver cup adorned by his initials in applied strapwork, ingeniously entwined. Grace, knowing all too well Jamie's propensity to fling his tableware to the floor, was in anguish until he was induced to relinquish it in favor of another, less valuable present: a painted clay nodder in the form of a Chinese horse and its

Chinese rider. The horse's head and tail nodded; the rider's head and hands nodded; and the rider could be lifted off his mount and made to stand bowlegged on his own. This toy, Grace knew, was also unlikely to survive Jamie's ardent attention for long, and she hoped that both Jamie and Dan would retain their equanimity whenever the inevitable should occur.

"Everything else in this chest is for you, my darling," said Dan. "Fairings for the fair. First, these." He handed her two small silk-upholstered boxes, each no broader than the palm of her hand. Inside the first, nestled in a fragrant packing of camphor-wood curls, was a fragment of chalky white stone, from which protruded three perfect blood-red crystals, each nearly an inch in length, and clear as gems. "Oh, are they?" asked Grace eagerly. "So large and perfect?"

Smiling, he nodded yes; indeed they were. "Now the other," he said.

The second box contained another mineral specimen: rising from a dimply matrix of tiny pink crystals was a small thicket of deep golden crystals, two inches long. "Oh, Daniel," said Grace. "They are exquisite, the most beautiful and the largest that ever I saw, like jewels."

"Much too beautiful to grind up for use, I'm afraid—so I have brought you the ground pigments too. Open this." The little box contained a packet of dark-red powder: ground cinnabar; vermilion, in fact. And a packet of golden powder: orpiment. Grace took a tiny pinch of the dark-red powder between thumb and fingertip, and closed her eyes, the better to feel how fine was the grind: silky, so fine as almost not to be felt at all; impalpably fine.

"Mine," said Jamie, reaching for the cluster of golden and pink crystals, as mouthwatering as Venetian sugar crystals displayed in a confectionery window. Dusting her fingers against her skirt, Grace held up the mineral specimens for him to see, both cinnabar and orpiment crystals in their matrices, just out of his reach. "Look, but never touch, darling," she told him.

"He won't hurt them," said Dan.

"He puts everything into his mouth," said Grace. "And they're deadly poisonous, both of them. Cinnabar is mercury, you know—and orpiment is arsenic."

"What an unlucky present to bring home to one's bride! Don't tell anyone!" said Dan. "What about these?" he added, presenting her with yet another packet. This proved to contain a goodly supply of rough amber-colored nuggets, not as heavy as they looked. The little nuggets resembled droplets of petrified amber, or caramelised sugar, good enough to eat. Grace sniffed them and then put one in her mouth, just as Jamie would have done. Immediately it began to dissolve, thick and gluey, and just faintly sweet, less sweet than the drops of caramel sugar it so much resembled. "I wasn't quite certain whether you preferred your gum arabic in powdered form," Dan was saying.

"Oh, no, I always prefer the raw tears themselves," Grace assured him. "This is the real thing; one never knows how the powdered stuff may have been adulterated." These were undoubtedly the actual droplets, the hardened sap that oozed from the slashed bark of certain acacia trees in the Arabian desert. "Here, Jamie, this you may safely taste," said Grace, and she popped one of the clearest and palest of the little teardrops into his mouth. "Gum arabic never hurt anyone, and it's sweet, too. Thank you, dearest—what a handsome present. And enough to supply me for years."

"There's more," said Dan; and so there was:

A dozen large chintz Bengalese kerchiefs known as bandannas, of the kind most coveted just now by every fashionable lady in Philadelphia, Boston, and New York, in shades of madder, indigo, saffron.

Three packets of perfect ivory blanks; ovals and the newly fashionable rectangles, sliced thin, translucent, the characteristic netted matrix perfectly even and nearly imperceptible, and polished smooth, ready for paints. Grace ran her fingertips across them, and around their edges. She loved ivory, the warm smooth hardness of it; its faint networked grain; the nobility of it, derived from the nobility of elephants—for who could not love and revere elephants? These disks were very thin, very smooth and white; far better than any that Grace had been able to buy through any American supplier.

A gorgeously figured tortoiseshell tea caddy mounted in silver with an ivory escutcheon, each of its two inner compartments ready-filled with tea: with beautiful Bohea and fragrant Congou.

An entire bolt of utterly translucent Dacca muslin gauze, in the exquisitely fine weave called *baft-hana*: woven air. Upon unwrapping this, Grace glanced sidelong at Daniel, wondering if he knew its reputation as suitable for the clothing of courtesans, whose fleshly charms were not so much concealed as heightened by seven or eight layers of this ethereal stuff. How was she to use this, here, in dour America? Yes, he knew just what it was, she concluded; for he raised one eyebrow a little as he met her glance for a long moment.

A carved lacquerware box, in the old Chinese style: cinnabar-red, deeply carved in an exquisite design of birds perched amid plum blossoms, carved through the dozens upon dozens of layers of lacquer, so that the carving revealed the edges of other thin layers beneath—green, gold—over a black ground. The interior of the box was fitted out for a scholar, with neat close compartments containing an inkstone, a calligraphy brush with a carved cinnabar lacquer handle, and two bowls of the same material. "Daniel, dearest!" said Grace. "It is fit for an emperor!"

"I thought you'd rather have a scholar's paintbox than a workbox," he said.

"Infinitely," she said. Needlework was no joy to her.

"And here is one last present for you," he said then, reaching into the very depths of the crate to draw up still another rectangular twine-bound bale of straw, "though it is not from me. It is from Mrs Fleming, a belated wedding gift. She told me that she had ordered it at the time of our marriage, but it was unfortunately not ready until some weeks after we had sailed."

Mrs Fleming was Grace's stepmother, now remarried and accompanying her merchant husband on his voyages between three houses on three continents. They had been parents to her, had reared her. The rice-straw covering made a thickly rounded layer, like an enormous silk cocoon, and the hemp cordage was neatly tied in handsome knots devised by Chinese artisans. Dan cut the cording for her, and Grace pulled apart the straw packing, letting it fall with the rest to the parlor floor, which by now resembled a freshly bedded horse stall. Inside the thick layer of straw she came to another layer, a wrapping of quilted blue cotton; and upon unwinding this, the wedding gift was revealed: a black-lacquered traveler's desk, a writing slope, its every surface inlaid with mother-of-pearl butterflies and blossoms. "Oh!" breathed Grace.

"That is handsome," admitted Dan.

"It is just like her own," said Grace. "Mr Fleming gave her a japanned writing slope very like this—mother-of-pearl set into black lacquer—when they were married, and I always coveted it, admired it, longed to own just such another! Hers was inlaid with birds, and leaves—tea foliage, in fact, with the buds and flowers and seedpods all perfectly depicted. She knew that I doted upon it. But this one is more beautiful still—these butterflies! Look, here is a sphinx moth, quite unmistakable! And those three cannot be anything but silk moths. See this fat caterpillar, strolling among the blossoms—oh! and my initials, worked into the branch of this gnarled tree. Oh, it is beautiful! But where is the key? It must be here; I hope I have not dropped it?"

A dismaying quantity of rice straw and camphor curls littered the parlor floor. And though Grace and Daniel and Rawley and Jamie picked minutely through this dross as Rawley swept it up and carried it out to the yard behind the house, still the missing key could not be found, and Grace felt ashamed at how disappointed she felt; at how her pleasure was curdled by a mishap so tiny as this, a mishap which a locksmith would certainly set right in a matter of minutes. Command yourself, she thought; and she gave Rawley one of the bandannas, a bright azure one.

· · ·

WHAT DO GIFTS MEAN?

How silly, this question! Gifts are—gifts, of course, tokens of affection and esteem! Simple as that!

Oh, but are they indeed? Think again. Gifts are never so simple as that. There are wonderful gifts, and there are terrible gifts—and a vast range of banal gifts too, between the two extremes. Worst of all are the gifts given as reproaches, as hints for change or improvement. Here; read this, to amend your ignorance, your wrongheadedness. Here, wear this; your appearance is an embarrassment. Here are tickets; now you are bound to attend this lecture, this sermon, this play—and let it be a lesson to you, a lesson upon your shortcomings. And, insult piled onto injury, the recipient is obliged, even by such gifts as these, to thank the giver, for this not-very-subtle reproach, disguised as gift!

Only slightly better are the gifts which prove the giver either oblivious or indifferent to the true nature and temper of the recipient. The giver has never noticed, or does not care about, the recipient's particular excellencies of character: her discerning taste; or his formed and nuanced judgment. Ill-suited gifts are a rude snap of the fingers under the recipient's nose.

Equally disappointing are the gifts which are nothing but keepsakes, to remind one of the giver: think of Me, remember Me, who gave you this.

Oh, but it's the thought that counts.

Very well, then; just what was the thought? The insulting, careless, selfish thought may be only too apparent.

Hence, the offering of gifts is fraught with dangers, riddled with pitfalls, and not to be undertaken lightly.

What did these presents from Daniel mean? To Grace, these presents proved that her husband knew and loved her actual red-haired, imperfect self; that though he saw her clearly, he saw nothing he would change.

. . .

WITH HER FINGERNAIL GRACE SCRAPED AT THE SILVERY LITTLE man's waistcoat—the pale stripes now yellow, the dark ones green—but inflicted no scar. Thanks to skill, patience, and gum arabic, her transparent watercolor tint was stuck fast to the silver surface. The serious bespectacled face had now a scarcely perceptible hint of color too, more evanescent than the lining of a scallop shell. Technically, the experiment was a success. But was it a success artistically, aesthetically? Did color improve the silvery miniature? She thought not.

Grace loved color. It was as pleasurable as music. Indeed, it was sometimes not entirely clear to her whether she was seeing colors, or hearing them. She sometimes felt colors as notes, and juxtapositions of colors as chords. Red—green—gold (the Turkish rug on her floor, for example) might fall upon her eye much as *sa pa ga—do sol mi—en e o—A E C*—fell upon her ear. And for her, individual colors, like individual notes, had each their own particular flavor, pitch, meaning and tone; their own *rasa*: juice. In India, where she had spent her girlhood, it was generally known that colors, like notes, had distinct attributes—though not everyone agreed which qualities attached to any particular color (for tastes vary, and different mouths might discern quite different flavors in the same dish; to some tongues, even bitter melon is not bitter). Still, there was general agreement that red, the color of blood, signifies life, in all its fertility, sexuality, valor. Green was Dan's color, for green means commerce, prosperity, travel, trade. Yellow is for religious fervor. Blue is vulgar; black is inauspicious; and white stands both for death and for purity: the death of desire.

Why, then, was the little portrait less satisfying now, tinted, than it had been when only black, white, and grey? Grace had expected that the silvery miniature would, like a skilfully tinted engraving, become more satisfying with the addition of color. But it was not.

Grace took it downstairs to show it to Anibaddh; but learned from Rawley that Anibaddh and her sons had gone out to inspect several houses to be let for short terms. Then Grace set out for the address on South Eighth Street given her by Mr Cornelius. There the door was locked, and no one came when she knocked. She waited several minutes and rapped at the door again. At last, she heard someone coming, and Mr Cornelius himself opened the door to her. "I beg your pardon, Mrs Pollocke, for keeping you waiting," he said. "But I'm here alone at the moment, and was in the middle of a ticklish operation I couldn't leave off. As soon as I open for business in earnest, I guess I'll have to hire an assistant to let the people in."

Grace noticed that his hands were red and sore-looking, and as she stepped inside, a chemical stench enveloped her, a horrible miasma of smells. What was it? Unbidden came the memory of a Scottish beach at low tide on a rare hot midsummer noon, when the kelp lay rotting, stinking. Aye, that was part of it; and something else too, a farmyard reek, not the dung pile but something worse: billy goats. There were no goats to be seen, but Grace noticed a half dozen brown glass jugs containing a dark liquid lined up against one wall, their mouths corked and sealed with wax.

"This will be the reception room," Mr Cornelius was saying. "Though just at present we're storing chemicals here, until we get a lock to the storeroom in back. There's our workroom, and beyond it a closet, without windows, to be our darkroom—oh, yes, several of the operations have to be performed in darkness. And through here—please, this way—this is our studio."

Grace saw a straight chair for the sitter, set not on a platform, but on the floor; and angled toward the large south-facing window. This sitter's chair was just now occupied by a plaster bust—oddly blue—elevated atop a pedestal of books. Nailed to the wall behind was a length of sailcloth. Between chair and window there hung from the ceiling a large thick glass disk, of deepest blue. In the private fenced yard just outside the window, a large mirror upon an adjustable wooden stand threw dazzling sunshine into the window, through the suspended dark disk, and onto the subject inside. Of course the bust occupying the sitter's chair was in fact plaster-white, not blue, Grace realised; it appeared blue only because it was bathed in the blue-tinted light passing through the glass disk. Some five feet in front of the chair—where painter and easel would have stood—was a bureau, hip-high. Atop this rested the camera itself, an oblong mahogany box, six or seven inches high and wide, eighteen inches long; and pierced at the sitter's end by a round glass lens with brass ring fittings.

"I won't presume to explain the mysteries of a camera to you," said Mr Cornelius politely. "I guess you must know all about them."

"A little," said Grace. "I think I was seven or eight years old when I was taken to see the big camera obscura at the observatory on Calton Hill in Edinburgh, but I remember marveling at the dim image of the city skyline cast upside down, flattened, upon the wall opposite the aperture, the lens. And then years later, my teacher in Macao—Mr Chinnery, who taught me to paint—Mr Chinnery owned a camera obscura that was intended to be portable. Portable indeed! I always thought it the most awkward thing in the world, and weighing as much as a campaign bedstead. An extra coolie was required just to carry the monster. It was invaluable for making accurate tracings of landscapes, I suppose, but it scarcely seemed worth the trouble at the time. Your camera, here, is very nice and neat by comparison. The silver plate, I suppose, must be inserted at that far end, where the focused image falls?"

"Exactly. The plate—silver on copper, as you saw—first has to be polished to a fare-thee-well with a pumice slurry, until the silver is like a mirror. That's the first operation. Then in the second operation, the silver is sensitised to light by exposing it to the fumes of—of a halogen. Mr Daguerre's process calls for iodine, but my partner has found—well, I'd better not say. He's continually reminding me not to talk about it, lest everyone leap onto his discovery—but he has found another substance whose fumes make the plate far more sensitive to light than mere iodine. When it has been properly fumed—tricky to judge, especially by dimmest candlelight!—the plate is fixed into the apparatus at the back of the camera obscura, just as you observed; and the plate, safely inside the camera, can then be uncovered. All that is the second operation, which I was just finishing when you came to the door. Now for the third operation, the most thrilling of all; that is, uncovering the lens to make the drawing—or rather, to let the light make its own drawing upon the plate. Unfortunately I'm without a sitter today—reduced instead to making pictures of this bust of Mr Jefferson. But here you are, Mrs Pollocke, by some providence—and the light still strong! You won't refuse to sit for me, I'm sure! It'll take only a moment—less than a minute to expose the plate—and then, if you can spare a few minutes more, I'll demonstrate for you the fourth and fifth operations too: bringing up the image; and fixing it for all posterity. There, Mr Jefferson and his tower of books are set aside. Do oblige me, Mrs Pollocke."

That was how Grace found herself sitting in the chair and gazing into the lens of the camera five feet from her face. Brilliant April sunshine splashed across her right shoulder and right cheek—not quite in her eyes—reflected from the mirror outside the window. The light was blued and cooled by the suspended blue glass, so she was not completely dazzled, and could see bright whirling motes of dust, weightless.

"That devious old sun has moved again already; I ought to go out and readjust the mirror," said Mr Cornelius to himself. "But I must not wear out your patience; this will just do, I think."

Grace was wearing a neat dark dress with wide sloping shoulders and full sleeves. One of the pretty calico kerchiefs Dan had given her was tied loosely around her neck, its ends cascading in front of her collared lace bodice. Her hair, for once, was smooth and neatly plaited at her ears. She composed herself, as she composed her sitters: several deep breaths; lips gently closed, jaw relaxed; shoulders down, soft . . . and now think of the one you love.

"Three-quarters of a minute should do it, I guess," said Mr Cornelius, taking out his pocket watch. "And don't blink or sigh if you can help it. Ready?"

"Yes," said Grace.

He gently removed the lens cover, and noted the beginning time on his watch. Grace gazed steadily into the lens, quite a wide one, perhaps two inches across, a black bulging eye, like the eye of a whale. She had looked into a whale's eye, once, years ago, upon the China Sea . . . but think of Jamie, think of Dan . . . and do not blink, if you can help it! Where was Dan just now? Down at the docks, she supposed. She was tired; she had been tired all day; she had not slept enough. It was a great comfort to wake in the night and feel him there beside her—but so many wakings! He was not a quiet sleeper, and he took up so much of the small bed! She needed to blink now, needed nothing in the world so much as to blink!

Mr Cornelius looked up from his watch and smoothly replaced the lens cover. "Very good," he said. "Thank you; you are at liberty to move, and blink, and swallow. Now I cover the plate inside the camera by closing these levers. Then I can open the camera and remove the covered plate. Would you like to come into the darkroom and see the image come up? Of course you would, Mrs Pollocke!"

There was only one wax taper for light in the closet; he struck a match and lit it, then shut the door. "Now," he said, "your image has been imprinted on the plate, but it remains invisible until it's exposed to the fumes of mercury, inside this box made for the purpose. I set the plate above the fumes, just so; and now I'll light the spirit lamp underneath, to heat the mercury. And a good tight lid, as breathing mercury fumes is not at all recommended. It should take only a few minutes, as it's still warm from my earlier experiments. We can watch through this glass window as the image develops—but it's best not to bring the candle too near, at this stage . . . oh, the chair! Sorry, I should have warned you. But sit down if you like. No, I'll stand, it's only a matter of a few minutes. In a moment I'll venture to bring the candle near and we can have a look."

Presently he did so. "Ah! Now look, Mrs Pollocke, look at that!" said Mr Cornelius. "Here is the shape of the head; and there is your white lace coming up already!" Grace could see them too, in the faint wavering candlelight. "A few more minutes should do it, I guess. The mercury is up to a hundred forty degrees already, so I'd better put out the spirit lamp."

They waited in silence until, in the fullness of time, the mercury had cooled and Mr Cornelius deemed the picture properly ripened. He removed it from the apparatus, saying, "So that is the fourth operation, Mrs Pollocke. Now for the fifth: a bath in salt water, to remove the remaining light-sensitive coating. Quick and easy to do, and no stinking poisons either. Last of all we pour clear water over, like this, very hot from the kettle, so that it runs off and quickly dries, leaving no spots—we hope. There, that should do the trick. Let's go have a look, out here in daylight. Well! What do you think, Mrs Pollocke, eh? A few tiny spots there on the plate, that's a pity; might be dust inside the fuming box. I did shirk on wiping it out. Too much light on the shoulder and the background, it's burned out completely. But it's about right on the face."

He handed her the little silvery picture. Grace was shocked, but there was no gainsaying this portrait. No artist's eye, no artist's hand had intervened; the very light itself had inscribed the plate. This was herself: her hair smooth, its redness not apparent; and her dress nice and neat. But was that truly her air? So fatigued, so annoyed, so resigned? The silvery background behind the image reflected a bit of her real self at this moment, much larger than the image—her nose, lip, eye—in her true color, behind her small grisaille self. "Prodigious. Marvelous," she said. "This will mean the end of painted portrait miniatures."

"Oh, but we are not able to reproduce colors, and—ah!—did you succeed in applying colors to the plate I left with you?"

"I have not only applied them, but even made them stick. Still, I don't think there will be much demand for tinting," said Grace, giving him the little colored portrait. "See for yourself; it is no improvement upon the grisaille image."

"You don't think so?" he said, examining it.

"No," said Grace.

"What's wrong with it?"

"It looks . . . mistaken. It's what happens when more than one painter has had a hand in a painting: awkwardness; crudeness and conflict. As though one musician fingered the frets of the lute, while another plucked the strings."

"It's not quite what I'd expected," admitted Mr Cornelius, examining the tinted portrait still, tipping it this way and that. "The effect isn't entirely pleasing, is it?"

"Not entirely," agreed Grace. In many academies of painting, the passing master armed with an authoritative brush might, with a few impatient strokes, correct a student's efforts—for the better, usually; but sometimes, it must be said, for the worse. But on this silvery miniature, it was as though she, a callow student, had daubed over the master's exquisitely correct drawing.

"All the same," said Mr Cornelius, "I guess some people will want colors. Will you do it, if a sitter requests it?"

"Oh, yes, I suppose I will."

"At a fair rate of pay."

"What I should like best, Mr Cornelius, is to learn to make daguerreotypes. You can pay me by instructing me in the performance of these five operations."

"If you like. You might begin by studying this little instructional manual. It is Monsieur Daguerre's own account of the processes—translated into English, of course—with excellent illustrative plates. Just a moment; I'll write my name and address here, on the flyleaf—do take your time with it, but I'll be very glad to have this little book back again, when you have read it."

"I shall certainly return it," promised Grace.

"Oh—and you're not English, I hope?"

"Scottish," said Grace.

"Well, that's all right, then. The process is a gift from the French government, you see, free to the world—*offert à l'humanité, libre de droits*—except in England and Wales, where Mr Daguerre's patent is to be respected, and paid-up licenses to be issued."

. . .

MRS AMBLER WAS ONLY TEN MINUTES LATE FOR HER THIRD sitting the next forenoon, and her sister came with her once again. "Well, Mrs Pollocke," announced Mrs Ambler, as she settled into her pose, "I'm bringing you some new business, what do you think of that? My sister is thinking of getting her likeness taken too—if it can be done quick enough, before she has to go back to Virginia."

"How long do you remain in Philadelphia, Mrs MacFarlane?" asked Grace.

"Well, it's hard to say just how much longer my husband's business might keep us here," said Mrs MacFarlane. "It might be only a few more days."

"A watercolor miniature on ivory could be completed in three sittings, four at most—and finished within a few days," said Grace.

"Could it? How much does a miniature cost?"

"Here is my price list," said Grace; and she handed Mrs MacFarlane the card on which her present prices were neatly written out, for every size, from miniature to full-length—one hand, two hands, or no hands. No one had ever ordered a full-length.

Mrs MacFarlane studied the card.

"You won't get it done cheaper anywhere in Philadelphia, Clara," her sister assured her. "I compared pretty thoroughly before I settled to get mine done here. All the gentlemen painters charge more than Mrs Pollocke, even though their likenesses don't turn out any better, or even so good, sometimes."

Thank you, thought Grace; and chose another brush for the highlights on Mrs Ambler's glossy ringlets. It was quite true. Mr Sully's pictures of eminent men seldom resembled their originals so much as they resembled each other. Mr Neagle's likenesses were not bad, but he was busy and expensive. Mr Inman's sitters sometimes ended up with comically elongated necks, not swan-like so much as camel-like—and in any case, he had by now left Philadelphia for New York. And Mr Douglass, whose likenesses were good and prices moderate, had sailed for Europe, where even white people might sit to colored painters.

"Oh, it's not a matter of the expense," said Mrs MacFarlane. "I was even thinking I might get two of them done: one for my husband, and the other for Papa, as a birthday present."

"Why, Clara, that's a handsome notion! I could have one done for Papa too."

"If you wanted a miniature, Mrs Ambler," said Grace, "I should take your likeness from off this half-length. There is no need for you to sit again."

"Wouldn't that be a right elegant birthday present, if all of us sisters could sit for our pictures, to give to Papa, all in a set?" said Mrs Ambler.

"Why not James and Charley, too?"

"Oh, I know, Clara!" cried Mrs Ambler. "We could have a group, a conversation piece, with all of us, in front of the house! When we're all there for the revival!"

"I don't know if our sister Pratt is coming, though, so soon after her confinement," pointed out Mrs MacFarlane. "And I'm sure James won't come. He never does."

"It would do him good," said Mrs Ambler.

"And where in the world would we get a painter to come and paint us all?" said Mrs MacFarlane. "A good painter, I mean."

"Maybe just the miniatures of me and you, then, after all," said Mrs Ambler.

"It's awful hard to get everyone to act together, so many of us," said Mrs MacFarlane.

"Just about impossible, I guess," agreed Mrs Ambler.

"Do you have lots of relations, Mrs Pollocke?" asked Mrs MacFarlane.

"No," said Grace. "And those few are a great distance from here."

"That's too bad. We're five sisters and two brothers, all living. And Papa still with us too, and Aunt Bella."

"I daresay it must be a great comfort to have one's family all about one," said Grace.

"Don't that sound elegant, Anne, the way she says that: 'One's family all about one'! I swan, she talks just like a book! I wish I could sound like that. Wouldn't Mr MacFarlane laugh, though, to hear me!"

"WHO ARE THOSE LADIES?" demanded Anibaddh, accosting Grace on the stair landing as soon as Mrs Ambler and Mrs MacFarlane had gone away.

"What? Oh, nobody, just a sitter; and her silly sister, who comes to distract her with foolish chatter."

"But what are their names?" said Anibaddh.

"Their names! The elder is Mrs Ambler, if you will know; and her sister is Mrs MacFarlane. But why do you ask?"

"Do they live here, in Philadelphia?"

"Mrs Ambler lives up on Arch Street; but I believe her sister is here for a visit of only a few weeks."

"And the elder—is her Christian name Anne?"

"But what can you mean, my dear, by this cross-examination?" asked Grace, frightened now; for she saw that Anibaddh was agitated.

"Is her name Anne?" demanded Anibaddh again.

"I think it is. I have heard her sister call her Anne. Can you possibly know of them?"

"And the younger, is she called Clara?"

"Aye."

"They are the Grants," said Anibaddh. "Their father is Judge Grant of Grantsboro Plantation, who thought he was my master. They are your cousins."

CHAPTER
4

"Cousins in Virginia!" cried Dan, when Grace explained it all to him in a low voice, in their bedroom that night.

"Shh!"

"Cousins you've never met! But why didn't you ever mention it?" he whispered.

"They are not the sort of people one wishes to know. Not the sort of people whose good opinion is any compliment—contrary to their own view of the matter."

"But how could you know that, if you'd never met them?"

"I did meet their terrifying old aunt in Edinburgh when I was just a lass. That was enough, and more than enough, for me. Aye, it was she who came to claim me for my uncle, to take me back to Virginia, there to be brought up among my cousins. And when my stepmother would not assent, the old harridan—Miss Johnstone was her name—actually kidnapped me for a matter of several hours; and very bad hours they were. It was Anibaddh who saved me, and herself too, by running away with me. Aye; Anibaddh had been Miss Johnstone's slave, but she took her freedom then and there, in Scotland—and returned me safely to my stepmother—and ended by sailing to India with us. I realise now that my stepmother's decision to leave Scotland—an exceeding sudden decision it was too!—might have been taken, at least in part, to remove me from the reach of that dreadful woman. I am sure I have told you of this."

"I guess you did refer to it in some oblique way; or maybe I was listening with only half an ear—hearing only of a grudge you bore against me for being American, a prejudice that I was bound to overcome so as to win you. Somehow I didn't quite absorb the details;

didn't quite understand that your wicked old witch was a thoroughgoing fact."

"I'm afraid that she, and my Virginia cousins, are as factual as anyone."

"Weren't you ever tempted, all alone here these last two years, to send and let them know that you'd come to America after all?"

"Never indeed! I was lonely, but never so abject as that," said Grace.

"Ah; lonely! My darling! So was I. Gracie, let's not be separated again," he said, drawing her to him. "Wives and children may thrive in China, as well as anywhere. Mrs Fairlie down at Macao was brought to bed twice, within fourteen months—and delivered of two bouncing daughters."

"And poor you, with only a single son to show, for the same time!"

"Though it must be admitted that Fairlie was unable to attend to business, nor to put in the long hours that I did. Consequently his capital did not increase nearly so successfully as his family. Indeed, I think he has little to show for his pains during the last three years—except those little girls. His expenses were heavy with two establishments, and Mrs Fairlie no manager; and then, while up at Canton, he would deny himself nothing that might assuage his anxiety over them, eighty miles away. You ought to be proud of me, Gracie, dear; my only indulgence, my only unnecessary outlay, was for a little scull, in which I went out for a pull each morning; and when I came away, I sold her for just what I'd paid. I was sorry to part with her; she was a good companion to me, and very good for my health too—though not nearly as good as you."

"Ah, rowing! That explains these arms, this chest," said Grace, laying her hand against the front of his nightshirt. "I always did admire the arms and shoulders of sailors!"

He picked up her hand; turned it over and kissed the palm. "But if—if all goes well, Gracie, it will not be necessary that I should go there again. If this cargo sells well."

"Nothing is selling well, I should think," said Grace. "Has anyone any money to buy with?"

"I have received offers."

"Actual money?"

"Terms."

"Drafts payable three months hence, I suppose," she said. "And those to be renewed for three months longer, when it is explained that the original drafts cannot be honored, due to some third party's failure to honor his debt, when it fell due? There is no actual money to be had. Even houses and property are now sold upon a promise to pay at some future time, when money shall somehow have welled up again." Abruptly she fell silent.

"What's the matter?" he asked, after a moment.

"Nothing. I was only listening." Jamie's little bed had been moved to the tiny room directly beneath this. Would she never again exist in only one flesh, her own flesh? Or would part of her mind forever follow her child? She might never be single-minded again. If she were to bear another baby, would she be split yet again? How did the mothers of many children ever exist in only one place, one body?

Dan lay back. Presently he said, "But how astonishing, Gracie, that they should have happened to come and sit to you, of all the painters in the country! What are the odds? Can they possibly suspect who you are?"

"Not in the least; no more than I suspected them. And if Anibaddh had not heard their voices—"

"Did they see her?"

"No. She heard them first, chattering away in my studio—they are loud and assured as parrots, the two of them—and instantly she knew their voices, unchanged all these years. When they came downstairs, she took the opportunity to look out through the crack at the hinge side of the door."

"If she could recognise them so positively, after all this time, we must suppose that they would know her too. Supposing they had happened to meet, face-to-face?"

"The blood runs cold in my veins to think of it—although it is quite certain that Anibaddh is free in law, and so are Jeebon and Bajubon. But Ani tells me that she has concluded to take Mr Forten's house in Christian Street for the coming quarter, so she will not frequent even the same part of the city as my cousins—and certainly need never again find herself under the same roof with them."

"Ah! Speaking of roofs," said Dan, "I've got a slater coming to see about ours. How long has it been leaking?"

"Only since the day you came home. A feature of my warm welcome to you."

Grace blew out the candle. Darkness enfolded and concealed them; licensed them. Still, silence was enjoined, for there were others in the house: not only Jamie directly below, but also Anibaddh, Jeebon, Bajubon, Miss Babcock, and Rawley. The house was full of people.

GRACE KNEW JUST WHEN Dan slept, by the slower, deeper rhythm of his breathing. Through the window beside the bed she could see dark sky, star-studded, and no moon tonight to wash them out. There were the constellations of the Centaur and the Crow; but her own stars, her beautiful and comforting Kritikas—the Pleiades—were winter stars, not to be seen at this season. Philadelphia had gaslights lining its streets now, stinking and shining all night. The lights reassured those who feared darkness, or feared what men did in the dark. Some people felt safer, she supposed, because lights burned all night outside their windows, but Grace did not like it; she loved the nighttime. The gaslights did not illuminate what was to be seen at night; quite the contrary. They swamped the starlight. They threw shadows. They dazzled, so that one could not see beyond them. And it was unnatural. Night was for darkness; that was the proper way of things. She closed her eyes, to make darkness.

She could hear better thus: her own heart, pumping; Daniel's breathing, slow now and easy. And, between Daniel's breaths—if she held her own breath—she fancied she could even hear Jamie below, through the floorboards. She knew, having shared her room with him until he was weaned, that Jamie was a restless sleeper. He squirmed and turned and murmured all night, between wakings; and twice or three times she had heard him laughing in his sleep. She fancied now that she could hear him murmuring something; or perhaps she truly could hear it, between Daniel's nearer, louder breaths. To hear music better or to taste a food more thoroughly, Grace often closed her eyes. She preferred to blow out the candle when they made love, not from bashfulness, but to retire her eyes, just temporarily; to retire the greedy domineering eyes which swamped all the senses otherwise. Those eyes knew how to see pictures, how to direct the hands to make pictures; hungry, busy, demanding, diligent, those eyes. It was a relief to rest them and let the other senses play. Beside her, Daniel stirred, sighed. She could smell his hair.

Had she borne Daniel a grudge, for being American? No, not a grudge; only a certain reserve at first, which had evaporated long ago. She had hardly known, then, what constituted Americanness, had scarcely yet perceived how different were the Americans from the Scots and English and Indians among whom she had lived hitherto. The differences had become clear to her only after she had come to live here. And while she had been discovering this—discovering that she disliked America, and Americans—she had been alone, Dan far away in China.

Americans! How could she be married to one? Grace had been brought up with the Scots conviction that the inhabitants of Edinburgh spoke a purer, more correct, and more elegant English than ever the English did; and she considered that American speech scarcely qualified as English at all. Would Jamie sound like one of them? Would he say "fix" for "arrange"—"done" for "finished"—"reckon" for "suppose"—and "ornery" for "ordinary"? Would he sound like Rawley, who talked to him constantly? They took a competitive pride in their original and colorful locutions, these Americans; and the more garish the better. They relished opportunities to pronounce something or someone savagerous, rambunctious, highfalutin, poor as Job's turkey, or crazy as a loon. Grace had heard a man declare that a stolen thing had been "bodaciously absquatulated," and something else "catawamptiously exfluncticated"; had heard a fast horse praised for being "quick as a blue streak of greased lightning," and a small child said to be "scarce knee-high to a mosquito."

They admired prolixity, too; the longer the speech, the better. Their newspapers conscientiously cited the duration of any public man's address, but seldom troubled to report its substance. Any senator of theirs who could by his quacking hold the floor for two hours or more was esteemed a latter-day Cicero; no matter that he made as much sense as a duck.

Were a people who so valued hyperbole and flamboyance even capable of any subtlety or precision of thought? It seemed to Grace that they were not; that all nuance was lost on them. What she had seen thus far of American arts, letters, and politics was as careless, hasty, inconsistent, childish, and showy as their discourse.

Daniel turned over; his mouth fell slightly open; and he snored gently. As sleep was not just now within Grace's reach in any case, she forbore to nudge him.

At least he did not spit. She had been astonished to discover, upon arriving in Philadelphia, that nine men out of ten were copious public spitters. Fortunately her husband was, in this respect at least, an unusual specimen of American manhood: the one out of ten who abstained. Grace could never have loved a man who would spit. In Bengal, where men chewed *paan*—betel with lime—and spit bright-red saliva everywhere, she had never become inured to the repugnant crimson-spattered pavements and walls. Here in America, the quids were of tobacco leaves, and the expectorate was not scarlet but dark brown.

But there was no escaping the reciprocal conclusion: just so wrong as Americans seemed to her, so wrong must she seem to them.

Had Daniel foreseen this? Had he quite known, in China, what a singular figure she would cut, among American women? Had he foreseen his mother's disappointment, upon becoming acquainted with the bride he'd brought home? He must have known that his wife's continuing to paint heads for money would degrade him, would even render him ridiculous; nevertheless, he had explicitly said that she might, and had defended her right to do so despite his mother's disapproval. Grace had not anticipated how curious this would appear; had not known that her painting of heads would seem, to his neighbors, a humiliation and reproach to him. But he must have known.

Who was he, this beloved and trusted other self, this stranger, lying here beside her? She studied his unconscious profile. How little time they had spent together, these last three years! But now that they had time, what might emerge?

What if she should disappoint him, as she disappointed his mother?

In China, Grace had known Daniel to reject a consignment of tea which failed to live up to the promise of the samples which had been furnished him, the samples which had induced him to contract for it. He had sent back the chests, fifteen of them, and lodged a complaint with the Hong, alleging that the merchant was attempting to commit a fraud upon him; and that he, the barbarian Pollocke, would require the merchant to furnish that same first-chop tea which he had sampled—and at the contracted price—and not to attempt to deceive him with an inferior sixth-chop substitute! Was he, the barbarian Pollocke, to be taken for one of those Foreign Devils to whom all tea was the same? For one of those who could not discern a Congou from a Souchong, a Canton Bohea from an Up-Country Bohea? He was not. This was not the tea he had engaged to buy. He had prevailed too; the Hong had apologised, and the duplicitous tea merchant had been beaten, banished from Canton, and barred from any further adventure in the profitable trade with the Fan Kwae, the foreigners.

Supposing Daniel now made the discovery that she was not just the first-chop wife he had bargained for? That here, in America, she really would not do after all?

And what if he should disappoint her? *Sonā jāne kase aur mānus jāne base*: Gold is known by the touchstone, and a man by living with him.

But this living-together by husbands and wives was fraught with risks, it seemed to her. How could love—that fragile, ephemeral blossom—withstand the inevitable trials of cohabitation, great and petty: ill temper, fatigue, impoverishment, anger, drunkenness, sorrow, boredom, children, sickness, resentments—and an intimate knowledge of the faults of the loved one?

· · ·

"LOOK, THE FIRST OF THE ERRINDY," ANIBADDH WAS SAYING, pointing out to Grace a robust castor bean seedling. "Here; and here. Here's another. Yesterday, nothing; this morning, dozens pushing up."

Exquisite, that strong brittle yellow-green curved neck; arching up, pushing upward, from glistening wet black soil! Grace stopped to gaze; heard the yellow-green on black as *ni sa*: seventh, octave.

Gravel crunched under their feet; a new gravel path ran down the middle of the large fenced south-facing yard behind the tall house Anibaddh had leased in Southwark. She had also taken the deep vacant lot beyond—vacant except for a large shed which had formerly been a rope maker's workshop. In a scant fortnight, she'd had the fence separating the two yards taken down; the ground dug by a crew of day laborers; wagonloads of manure hauled in; long furrows dug; and each furrow sown to errindy: castor bean; *Ricinus*; Palma Christi.

A baby avenue, a double row of pale-barked saplings, had been planted too, along both sides of the new gravel path leading to the old rope shed, where someone inside was using a hammer energetically: bang! bang! "And look: my mulberries are leafing out too," remarked Anibaddh, fingering a fat green bud erupting from one of the flexible grey sticks lining the path.

Mulberry saplings, of course. Of the thousands she had brought from China, the Rani had caused some fifty of them to be set out. Grace could see tall stacks of other doomed saplings piled against the far fence; unplanted, not so lucky as these. A small single-wheeled seed drill of the kind used by Bengal peasants leaned against the fence too.

"The rope shed will make a fine wormery," Anibaddh was saying as they entered. Inside, Jeebon and Bajubon were tacking up lengths of coarse muslin over every opening to serve as screens. From a ladder Jeebon wielded a hammer, while Bajubon passed him nails and held the flimsy fabric in place.

"You have not lost a moment, any of you," said Grace. "But isn't it still very early? Supposing there's another frost?"

"No harm to the mulberries. As for the errindy, I should simply sow again. I've plenty of seed," Anibaddh said. "Bushels of it." Removing the lid from a large stoneware crock, she plunged her hand into it, bringing up a streaming handful of castor beans, and let them fall— click-tick-tick—back into the crock.

"How beautiful they are! Yet hideous too," said Grace, running her fingers through the seeds: dry, shiny, smooth, hard-shelled. She took half a dozen into her palm, and turned them over with a finger, examining them. In size, shape, and markings, they exactly resembled fully engorged dog ticks; hence their Latin name. Each was exquisitely mottled, netted, stippled, and spotted in rich mahogany or maroon upon an ivory or tan ground; each differed from all the rest. The moire markings were not symmetrical, but were nevertheless pleasingly balanced: like watered silk, like marbled papers, like wootz steel, like the labia of orchids. "They remind me of cobras," said Grace. "So lovely; and so deadly."

"What is deadly may also be very useful," said Anibaddh.

"I daresay it may be useful because it is deadly," Grace said. "You must remember, at Patna about ten years ago, that young wife who was suspected of feeding them to her tyrannical old mother-in-law? No? Nothing was ever quite proven against her, and she went free at last. It was suggested rather convincingly that the spiteful old woman had eaten them of her own volition, knowing that suspicion would fall upon her daughter-in-law."

"Mm," said Anibaddh.

"There was another case too," said Grace, "a Mohammedan, who had been talking of taking a second wife. But the man suddenly died, and the first wife—the widow, I should say—was found to have poisoned him by stirring a handful of castor beans into his *lobhia aur khumbi*. She claimed that she had prepared the dish for herself, intending to commit suicide in her jealous misery, but no one believed her." There was no knowing how many tragic deaths ought to be attributed to these pretty beans found along any roadside—in India, at least. A digestive disorder; a dysentery; a bloody flux, a rapid failing—what could be more common?—and then all is over. Suspicion does not even arise.

Anibaddh, rifling through a thick dossier of papers, appeared not to have heard any of this. She said, "Look: here is my advertisement in the *Silk Culturist*. It is to appear in the *Silk Record* too, and the *Farmer's Gazette*." It was a large and attractive advertisement, with several levels of headlines using every style of type available to an enthusiastic compositor:

PALMA CHRISTI SILK
COMPANY.

...

ERRINDY SILK CULTURE FAR SUPERIOR TO
MULBERRY CULTURE IN EVERY RESPECT.

...

Errindy silk prized in the Orient.

The robust Eri silkworm feeds on the Palma Christi plant (called in the
Orient Errindy)—& produces large cocoons which may be spun as easily as
cotton into the extremely useful—strong—lustrous Errindy Silk. Besides
providing fodder for these valuable silkworms, Palma Christi plant is the
sole source of the useful Castor Bean, from which Castor Oil is expressed,
prized for its medicinal qualities, and for fuel, lamp oil, and lubrication of
machinery. Unlike expensive & ill-suited mulberry TREES, Palma Christi
plant is of rapid and easy cultivation anywhere in the U. States—is often to
be seen thriving by the roadside, a common weed. Crops of BOTH Errindy
Silk and Castor Bean, for domestic use or as cash crops, may be produced in
a mere matter of WEEKS—requiring only little ground and small outlay.
A ready market, for Errindy Silk and for Castor Bean, is already well-
established in the U. States and abroad.

**EGGS—WORMS—SEEDS—COCOONS—MAY BE ORDERED
AT ADVANTAGEOUS PRICES, FOR IMMEDIATE SHIPMENT.**

*An interesting and useful instructional pamphlet
will be sent with all orders*
at
NO ADDITIONAL CHARGE.

INTERESTED PARTIES ARE INVITED TO INQUIRE
OF THE SUBSCRIBED:

. . .

PALMA CHRISTI SILK COMPANY.

CHRISTIAN STREET.

SOUTHWARK—PHILADA.

"I've never noticed castor plant growing here," said Grace. "But I've yet to venture outside of Philadelphia, sorry to say."

"I remember it in Virginia," said Anibaddh, "growing in the waste ground, very rank and weedy. But the race I've imported is vastly superior, bred for luxuriant foliage and oily beans. And after pressing out the oil, the spent bean mash can even be fed to pigs, if it is sufficiently cooked to drive off the poison."

Grace said, "We painters like castor oil too; it's a fine substitute for linseed oil. They are exceedingly tempting, these beans, aren't they? One wishes to pop a handful into one's mouth! And what a satisfying crunch one imagines between the teeth—like hazelnuts, perhaps! Here, I had best distance myself from temptation. And the Eri silkworms? Are they raised like mulberry silkworms?"

"Easier by far, and triply productive. Oh, but they are, Miss Grace; do not give me that skeptical frown! Mulberry silkworms produce only one generation in a year, but Eri silkworms will easily produce at least three. And as their cocoons are never reeled, but only spun—like cotton—even Americans ought to be able to make satisfactory thread." She untied the ligature from a hessian sack and, rolling down the top of it, revealed cocoons, elongated ovals, not two inches long, downy, firm, white. "Errindy cocoons," she said, and offered a handful of them to Grace. They weighed almost nothing, and resembled mulberry silk cocoons which Grace had seen before—except in one gaping respect: one end of each errindy-silk cocoon was open, a hole about a quarter-inch across, and the cocoon was hollow, a void; the moths flown and gone. "As errindy silk cannot be reeled in any case—it must be spun—there is no disadvantage in permitting the moth to emerge," said Anibaddh. "It does not spoil the cocoon. It can still be spun." The *himsa*, the violence, of conventional mulberry silk production had always distressed the Rani; Grace knew that she hated smothering newly completed cocoons to kill the moth forming inside, before it could pierce its cocoon and emerge.

"Mmm," said Grace, and watched Anibaddh's profile as she tied up the bag again. "One takes the Eri cocoon, then, only after the moth has finished with it; has abandoned it? Aye; errindy silk is *ahimsa*, then."

Anibaddh's hands fell still for a moment. Then, without looking up from the tie, she said, "Even an insect, a lowly worm, ought not to be robbed of her labor."

JEEBON AND BAJUBON finished their task and then, having put away the ladder and the bolt of muslin, they carried the hammer and nails up the new garden path to the house, where, their mother told them, they would find their tiffin laid out for them by Miss Babcock.

Now that it had all been explained to her, Grace thought it more incomprehensible than ever: this tremendous undertaking, this substantial investment, this Palma Christi Silk Company established here, in these rented buildings, upon this rented ground. How long did the Rani expect to remain? Was she not in transit to London, to educate her sons and seek justice for her husband? Hadn't she taken the house for only the quarter? "It looks as though you mean to remain here a good long while," said Grace.

"And why not?" said Anibaddh. "There is ample scope. I mean to establish errindy and Eri silk in America. It is not an undertaking to be accomplished without effort. It will require a great deal of effort, and investigation, and considerable travel too, I daresay."

"But why, Rani?"

"Haven't I just been telling you? Eri silk is far better suited, in so many respects, to American conditions—the climate, the people, the mills—than mulberry silk. I daresay that errindy will grow nearly year-round in the warmer southern states. It is exceedingly useful; and it is my purpose to establish it here."

"Oh, useful! Aye, it is that, certainly! Notorious for its usefulness—in so many ways! 'The Friend of Downtrodden Wives'—isn't that what errindy is called?"

"I never have heard it called that," said Anibaddh calmly. "Castor oil is called the 'King of Purgatives' in Ayurveda; an invaluable medicine."

"I wonder that plantation owners—that any slaveholder or tyrant, or cruel husband, even—should tolerate this pretty weed. I should think they would be well advised to eradicate it wherever it may spring up, valuable cash crop or not!" exclaimed Grace. For an instant, she perceived in Anibaddh's eye the glint of something sharp: Malice? Or was it humor?

Then it was concealed again behind that bland earnestness she had assumed. "I mean to establish it wherever I can," Anibaddh said evenly. "It is a gift, an endowment from the hands of the gods to all human-kind, this Palma Christi."

. . .

THESE, MY VIRGINIAN COUSINS! THOUGHT GRACE, WHEN THE Grant sisters came again. They looked quite different to her this time as they came into her studio, and shed their shawls and gloves; and settled themselves, noisy and bustling as ducks landing on a pond. That round forehead of Mrs MacFarlane's—the nice comma of Mrs Ambler's nostril—weren't these a little like her own?

"My husband says his business may draw itself out for another week or ten days, so I think I might just as well go ahead and have my likeness taken after all, if you really can do it so quick," said Mrs Mac-Farlane as Mrs Ambler arranged herself. "Heavens! What a deal of trouble these runaways have caused us all!"

"Runaways?" asked Grace, taking up her palette.

"Oh, it's a constant trouble," said Mrs MacFarlane, wearily. "If only the line was further away. But no; it's just near enough to tempt them all the time. They can't get it out of their woolly heads. The grass looks so much greener, I guess. It is too bad."

"I suppose the grass is greener, though, isn't it?—in the condition of freedom," said Grace.

"Oh, but Mrs Pollocke, some people don't know when they're well off," said Mrs MacFarlane, shaking her head. "Fed, clothed, cared-for, from cradle to grave. But no; they will steal off—and soon enough they find themselves starving, in rags, and shivering in the alleys. Some of them do think better of it, and come creeping home again, you know. Oh, but they do, I assure you! They come creeping back home again, for the sake of three good meals a day, and a roof over their heads!"

"I wonder that there should be any occasion for employing slave-catchers, then," said Grace.

"Some of them are so ignorant they can't find their way home again even if they want to," said Mrs MacFarlane. "Mr Whitehead, who has brought back a number of our people, says they're positively glad to see him, sometimes; they even beg him to take them back home again."

"Do they, indeed?" said Grace.

"Sometimes they do," maintained Mrs MacFarlane stoutly. "Or they miss their relations, and come back for the sake of living near them again."

"Have you ever lived in the southern states, Mrs Pollocke?" asked Mrs Ambler.

"No, I have not," admitted Grace.

"Or visited there?"

"No," said Grace.

"There's a great deal of prejudice on the subject," said Mrs Ambler. "But anyone who hasn't lived among us, in the South, is in no position to understand the situation. We grew up in Virginia, you see, my sisters and I, and I lived there all my life, until I married and came to live in the North with my husband."

"A lot of those negroes aren't even Christians, Mrs Pollocke, do you realise that?" broke in Mrs MacFarlane. "They're still heathens! They still steal off to the forest, some of them, to do their heathen practices and witchcraft, their devilish juju business. I swan! It makes my scalp prickle, sometimes, when I think of all those savage negromancers among us."

"What are mancers?" Grace asked, genuinely baffled for an instant, before she realised too late what Mrs MacFarlane meant.

"Why, you know: negromancers. It's in the Bible. It means negro practitioners of sorcery and witchcraft, and shameful practices as are done under the covers of darkness. Sometimes I can hardly sleep at night, for nerves about it, even though Mr MacFarlane is always careful to put the chain on the bedroom door before we blow out the candle."

Mrs Ambler said, "Of course, we hire preachers to come and baptise them, and teach them what's right. And when there's a revival meeting, there's a part of the grounds that's set aside specially for the negroes. But they don't learn fast, Mrs Pollocke. It's not their fault, I don't blame them. It's just that they're not really capable of it, and it's a mistake, as our father always says, to expect too much from them. They'll only disappoint you, always."

"Anne, I have the most brilliant notion," broke in Mrs MacFarlane suddenly. "Why shouldn't Mrs Pollocke go home with us, for our revival meeting? She could paint a miniature of poor Mamma, from Mr Stuart's full-length that's in the dining room! All of Mr Stuart's portraits, Mrs Pollocke, are very much celebrated, you know. And take Papa's likeness too—who can say how much longer Providence may spare him to us? And maybe even paint the house, like that picture of Butler Place. Oh, Mrs Pollocke, do come with us! You must!"

"I thank you for your kind invitation," said Grace, "but it is utterly out of the question."

"But why should it be out of the question, Mrs Pollocke?" said Mrs Ambler. "You could come back up to Philadelphia with me, afterwards. And I'm sure you'd like it ever so much, and Mr Stringfellow's preaching is so . . . so affecting! Why, the confessions! The saving! I've never heard any preacher here in Philadelphia who could even come close to him for eloquence and sense."

"It's like standing at the gates of heaven itself, and the gates opening before you! Do come, Mrs Pollocke!" urged Mrs MacFarlane.

"It is quite impossible," said Grace. "I could not bear to separate myself from my little boy. And as my husband has only just returned from a very long absence in China, I could not think of going away just now."

Mrs Ambler's faint moustache was not so very faint after all. Some people, Grace knew, considered this feathery shadow on a woman's upper lip attractive, even erotic. Was Mr Ambler among them? Grace picked up just such a shadowy tint on her brush, wiped it nearly dry; raised it—stopped there, poised just an inch from her canvas, an inch from Mrs Ambler's upper lip. No. She did not trust herself just now. "That will do for today, Mrs Ambler," she said, putting down her brush.

"Well, I beg you will think over the invitation, at least," said Mrs Ambler, "before you make any definite answer."

. . .

"To VIRGINIA? THEY INVITED YOU TO GRANTSBORO PLANTA-
tion?" asked Anibaddh, over her shoulder.

Up, up the four flights of stairs to the very top of the rented house,
Grace followed Anibaddh, who was carrying a basketful of leaves. "Aye,
they wanted me to go with them," said Grace, "to see the glories of
springtime in Virginia, and to see for myself how light is the burden
of bonded servitude, how enlightened the institution itself. And during my residence, I was to be commissioned to paint a miniature of
their dear departed mother—whose likeness I was to copy from a life
portrait by the Celebrated Mr Gilbert Stuart. And do a head of their
father too, who is now, I understand, a pitiful invalid. Furthermore,
though they have not admitted this, I think they hoped that the minister who is to preside at their revival meeting might by the eloquence
of his preaching save me from the error of my impious ways."

From the window over the stair landing, Grace could see the long
sunny yard below. Already the castor plants growing at perfect eight-
inch intervals in their long rows were much larger; far more green
showed, and much less black soil between them. The green had darkened too; it had more blue and less yellow, Grace noted; not so much
now like *ni sa*, but more like *pa sa*: fifth, octave.

The attic was warm and bright, with sunshine streaming onto the
trays set out under the dormer windows. "Look; they're hatching," said
Anibaddh. Laid out upon the trays were drifts of dry leaves stippled
with flat grey dots like poppy seeds: silkworm eggs. And among the
eggs Grace could see several minuscule animated black threads, not
half as long as her smallest fingernail. As she watched, another infinitesimal black thread struggled free of its tiny shell. Anibaddh tore a
small piece of mulberry leaf and laid it atop the tiny black threads.
"The mulberries aren't quite as far along as I'd like, but plenty of
them," she said. "And the errindy is thriving. If the weather remains
warm, the leaves should just stay ahead of the worms. Look, the Eri
worms are hatching too." She tore an errindy leaf to bits and dropped
the pieces gently onto several other trays.

Like the mulberry silkworms, the new-hatched Eri worms had
black heads, but their minuscule bodies were hairy and pale. Walking

on nearly indiscernible legs, the larvae approached the fresh leaves, clambered aboard, and began, Grace judged by the motion of their heads, to eat. "Try this," said Anibaddh, offering a magnifier. Through the lens, Grace could actually see the worms' infinitesimal jaws working, and minute dents and dimples in the leaf's surface gradually appeared as the worms ate.

"Are you going?" said Anibaddh suddenly.

"What?"

"Are you going with them to Virginia?"

"Of course not. I thanked them for their kindness but it was out of my power to avail myself of the pleasure: responsibilities as wife, mother; previous engagements which must be honored, et cetera, et cetera."

"You have never let them know who you are?"

"No, they cannot have the faintest idea," said Grace. She was not sure why she had kept this secret, or how much longer she might keep it. "I am wanted only on account of my wrong opinions—for the merit they hope to win by reforming me—and for my skills as a painter, of course. I will admit to some curiosity; I should dearly like to see my uncle, my own mother's brother. But it is out of the question that I should turn itinerant painter—and so I have said."

"Oh, but Miss Grace, supposing you went—and that I went too, as your servant."

"What! Preposterous! Why should you propose anything of the kind?"

There was a long silence while Anibaddh considered how to reply. Grace waited, looking at her, looking into her. For the first time since her return, Anibaddh allowed this.

"What is all this about, then, Rani? All this!" Grace swept her arm, to indicate everything around them. "House—furniture—plantation— wormery—your Palma Christi Silk Company! My dear, I have no head for business, and perhaps I am only being very stupid indeed, but— but—I do not quite understand. I do not understand at all. It is such a permanent sort of investment—and in a rented property—and that property rented for a term of only three months! My husband says that you have hired tutors for Jeebon and Bajubon—"

"John and Benjamin. Those are their English names, now."

"I beg your pardon. Their pardon. But you have indeed hired tutors?"

"I have."

"Why should you pour out your efforts upon *this* ground; exert your gifts *here*? You owe nothing—less than nothing—to America, to Americans. The interests of your sons and your husband would seem to require that you proceed to London with all possible speed. Instead, you have dug yourself in here! Why, Rani? Why did you come back to these States? The truth."

Anibaddh did not reply for a long moment. At last she said, "I left something here, years ago, that I want to get. If I can find it."

She was not here to sell silk. Not to establish errindy and Eri silk culture in the United States.

"What on earth could be worth the time—the trouble? The risk?" whispered Grace.

"Can't you guess?" said Anibaddh. "I thought you might have guessed, by now." Then she made herself opaque again, like a turning-away, so that Grace could see no distance into her soul.

No; Grace could not guess.

"WHERE IS JAMIE?" CALLED GRACE DOWN THE BASEMENT
stairs to Rawley, who was singing as she ironed. Grace could tell by
the smells of steamy cotton and hot iron; and by the song, the one
Rawley always sang while ironing.

"What's that, missus?" Rawley called back.

"Where is Jamie?" she called again.

"Well—ain't he with you?"

The kitchen door, the door leading out to the backyard, stood ajar.
Grace hurried out, her heart burning. He was not among the straw-
lined rows of peas and beans. The lid of the cistern appeared undisturbed, and surely he was not strong enough to move it. He was not
behind the wee house at the back fence; nor inside it. "Jamie?" she
called into the warm awful afternoon. "Jamie!" Time stuttered; the
entire universe was about to be torn to pieces; that instant just before
she knew that he was lost had been the last happy instant of her life.

There was a rough scuffling against the board fence, against the far
side, where the neighbors' pig lived. "Jamie!" she called again. There
was a very small gap under the bottom board, only a few inches high,
far too low, surely, for a small child to wriggle under.

"Mamma?" said his voice, from the far side of the fence. "Mamma,
Mamma!"

She dropped to the wet ground to look through the gap. She could
not see him. But there was the pig, just raising its massy head from the
muddy straw bedding in its little shed against the far wall of the yard.
Its snout twitched in her direction, and its ears flopped forward over
its tiny eyes. It grunted, twice, and heaved itself to its feet, to stand
staring and snuffling. This was not the greedy young pig that had

raided Grace's cabbage patch; this was a tusked boar, with a ring in its nose.

Grace leapt to her feet, and jumped to grab the top of the fence, six feet high. Scrambling, she got one elbow and then the other onto the crossbar near the top. Then she heaved herself upward and threw one arm and one leg over. There was Jamie, just below her, looking up. His upper lip was slimy, and his fair hair full of mud. "Go under!" she ordered him, fiercely, hoarsely. "Climb under the fence. Right now!"

"Can't," he said, and began to cry.

The big boar snorted, and stamped its front feet.

Grace slid herself painfully along the top of the board fence—six inches, a foot—then got her other leg over, and dropped awkwardly to the ground next to her son inside the pigpen. She landed badly, one ankle twisting painfully under her, and knelt beside him.

"Mamma," he cried, and threw himself into her arms, hanging around her neck. The boar grunted loudly and ran two or three steps toward them, before stopping again. Grace stood with her back against the fence. For so short-legged and ungainly a creature, it was frighteningly quick on its little cloven hooves. Its long curved tusks were stained brown as though it chewed tobacco, and the ring in its nose looked old and corroded.

She could not climb over the fence with Jamie in her arms. She could not throw him over it. She dared not carry him across the boar's pen to the stout gate, latched in any case from the outside. Could she perch him on top of the fence, hang him there, tell him to hold on, and then climb over again herself, to reach him down from their side? "I'll put you safe, up on the top of the fence," she told him, and tried to pry his arms from around her neck. "We'll both climb over."

"No, no, Mamma," he cried, and clung all the tighter to her.

Under, then? She squatted in the mud, one arm around Jamie, and half an eye for the boar, feeling under the fence. Here was the little opening where her son had wriggled through, somehow. She clawed at the filthy ground; could she enlarge the gap? She scraped with her fingernails, felt a rock, dug around it, clearing away around it, and pulled it free. The rock was only a little larger than her fist. She set it aside and went on clawing at the little opening. The gap was bigger now, but was it big enough for a baby to fit through? Babies could make their way through very small openings, she knew from painful experience.

"There, my dear," she said to Jamie. "Now it is big enough for you to crawl through again. Here you go, home again, headfirst."

"No," he said, clinging to her and wiping his nose against her neck.

"Missus! Is that you?" called Rawley's voice.

"Rawley!" cried Grace. "Quick—here, under the fence. He won't let go of me, you'll have to grab on and pull him through." Jamie screamed and fought as she detached him from around her neck, and screamed as she pressed him facedown, headfirst down into the muddy gap, and continued to scream, ever louder, as Rawley's strong black hands appeared through the opening, gripped him, and pulled him through, kicking.

Grace had turned her back on the boar. When she looked again, it was nearer, its head swinging from side to side very low, and snout twitching. She felt for the pitifully small rock she had set aside, and stood up. The boar snorted loudly, and stamped its feet again. The high fence behind her was sheer on this side, with no high crossrail to scramble up to. She knew that she threw very badly; if she threw the rock and missed, she would be left empty-handed. In any case, it was a puny rock. "Thou art unclean! Unworthy to pass between me and the sun!" she declared fiercely to the boar in Bengali, putting as much threat into the words as she could; and it squealed shrilly, taking the offense she offered.

"Who's there?" shrieked a woman's voice, cracking. "Oh, no, get out, he'll kill you! Tom! Tom, come quick, and bring the dog!" A woman's bonnet appeared, just above the sturdy gate on the far side of the pen. "Tom, come quick!" shouted the old woman again over her shoulder.

"Flap something at it, your shawl, or your bonnet," Grace called to her. "Distract it!" After a moment, the woman seemed to understand; she took off her bonnet and waved it above the gate. The boar grunted, and whirled, to get a look at this new threat.

Then a man's face appeared above the gate too. "Don't move," he called to Grace; and to the old woman, "Go unchain my mastiff!" She disappeared. Grace did not move. Presently the man opened the gate, and a heavily muscled dog charged into the pen. The boar wheeled to face it. The dog stiffened; the boar snorted loudly; but they did not close upon one another.

"Come on now! Run across!" the man called to Grace. "Quick, run!" He did not want to venture into the pen himself, it seemed. It was only twelve feet across to the gate. Grace plunged, on her painful ankle; out; safe! The man slammed the gate shut behind her. There was a terrible shrieking, an earsplitting screaming; it was the boar, whose ear was now torn and bleeding. There was blood on the jaws of the dog too. The man had much ado in getting his dog to come at his command; but at last, after considerable threat and cursing, it too retired to safety outside the gate, and was returned to its chain.

"If no one keeps boars, Mrs Pollocke, how are we to get pigs?" said the man reasonably, as he walked Grace back around the block to her own front door. "And without pigs, where's bacon to come from, eh? And ham? You'd best keep a closer watch on that little boy of yours."

LATER, THOUGH—after the gap under the fence had been filled with large stones well mortared—after Jamie had been bathed and kissed and put to bed—after Grace's scrapes and splinters had been cleaned and dressed—then Grace realised that she knew after all why Anibaddh had returned to America.

I left something here that I want to get, Anibaddh had said.

What on earth could be worth the risk? Grace had asked.

Of course she knew the answer; had known ever since she had given birth—had given a hostage to fortune—the one cause sufficient to risk anything, everything.

She tried to imagine asking Anibaddh what made her think or hope it was still here, the "something" that she wanted to get; how she proposed to get it back.

Horrible to imagine Anibaddh's private distress, all these years.

Terrifying to know that she herself was obliged to do anything, everything, to help.

. . .

"WHAT DO YOU THINK OF MY DRESS, MRS POLLOCKE?" ASKED Mrs MacFarlane.

"Most elegant, and suits you exceedingly well," said Grace as she placed a small table under Mrs MacFarlane's elbow.

Mrs Ambler was pawing through Grace's kit, set out on a paint-streaked stand. "So this is the palette you use when you are painting a miniature? How sweet, it is so very tiny! And that is your little brush? Oh, and a magnifying lens; yes, I see. And so there is the disk of ivory, a slice of an elephant's tooth, isn't it? So thin, hardly thicker than pasteboard!"

Grace induced Mrs Ambler to sit down too.

Mrs MacFarlane was not quite so handsome in feature as her sister, but there was a rather attractive softness about her chin and jaw; less hard resolve showed itself there; less intelligence too. Quick to smile, she often appeared pleasantly, softly confused, a bit addled; even a bit sleepy, for her eyelids were long. She was fair, and no faint shadow lined her upper lip. Her dress, of a melon color, flattered her pale neck and throat, throwing a rosy light upward under her chin. Grace started by studying and sketching the shape of the face; the shape of the chin and the forehead, round as Grace's own; then the correct proportion at the greatest width, across the cheekbones.

Mrs Ambler was telling Grace about the sermon she and her sister had just heard, and the preacher who had delivered it. It was a Tuesday, but the sisters took themselves to a church service almost every morning; and twice on Sunday. "Well, it sure was interesting, I thought," said Mrs Ambler. "Didn't you, Clara?"

Mrs MacFarlane agreed that it had been downright interesting, and added that the preacher had a resonant voice, very pleasant to hear, nearly as pleasant as Mr Stringfellow's.

"His text was the plagues of Egypt," explained Mrs Ambler to Grace. "Starting with all the water turned to blood—only Pharaoh insisted it wasn't really blood; it only looked dark red, like blood, and smelled bad, just like any stagnant water might."

"And the frogs," said Mrs MacFarlane. "I swow, the very idea makes me laugh, frogs being so comical, don't you think, Anne? Who could be alarmed about frogs?"

"I guess you wouldn't care for them in your bed much, though."

"I guess not; and toads are worse."

"But as for Pharaoh," continued Mrs Ambler, "he just said there might naturally be a big frog hatch after a spring with lots of standing stagnant water. You see, Mrs Pollocke, Pharaoh was being advised by his court magicians, who were alchemists and negromancers and that sort of thing, who insisted that all these dreadful plagues was only to be expected in the natural course of events, being atheists who pretend that everything can be explained by science, and refuse to see the hand of God, be it ever so."

"Oh, indeed," said Grace.

"When the flies came, Pharaoh and his magicians said it was only to be expected, from all those dead frogs a-lying around in big heaps. And then the very grievous murrain, and the boils, but Pharaoh said that diseases just happen naturally sometimes, especially when there's been lots of flies and mosquitoes about, like when there's a outbreak of the glanders, or distemper—and he denied that it was a punishment from the hand of the Almighty. Even the hailstorm, with hailstones as big as—as—"

"The biggest ones I ever saw was about like hens' eggs," said Mrs MacFarlane. "And that was plenty big enough. Remember, Anne, how it flattened the wheat, and knocked down all the peaches?"

"And we ran outside after, when they were melting? And threw them at each other, and Charley caught one on the nose, and his nose bled and bled, and he set up such a howl!"

"Ha ha! Served him right!"

"But God whispered in Moses's ear that He Himself was hardening Pharaoh's heart, and making him so prideful and skeptical, as—well, as an opportunity for God to show what He was capable of if He was provoked."

"Such as locusts," said Mrs MacFarlane helpfully. "But Pharaoh's infidel magicians predicted the locusts wouldn't stay long because there wasn't a thing for them to eat, not after the hail. And when the wind changed and blew them away, Pharaoh said, see, told you so—"

"And darkness, three days of thick darkness, wasn't it, Clara?"

"Yes, 'even darkness which may be *felt*'—but old Pharaoh, him and his magicians pretended it was just a—a eclipse, isn't that what the preacher said?"

No, thought Grace; a palpable darkness lasting three days was a dust storm, not an eclipse. And as all green growing things had already been destroyed by hail and locusts, it did not take a Jehovah—nor even a Pharaoh or a Moses—to predict that a dust storm was likely to follow. Forbearing to express her Pharaonic doubts, however, Grace held her tongue, and only considered the folds in the sleeves of Mrs Mac-Farlane's dress.

"And again God hardened Pharaoh's heart, because He wasn't done with His mighty demonstration yet, as He was saving the best for last—and that's when He smote down the firstborn in all the land," said Mrs Ambler.

Mrs MacFarlane said, "I guess that showed old Pharaoh, and his magicians! They could hardly pretend that was just a natural occurrence!"

Indeed, Grace had to concede that this catastrophe—if accurately reported—was not easily dismissed as a recurring phenomenon in nature. "But," she said, "how are we to muster a solemn reverence for any Divine Power which would summarily extinguish so many innocent and unoffending lives in a fit of pique; merely as a demonstration of puissance; and especially if this Divine Power had indeed—as boasted—manipulated the Pharaoh's heart and mind, thus contriving a pretext for this—this crushing and unjust blow?"

"I swow!" cried Mrs MacFarlane. "You sound as if you was taking Pharaoh's side!"

"Oh la, Clara, I'm sure she don't. Who could be so wicked? You don't take Pharaoh's side, do you, Mrs Pollocke?"

"No, I do not," said Grace. "A plague on both their houses. I think that the Egyptian natural philosophers were quite right about the causes of the troubles afflicting the Nile Valley that year. But I cannot sympathise with them, nor with any regime that tolerates the holding of humans as property, in hereditary and perpetual bondage. And it seems clear that Jehovah disapproved of them on the same account—"

"Heavens, Mrs Pollocke!" interrupted Mrs Ambler. "No, no; you've misunderstood from start to finish. I don't say you're at fault, for these misunderstandings will arise here in the north all too often, where the atheists and abolitionists are so bold and shameless. I wish you could have heard the preacher this morning, because he put it very clearly. No, no; God's quarrel with the Egyptians was not on account of their embrace of slavery; far from it!—as He has clearly ordained and decreed the institution Himself! No; it was on account of Pharaoh's prideful setting up of himself in opposition to God's will, you see. Pharaoh relied on his infidel advisers—his magicians—negromancers—alchemists—those who pride and puff themselves up on their own cleverness, atheists who pretend that the handiwork of the Lord—all Creation—is only nature and chance."

"The leatherheaded fools; why do they guess it's called 'Creation,' then?" put in Mrs MacFarlane.

Her sister hardly faltered, but only finished by saying, "In their sinful pridefulness they deny the very hand of the Almighty, Mrs Pollocke, and refuse to bend their necks under His yoke."

"That was very well put, Anne," said her sister. "Not even Mr Stringfellow could have said it better. Now, don't that place it all in a much clearer light, Mrs Pollocke?"

"Speaking of a clear light," said Grace, "I must draw this curtain just a little, I think. There; that is better." She considered the disk of ivory on which she had captured, she thought, some of Mrs MacFarlane's characteristic look of sweet-tempered confusion. Then, her minuscule brush poised an inch above the ivory, Grace paused. Had she the courage for this? She leapt from the precipice, saying offhandedly, "Perhaps you can shed some light too, upon another part of scripture which has always baffled me. I mean those verses in which Hagar and her infant Ishmael are cast out into the wilderness by Abraham, on account of Sarah's jealousy. Having exhausted what little food and water she had been given, Hagar, we are told, 'cast the child under one of the shrubs,' and went to sit down some distance away, out of earshot, so as not to hear the infant's distress, nor witness his death. Well! But what are we to make of this—this unnatural conduct? Could any mother bring herself, do you think, to abandon her baby under such circumstances?"

"It is dreadful," agreed Mrs MacFarlane complacently.

"Well, but she was an Egyptian bondwoman, wasn't she?" said Mrs Ambler. "Which is the same thing as an African slave. And negroes really don't look after their children like regular people do, Mrs Pollocke, or have the same feelings about them. It's just their nature, you see, and here's a proof of it from Holy Scripture. It's not their fault, and we don't hold it against them. It's just how Divine Providence hath seen fit to make them."

"I cannot believe it," said Grace. "What mother could bring herself to do that?"

"Oh, you'd be surprised, Mrs Pollocke! You mustn't go supposing that their feelings are like yours. They just don't have those tender natural feelings that civilised Christians have. But they don't, Mrs Pollocke, no more than a cow does! Why, when you take away her calf, a cow walks around for a day looking for it, and lowing—but by the next day she's forgotten all about it! And that's how it is with negroes. I know it's hard to believe until you've seen it for yourself."

"But have you in fact ever known a slave mother to abandon her child?" said Grace.

"Well," said Mrs MacFarlane, "if you was to press me, just at this very moment—"

"Oh, yes, there was!" cried Mrs Ambler. "Don't you remember, Clara? That maid of Aunt Bella's that ran away, when Aunt Bella took her abroad? We was just girls then, it was years ago. That was Annie, Annie Bad; you must remember her!"

"Oh, Annie Bad," said Mrs MacFarlane. "That's right."

"How did that happen?" said Grace. She succeeded in making her voice sound as it usually did, but her hand holding the tiny brush was trembling. She set down the brush and wiped her palms at her hips on her smock.

"We was just girls then, and it was pretty shocking, I guess; they didn't say much to us children about it. But our Aunt Bella had to go abroad, for something or other. . . . What was that about, Clara?"

"Wasn't there an orphan somewhere, some kind of cousin, that was supposed to come and live with us?"

"That was it. Well, anyhow, of course Aunt needed her maid to go with her. And since the maid had just had a baby, Aunt guessed she wouldn't cause any fuss about stealing herself away, and all of that, not with her little baby waiting for her at home. But that girl—"

"Not the faintest natural feeling."

"—that girl ran away anyhow, it was in England somewhere, I think, where they don't understand this sort of thing at all, and Aunt couldn't get anyone to help. She finally had to give up and come on home without the maid. We never did get her back."

"What became of the poor little baby?" asked Grace.

"Well, let me think. . . . Clara, that must have been—must have been Diana, wasn't it?"

Diana.

"Sure it was," said Mrs MacFarlane. "I guess some mammy must have looked after her while she was little. I don't exactly remember. But you see, Mrs Pollocke, that's what generally happens if a baby loses its mother."

"There's always plenty of old mammies around the place to look after the little ones, and aren't they a sight!" said Mrs Ambler. "Playing, and quarreling, and tumbling over one another, always fighting and biting just like a litter of puppies, and just as happy."

Grace did not dare to trace the further fate of the infant Diana by more questions just now. Instead, she made a feint in another direction: "And what of the cousin, the orphan? Did he ever come to live with you?" But even as she uttered these disingenuous words, she rendered it impossible ever to reveal to these cousins their kinship. If ever she were going to suddenly exclaim, to remember them, to recognise them—to claim them as her long-lost cousins—this was the time; this, the last possible moment.

And now the last possible moment had slipped away.

"No, nothing ever did come of that," said Mrs MacFarlane. "I wonder why not. I'll have to ask Aunt Bella when I see her again."

"I think it was a girl—the cousin, I mean," said Mrs Ambler. "Because I remember thinking we had plenty of girls in the family already, and I didn't much care for the notion of sharing my dolls with any orphan."

Grace took up her pencil again. Her hand was steady now. She looked hard at Mrs MacFarlane—who blushed, then laughed, hand over her mouth, and looked away. "I declare, Mrs Pollocke, you look like you're going to eat me up, when you do that!" she cried. "I knew I wouldn't be able to bear being looked at so hard! Anne, how did you tolerate being looked at so hard?"

"Oh la!—you must just pretend it is Mr MacFarlane looking at you," advised Mrs Ambler.

THE NEXT MORNING was Rawley's half day, so when Grace went down to Christian Street in Southwark to call on Anibaddh, she took Jamie with her. It was slow going, because Jamie was no longer content to be carried on her hip; he wanted to walk on his own feet, holding her hand. But he was not quite tall enough to reach her hand unless she walked bent over; and he could not walk fast, for his legs were short and the curbs were high; and he was distracted by everything he saw on the ground, so much nearer and more fascinating to him than anything else. Leaves; rubbish; an eggshell; a discarded pamphlet in the gutter; a length of twine; these all delayed them, and he had to be tactfully convinced that they were not to be picked up and tasted, or collected and carried along. Grace held on to her patience with both hands, and it was a lovely spring day; why hurry? In any case, she did not anticipate this visit with any relish. The more delay, the better; for she had not yet thought of how to open the subject.

Nevertheless, they arrived at Anibaddh's doorstep at last. "Hello, Master Benjamin," she said to Ani's younger son, who admitted them. It was difficult not to call him Bajubon. "How go the studies?"

"Very well, ma'am, thank you," he said, but ducked his head, still bashful. Neither he nor his elder brother had yet attained any degree of manly address. He sounded neither Khasi nor British nor American, but a peculiar blend of all three. Had he any idea, Grace wondered, why his mother had brought him to America on their way to London? Did he suppose it was to advance her silk interests? She inquired for his mother, and was told that she was in the wormery. Ushering her through the house to the garden behind, Benjamin walked with her through the plantation, where the castor bean plants were thriving; the planted mulberries too. She could see the unplanted mulberry saplings piled against the back fence. From every node and bud, those doomed saplings had sent forth leaflets and shoots into the spring sunshine—but already these were yellowing, dying.

Benjamin left her at the door of the former rope shed, now the wormery. Lined up along the walls inside—but not quite touching them—were multitiered tables, étagères, each tier bearing trays of leaves—and the leaves all gnawed, richly infested by caterpillars: silkworms. Each table leg stood in a shallow tin dish, and at the far end was Anibaddh, with a spouted watering can. She was pouring water into each dish, filling small moats: an India method for discouraging ants.

"Ah! You have found me," said Anibaddh as she straightened, holding her necklace, a handsome strand of dark irregular pearls. The tremendous emerald on her finger gleamed, and light danced off her little ruby eardrops. "Among my babies. Look, third instar already." And so they were, the caterpillars upon the trays upon this table; a week older and larger than at Grace's last visit, they had changed color. No longer tiny black newborn threads, they had outgrown and shed their baby skins. Now they were like moving grains of hulled rice, with whitish bodies and wide black faces.

The Eri silkworms had grown too. They were distinctly corrugated now; spiky and greenish. At the far end of the shed Grace could see several trays of yet other worms, green ones, small and large, feeding on other leaves. "What are those?" Grace asked.

"Just some American caterpillars which I have collected, for study; even they may prove of use, eventually," said Anibaddh, coming forward.

"Look, Jamie; see the worms?" said Grace. The white silkworms regaled themselves amid a paradise of tender leaves continuously and miraculously renewed and refreshed, by an unseen and unguessed-at providence.

"Here is a penny for your little caterpillar," said Anibaddh, handing a large copper cent to Jamie, who received it reverently, awestruck at so valuable a gift.

"Not in your mouth," Grace warned him; and she asked Anibaddh whether the Palma Christi Silk Company's advertisements had sparked much interest.

"Yes, I have had numerous inquiries," said Anibaddh. "Enough to encourage me to think of traveling, to demonstrate and offer samples."

Grace guessed from Anibaddh's elaborately casual manner just what the answer would be, but she was obliged to ask nevertheless: "Where? Where will you travel?"

"Down through Maryland, and into Virginia, at first," said Anibaddh, "where the warm weather is coming on already."

"Jinya," said Jamie unexpectedly, squirming on Grace's hip. "Jinya."

"Rani, no," said Grace. "You cannot go there, my dear. Not even for—for . . . I know, now, what you left behind, and why you have come back to America. I came to tell you that I will do anything to help you to get her back; anything you ask of me."

Anibaddh's face became still, hard as basalt. Terrifying.

"Diana," uttered brave Grace. "Her name is Diana. My cousins spoke of her."

Anibaddh turned away; poured water into the next dish. Her hand shook; the water sloshed out of the dish, and she let fall the watering can. She leaned against the doorframe.

"Uh-oh," exclaimed Jamie. "Spilled!"

Grace reached for her hand, tried to turn her around, but Anibaddh still twisted away, covering her face with her other hand.

"My dear," said Grace. "Dear Rani. Don't cry. I am so sorry. Everything has been so dreadful for you. We will get her back." Grace felt her own tears now, and blinked them back as best she could.

"Mamma cry?" said Jamie. "Rani cry? Don't cry."

"What did they say?" choked Anibaddh.

"Only her name."

"She's alive, then? She's there, at Grantsboro?"

"I cannot be sure. I did not dare to ask any pointed questions. Rani, I know of a lawyer who could advise us. Let us go and consult him," Grace urged Anibaddh's back. "But you must not think of setting foot in Virginia, not even for this."

"There is not a day to be lost. She may have had babies of her own by now. I must find her as quickly as possible. She may be pregnant at this very moment. It becomes only more difficult."

Grace had not thought of babies: another generation born into slavery. She started to say, "But a lawyer's advice—"

"I am still not a fool, Miss Grace. Of course I have had a lawyer's advice," interrupted Anibaddh fiercely. "There are a few men—and women—in this place who are not afraid to help. They are not hard to find, if one knows where to look." She dashed the tears from her eyes. "And upon their recommendation, I have written out a letter stating the particulars of my situation, and that letter has been forwarded under cover to a lawyer in Washington City, who has been able to manage other cases not so different from . . . mine."

"But surely this lawyer, whoever he is, does not advise that you should venture into Virginia!"

"Should you like to know what he advises? Wait here while I fetch his reply, and you shall read for yourself."

While Anibaddh went up to her house, Grace tried to calm her breathing. Her heart was thumping very hard in her chest, and she was trembling a little. She tried to calm herself by chatting to Jamie, and admiring Liberty's handsome profile, on his cent. But her heart was still pounding when Anibaddh, looking like thunder, returned after a few minutes and handed Grace the letter.

Mrs A. L.—Dear Madam:—

My interest and my sympathies are strongly aroused by your letter of the 22nd inst., arrived to hand just now under cover from the faithful friend to whom you confided it. It is perfectly true that I have more than once had the satisfaction of successfully concluding negotiations resembling that into which you now propose to enter with the object of securing the freedom of your daughter D____, and of any children who may have been born to her.

Naturally you will understand that the undertaking you propose may be fraught with disappointments and dangers, some of which may be foreseen and guarded against; and others, which may not easily be foreseen. My experience has taught me that only the most carefully framed inquiries are likely to meet with success, and that in a case such as this, too great a haste will only place in jeopardy the likelihood of successfully concluding the transactions in question.

The man you name as having been D____'s master 18 years ago is known to me only by reputation. To the best of my knowledge, he still resides at his plantation near Leesburg, though he has played little or no part in public life in recent years. It is rumored that he is now sorely beset by the afflictions of old age and declining health, and by a marked ebb in his fortunes. It is reasonable to hope, therefore, that a cash offer such as you propose might indeed be successful, if in fact your daughter D_____ (and her children, if any) remain still under his control after the passage of nearly two decades.

Particular facts must first of all be positively and independently ascertained, however, before opening a correspondence or entering into negotiations of any sort: namely, the present whereabouts of your daughter D_____ and the identity of her present master; and the whereabouts, names and ages of D_____s children, if any have been born to her, and the identities of the masters of any such children.

I must advise in the strongest terms against applying for such information to the man you have named, as I have known of diverse cases where so premature an approach has proven fatal to the eventual success of the enterprise. It is far more prudent to ascertain such facts from independent sources, before commencing any overture.

I am fully cognizant of the difficulties of ascertaining the forgoing, after so long a period of time, and under the particular circumstances of your situation. Certain prudent and discreet friends of mine, however, may be able to shed light on this business; and if a suitable opportunity offers, I will institute inquiries on your behalf, if it can be done without compromising the likelihood of future success.

You, madam, will of course continue meanwhile to investigate any avenues which Providence may open to you, and will communicate to me anything you may learn. And permit me, in closing, to repeat that it is of utmost importance in a case such as this to avoid raising any premature conflict or suspicion.

Yours Truly,
J. Bigelow, Esq.

Grace refolded the letter and gave it back. "You might have confided in me," she said. "You might have asked my help."

"No," said Anibaddh. "I couldn't."

No; of course she couldn't. There was too much shame in the matter; shame and confusion of nearly twenty years' standing. Grace could imagine the long-ago shame of the gross belly, growing only more prominent upon the tall thin girl as weeks and months had passed.

There might have been shame too in the infant's paternity. Who was the father? Had he been some irresistible ardent boy, of Anibaddh's own age and race; and the baby a badge, a memento of passionate desire, even love? Or had he been a man in a position to compel or coerce submission in a slave girl? In such a case as that, how was Anibaddh to cherish the resulting infant? How was it to be anything but a loathesome reminder of the miserable circumstance of its conception? Such an infant—poor innocent though it was—might certainly be abandoned. Poor infant! Innocence was no shield in this world. So might Hagar the slave girl have put away from her the infant Ishmael.

Piled atop all this, there was Anibaddh's present shame at having abandoned her own helpless infant; of having failed to love, refused to cherish this blameless child.

"I was only fifteen when she was born," said Anibaddh, as though she could hear Grace's thoughts. "I didn't want her, then. I didn't love her. I was ashamed of her, and of myself. For a long time, I never let myself so much as think of her. It wasn't until my other babies were born . . . that I found out how much I loved her, even her, the one I didn't want, the one I left. I couldn't forget her. And my aching for her has only increased, all this time, with every breath, with every mouthful of food, with every morning's waking. I told my husband about her years ago. When he gave himself up to be imprisoned, he told me to go and get her. I must find her. And if it means going into Virginia—why, then I will go into Virginia."

"That you must not do, Rani; too much, too many, depend upon you now: your children, your husband. But I can go there. I will accept my cousins' invitation, after all. I will go with them to Grantsboro Plantation, and while I am there, I will try with all my might to find out what has become of her; and I will write to let you know everything, anything that I can learn. When my cousins come this afternoon for their last sitting, I will get them to repeat their invitation; and this time I will accept it. They are leaving within this week."

"Sweek," said Jamie. "Get down," he added, pitching himself groundward so that Grace nearly lost hold of him.

She set him down. "Don't touch; just look," she told him.

"You would do this for me?" said Anibaddh.

"I would. I will."

"And Mr Pollocke—what will he say?"

"He will not try to prevent my going," said Grace, with more certainty than she felt.

"They don't know who you are, those Grants?"

"No," said Grace. "I have not told them. I gather that terrifying old *cailleach* Miss Johnstone is still among them, at Grantsboro; they call her 'Aunt Bella.' But she cannot possibly recognise me. She scarcely laid eyes on me all those years ago, and that for only a few hours—and in any case, I flatter myself that my appearance has improved out of all recognition since I was eight years old. I only hope that if I do quake with terror upon meeting her again, I shall be able to conceal it."

"She is vile," said Anibaddh, "though she lets on to be very good. That is the only thing she fears: being found out."

"I shall remember that," said Grace. "Jamie, don't touch."

"Write to me under cover to Mr Pollocke. Every particular that you can find out: where she is; who is her master; whether she has any children. Then I will let Mr Bigelow in Washington City know all about it—and he will write the offer to buy her, and her children—my grandchildren. Only his name appears in the business. They need never find out who is behind it all."

"I shall be very discreet," promised Grace. Jamie had made his way out to the rows of castor plants, and Grace stood in the open doorway where she could watch his straw-colored head above the foliage. Presently she added, "It is loathesome, though, this business of buying anyone's freedom—of actually engaging in that trade of human beings. I detest the thought of rewarding a slaveholder in his wrongdoing, as though I actually acknowledged his right to own human property. It is a gross violation of principle."

"Oh, principle," said Anibaddh disdainfully. "If you are going to cling to that—perhaps you think it is more principled to steal her away?"

"Well; oddly enough, I do."

"But it is far more risky," said Anibaddh. "And I don't care about principle. I am not so proud as to stand upon principle, when my daughter's freedom is at stake."

"I mean only that it is infamous to engage in buying a human person," said Grace.

"Certainly it is infamous," said Anibaddh. "It is disgusting. Shall I tell you? Mr Bigelow will propose to send an appraiser to establish her value, and will guarantee a ten percent premium above her appraised value to sweeten the deal. But I will do anything to get her back. Anything. What use is all my money, if I cannot get her? Even if they say a thousand dollars, I have money to buy her freedom. And her children too."

Grace had been shocked to see newspaper advertisements offering rewards for the return of runaway slaves. The rewards offered were generally several hundred dollars, occasionally as much as five hundred; but this surely was less than the full market value of the slave. Surely Diana's master—whoever that might be—would not hold out for as much as a thousand dollars, even if she had a baby by now. Or two. Grace said, "How will I know her, your Diana?"

"I think I would know her," said Anibaddh, and for a moment a small private smile lit her eyes. "Six months old when I left her, only half weaned, but I would just know her, wouldn't I? Like smelling her. She'll be eighteen years old now, my baby girl."

"Will she resemble you, do you think? In feature? Height? Complexion?"

Ani's smile faded. "She gave promise of being tall. She had such long legs, even then! She was not very dark—but babies aren't, sometimes. Sometimes they begin light, and grow darker. Unlike silkworms."

"And in feature?" Grace's question meant: Am I to look for a girl whose father too was African? Or am I to look for a girl whose features suggest . . . some other paternity?

"She wouldn't pass for white," replied Anibaddh after a moment.

. . .

GRACE STARTLED AWAKE: A CRASHING IN THE STAIRWELL. IT was Dan, come in at last from a gentlemen's dinner party. A glance out the window over her bed showed how late it was: the stars had wheeled around, and the sky was no longer quite black. He fumbled at the latch of the bedroom door, and then the sweet fetid smell of alcohol wreaking its havoc in a human body came in with him. He lurched against the blanket chest at the foot of the bed, where it always stood, and swore: "Damnation!" Then, "Sorry. Are you awake?"

"I am now. Be careful; there is a trunk in that corner too," she warned him—too late, as he banged against it.

"Dash it! I couldn't get away any sooner. It turned out that I was the guest of honor. Which I wish I'd known beforehand." She could hear the whisper of broadcloth as he undressed. "Any number of toasts. You mustn't scold me, Gracie, for staying. I couldn't be the first to go away from dinner given in my honor, now, could I?"

"When did I ever scold you?" said Grace, and added, when he slid into bed beside her, "You're very cold."

"Had to walk it. Never a hack when it's wanted. Law of nature."

Brandy, Grace decided. "Far?" she whispered.

"No; he boards just over on Sixth, below Chesnut." He slurred it: Cheshnut.

"Oh! I had supposed he was a married man."

"Well, now, I believe he is," said Dan. "Though I've never met his wife."

Grace could not reconcile herself to this American practice. In any comfortably civilised place, husbands and wives, upon marrying, established private households of their own. These households might be— indeed ought to be—very modest where means were modest; but they were indubitably private, not mere lodgings in boardinghouses. In civilised places, when a gentleman gave a dinner to his friends, it was at his own table, in his own dining room, no matter how small; and his own wife presided as hostess. Furthermore, in civilised places, no one dreamed of inviting a married man to dine without his wife; nor did any married man dine where his wife was not invited. As a consequence, in civilised places, dinners broke up before breakfast time; gentlemen took their brandy in moderation, or, at least, not greatly in excess of it; and the conversation might be rational, well informed, interesting—or, with luck, even clever.

"Tobacco too," observed Grace.

He had nearly dropped into sleep, but he roused enough to say, "I did have a quid. Only to be sociable." Then, more fully awake again: "Why is that trunk out? Is someone going somewhere?"

"Aye," said Grace. "I am going to Virginia with . . . my cousins. The day after—well, no—this is tomorrow. On Wednesday. I have just settled it with them."

"What! Why? Only last week you so roundly despised them. Have you made yourself known to them, after all?"

"No, I have said nothing of our kinship; nor must you, my dear, not to anyone. It is a deep secret." It had been absurdly easy to make them renew their invitation to Grantsboro; and they had been hugely gratified—even triumphant—at her acceptance.

"You'd go all the way to Virginia, just to paint their silly heads?"

"They want me to come and paint their father, and the old mansion. And copy an old portrait of their mother, painted by Mr Stuart; I will own that I should like to see that. And they want me to attend their revival meeting too. I'm afraid I have given them some cause to doubt my piety, and I daresay they hope to convert me."

"Excellent reasons to stay home, I'd say," said Dan, his hand tracing her waist; her hip. "We want you here, Jamie and I."

"Jamie is weaned, and Rawley is very good to him," said Grace. "Your mother will not mind looking in every day, I am sure. The Rani and Miss Babcock have offered to be of use too. And it will be only for a matter of weeks, perhaps three or four weeks."

"But why, Gracie? Is it the money? We're going to be all right for money. I've got offers for the chinaware and the furniture; and tonight, a signed contract for all the Hyson, rather better than I expected. And the rest is only a matter of waiting for the right buyer."

"It's not the money," said Grace, and paused.

"What, then?" he said. "Why do you want to go away from me so soon?"

"Oh, my dear—it is dreadful timing, isn't it? I don't want to go in the least, to tell the truth." Again she paused. "I am terrified even to think of it," she said at last. "But I cannot see any other way. There is a very good reason; I must go. If I tell you, will you keep the secret? It is a matter of gravest importance."

"Well, what?" he said.

"Only if you promise to keep the secret," she said. "From everyone. Every one."

"How can I promise if I don't know what it is?" he said.

"How can I tell you if I have not your promise first?" she said.

An impasse. What did she, or he, know of how connubial life ought to work? Ought there never to stand secrets between wives and husbands? Or were there many? Great swathes of his life were mysteries to her, blank, because the two of them had spent so much time apart, and because the spheres each inhabited were quite separate and quite different, as different as starry night from bright day. She knew little of his merchant life; as little as he knew of childbearing, childbirth.

Would sharing her burden make it lighter? Did burdens lighten by half when they were shared—or did their mass only increase as they spread?

If she could not keep her own secret, how could she expect anyone else to keep it for her?

He snored; roused; turned over; settled again, fast asleep. Her secret—Anibaddh's secret—remained untold. It was safer thus.

"DANNY TELLS ME you're set on going down to Virginia, for a revival meeting," said Mrs Pollocke, who had stopped in about midday. "Impossible, I would have said; but he assures me it's true."

"It is not for the revival meeting that I am going, precisely," said Grace. "But to paint several portraits for a family there. But there will be a revival meeting while I am there, I am given to understand. Or is it a camp meeting? Are they the same thing?"

"A camp meeting is held out-of-doors. A little early in the season for an outdoor meeting, I would have said. What ministers are coming to preach?"

"They have mentioned a Reverend Mr Stringfellow," said Grace. "A Baptist minister, I believe."

"I never heard of him," said Mrs Pollocke. "What a strong smell! Fish?"

"Shad," said Grace. "Won't you join us?"

"Oh, I couldn't put you to the trouble," said the elder Mrs Pollocke.

"It is no trouble at all," said Grace politely. "And there is plenty."

"Well, I don't mind if I do, then," said Mrs Pollocke. "Nothing beats shad, does it, for delicacy of flavor? I've had to cater for myself for weeks now, and Cook still shows no sign of improving. I do hope she recovers soon."

AS GRACE PACKED her belongings—her clothes and her painting supplies—her eye fell upon the exquisite lacquered travel desk, the gift from her stepmother. Such a thing would be so convenient for this visit—if only she had the key! She wished she had taken it to a lock-smith and had it opened, and a new key made; but now there was no time before her departure. It would have to wait until her return from Virginia. She replaced it in the blanket trunk at the foot of her bed for safekeeping.

"**I**S MR MACFARLANE NOT TO ACCOMPANY US?**" ASKED GRACE—
for he had escorted the ladies only so far as the door of their compartment, and had there placed them and their parcels under the care of the railroad carriage attendants: two fat negro matrons, each of whom pocketed a dime tip.

"Oh, no; him and Mr Whitehead will ride with the other gentlemen in the regular cars, where they can smoke and chew to their hearts' content," explained Mrs MacFarlane as she settled into the seat beside the window. "And we'll be perfectly comfortable here, in the ladies' compartment, away from all that smoke, and the noise."

"He'll want to keep a sharp eye on Othello and the others too, I guess," added Mrs Ambler, as she tested the latch on the window of the railroad car.

"Who, or what, is Othello?" asked Grace, tucking her valise under her seat. A favorite dog or saddle horse, perhaps, to be carried home in the cattle car? The ladies' compartment seemed moderately clean; the windows could be opened and shut; and the floor had only a few stains from tobacco spittle. In truth, Grace was glad to be spared the company of Mr MacFarlane, for she had disliked him on sight and without, she now reproached herself, any justification. What characteristic had so disturbed her? She hoped that she was not so petty-minded as to have been disgusted by his very slight limp or by the dandy's walking stick he sported. Even if his expression had a hint of sneer, no man was to be held responsible for the cut of his nostril. He spoke very deliberately, which aroused her impatience, and she had disliked his drawling Virginia pronunciation; but she had best accustom herself to that. Most of all, she decided, she had disliked his very light brown eyes—

nearly yellow—very steady behind their hooded lids; reptilian. It was not that he avoided her glance; quite the contrary. But his look had been full of appraisal—and then, dismissal.

"'Who is Othello'! Oh la, Mrs Pollocke, don't you ever look at a newspaper?" exclaimed Mrs Ambler, arrested in the act of drawing off her gloves.

"It's been all over the Philadelphia papers these past two months, this trouble of my husband's, in recovering our property!" added Mrs MacFarlane. "How could you miss it?"

"I was so afraid that dreadful Mr Brown might prevail, after all," said Mrs Ambler. "With all his objections and his delays, and sowing doubt and confusion all about! But no; Judge Lewis saw through all that, I guess; and justice is done at last, heaven be praised and thanked."

"Well, my husband deserves a deal of the credit too, Anne. He went to an awful lot of trouble and expense to get them all back. Papa will be so much relieved."

A prickling heat ran up Grace's back as the truth broke in upon her at last. Since before Easter, she had been averting her eyes from the sensational newspaper accounts, and closing her ears to her mother-in-law's gloatings; for it was all too monstrous to be dwelt upon. Still, certain details about this notorious court case had penetrated her guard, to fester in her mind. The gist of it was that a band of fugitive slaves from Virginia had been hunted down by Philadelphia slave-catchers; captured; dragged before a judge; and eventually, upon that judge's decision, restored to their master—actually re-enslaved!— despite all that Mr David Paul Brown's silver tongue could do, by dint of the unctuous tenacity and perjured witnesses of the Virginia lawyer, who was also the master's son-in-law. Now, suddenly, Grace under-stood: the Virginia lawyer called by the newspapers "Mr M___" was Mr MacFarlane; the slavemaster "The Hble. Mr G___" was her Uncle Grant; and the re-enslaved band of fugitives was now aboard this very southbound train. With a shriek of its steam whistle, the train began to move.

"Where are they—the poor captives, I mean?" said Grace.

"Well, in the baggage car, of course," said Mrs Ambler. "Where else would they be?"

"There they sit, at their ease, which is far better than they deserve, the wicked creatures," said Mrs MacFarlane. "Let them walk it, I said to Mr MacFarlane. They ran north fast enough; I guess they can walk south again! But no; he said it would take too long, and the spring sales at Alexandria are coming right up. And of course we'll need to get ourselves comfortably settled at home again as soon as ever we can."

"The sales! Do you mean to say that your husband has taken all this trouble to reclaim these poor people as his property—only to sell them into a heavier bondage at the first opportunity?"

"Well, they belong to Papa, actually, not to my husband," said Mrs MacFarlane. "That's one of my father-in-law's peculiarities, you see; he won't own slaves, and since he still owns a half interest in Arrochar—that's the name of our plantation—oh, it's the most ridiculous thing—but my husband won't go against his father on this, even though the other half interest is his own, it having come to him when his mother passed away."

This was horrible; but Grace told herself to hope. Though some owners refused to sell, citing moral scruples, it appeared that Grantsboro slaves were sometimes sold; so it was conceivable that an offer for Diana might be accepted.

"La! Don't tell me I forgot my book!" said Mrs Ambler, peering into her satchel. "My stupid girl must have put it into my trunk instead."

"Never mind, Anne, you can borrow mine," said Mrs MacFarlane. "Here, it's *The Heart of Midlothian.* I don't guess I'm feeling quite chirk enough for reading anyhow."

"Oh, that one. I don't think it's quite nice," said Mrs Ambler. "Isn't that the one where—"

"Don't tell me! You'll spoil it!"

"It's the milkmaid one, though, isn't it? Where she walks to London and back, to ask the Queen to pardon her sister, who's no better than she should be? It was awful vulgar, I thought: milkmaids and cowherds and schoolmasters and criminals, and girls without husbands having babies, and then murdering the poor fatherless babes too. La, Clara, I wonder at you, wanting to read it, under the circumstances! I didn't finish it, even. What was her name, though, the milkmaid?"

"Jeanie Deans," supplied Grace, in spite of herself.

"I liked *Ivanhoe* ever so much better," said Mrs Ambler.

"Oh, me too," said Mrs MacFarlane. "And *The Lady of the Lake!*— why, that's my favorite of all. I've got parts of it by heart:

> Mild and soft the western breeze
> just kiss'd the lake, just stirr'd the trees
> and the pleased lake, like maiden coy,
> trembled but dimpled not for joy;
> The mountain shadows on her breast
> Were neither broken nor at rest—

Now, that's what I call sublime, don't you, Mrs Pollocke?"

Grace said that she liked *The Lady of the Lake* very well.

"But my father-in-law only laughs at it," Mrs MacFarlane said. "He says there never was anything romantic about Scotland. He says it was awful cold, always; and dirty and poor. Well, I guess you would know something about that yourself, Mrs Pollocke; what do you say?"

"I have never seen Loch Katrine, nor the Trossachs, nor any of those romantic places from the poem," said Grace. "I have not been in Scotland since I was a child; and if it was cold and dirty and poor, I must have been too young to take any proper notice of it. I do remember very well that there was always music—songs, fiddles, bagpipes—"

"Oh, don't talk to me about bagpipes!" cried Mrs MacFarlane with a pained grimace. "I don't see how anyone can bear it. Well, Mrs Pollocke, you'll see what I mean when you meet my father-in-law; oh, yes, he still lives near I and Mr MacFarlane—and a crosser-grained old man never drew breath."

GRACE RESORTED TO the book she had brought, the one lent her by Mr Cornelius: *An Historical and Descriptive Account of the Daguerreotype and the Diorama*, by Daguerre. She skipped directly to Monsieur Daguerre's practical description of his process, and by the time the train halted at Wilmington, she had studied it twice through. M. Daguerre's instructions occupied fewer than twenty pages, even including the figures and their explanations. The translation was no worse than most, and the procedure was explained with perfect clarity, sufficient even for those who had not had the advantage of seeing it performed by Mr Cornelius. M. Daguerre had held back no secrets; anyone could perform this marvelous operation and expect success.

Then she paged back, to skim over all the self-congratulatory non-sense—committee reports, extracts of letters—which filled the first sixty pages. Oh, the French! And their darling bureaucracies! Still, it was they who had purchased from Monsieur Daguerre his invention, and made a generous gift of it to all the world—excepting only their old enemies, the English. And for his reward, she read here, Monsieur Daguerre was granted a pension of 6,000 francs annually, for life. By Grace's calculation, this equaled some 480 sicca rupees; or 240 pounds sterling; or about 1,200 dollars American: a handsome annuity, a comfortable competency in any currency—unless compared to the 13,000 pounds sterling paid each year by his grateful country to the Duke of Wellington. It was in any case far more than Napoleon gave poor old Joseph-Marie Jacquard to compensate for having appropriated his brilliant loom as public property, to the benefit of the Lyons weavers. Monsieur Jacquard had had to satisfy himself with an annual pension of 1,500 francs, and a small royalty (no doubt mostly theoretical) for every loom erected to his design during the subsequent six years—oh, yes, and the Croix de la Légion d'honneur. Or so Grace, when a mere girl, had been told by her stepmother's brother, a man who understood looms and inventions and patents.

RAILS HAD NOW been laid without break all the way to Washington, crossing wide creeks and inlets upon low causeways of a terrifying spindliness—except where the broad Susquehanna River had to be crossed just above Le Havre. There, everyone piled out of the railroad cars and onto a steam ferry to cross the river, and then back into waiting railroad cars again on the south side. During the disorderly move from the cars to the steam ferry, Grace succeeded in getting a look at Mr MacFarlane's band of recaptured slaves. There were four of them, men. They were shackled to one another at the ankles, and walked at a slow shuffle. Their faces showed nothing at all, like a row of houses with shutters closed over the windows.

The train arrived at Washington late in the evening, and the

Grantsboro party was met by a wagon which carried them and their baggage—the shackled slaves trotting behind—to a large but ramshackle timber-built hotel. The slaves were led off to the cellar, where, Mrs MacFarlane assured Grace, there were secure pens for the convenience of travelers such as themselves.

Though it was long after the usual dinnertime, platters of fowls and potatoes were laid out for them in the hotel dining room. This "light collation," as Mrs Ambler called it, had a faintly tired and picked-over air, as though it had made a previous appearance, for earlier travelers. The Grantsboro party was waited on by a couple of negro women, very much alike; were they sisters? Were they slaves or free servants? Suspecting that they might be slaves, Grace felt horribly abashed and ashamed at being waited upon by them. Though she had been hungry, her appetite now failed her and, pleading fatigue, she soon excused herself to retire.

The hotel was large, with long corridors whose warped shrunken floorboards creaked badly, so hastily had the building been erected, and with such ill-seasoned timber—for the Americans did everything so very rapidly!—yet with wasteful haste, with inadequate care, it seemed to Grace. Carpets lay across the floors in most of the principal rooms, but these were disgracefully stained. A spittoon stood in every corner of every room, and upon every landing of every stair; but still the floors and rugs were vilely filthy. Even the black-mouthed Bengali betel-chewers were not so careless as American men.

Silk too was saliva, Grace knew; the saliva of silkworms. But that was a clean and useful sort of spit.

Feeling nauseated and dizzy with fatigue, Grace made her way upstairs to the bedroom which she and Mrs Ambler were to share. Her portrait miniature of Dan was in her dressing case: a comfort. If only she had a daguerreotype portrait of him! She would make one when she returned to Philadelphia, she promised herself; and one of Jamie too—if he could be induced to sit still.

THE VISITORS' GALLERY of the Senate chamber was high, hot, and airless, but what did ladies carry fans for, after all? They had been told by the Virginia delegation secretary whose responsibility they were that they had been lucky to get tickets. He was a very young man whose name Grace had not caught.

"Did Mr MacFarlane not wish to come too?" Grace whispered to Mrs MacFarlane as they settled into their seats.

"Oh, but he couldn't. Him and Mr Whitehead had to leave before breakfast, and I don't expect them back until after dinnertime," replied Mrs MacFarlane in a loud whisper. "Well, to cross over to Alexandria, and consign those boys to the auctioneers, of course, just in time for the spring sales! I swow, what a relief it will be to have those trouble-makers off our hands at last! Oh, look, look, Anne; there's Mr Roane! Mr Roane is our senator from Virginia, Mrs Pollocke, and he was very attentive to our father, in the old days, when Papa still sat on the bench."

"Oh, and there, Clara!" said Mrs Ambler, pointing. "Isn't that Mr Calhoun? Oh, it is! What a splendid head! What a presence! Now, that's what I call a fine figure of a man. What do you make of such a head as that, Mrs Pollocke—as a painter, I mean?"

But Grace did not reply. She was trying to hear the senator who had the floor, for he had just said something about the state of Penn-sylvania: ". . . the honor to present the petition signed by numerous citizens of the state of Pennsylvania, praying the abolition of slavery and the slave trade in the District of Columbia," said the senator.

"Moved, that the petition be received," someone called out.

"Objection to any motion to receive the petition!" cried the man who was Senator Calhoun. He had remarkable iron-grey hair bristling straight up from his forehead like iron filings atop a magnet, and he spoke in impressive tones. "The Constitution prevents Congress's interference in this matter."

"But whose responsibility is the governance of the District of Columbia, if not Congress's?" whispered Grace to the secretary behind her shoulder.

"Moved, that the motion to receive the petition lie on the table," cried another voice.

At this, the president of the Senate tapped his gavel on his desk and said, "Ordered, that the motion to receive the petition lie on the table." No one objected to the presiding officer's order; and the United States Senate then proceeded to the next order of business.

"Is the petition not even to be received?" whispered Grace to the secretary, doubting whether she had understood what had just passed.

"Oh, ma'am, that's how they always deal with petitions of this kind. That's just how it's always done," explained the young man.

"But there is a right, the explicit right of citizens to petition the government for a redress of grievances! It is in the first clause of your bill of rights," whispered Grace. In her mind's eye she could see the very phrase: near the right margin of the page, in the worn misaligned type of the little edition she owned.

"Oh—well—there is a right to make a petition, ma'am, certainly; and circulate it, and sign it, and send it along—but of course it must be perfectly obvious that Congress is under no compulsion to receive every petition that comes its way!"

"Of what use is the right to make a petition, if Congress will not receive it?"

"Why, what an absurdity, ma'am, if Congress was obligated to debate every petition that anyone made up his mind to send along. There ain't enough days in the year! No, our public men have far more pressing calls upon their time. Oh—well, the banking situation is dire—and there is the bankruptcy law which must be reformed; and the great question of distribution; and an absolute torrent of claims to be sorted out—many of them fraudulent—in the aftermath of the burning of the public records during the Late War with Great Britain."

When Americans referred to the Late War with Great Britain, Grace knew, they meant the hostilities of 1812—concluded some twenty-six years ago, about the time she had been born. Nevertheless, she sensed that she, a Briton, was meant to feel herself included in this rebuke; as though she herself had by some power of national proxy destroyed the records of the American government—thus inspiring some of its more enterprising citizens to take fraudulent advantage of the situation.

But Grace, hearing the business that the Senate did find worthy of its attention that afternoon—a new deputy postmaster at Columbia, Tennessee; a new agent to deal with the Sac and Fox tribes near the Mississippi River in Iowa Territory; an hour's debate upon whether the business of the Senate ought to be commenced at an earlier hour of the morning, at eleven o'clock rather than noon, during the remainder of the present session—could only conclude that the Americans were bent upon spending their time and breath on trivialities, so as not to have to take up the one great burning question of the day. Unbidden, her mind's eye pictured those fettered men, consigned even now to the slave pens, the auction blocks of Alexandria.

Blinking hard did not dispel this image of misery; nor did willing it away; and she was obliged at last to resort to the contemplation of Mr Calhoun's fine head. Even if she had not known his name, she would have guessed him to be of Scottish stock. He was tall, gaunt, his bearing conspicuously upright; and his erect steel-grey hair made him taller and fiercer still. His face was long, his features chiseled. It would be an interesting head to paint, Grace thought, but a marble bust would suit him best—for he was cold and adamant as stone. Where was humor? Where were diffidence, discrimination, moderation, patience? In his argumentative canting habit of speech Grace thought she discerned a sanctimonious self-righteousness. That was one of the qualities she found most repulsive, in anyone, anywhere—and far too common here among the Americans.

Even these august senators spat on their handsome carpet.

Later, as the three ladies followed their young secretary out of the Capitol, he stopped suddenly, throwing both his arms out sideways, so that Mrs MacFarlane trod on his heels. There was a commotion in the wide unpaved street: dust, hallooing, men running, dogs barking. Craning to see around their protector, Grace made out what she first took for a bull-baiting. But no; when the dust cleared for a moment, she saw that it was only an exceedingly active and enterprising cow. One man with a noosed rope tried to toss the loop over the cow's horns, just as another man seized her tail. The cow ducked the rope and kicked the man at her tail, knocking him flat—then galloped away down the street, with dogs and men streaming behind her in enthusiastic and noisy pursuit.

Nothing could have expressed more poignantly the differences between America and India. At this moment, Grace felt a great yearning for Calcutta, where peaceable cows sauntered from one market stall to another, picking out choice morsels. Cows were sovereign; no one thought of owning a cow. They went unmolested, not merely tolerated but welcomed. What they ate was an offering, a deposit in the great bank of karma.

"THE PATENT OFFICE is certainly one of the sights every visitor ought to see," declared Mr MacFarlane, as they all stood before it the next day. He tapped his walking stick to lend emphasis to his more important nouns: "It is truly a temple of American Invention and Ingenuity—and a veritable phoenix as well, this Glorious Monument now being resurrected from the ashes before our very eyes." The walking stick was a malacca cane topped by an ivory handle carved to an unusual swelling shape, like an arum. His cheek was distended like a chipmunk's, but Grace suspected neither toothache nor acorn, but only a plug of tobacco.

"Alas, did the Patent Office burn, too?" asked Grace; and some devilry made her add, "In the Late War?"

For a moment his yellow eyes fixed on her in reassessment. Then he spat and said, "No, it was about three years ago. It was burnt to the ground when the clerks whose duty it was to clear the ashes out of the stoves left them—where do you think? In wooden boxes—in the basement."

It was an enormous building; or rather, it was destined to be enormous whenever it should be finished; but, like so much in this stark staring-new capital city, it was very far from finished. It reminded Grace of a flat for a stage set, for only one vast classical elevation had been completed; behind this ambitious front the rest of the building was still under construction. How aspiring these Americans were! How earnest! It was very impolite to notice the national absurdities of these people from whom her husband was sprung—though he, of course, was not at all typical of them. But how could one fail to notice?

When they had finished admiring the false front, they went inside to saunter through the gallery of models, good and dutiful tourists. Presently Grace found herself standing before a glass case which contained a model of a steam-powered device for unwinding silk cocoons; twisting the filaments together; and reeling the resulting thread onto spools: a silk-reeling machine. Could it indeed replicate the patient skill of a Cheh-Kiang peasant or a Bengali ryot?

Someone owned this design. It was the actual property of the man whose name was written upon a little pasteboard card: Obadiah Hale. Without Mr Hale's permission, no one could own nor use—nor even build by his own hands and ingenuity—a device which operated by the same principles.

Mr MacFarlane appeared at her elbow and said, "A remarkable example, you'll have to admit, Mrs Pollocke, of American enterprise and ingenuity. Especially when you consider that it has been only three years since the old Patent Office burnt down."

"Quite," said Grace. "But perhaps a great deal was saved, from that fire?"

"Oh, no; not a single thing was saved; everything was burnt to ashes, everything. Every patent; every model. Just imagine: some ten thousand patents had been granted, since the founding of the United States; ten thousand patents, lost, destroyed. Ten thousand inventions, ten thousand properties, and with them, every deed of ownership." He paused long enough to expectorate toward—though not quite into—a nearby spittoon, then continued, "Immediately, however, this Great Nation has set about the work of reconstruction—not only of the Edifice itself, but also of the records that had been contained therein. Everyone already in possession of a patent was instructed to send it to Washington, so as to have it copied and rerecorded. Already some two or three thousand have been resubmitted, and restored."

"And the other seven or eight thousand? What of those patents?"

"They are canceled."

Might ownership indeed be canceled thus, by a mere accident? Incinerated?

THE GRANTSBORO OPEN carriage standing in the street before the hotel was of a size and style that must have been first-rate and downright handsome (to use the American phrase) some thirty years since; but now, as she and her cousins mounted the step and took their seats, Grace saw that horsehair was bursting through its perished upholstery, and where the paint was not frankly peeling, it was faded, gone milky with age. It was drawn by a pair of greys, well matched and well bred; but to judge by their near-whiteness, they too were some years past their youthful prime. The elderly negro coachman on the box was nearly as grizzled as the horses. A baggage wagon had come from Grantsboro as well, drawn by a pair of stout workhorses and driven by a much younger and blacker man. The two footmen were younger still, black and shining and noisy as ravens, laughing at nothing at all, it seemed to Grace. What fine teeth they had! The joy with which they greeted the returning travelers was noisy—familiar—childish—and, seemingly, perfectly sincere. At length, everything was loaded: trunks, boxes, cases, valises, workbags, and parcels. Everyone was seated, an extra cushion was found for Mrs MacFarlane, and the coachman shook his whip over the backs of the greys, wheeling them southward.

The flimsy timber toll bridge across the wide Potomac creaked alarmingly under the carriage wheels, but it was no worse than the railroad bridges. Grace was called upon by Mr MacFarlane to admire it. Apparently it was called Long Bridge. How thoroughly they had mastered the obvious, these Americans! "Upwards of a mile in length; lengthier than any bridge in London or Paris, I'll wager," Mr MacFarlane declared. Grace agreed that it was indeed a remarkably long bridge; and privately she resolved to teach Jamie that speakers of English said "longer," not "lengthier." Upon gaining the Virginia shore, the carriage turned westward onto the turnpike, and soon the morning sun was warming the backs of the travelers.

"Ah! My sweet Virginia countryside, at last! It does me good already! How I've missed it!" declared Mrs Ambler. "Well, Mrs Pollocke, how do you like Virginia—so far, I mean?"

"It is perfectly charming," said Grace, as she was bound to do. And it was lovely, like the prettiest, the most bucolic countryside she had ever seen in life or in painting; like an English landscape by Mr Constable or one of his imitators.

"And how do you like our new turnpike?" asked Mrs MacFarlane.

Grace praised it too, as she was bound to do; praised its straightness and width. It was wide enough in most places to allow two wagons to pass in opposite directions; and the tollgates set across at intervals were attended, and punctually opened by their attendants upon payment of the twenty-cents toll.

"The road that crosses the mountains west of Cumberland—what's that called?" Mrs MacFarlane asked her husband, who was dozing with his hat pulled down over his eyes. He had laid aside his walking stick, and now Grace could see that it was only a half-bark malacca; the lower part of the cane had been shaved, stained, and varnished to resemble a superior grade of stick.

"The National Road," said Mr MacFarlane from under his hat.

"No, no; I mean the paving of it, the surface."

"Macadam," said Mr MacFarlane. "For the man who invented it, John Loudon McAdam."

Grace was transfixed by his walking stick. What was that peculiar shape which formed its carved white handle? It had slid a little nearer, turning with the motion of the carriage, and all at once she recognised it: a cobra, its hood spread wide. The mere shape had been enough to fill her with unease.

"Connected with our Loudouns, I guess," Mrs Ambler was saying. "Our county is called Loudoun County, you know, Mrs Pollocke, named for Lord Loudoun, who was the . . . well, he was the governor of Virginia, before the revolution, wasn't he? An English lord, I guess."

"Oh, never English," said Grace. "The Earls of Loudoun are peers of Scotland, and they have always been Campbells; the present Countess of Loudoun is the Right Honorable Flora Muir Campbell, the great-niece of your Lord Loudoun; and her husband was Lord Hastings, who was the governor-general of India—" She broke off, not saying: in 1822 when I first went there, and finished, "formerly."

"I wish they'd put macadam on this road," said Mrs MacFarlane. "It's awful rutted."

"McAdam . . . now, that would have to be a Scotch name, I guess," Mrs Ambler said to Grace.

"Formerly MacGregor, I have no doubt," said Grace, "and changed to McAdam when King James proscribed the MacGregors for beheading his forester." It was a nice defiant touch to claim descent direct from Adam himself. Had the King imagined that if he banned the name, the race would die out? Every married woman changed her name. She hoped no one would ask her maiden name. No one did. It had been MacDonald.

The carriage lurched hard, and Mr MacFarlane's walking stick fell to the floor at Grace's feet. As she picked it up, Grace saw that the head was carved not of ivory, as she had supposed, but of bone strips pieced together; probably camel bone. She handed it back to him.

"I swow, someone ought to tell the directors about macadam!" declared Mrs MacFarlane.

"Just what is it, though?" asked Grace.

Her cousins looked blank, and it was Mr MacFarlane who replied, "It only means that the crown of the road is built up, with a ditch on either side; and the surface of the road topped with a thick bed of rough sharp rock, first a thick layer of large rock, and on top of that thick layers of smaller rock"—he gestured with his hands, laddering them, stacking them to indicate layers—"all sharp, you understand, not round gravel, which only rolls away—and all watered well and packed down by heavy rollers, until it is solid as can be. Nothing could be more obvious, if you think about it—and why the man supposed he should be entitled to a patent on a thing so self-evident as that is a mystery."

"I don't see how can anyone pretend to own something like that," said Mrs Ambler. "You might as well try to patent the curing of ham."

"But if he has created it himself?" said Grace, thinking of M. Daguerre's process. "Isn't a man entitled to enjoy the fruits of his own ingenuity, his own labor?" Oh, dangerous ground! And provocative question, here on slave-state soil! Increasingly, Grace's futile indignation over the infamous wrong was supplanted by a burgeoning curiosity: just how did slaveholders justify themselves, apparently to their own complete satisfaction? But no one was attending to her.

". . . not even for the specified brief duration of the patent," Mr MacFarlane was saying.

"What is it, twenty-seven years? Why twenty-seven, I wonder?"

"The period of a generation," he said, and replaced his hat over his eyes.

THEY DROVE AS FAR as Dranesville that day, and put up at the busy tavern there. The next day's drive took them through Leesburg— where they left Mr MacFarlane to attend to some courthouse business—and into the rising ground beyond. So exquisite a day, at the end of May! How lovely, how sweet the fertile fields rolling away on either side of the road! The hills were gentle swells, soft as shoulders, sweet as décolletage; ahead, in the distance to the west, blue mountains reared up. Magnificent trees outlined the boundaries of each field, and as the carriage passed from time to time under their dappled shade, Grace feasted her eyes—and nose—on the flowering trees and verdant shrubs and vines that flourished in their shelter. "What is that lovely blooming tree?" Grace asked Mrs Ambler.

"What, that? The little one with white flowers? That's our Virginia dogwood," was the reply.

Dog-wood! Who but Americans could blight so exquisite a tree with so degraded a name? Would they call the lotus 'muck-weed'? "And what is that handsome shrub growing everywhere under the trees?" Grace asked. "The one with the shiny neat leaves, like oak leaves, and so vivid a green?"

"That, handsome! Oh la, Mrs Pollocke, you'd better stay away from that! That's poison oak—and over there, with those pointy leaves, that's poison ivy. Never go near them, not even the slightest touch, or won't you be sorry! Did you hear that, Clara? Mrs Pollocke didn't know the poison oak! And she thinks it handsome!"

Mrs MacFarlane said, "Just the barest touch from the leaves or the twigs makes most folks swell up in a terrible rash, with blisters and oozing pus, and such itching, I swow! You can't imagine! Anne, do you remember that time James—"

"Of course," said Mrs Ambler.

Mrs MacFarlane explained to Grace nevertheless: "One time—oh, years ago now, I was just a girl—our brother, our eldest brother, James, he must have been maybe eighteen, old enough to know better, but somehow he got himself into the poison oak one night—and wasn't he sorry! His whole face swelled up, and his eyes swelled shut, and it was all over his, ahem, his person too. Somehow he'd got it everywhere, though how he could, unless he'd gone diving into a thicket of it without his clothes on, I don't see. He suffered for weeks, didn't he, Anne? And willow-water poultices all over him, day and night, and the doctor called in, not that he could do a thing for it, it's just one of the trials that a body has to suffer through. No, Mrs Pollocke, you want to take a good look at those leaves, so as you'll know it when you see it—and be sure you give it a wide berth."

It was like the Oriental lacquer tree, then, thought Grace; that tree whose sap at merest touch triggers a horrible oozing itching rash. Yet that very sap is lacquer; when dried, it becomes the highly prized lacquerware of China, of Japan and Burma. Her beautiful present from Dan, the carved scholar's paintbox, was made of lacquer tinted with ground cinnabar (vermilion; mercury ore, so poisonous, so useful, so beguilingly beautiful). The tinted lacquer was painted over a base of bamboo, one thin layer after another; then carved and polished. Grace looked well at the poison oak and poison ivy, so as to know them in future. She had plenty of opportunity to study them, for they grew up the trunks of tall forest trees and made luxuriant thickets at eye-level.

The carriage forded a shallow stream, and the horses strained to drag it up the far slope. "Ah! Now we are on Grantsboro land, Mrs Pollocke," announced Mrs MacFarlane. "It's nine hundred good acres here, at the home farm; and another five hundred acres—nearly—up at Arrochar. Still the best crop land in three counties, my husband says, because we are always very careful to manure in exact rotation."

"Virginia tobacco is famous everywhere," said Grace politely.

"Oh, well—tobacco! Nobody grows tobacco much anymore," said Mrs MacFarlane. "It's awful exhausting to the land, my husband always says, and we don't grow any at all, up at Arrochar. Wheat's far more profitable, and it don't require near as much manuring. But my father still grows some tobacco here, his own particular breed: 'Grant's Pride,' it's called. Just an acre or two, and very proud of it he is too. On the richest bottomland, always, and better manured than any other field on the place. We'll be passing it in just a moment, here. . . . Look; there it is; that's his own young tobacco, and up just a few weeks ago, I guess. And in amongst it, you see, he grows his spotty beans, too— no, the leaves are just plain green, but the ripe beans in the pod will be spotty, like ink spattered on paper. The beans furbish up the soil, and the vines climb right up the tobacco stalks, so as nobody has to set out sticks for them to climb up on."

To Grace, the deep green of the young tobacco seedlings against the fresh-cut red soil was an especially delicious color interval, like the taste of saffron with rosewater; like the sound of an open fifth, E played against the A drones of the pipes; *sa pa*. In a further field on the next hill, she could see a crew of black laborers (slaves, she told herself, men and women slaves) bent over their hoes among the rows of some vigorous low-growing vining plants; pumpkins, perhaps. The carriage now turned up an avenue of stately beeches lining both sides of the road leading up a mild hill. Ahead Grace could see a stand of majestic elms shading a large handsome brick mansion and its outbuildings. In a few moments the carriage drew to a halt in the wide gravel drive before the great house itself.

As a picture, it was quite satisfying. If Grace were painting it, she would simplify a little: put the carriage house somewhat further down the slope; furbish up the camellias, which didn't quite conceal the smaller brick offices behind the house: kitchen, dairy, stores, woodsheds.

A long double row of trees overhung a drive which led northward, terminating at a village some two furlongs off, a cluster of small cabins on lower ground. Those might be the slave quarters.

Grantsboro.

How different her life might have been, if her stepmother had relinquished her; had let her go to live here at Grantsboro, an eight-year-old orphan among her cousins. And how astonishing that she was here, now, after all. As Grace descended from the carriage, she had a peculiar sensation of seeing herself from a considerable height and distance, as though from a box seat at the theatre—a gods'-eye view, watching her own self stepping down now onto the gravel; onto the very soil of Grantsboro Plantation after all, and after so many years.

Some ten or dozen black folk had appeared from somewhere, and more were gathering; they cried out greetings; they laughed; they grinned, strong teeth bright in black faces. They were all very old, or quite young; there were little coal-black children wearing only shirts, clinging shyly to the legs of old ashy-haired wrinkled black grandmothers. Immediately, unasked, the grown folks began unloading the baggage. Grace saw her own trunk dropped rather hard, and a crate was let fall against it, gouging a ugly gash in the side. The case containing her painting supplies came next; Grace flinched as it landed.

"Careful with that plunder, there!" said a tall mulatto butler with marvelous side-whiskers, too late. Very quickly everything was unloaded into a disorderly heap on the gravel drive. Then, under the direction of the butler, the baggage—the "plunder"—was picked up by all and sundry, to be carried up the wide front steps of the mansion. What was to be taken where? No one knew; no one cared; all was confusion, noisy, busy, cheerful. Grace saw a couple of small girls pick up her painting case to carry it off between them, and then stagger aside when a well-dressed old lady, a white lady, came trotting down the steps from the house.

"Aunt Bella!" cried Mrs MacFarlane.

"**D**EAR AUNT BELLA!" CRIED MRS AMBLER, THE NEXT TO embrace her aunt. "Let me present our visitor. This is Mrs Pollocke of Philadelphia, who has kindly agreed to come and paint all our heads— miniatures, you know, our birthday present for Papa. Mrs Pollocke, let me introduce Miss Arabella Johnstone, our Aunt Bella, who you've heard us talk about so often. She's been—oh!—just another mother to us all."

"How do you do, Mrs Pollocke?" said Miss Johnstone. "And welcome to Grantsboro Plantation."

This was no Gorgon; only an old woman, smaller than Grace, dry as leaves. "How do you do, Miss Johnstone?" said Grace, making her curtsy. Grace would not have recognised the face, now much faded and lined; but the voice retained a timbre and tone—and that languid Virginia drawl!—which Grace had never forgotten: imperative, imperious, even in welcome. Still, Grace felt her dread ebbing away, for Miss Johnstone took not the slightest interest in her; with no more than a nod she had turned again to Mrs MacFarlane. Grace knew herself to be an inconsiderable sort of guest after all, a hired person come to perform a service for the family, on about the same footing as a doctor or a lawyer; or rather, as female, somewhat lower.

"How does poor Papa, Aunt? Can we go right in and see him?" Mrs Ambler was saying.

"No, he's resting now, heaven be thanked," said Miss Johnstone. "He had a bad night again, I'm afraid. And Miss Clara, dear, you must come upstairs and lie down straightaway. I won't hear a word of argument." With this, Miss Johnstone tucked Mrs MacFarlane's arm under her own and led her away.

"Oh, well then, you'll meet Papa at dinnertime, Mrs Pollocke," said Mrs Ambler. "He's a martyr to the gravel, I'm afraid, and has been poorly for a long time. Come along and I'll show you over the house. Hall, of course; and there's the mailbag for any letters you may wish to send; it goes in twice a week. Here's the parlor . . . here's the library—ah! and just as I expected—Julia, in her usual chair! Get up, dear, and be introduced to Mrs Pollocke, who's come to paint all our heads. This, Mrs Pollocke, is our pet, our darling baby sister Miss Julia Grant. She's a terrible bluestocking, and if you ever want her, you'd best look here first, in the library."

Grace saw thick black hair and downcast eyelashes, skin as creamy as dogwood blossom. But perhaps this sister was bashful?—or proud?—for she was slow to rise. After a moment, however, she did rise, and tried to look at the visitor; then Grace saw that Miss Julia Grant's right eye looked off to the side while the left met Grace's glance. Ah, poor blighted beauty! The eyes were large, violet-blue, and deeply fringed in dark lashes; and her black hair formed a vee above her smooth white forehead—a "widow's peak," as some called it.

How was this one to be painted?

They murmured how d'ye do at each other; then Mrs Ambler drew Grace through the library, to another room built off it. "This is Papa's tearoom," explained Mrs Ambler. It was small, octagonal, and win-dowed all around. "He modeled it after Mr Jefferson's at Monticello, excepting we don't have busts of eminent men on the walls, only Papa's sporting pictures instead. And I don't guess we've ever once drank our tea in here. But what do you say? Will it do for a portrait studio?"

"It will do admirably," said Grace. She had only a moment to take in the paintings—horses, greys mostly, with large barrel-shaped bod-ies, long thin necks, and tiny heads and hooves—before Mrs Ambler drew her away again, back through the library, and down the hall.

"And here's the dining room," said Mrs Ambler. "Breakfast at half-past nine, and dinner at four o'clock sharp. Aunt Bella's a stickler for punctuality, so consider yourself warned. Then we generally have our tea in the parlor between seven and eight, or sometimes later in sum-mer, when the evenings draw out so long." A pair of three-quarter-length portraits hung on either side of the fireplace opposite the windows: a gentleman and a lady, both of about Grace's age but from perhaps thirty or forty years ago, to judge by the dress and poses, the props and frames. The gentleman stood with his hand resting upon a stack of books. His hairline formed a sharp vee on his forehead. In the pendant portrait on the other side of the fireplace, the young lady sat upon a red velvet chair. She was a striking blue-eyed, black-haired beauty, her coloring much like poor Miss Julia Grant's—except this lady had of course no walleye, and she had no widow's peak. "Ah, you spotted Mama," said Mrs Ambler. "Wasn't she the blooming young beauty? That's the one we want you to paint a miniature from—just the head, of course. When she and Papa was newlyweds in Washington City, they sat to Mr Stuart, a wedding present from her father. The Celebrated Mr Gilbert Stuart, you know. Now I'm sure you must be feeling tired and dusty, Mrs Pollocke, and I guess you might like to rest a little before dinner, so I'll show you your bedroom."

The staircase was broad and handsome, quite unlike the narrow twisting ladderlike stair in Grace's house in Philadelphia. On the landing was a mahogany console on which reclined an unclothed marble female.

Mrs Ambler laughed and explained, "She's awfully embarrassing; we all wish she had more clothes on. But she's Papa's pride and joy; he bought her when he was raised to the bench: his Cleopatra."

Not Cleopatra, thought Grace; for where were her attributes, her props? Where was her asp? No, this languid beauty held instead a pomegranate; this surely was Persephone, sequestered in the underworld, awaiting rescue by her frantic mother—or her mother's deputy. Grace only wished that she herself had the powers of a hero for the daunting task ahead.

"Aunt Bella has put you in the Chinese Room," said Mrs Ambler. "Your plunder's been brought up, I see—that trunk is yours, I hope? Good; these silly people so often get things mixed up. Remember, dinner's at four o'clock, and don't be late, if you want to make a friend of Aunt Bella. Some tea brought up now, if you want it? And someone to unpack for you? Oh, but it's no trouble at all."

The Chinese Room had a painted yellow wallpaper and a lacquered screen in the corner, but nothing else Chinese about it; the four-poster bed, the rocking chair in front of the tall window, the writing table, the washstand with its basin and pitcher, and the mahogany chest of drawers were all solidly American. The window overlooked a garden of patterned boxwood and gravel, a bit light-starved and sketchy under the high shade of the overhanging elms. Beyond, a green lawn swept down to a boundary of trimmed boxwood under forest trees. Grace sat, and looked, and thought, and rocked. Rocking chairs were one American innovation she thoroughly liked.

Presently there was a brushing at the door, an indistinct voice, and then the door swung open and a black maid (a slave! thought Grace) backed in, bearing a tray rattling with chinaware and silver. "Here's your tea, ma'am," said the maid. "I put it on the table, here? I pour it out for you, ma'am?"

No; Grace preferred to pour for herself.

"I unpack your nice things for you, ma'am?" said the maid (the slave, thought Grace).

At the door, still standing open, Grace glimpsed a movement; then there was a smothered giggle from the corridor outside, but no one was to be seen.

Such ugly words: slave; slavery. Like penury, perjury, plagiary; but they had a lascivious lewd sound too. And like a wild beast, like a tearing of flesh: slavering, salivating. Knavery; savage raving. Astonishing, thought Grace, that the Virginia gentry had not invented some more genteel term. They were able to say the word without flinching. They were able to command their slaves without flinching.

"Yes, do unpack, please," said Grace. "What is your name?"

"Cleo, ma'am," said the woman, and she set about transferring Grace's clothes to the chest of drawers.

"And who is the little child in the corridor, Cleo?"

"Go on downstairs, Cordie, you bad creature!" called Cleo loudly. "Go on down, now! Sorry, ma'am, I only bring her along to open the door for me 'cause of that heavy tray."

"Is Cordie your daughter?" asked Grace.

"Yes, ma'am, she is," replied Cleo without looking up from her work.

Grace sat still, watching the door. After a few moments the child peeked again; and this time, when she saw that Grace was looking at her, the child did not duck or giggle. She slowly crept forward until she stood in the middle of the open doorway, and gazed quite frankly at Grace. Her large eyes were pools of India ink. She was four or five years old, Grace judged.

It was Grace who looked away first, to pour more tea into her cup—and to release the transfixed child, to give her a chance to escape if she wanted. But when Grace looked back again, Cordie was crouched at Grace's feet, at her laced boots. The laces were of stout pink grosgrain ribbon. The child gently touched the ribbons with her fingertips, then stroked them, feeling their ribs. She ventured to glance up at Grace's face, but saw no forbidding there. Emboldened, she touched the hem of Grace's skirt, feeling the texture of the fabric. Just touching it.

A FEW MINUTES before dinnertime, Grace went downstairs to the dining room. The table was set for seven, but only six chairs stood ready; there was no chair at the head of the table. The cloth was well pressed; the old fashioned china and glass were handsome, the silverware polished. The dining room was at the northeast corner of the house, and by this hour the portraits on either side of the unlit fireplace were in shadow.

Grace studied the gentleman's portrait. This was her uncle, Judge Grant—when he had been about the age she now was. He was the elder brother of her mother, the mother who had died so young, so long ago, in Scotland; and he had emigrated from Scotland even before his sister had married. Her nearest living relative, if blood counted for anything—except for Jamie, Grace reminded herself. The young gentleman in the portrait looked confident; certainly Scottish, thought Grace, in his intelligent eye, his sharp sardonic eyebrows, his upright posture, his fresh ruddy coloring—such a neatly curled pink ear! so flat against the head!—but American too, in the cut of his coat and waistcoat, in his watch chain. His fingernails, resting atop a stack of books, were unusually broad, quite square.

Voices and footfalls approached in the corridor, and a curious sustained creaking. Then the side-whiskered butler Grace had seen earlier levered across the threshold a wheeled invalid's chair bearing an old man, bald and spotted as a toad, a blanket across his lap. Following close behind were Mrs Ambler and Miss Johnstone.

What havoc time and disease had wrought! Judge Grant's face and hands were much swollen, and his thick body slumped to one side in the chair. He wore slippers rather than proper boots. But he was able to shake hands when Mrs Ambler performed the introductions: this was her dear Papa, Judge Grant; and this was Mrs Pollocke, of Philadelphia, the painter, come to visit for a few weeks. The butler wheeled the creaky chair into its place at the head of the table just as Mr and Mrs MacFarlane hastened in with Miss Julia Grant. All were seated, and at the butler's direction, two maidservants (slaves!) carried in dishes and held them before each diner in turn. Both these maids were older than herself, Grace judged; too old to be Diana.

The butler decanted wine at the sideboard behind Miss Johnstone, who sat at the foot of the table, and then brought it to the table to pour, beginning with his master. By the time the butler had rounded the table and filled each glass, Judge Grant's glass was empty. "William," he said hoarsely, nodding at his glass, and the butler refilled it.

"I hope you're not too tired by your journey, Mrs Pollocke," said Miss Johnstone. "My girls tell me—I call them 'my girls,' you know, though I'm only their aunt—my girls tell me that you've never visited Virginia before. How do you like it?"

Grace's reply was obliging and civil; and then Miss Johnstone's attention was diverted by other matters, so that Grace ate her dinner undisturbed until the plan for having everyone's head painted came under discussion. Apparently this plan was no secret from Judge Grant.

"When will you start, Mrs Pollocke?" Miss Johnstone said.

"I am ready as soon as you please," said Grace. "Tomorrow morning, if you like."

"Well, who wants to go first?" said Mrs Ambler.

"Miss Julia?" said Miss Johnstone.

Miss Julia looked down, and Grace could see that she hoped to avoid being painted at all.

"Aunt Bella, why don't you go first?" said Mrs Ambler.

Miss Johnstone said, "Oh, not me! How could I, with such a terrible lot of work on my hands just now, all these comings and goings, and getting ready for the revival? Who'd want a picture of me anyhow?"

"La, Aunt Bella, we'll all be fighting over who gets to keep your picture," said Mrs Ambler. "We'll have to pass it among us, in six-month turns!"

"And as for being too busy, Aunt—well, you know you'll only get busier!" said Mrs MacFarlane. "Charley's coming, ain't he? Hadn't you best go first, before him and Mr Stringfellow and Eliza and her new baby all get here?"

"When is Mr Stringfellow coming? And Mrs Stringfellow?" asked Mrs Ambler.

"Mr Stringfellow should be here by the end of the week," said Miss Johnstone, "but Mrs Stringfellow won't be coming with him, I'm afraid, as she's been a little unwell lately."

Here was the butler's hand; in it, the decanter. It tilted; ruby wine swirled into Grace's glass. The back of his hand was ashy, but pink beneath. What unusual square fingernails he had, quite broad and blunt. He passed on. Grace looked up at the portrait of Judge Grant which hung just opposite her, behind Mrs MacFarlane. The shapes of ears and fingernails often ran in families, passing quite recognisable from one generation to the next; nor did they change with age. Grace could see her uncle's mottled swollen hands and their broad square nails from here: wrestling to get a knife through the chop on his plate. The chops—mutton, Grace thought—were not very yielding. Judge Grant's knife slipped. His ears were still flat and neat too, Grace saw, though freckled and yellowish now in his old age and ill health. His sardonic brow was heavier now, and his hair had receded halfway back over the top of his head.

William the butler bent over his master's chair to help him, and his profile aligned with the judge's. William's ears were neat and flat too, not pink but very dark brown. His tightly crimped black hair formed a vee on his forehead.

Do not leap to conclusions, Grace admonished herself.

"All right, then. Since you're all so urgent with me, I guess I'll submit to be painted first," said Miss Johnstone. "After breakfast tomorrow, in the tearoom."

———

THE DOUBLE PARLOR was filled with various tables and chairs and sofas; a chess table stood under a window, and an old piano at the far end. No gentlemen had come in for tea, but all the ladies were there.

"Where is the tea?" said Miss Johnstone, and pulled the bell rope. Within a minute or two, the maids who had waited at dinner brought the tea in a silver pot, and the cups and saucers on a tray. The sisters and their aunt had been discussing which guests were to sleep in the various bedrooms, but now Miss Johnstone abruptly changed the subject, saying loudly, "Well! it is a great relief to have all that troublesome runaway business finished at last, and justice done, and those wicked troublemakers captured and sold south where it's said the masters know better than to tolerate any nonsense. I guess by now those four must be regretting that they was ever so foolish as to run away from the comfortable wholesome life they always had here at Grantsboro, with plenty of food and decent clothes on their backs and on their wives' and children's backs too, and all at no expense to themselves! I guess they wish they was safe back here again, instead of walking down that long hard road to Mississippi!"

The maids setting out the teacups showed no sign of hearing this, and presently they both went out.

"There, that should get the word out," said Miss Johnstone. "Judge Grant never sold any honest servant south. But the dishonest ones can count on it. Their certain fate, swift and sure. Let them all know that."

"Do you mean that they are married, those men who were sent to the auction block?" asked Grace.

"Oh, married, Mrs Pollocke! These people don't marry, you know, not in any legal or moral sense," said Miss Johnstone.

"Very true, Aunt," said Mrs Ambler. "But Mrs Pollocke should know that lots of them do consider that they are married, and Papa has always been reluctant to separate any of those—except in a case of absconsion, like this. Those men abandoned their wives and children when they ran away—so why should Papa feel more scruples about their conjugal bonds than they do?"

Grace stifled her urge to retort, but had to abandon her cup and her seat. She rose and strayed to the piano at the far end of the room. It was an old six-octave square instrument of English make, and several thick piles of old sheet music lay upon it. Taking up a stack of these old dusty sheets, Grace paged through them. The most recent pieces were at least ten years old, quite out of fashion—though at the very bottom of the pile were some respectable sonatas by German composers which might be thought to transcend fashion. Grace laid her fingers lightly on the warm ivory keys (thinking of an elephant she had loved in India, a particularly patient, kind, and courageous old elephant, with marvelous tusks), and touched a chord, the wistful Neapolitan: two white keys outside, two black keys inside.

Ugh! The piano needed tuning, and F was feeble; probably one of its strings had broken. She splayed both hands and touched four octaves. It was very badly out of tune indeed, and one of the A's stuck; and yet the instrument itself had been a good one. Even now its tone was pleasant, resonant, well balanced—as far as she could judge, under the dissonance.

"Do you play, Mrs Pollocke?" called Miss Johnstone from the far end of the room, in her remarkable carrying voice. "How delightful! It's been a long time since we've had any musical evenings. I'm afraid our piano hasn't been tuned lately, but I don't think it can be very bad. It was said to be very valuable when my dear departed sister had it brought here—heavens! as a bride, all those years ago!—and Mr Stringfellow always used to say it was a remarkable good one. Do play us something, won't you?" And, having thus hushed her nieces, she clasped her hands in her lap and sat in an attentive pose of aesthetic expectation. Her nieces took up similar attitudes.

Grace could play, a little, and when she was alone she could sing. What to play for the Grants? She sat down and let her hands stray over the keyboard in the moment of choosing, letting them try a few more chords. Then she began to play.

What made her play this? Why did this come to her hands, just now: "The Philadelphia Firemen's Cotillion"? It had been published last year in Philadelphia by its composer, Mr Francis Johnson—Frank Johnson, Philadelphia's black African bandleader and composer, whose orchestra played at every high-toned public entertainment in Philadelphia. The jolly little tune had been all the rage for three or four months.

It was familiar to her because the sheet music (remarkable for the bad-
ness of the engraved cover sheet decoration: a fire hydrant, on a brick
sidewalk!) stood on her mother-in-law's piano. The tune was simple
enough, but that A would stick, which tripped up her triplets; and
middle F hardly sounded at all. Then she was distracted by the sudden
unbidden fancy of Mr Johnson himself seated here, at this piano, in this
Virginia parlor, playing his own composition for the entertainment of
these flowers of the soi-disant Virginia chivalry. In her sight, her own
pale freckled hands on the ivory keys were suddenly his black hands,
black as the ebony keys, coaxing music from this misprized old wreck
of a piano—and she missed a chord. With some effort, she banished
this vision, recovered her place, and pounded straight through to the
end without further mishap.

"Charming!" cried Miss Johnstone when the music had ended, and
clapped her hands, her nieces following suit. "Now, won't you just
remind us; what's the name of that piece? We can't quite place it."

Grace could never have explained what devil prompted her to reply,
"Just a little German dance of Beethoven's, of course. One hardly ever
hears it played, though I cannot think why, for it is, as you say, so perfectly charming!"

"Beethoven, of course. So bold, so powerful! You play pretty well,
Mrs Pollocke. I guess you must have had a good master. What a pleasure it is, to hear my sister's fine old instrument again! Won't you
oblige us with something else?"

Grace smiled a little, eyes half closed, and said, "Very well. I shall
play you a little piece by one of our Philadelphia composers. Perhaps
you have heard of him: Mr Francis Johnson. He is a black man, but I
think you will agree that his music is quite remarkable in every respect."
She saw from the corner of her eye Miss Johnstone's jaw take a firm
set; and then Grace launched into Beethoven's little German dance in
C, a very simple piece which even so unaccomplished a pianist as herself might render creditably. It was so brief that she played it twice
through, pretty certain that her audience would not notice; and got
through it without disgracing herself, or it—except for that sticky A
and the nearly silent F.

"Well!" said Miss Johnstone when she had finished. "A poor imita-
tion of what real music should be, but as an example of what negroes

are capable of, I guess it might hold some interest, for some folks. I guess you must be tired, Mrs Pollocke, so we won't expect any more music this evening. Maybe some other time. Now, Clara, dear, aren't you ready to go upstairs? It's been a tremendous long day for you."

"I hope you will excuse me too," said Grace. "If you will spare me a lamp to light my way."

Grace gained the refuge of her Chinese bedroom, and shut the door behind her. A tall black shadow rose, rustling, from the chair by the window, and Grace nearly gasped aloud—an instant of chill fear—until she realised it was only the maid.

"Sorry, ma'am, I didn't mean to give you a fright," said the maid.

Cleo, Grace remembered; she had said her name was Cleo. "What are you doing here?" demanded Grace.

"Just a-setting up to help you get undressed and into your bed," replied Cleo. "That's my duty, ma'am, that's all."

"I can undress myself and get into bed without help," said Grace. "So you may go, Cleo."

"Yes, ma'am," said Cleo, but she didn't go. Grace set the lamp on the candlestand, and waited.

"My little girl, she say you give her a ribbon, a yellow one."

"Yes, I did."

"I didn't think she'd steal nothing. Me and her father, we raise her to be a good girl, and always tell the truth."

"I'm sure she does."

There was a silence; and presently the maid said, "Some folks always tells the truth . . . and others doesn't, not always. And I'm a-wondering if it's true or not, that they catched my husband, and brung him back to the sales at Alexandria, and sold him south. They always say that they catch all the runaways, every one, and then sell them right south, but maybe that's just making fools of us. Could be he got off free and safe."

Grace's heart sank within her. "What is your husband's name?" she asked, dreading the reply.

"Othello," said Cleo.

"I am very sorry," said Grace, wretched and furious, "but it is true. It was in the newspapers in Philadelphia when the four fugitives were captured; and there were accounts of the courtroom proceedings too.

I saw them brought on the railcars as far as Washington City, and I—I noticed your husband in particular. There I was told that Mr MacFarlane and Mr Whitehead took him and the others across the river to Alexandria, and . . . I did not see them again after that."

Cleo walked out without another word, leaving the door to the corridor standing open.

GRACE HAD UNPACKED her kit and set up her easel in the tearoom before breakfast, and was ready to begin by the time Miss Johnstone came in, wearing her best.

"All very well, I guess, for young wives and unmarried girls to indulge in this sort of thing—primping and a-setting for their likenesses," said Miss Johnstone as she settled herself into the chair, and smoothed her lace collar, and touched her eardrops. "But a lady of my age and position has a great many duties, Mrs Pollocke. You might calculate it would ease my burden, to have my girls gather 'round for a visit, but it's quite the reverse, and I guess my burdens will only increase once the rest of the family gets here, so I might as well get it over with at once. I wouldn't do it at all, except my girls have begged me so, and I never have sat before, and I'm not getting any younger or handsomer—though I've always been very careful about the sun. I dread to think what Mr Stringfellow would say, if he knew: Vanity, thy name is woman! Well; and you must not try to make me look coy or girlish, Mrs Pollocke. I would have you paint me just as I am, a lady in the dignity of her maturity. It should be a portrait of character. I am not afraid of that."

"No, indeed, Miss Johnstone," said Grace. "I daresay you have nothing to fear there. Turn just a little more to your right, if you please. The hands may rest in the lap. Excellent, very handsome. I suppose it is a heavy responsibility to supervise such a household as this one."

"I've had charge of the entire establishment for a good many years now, ever since my poor sister died, and the people know that they're not likely to get away with much, so they don't try to put much over on me. They know by now what a sharp eye I keep, and everything noted down in my housekeeping ledger."

"Have you a large staff?"

"I'd say so. Housemaids, kitchen, scullery, laundry, dairy . . . Fourteen, fifteen, sixteen—seventeen in the house, counting William. And of course there's always the others around too, the little pickaninnies, the old mammies—I don't count them, as they never do a lick of work. We don't put them to work until they're twelve years old, Mrs Pollocke— unlike in England, where the poor little children are set to work in your mills and your coal mines. And our old folks, too old to work; they're well looked after too. Of course, I don't count the boy who brings in the firewood, as he's outside, and therefore Mr Boyce's responsibility."

"Is it Mr Boyce who manages the estate's business out-of-doors?"

"Yes, he directs the overseers and the negro bosses, now that poor Judge Grant is no longer well enough to supervise the day-to-day business. A plantation of this size—more than nine hundred acres here, you know, and five hundred more up at Arrochar—well, it don't make a profit all by itself; a great deal of clever management is required."

"No doubt. And a large labor force too, I suppose."

"Over a hundred head just here at Grantsboro; and then another fifty or so belonging to Judge Grant up at Arrochar, leased to Mr MacFarlane."

"You are quite a village unto yourselves, then," said Grace. "Chin down just a little, please, Miss Johnstone. Thank you. Births and deaths, I suppose, as in any village."

"Oh, yes; our annual rate of increase generally beats any other plantation in the county. Our situation is a remarkable healthy one, you know, and we're seldom bothered with mosquitoes, even in summer. It's different up at Arrochar. They're plagued by mosquitoes up there, ever since they dug that new pond. I calculate it may have something to do with my Clara's difficulties, and I wish she'd think of staying here this summer. Even the slaves don't do well up there, ever since that pond. Not a single baby has been born up there this spring—and that can't be natural or healthy, not so many young men and women together as they are."

"Does Mr Boyce keep a ledger, as you do? A record of all the people on the two estates?"

"Of course; all the births, and the deaths. Purchases and the sales too, but those are rare enough."

A maid appeared in the doorway, curtsied, and said, "'Scuse me, missus, but Cook send for the key for the pantry, to get lard and sugar."

"Pursued and hounded, Sukey, even here! Am I never to be left in peace? Tell Harriet she'll have to wait. She should have asked me earlier." The kitchen maid curtsied again and went away; and Miss Johnstone said to Grace, "Not that old Harriet—that's our cook—not that she isn't an excellent servant, quite a treasure. I'm sure nothing could induce us ever to part with her. She's of our own stock, a superior strain, born and bred here on the place. I only wish she was twenty years younger. And our trusty William too—the butler, you know— he's of the same breed; her son, in fact. It's mighty pleasant to have servants who can be thoroughly trusted, and that's not always the case at some houses. Well, just consider, Mrs Pollocke, the opportunities a disgruntled cook has! Criminal! It does happen from time to time, we all know it does, though it would never do to let on in front of the people. There was Mrs Cabell, over by Lovettsville, two years ago. Her cook refused to confess, and it never could be proved, but there was no room for doubt, and she got what she deserved in the end. Of course, poisonings are very rare, but not so rare as they used to be, and those wicked abolitionists are all to blame, going about sowing discontent and a false sense of grievance. I call it criminal, and that's the view Judge Grant always took too, formerly, when he was well enough to sit upon the bench and deal with such miscreants as made the mistake of straying into our county."

"Poisoners, do you mean?" asked Grace.

"I mean those abolitionists, spreading their criminal slanders and seditions." As she talked, Miss Johnstone's expression had become first animated, then aggrieved; and at last quite fierce. Her eyebrows lifted; her chin jutted forward. Grace worked quickly to capture this.

"How it can be criminal to express an opinion, Miss Johnstone— even an unpopular opinion, even a wrong opinion—when the right to do so is guaranteed by your Bill of Rights?"

"Well, I don't know about that, Mrs Pollocke, and I don't know what your personal views on slavery may be, but I will warn you that this is no place for abolitionist cant. It's not tolerated hereabouts. Our slaves are all very well looked after, body and soul."

Then, as the blaze in Miss Johnstone's eye began to dim, Grace threw a little more fuel on the fire, saying, "And then there is your Declaration of Independence too, which states that all men are born free and equal."

"Oh, how ridiculous! I'm sure it don't say anything of the sort, Mrs Pollocke. No, depend upon it, there's been some misunderstanding. It's easy for foreigners to misunderstand our institutions, and maybe you don't know that our Declaration of Independence came from the pen of Mr Jefferson, who was a Virginia gentleman. He can't have intended his words to be twisted around the way those abolitionists have tried to do. All men free and equal! No, Mr Jefferson was a man of far too much practical sense to say anything so silly as that. Indeed, Mrs Pollocke, what could be more obvious, if you look about you, than the fact—I speak of facts, now, you understand—the fact that we're all born into some dependence or other? Are we not all bound to obey the laws of the Almighty, and of nature, if not those of man? As for equality—well! It's perfectly clear that we're all born into pronounced inequality—as to birth, station, ability, intelligence, rank, money, beauty, health! Why, name me any two individuals that are born equal in these respects, Mrs Pollocke, if you can! Free and equal, indeed! No, no. But this is just the kind of sedition that those abolitionists are always trying to spread. There's an excellent pamphlet that you should read, Mrs Pollocke—I'll ask Miss Julia to find it for you. It sets out the whole matter in the clearest possible way."

In the silence that fell, Grace could hear a curious sound that had been going on for some time: *tink—tink—tink. Tinktink—tinktink— tink.* It seemed to come from somewhere just outside the house.

"No," said Miss Johnstone presently. "Our people are very well looked after, here."

"I wonder that any of them ever run away, then," said Grace.

"It's because they get false ideas in their heads, put there by those wicked abolitionists. They're too ignorant even to know that their condition here is vastly superior to what the poor laborers must endure in your country, Mrs Pollocke. And I know whereof I speak, from my own experience, for I've traveled in your country."

"Oh, have you, ma'am?"

"It was . . . let me see. It must have been twelve or fifteen years

ago . . . no, more than that, now. I make it eighteen years ago—back in
'22. Yes, I sailed to Scotland as a favor to Judge Grant, on a particular
errand of his. But I cannot say I was impressed, Mrs Pollocke, not
favorably impressed at all, by what I saw there. The servants are all so
pert, so bold and disobedient, so discontent with their lot! The patrols
and the police force are useless, not at all up to their work. The roads
are all but impassable, the horses and the carriages dismal, the food
poorly cooked, the weather vile. There was none of that genial hospi-
tality, that level of civilised comfort that we've become accustomed to,
here in Virginia. I had expected better, far better, from reading Sir
Walter Scott's novels. . . . But no—the modern leveling spirit had
already done its worst even there, as in France, and—and Europe.
We're determined to keep our Virginia safe from that poison. Why,
even so brief an exposure to that pernicious atmosphere instantly poisoned the mind of my servant against me—and I was there for less
than a month!"

"How was that?" said Grace calmly, though her brush hand was
vibrating in time with her pounding heart.

"Well, she ran away, absconded! I never did succeed in recovering
her, though I traced her as far as Newcastle. Oh—now what is it? Am
I never to be left in peace for the quarter of an hour?" exclaimed Miss
Johnstone—for the kitchen maid Sukey had appeared in the doorway
again.

"Beg o' pardon, missus," said Sukey, "but Cook says if she can't have
that lard and that sugar 'fore 'leven o'clock, those yeasty rolls won't be
rose up in time for dinner. She says it takes all day long for them to
leaven up at this season."

How very near her opportunity had been! If only the kitchen maid
had waited another few minutes, Grace could have led Miss Johnstone
to enlarge upon her experiences in Scotland. If only Miss Johnstone
had mentioned the baby left behind by the runaway servant, Grace
could have inquired as to that baby's fate.

"Never a whole hour to myself; you see how it is, Mrs Pollocke,"
lamented Miss Johnstone.

"It is an excellent start, however, ma'am," said Grace, "and we can
resume tomorrow morning, even if we must leave off now."

Miss Johnstone gathered up her skirt and rustled away. Grace heard her, as she passed through the library, ask Miss Julia Grant if she knew where the pamphlet by that clever Mr Dew might be found, to be lent to Mrs Pollocke; but she did not hear Miss Grant's reply.

Grace contemplated her morning's work. She had got perhaps a little too much of her sitter's animation; had made her quite indignant. She ought perhaps to relax the eyebrows a little, and soften the jawline somewhat; it was not her intention to draw in *caricatura*. But she had been looking at this long enough; her eyes needed refreshment. Passing into the adjoining library, she found it empty, the resident bluestocking gone.

The library was just what it ought to be: wood-paneled, the walls lined from floor to ceiling by open shelves and closed cases, packed with volumes and sets handsomely bound in calf or morocco; dark red, green, brown, and deep indigo. A faded Turkish rug covered the floor. The complete works of Sir Walter Scott filled an entire shelf, prose and poetry. A great many lawbooks, histories, biographies, travels, and geographies were here too, but in no particular order, it seemed: here were Macintosh's *Travels* and Le Compte's *Mémoires sur la Chine* next to a five-volume *Life of George Washington*. The library smelled dusty but dry; there was no whiff of mildew, that mortal enemy of books, though the fireplace was unused at this season. On the rug in the center of the room stood a large writing table with several drawers beneath. There were two upholstered easy chairs; the one nearest the window was frequented by Miss Julia Grant, it seemed, for the seat bore the imprint of much sitting, and a tall stack—a veritable tower— of books stood beside it on the floor.

Might the ledgers of Miss Johnstone or of Mr Boyce—the records of the Grantsboro slaves—be kept here, in the library? There were several closed cases which Grace would have liked to investigate; but not just now, when anyone might come in and catch her at it.

Over the fireplace there hung a large map of Loudoun County. Someone had outlined the extent of Grantsboro Plantation in dark red ink; and along the road leading northeast was another outline, somewhat smaller, to mark Arrochar. The county's northern boundary was the Potomac River, wide enough even here, well above the falls at Alexandria, to accommodate a few small stubborn islands set in its bed.

The books stacked beside Miss Julia Grant's chair were bristling with bookmarks. Grace took up the topmost book, expecting *Marmion* or something of that kind; but it proved instead to be *Chemical Instructor* by Mr Amos Eaton. Opening at random, Grace read, "It is much to be regretted that most of the celebrated treatises on chemistry, have so large a proportion of their pages devoted to useless compounds, which can never profit the scholar nor the practical man. Particularly those endless compounds with chlorine and iodine, which may be equally multiplied and extended with any other substance. This is surely trifling with the richest stores of human knowledge. . . ." Trifling, useless compounds! Surely not, thought Grace, and checked the date of publication: 1826. Mr Eaton must be forgiven, for daguerreotypy had not yet been invented, fourteen years ago.

The next book in the stack was *Chemical Pocket-Book*—published in Philadelphia, Grace noted. Beneath that was *Chemical Philosophy*, by John Dalton; also volume three of Thomas Thomson's *A System of Chemistry in Five Volumes*; and a single volume of Mr Robison's edition of the *Lectures on the Elements of Chemistry*, delivered in the University of Edinburgh, by the late Joseph Black, M.D.

Near the bottom of the stack was a catalog, a treasure trove, some fifty pages of laboratory equipment and apparatus, all of it named, numbered, and illustrated in beguiling detail. Grace had to admire the excellence of the drawings, all clear and correct: Pair of Scales and Set of Weights. Six Test Tubes. Wedgwood's Mortar & Pestle. Blown Glass Decanting Funnel. Filtering, Litmus, and Turmeric Papers. And all of this equipment and apparatus was offered for purchase, available to anyone who might send money to buy. As Grace paged through the catalog, a slip of paper fell free and fluttered to the floor. Retrieving it, Grace saw that it was a list, in a feminine handwriting. This, she guessed, must be Miss Julia Grant's list of desiderata, each item with its price, and totaled at the bottom: a shocking and impossible sum of $46.27, underlined and circled several times.

There was a swish of skirts and light quick footsteps. Looking up, Grace said, "Pray, Miss Grant, what is turmeric paper?"

"Oh, it is just—just for testing acids and alkalies," stammered Miss Grant, discomposed. "It changes color, you see, turning red in the presence of alkalies—and then reverting to yellow in the presence of acids." The blood rose to Miss Grant's pale cheeks, flushing her.

Is she turmeric paper herself, then, Grace wondered, and I an alkali, that she turns red in my presence? Miss Grant was embarrassed at being detected in her passion for chemistry, it seemed. "Turmeric, the spice from the Indies?" asked Grace.

"A strong yellow color, and a distinctive earthy aroma, like nothing else?"

"Aye, *haldi*," said Grace. "It is said to be especially good for the digestion, and for retentiveness of memory—and even for treating wounds. But I had no notion of its being useful in the laboratory."

"It's like litmus," said Miss Grant.

"Is that another spice?"

"No, it's derived from a—a lichen, if I recall correctly," she said, flushing still more highly; and abruptly she changed the subject: "But Mrs Pollocke, here is the pamphlet which my aunt thinks will interest you," she said, handing it to Grace: *Review of the Debate in the Virginia Legislature*, by Thomas R. Dew.

"Thank you," said Grace.

"I doubt you will thank me, once you have read it," said Miss Grant. "You must not suppose that it represents any views of mine. But I believe it does represent my aunt's views. May I come and see your morning's work?"

"Of course," said Grace, and returned with Miss Grant to the tearoom.

"That is very like Aunt Bella," said Miss Grant, after examining the miniature for a moment. "And she is just about to say: 'Merciful heaven! Am I never to have a moment's peace?' "

Miss Grant's eyesight was unaffected by the misalignment of her right eye, Grace concluded.

"I have tried to convince my sisters that it would be unsuitable for me to sit, in my turn," said Miss Grant. "But they are insistent; and so I must ask you, Mrs Pollocke, how a painter . . . how you yourself would approach the difficulty of painting such—such an unlucky countenance as mine."

"Permit me to look at you, Miss Grant," said Grace. "Pray, sit in that chair, as though we were to begin. Now you must look at me; and you must allow me to look at you. Mm. You are very like your mother, aren't you? In feature and complexion; and you have her shoulders. Turn this way, please; more, turn the shoulders. There. That is how I should paint you: looking over the left shoulder, the light on your left profile, the shadow on the right side of your face. I should paint the right eye just as it is; that is to say, in shadow, and therefore not distracting. You must allow me to look at you. You will become accustomed to it."

"Will I?" said Miss Grant; but she had flushed again and, rising from the sitter's chair, she said, "I was just going out for my walk. Would you care to join me?"

GRACE AND MISS GRANT STEPPED OUT THROUGH THE TEA-room's tall French door onto a lawn of mown grass, bounded by large hedges and balls of clipped boxwood. It was laundry day, and several of the slave women were draping just-washed bed linens across the clipped box, there to dry and bleach in the strong sun. Against the green-black foliage of the box, the white of the sheets was dazzling, too brilliant. "Perfectly blinding," said Grace, pulling the brim of her bonnet forward.

"Yes, thank you," said Miss Grant. "I'm awfully proud of our sheets; they're one of my chemical successes. I've induced the laundress to rinse in eau de Javelle, which I contrived to make up myself, from bleaching powder and water. Come, smell it. That's the scent of chlorine. It has the property of obliterating all color from anything it touches."

"My linens might certainly benefit from such treatment," said Grace. She always dreaded that her mother-in-law might call on laundry day, and take the dinginess of Grace's sheets as conclusive proof that Grace was an unfit wife and negligent housekeeper.

"I'll wrap up a packet of Tennant's bleaching powder for you take home, when you go," said Miss Grant. "And instructions for making up the solution; that's the tricky part. If you mix it too strong, you're apt to obliterate the sheets themselves. I did make holes in several old ones, I'm afraid, before I figured out just how strong to mix the liquor. Then the sheets must be thoroughly rinsed in clear water, and put to dry in the sunlight—which does the rest by virtue of its light and heat, two of my favorite imponderables."

"Imponderables! Are there such things? Things which cannot be thought of?"

"Ha! Your little joke!"

"No, indeed, you give me more credit than I deserve, Miss Grant, for I know nothing about 'imponderables.' To me, chemistry is just that: a mystery. I know nothing at all about it."

"Ah, well; the imponderables are those substances which cannot be weighed," said Miss Grant, "and they are four: heat, light, electricity, and galvanism. Everything else is ponderable; that is, subject to being weighed—given nice enough equipment. Which, alas, I have not."

"How fascinating to be a chemist," Grace said politely, "and study the real nature of things."

"If only I were! But no, Mrs Pollocke, I am not permitted to be a chemist; it is unseemly in a girl. I only make it my private study."

"Unseemly; I suppose so," agreed Grace. "Worse still than being a painter."

"Yet Madame Lavoisier was both chemist and painter, you know, rolled into one—and married, twice!—though childless, which makes a difference, I guess. Oh, I should have been born a Frenchwoman! I so long to visit Paris. Have you been to Paris yourself?"

"Never yet," said Grace.

"How I envy my brothers their freedom!" said Miss Grant. "And they make such poor use of it! They could sail to France whenever they pleased. They could outfit entire laboratories with every apparatus, the newest and the best; and spend from morning till night, day after day, conducting experiments! Perhaps even discovering new substances! But they do nothing of the sort. I don't think my father would mind, much, outfitting a laboratory for me, but my aunt has positively forbidden it. He would not begrudge the money, at least—if only he had it. My brothers are awfully expensive. Sons generally are, I believe."

"Can you indeed wish to spend your days toiling away in a laboratory, Miss Grant?"

"Oh, more than anything. Brilliant work is being done, and though it is a little sad to see those old medieval fancies draining away—like a unicorn's lifeblood—it is deeply thrilling to see it replaced, drop for drop, by the most strict and precise science. Chemistry has had such a dreadful reputation—for centuries, for ages, when it was still only alchemy—the black art, the forbidden art, the charlatan's art. That's partly why my aunt is so dead set against my dabblings in it. But even she cannot argue with the whiteness of our tablecloths and bed linens."

The curious *tink-tink-tink* that Grace had been hearing was louder here, and when they rounded the corner of the house, she saw heaps and ranges of old rubble and brick lying below the piazza; and squatting amid them, two aged black men wielding chisels and hammers. They were chipping old mortar from old bricks. Stacked off to one side under a grove of locust trees were the cleaned bricks, ready for reuse. Another pile, messier and much larger, was of bricks that had been broken and spoiled in the cleaning. The old men had been talking as they worked, and though they fell mute as the white ladies drew near, the steady *tink-tink-tink* of their hammers continued.

"Good morning," said Miss Grant.

"Morning, Miss Julia," replied one of the grizzled old men, and nodded, and grimaced a grin at them.

"I see that you are making steady progress, Walter."

"Slow but steady, Miss Julia. This mortar not s'posed to come off. When I built the ice house all that long time ago, I slake that quick-lime long and long. I make this mortar to stick on forever, till the Last Coming. I never expect to knock it all apart again."

The ladies walked on. Grace felt the very moment when the old men resumed their conversation, as soon as they had passed out of earshot. "Clover's coming along nicely," observed Miss Julia, as they turned down a dirt track along a broad field of clover, in bloom and humming with bees. "Let's go and have a look at the foals, and I'll tell you just what you should say about them to my father. Do you know anything about horses?"

"I know them to be large, dangerous, unpredictable, and untrustworthy—though very beautiful."

"Ah; you know nothing, then," said Miss Grant. "Be sure not to pretend otherwise. First of all, you must understand that all the horseflesh on the place—not the workhorses, of course, but the bloodstock—all are descended from Diomed, one way or another, and there is no better bloodline in America than Diomed's. Not even the Carter and Fairfax families, blue-blooded though they may be, are better bred than my father's horses. Look, you can see this year's foals from here, and quite a nice crop of them too. My father breeds for bottom and endurance, of course—but also, you see, for color."

In a close-fenced pasture near the stable, some dozen mares and their foals were turned out to graze in knee-deep grass. All the mares were greys, ranging from dark steel or roan to pure white, depending on their age. The foals, however, were all shades of red, brown, and black; most of them would turn grey as they matured.

As Grace and Miss Grant approached, the mares raised their heads. Friend or foe? Or of no interest at all? Quickly the mares decided that these visitors were of no interest at all and put their heads back down to resume their business, which was to crop grass as greedily as they could. The foals were capering with one another or napping in the sunshine, flat on their sides. One was nursing, roughly bumping its mother's udder to make the milk come. The mare flinched but tolerated this rudeness, and the foal suckled for a minute or two before coming out from under its mother's belly to have a look at Grace and Miss Grant. As it emerged, it revealed long comical ears.

"That's not precisely what was intended," said Miss Grant, nodding toward the mule foal. "A donkey stallion is a necessity, so as to get mules for the farm—but he's not supposed to get them on the blood mares. He's of an intemperate, devious, and determined disposition, though, our jackass, and this is not the first time he's surprised us all with an unexpected little success of his very own. It makes my father wild—as a surprising number of people imagine that a mare who's once produced a mule is debarred from ever producing a purebred again. That mare is called Madge Wildfire—uncommonly apt, I'm afraid, under the circumstances. All my father's bloodstock is called after characters from Sir Walter Scott's novels—well, yes; he actually ate a dinner over the same table as Sir Walter once, in Edinburgh, when they were both callow youths, centuries ago. You might ask him about that, if you like; he's always happy to retell that story. Nothing is better than a new ear to pour old stories into. That swaybacked old mare is Rowena, and she is the apple of his eye; and that one, over there, is Flora Mac-Ivor. We are running a little short on suitable names, though, after nearly forty years of this; and I believe that one of this year's crop has drawn the unfortunate name of 'Dumbiedikes'!"

Fascinated and curious, the foals ganged up; and together they grew bold enough to advance little by little. Gradually they edged near the fence to stare at Grace and Miss Grant, their little pink-lined nostrils flaring at the scent of these strangers. Then, all at once, they lost their nerve and bolted back to their placid mothers, who did not bother even to raise their heads.

Miss Grant led the way past a large kitchen garden surrounding by palings, to keep the rabbits out, Grace guessed. It was well weeded and well watered, though deserted just now. Presently they emerged into a narrow red-dirt lane with cabins on either side. Some of the cabins were built of logs, others of rough boards; all were innocent of paint. Some were of two stories, but most were only one. Each had a chimney built of round river rocks, or else stuccoed in red mud.

There were voices, high-pitched excited voices, from behind the cabins: much screaming, shrieking—and laughter too, rather hysterical. Grace and Miss Julia made their way between cabins and came upon a cluster of stinking pigpens. In the nearest enclosure, a mob of young pigs huddled in one corner, at least a dozen. In the opposite corner were the backs of ten or so negro boys and a few elderly men crowded together, bent over something on the ground, it seemed. There were excited dogs too; several whip-tailed curs circled the perimeter of this group, trying to penetrate—but the boys kept kicking them away. Then there came a shrill horrible shriek, a prolonged scream, and something—a shiny greyish egg-sized object—came flying on a high arc, thrown clear. It landed in the red dirt not far from Grace and Miss Julia; instantly a dog pounced, and devoured it in a single gulp.

Grace suddenly understood what was happening, just as Miss Julia said, "Oh! Oh, they are, ah . . . perhaps we had better—I beg your pardon . . ."

Just then one of the boys glanced around. There was a bright smear of fresh blood on his dark brown cheek, and in the instant before his face changed—like a blind coming down—Grace saw his hot excitement, the brilliance shining in his black eyes. But he tugged on the arm of the man nearest him, turning him too; and then half a dozen black faces turned toward Grace and Miss Julia, each black face shiningly animated until the instant of seeing the white ladies. A silence fell, except among the new-gelded pigs, who knew no better.

"We'd better go along, I guess," said Miss Julia, and they went away, saying nothing, as though they had neither seen nor understood. Leaving the slave quarters behind, they turned once more toward the mansion house set upon its eminence.

The lane here was overhung on both sides by a double avenue of old trees whose branches met overhead to form a long shady tunnel. The branches and trunks were thick, rugose, gnarled, light grey. The light green leaves overhead were nearly the size of Grace's hand, and delicate catkins drooped from the branches. Grace thought she recognised the trees, and guessed aloud: "Mulberry?"

"Ah! very good, Mrs Pollocke. Perhaps you will not be surprised to hear that we call this lane—well, what do you guess?"

"I don't suppose it could possibly be called . . . Mulberry Lane?"

"How predictable we are. These were planted nearly a hundred years ago, long before my father's time. The planters in those days had high hopes of cultivating silk here, as is done quite successfully in France, around Lyons, I believe—and anything the Frogs can do, we active and enterprising Americans can do far better, if only we bother to turn our hand to it—or so it is generally supposed. Lots of the plantations hereabouts have old mulberry trees. I gather that there was a bounty in those days, a quite serious attempt at establishing a silk industry. It was thought that feeding and tending silkworms might be a suitable task for the pickaninnies—the littlest black children, you know—too young for any other work. But the trees thrived better than silkworms ever did."

AFTER THEY HAD returned about midday, Grace went alone to contemplate the portraits in the dining room. She placed a chair and sat down in front of Mrs Grant, situating herself at precisely the point where Mrs Grant's gaze was fixed. For a while Grace only looked at her; and unlike any live sitter, the very young Mrs Grant in her red velvet chair gazed back unabashed under Grace's intent scrutiny. How young and handsome Judge Grant and his wife had been, in the morning of their lives! And how fortunate, to have been sufficiently prosperous even in their new-wedded youth, to sit to the Celebrated Mr Stuart!

Mr Gilbert Stuart had lived and painted in Philadelphia for some eight years, and many of his pictures were still to be seen there by anyone who took the trouble to seek them. Grace had seen several pairs of his portraits very like the pair in this room: prosperous couples from good families. She had also seen the superb full-length picture of President Washington belonging to the Academy of the Fine Arts, and some Campbell Stewart family pictures which were sometimes loaned for public exhibition. Mr Stuart had worked in Philadelphia until 1803; then he had gone to Washington City for a year or two. It was not until 1805 that he had removed himself and his practice to Boston, where he had remained for the rest of his life. How relieved Philadelphia's other painters, Mr Sully and the others, had been when old Stuart had at last gone north, and left some sitters—a few!—still unpainted, for them to portray! His own portraiture practice, Mr Sully had once told Grace, had not flourished until the eccentric, irascible—and celebrated—old master had finally removed himself to Boston, well out of their way.

These paintings were undated and unsigned, as was quite usual for Mr Stuart.

But the longer Grace looked, the more dubious she felt.

She rose to consider the portrait of the young Judge Grant. She stepped up very close, close enough to examine the brushwork on Judge Grant's ear. Then she returned to Mrs Grant, whose face and arms were oddly opaque and dull, quite unlike Mr Stuart's usual lively transparent flesh, in which the very blood could be seen coursing under the skin. The skin colors, Grace saw, had been too thoroughly blended upon the palette, rather than applied to the canvas one by one in transparent glazes.

And that red velvet chair? It was of a shade which Grace had never seen in a picture of Mr Stuart's. Red, aye; he had loved red—especially brick, pink, scarlet, vermilion—and had used them whenever he could, but his reds never—no, never!—had so much blue in them as this. This red was as ill-tuned as the old piano in the parlor.

As for the eyes: they did not glisten. They lacked the lively wet gleam which Mr Stuart always gave the eyes of his sitters. He accomplished this by means of a particular little trick of his own which Grace had first noticed several years ago in one of the Campbell Stewart pictures, and which she had since noticed in every portrait she had seen from Mr Stuart's brush; namely, he placed a minuscule white highlight just inside the lower lid, marking the inner curve of the lower lid where it lay against the iris of the eyeball; a meniscus, wet. Always. Every time.

But not here. Not for Mrs Grant; and not for Judge Grant.

She surveyed Judge Grant again, examining the hand resting upon a stack of five books. Far too often, Mr Stuart had made little curved paws with small tapered pink fingers; he had seldom troubled to portray the sitter's own hands. But this hand with its blunt square nails was more skillfully rendered than usual. The titles on the spines of the five volumes were in gold, sketchy, but perhaps just legible. Grace peered very closely with her head tilted sideways to make them out: *Life of George Washington.* At the base of the spine was the name of the author: Marshall.

Weren't these the very volumes she had noticed in the library? If she closed her eyes, she could picture exactly where they were shelved.

The library was deserted; not even Miss Grant was there. The five volumes of Mr Marshall's *Life of George Washington* stood just where Grace remembered having seen them. She took down the first volume—handsomely bound in full tree calf—and opened it. The first leaf inside the front cover had been inscribed by the author to Judge Grant, in India ink, in a precise hand: 'To my respected colleague the Hon. A. Grant / from the author in token of his esteem / John Marshall. Baltimore, 22nd June 1808.' Very cordial.

The following page bore the full title: *The Life of George Washington, Commander in Chief of the American Forces, During the War Which Established the Independence of His Country, and First President of the United States: Volume 1.* By John Marshall. It was no wonder that the life filled five volumes, if the title alone required five lines. She was looking for a publisher's name, a date, and found it: C. P. Wayne, Philadelphia, 1804.

And the fifth, final volume? She took it down, opened the cover—it made a stiff crackling noise, as though it had never been opened—and found the date: 1807.

Fetching her kit from the tearoom, Grace selected an ivory disk, a smooth oval. Then on her tiny palette she laid out the pigments she would need in a crescent around its perimeter, arranged as carefully as the Indian foods upon a figured *thali*, and set to work. She intended that her miniature copy should be faithful, but not abject; and she knew a trick or two quite beyond the painter, who was probably not Mr Stuart.

"NOW, CHARLEY, COME and be introduced to our guest," said Mrs Ambler to a tall man, when Grace came downstairs to the parlor where the family had gathered shortly before dinnertime. "Mrs Pollocke, this is our brother Mr Charles Grant, just up from Richmond a scant hour ago. He's our great pet and we've terribly spoilt him, I'm afraid, on account of his handsome side-whiskers! Charley, this is Mrs Pollocke, who's visiting from Philadelphia."

This new cousin made his bow, rather sketchy and negligent.

"Mrs Pollocke is here to paint all our likenesses, as a present for Papa," explained Mrs Pollocke. "You should get yours done too, Charley; do! Such an opportunity!"

"Oh, there's a painter on every corner, in Richmond," said Mr Charles Grant, as though painters were the most tedious thing in the world. "But a lady painter—well, that's a novelty, I guess. Would you say that you're any good at capturing a likeness, Mrs, Mrs . . . ?"

"Pollocke," prompted his sister helpfully.

"I guarantee it, Mr Grant," said Grace. "But I have a great deal of work on hand already."

Judge Grant did not appear for dinner. No one remarked on this, so Grace concluded that no one else expected him. She was seated once more where she could see the pair of portraits; but there was a tiny skirmish over the patriarchal place at the head of the table. "No, I wouldn't think of it, not when you're here, Grant," said Mr MacFarlane, bowing himself away from the seat of power.

"It don't make the slightest difference to me, MacFarlane," said Mr Grant. "It ain't the kind of thing I care about, you know." But then he did seat himself there, so Mr MacFarlane ended up next to his wife— who was looking, Grace noticed, just a little wan.

———

MR CHARLES GRANT came to the ladies in the parlor in the evening, asking for tea. When his sister Mrs MacFarlane had served him, he thanked her by declaring for all to hear, "Well, Clara, I must congratulate you on your prospects. I'm told you expect to be in the straw sometime about the end of the year, eh? I wish you luck. I'm sure you've had enough disappointments, and you'll take no chances this time around! No jumping off tables this time, now!"

"Charley! What a vulgar expression!" cried Mrs MacFarlane. "I beg you will never use it again in my hearing!"

"What?"

" 'In the straw'!"

"Well, what's so vulgar about it?"

"It's vulgar, and disgusting!" insisted Mrs MacFarlane.

"What am I supposed to say? 'Brought to bed'? 'Confined'? 'Lying-in'?"

"Why must you say anything at all?"

"If you must mention it, Master Charles," Miss Johnstone suggested, " 'accouchement' is more genteel."

"I only wanted to congratulate her, and wish her better luck this time! But you're all determined to put me in the wrong, every time! It's no wonder that James don't ever come here if he can help it!" He set down his cup and strode out.

Mrs MacFarlane promptly burst into tears, and was helped from the room by her aunt. From her chair near the window, Grace saw Mr Grant emerge through the piazza and onto the lawn in the dusk. He lit a cigar, and the glowing ember at its tip marked his progress as he walked up and down the lawn in the gathering darkness.

"Oh, dear! Well, Mrs Pollocke, as you're a wife and mother yourself, I guess I'd better explain," Mrs Ambler said. "My sister, you see, has just learned that she's in a—a delicate and interesting condition. She's been in this way before, but nothing's ever came of it, and it's been a great sorrow to her and her husband. She suffered grievously this January, just past, from just such a disappointment. She's been married for about four years now, and nothing to show for it. You can't imagine how many times we've been filled with joyful hopes and expectations—but always followed by the most painful disappointment. Dr Woodward says there's nothing wrong, no reason why she shouldn't have a baby—so we're encouraged to hope once more that this time all will be well."

"I hope it will," said Grace.

"Of course, she mustn't tire herself, so that's why my aunt wants her and her husband to stop here for a few days instead of going home to Arrochar, especially as Mr MacFarlane always has plenty of business to get through, with my father."

ON HER WAY TO BED, Grace went to the library and retrieved the pamphlet by Mr Dew found for her by Miss Julia Grant. Then—after pausing to listen for anyone approaching—she tried one of the closed cases which had earlier attracted her curiosity. It was unlocked—but to her disappointment, it contained only old newspapers; as she eased open the door, an avalanche of them slid onto the floor at her feet. She stuffed them back onto their shelf. The plantation ledgers on which she pinned her hopes must be kept elsewhere.

As she ascended the stairs, she considered whether she dared ask Cleo whether a slave known as Diana worked somewhere on these two plantations. But as Grace had declared herself capable of dressing and undressing without help, Cleo was not waiting up in Grace's bedroom.

In bed, Grace took up the pamphlet recommended by Miss Johnstone: Mr Dew's *Review of the Debate in the Virginia Legislature*. The subheading, Grace saw, turning to the title page, was *Abolition of Negro Slavery*. Abolition! She had hardly expected to see that inflammatory word here; and at first she took heart at finding the question under discussion, at least. But as she read, she soon saw that there were no grounds here for encouragement. Still she read on, fascinated and horrified. She had been very curious to know just how these southern slaveholders justified their peculiar institution—for entirely justified they certainly considered themselves, to judge by their manners, their so-evident complacency; as justified as the sternest of the Scots predestinarians. What were they thinking? How could they so successfully blind themselves to the grotesque injustice of their practice? This pamphlet answered that question.

GRACE READ AS MUCH as she could bear, and then laid aside the pamphlet. She felt as though she lay in a jungle clearing, with only a small fire for light, comfort, warmth, and safety. During the day she could hold dread—that wild beast!—off at a safe distance, at the perimeter of the clearing, at bay; but at night she felt it creeping in closer, watching for its opportunity, watching until her defenses should slacken for a moment, so that it might rush in and seize her at the back of her neck. She extinguished her light and lay in darkness, turning from one side to the other as each position became unbearable, trying to breathe deeply enough to relax the tight band that seemed to constrict her chest. I am not brave enough for this, she thought. I am not clever enough for this. I cannot see my way through. How ignorant and foolish and reckless I have been, to attempt something so daunting as this! It will all go awry, a ship smashed on a reef, lives ruined or lost; and it will all be my own fault. Anibaddh, how will you forgive me? My Jamie! My Dan! I am so frightened, and so stupid.

When she did succeed at falling into sleep, it was a thin light sleep; and when she awakened, too early, it was a struggle upward, out of a dream in which she had been painting a picture. She opened her eyes upon the Chinese wallpaper, drained of all color in the dimness before dawn. The painting in her dream remained far more vivid, although the colors on her dream-palette in her dream-hand had been dark and muddy. It was a large canvas, about three feet high and four feet wide: a bucolic landscape, hills enfolding an inlet of water in the background, and tall dark trees framing the subjects themselves in the center of the picture. The central figure was Judge Grant, seated in his invalid's chair, solemn. And all around him were gathered his family—not her cousins, the human family, but a grotesque animal family instead. Here was a cow; and beside her, her handsome young offspring, a minotaur. Here a mare; and there, a lusty centaur. Here a she-goat; and beside her, her dancing faun—or was it a satyr? Here were the female animals upon which Judge Grant had bred; and with them, their fantastical half-human offspring. Most disturbing of all, here was William the handsome mulatto butler, with his ears and his hairline, his eyebrows and his fingernails just like Judge Grant's; but his mother Harriet was not in the picture.

Rising from her bed, Grace went to the window and pulled back the curtain, blinking away this unwanted vision. It was before sunrise, but she drank up the sight of the dark trees and grass outside her window, eager to obliterate that savage painting of her own imagination. Her eyes felt dry and tired, underslept. In the lavender half dawn, something moved among the locust trees out at the edge of the clipped grass; something large and dark, with a flash of white. For an instant it seemed to be the centaur of her dream-painting—but then it trotted out from under the dark trees, and resolved itself into a bay horse with a blaze and two white feet, head high, bridled but saddleless, with broken reins trailing from the bit. Even from here she could see the dark scarlet lining inside the flared nostril, the nervous ears flicking forward and back.

Then a second horse emerged from the shadow of the trees, this a grey, also bridled and barebacked. Its stride was high and springy from excitement. Grace could see that they both were lathered with sweat, their necks wet and corrugated with sweat and dried salt—and their backs were dark too, where some rider had clung, but there was no dark girth mark. For a moment, the horses circled, looking all around, and Grace heard the bay snort. Then the grey savagely tore up a mouthful of the grass underfoot and stood chewing it around the inconvenient bit, drooling green foam, still gazing about. Within a minute, they both had their heads down, greedily grazing on the lawn. The bay trod upon one of the broken reins trailing from its bit, thus startling itself and its companion. They leapt without thinking—when did a horse ever think?—and galloped off down the slope toward the carriage house and stableyard, leaving great divots in the lawn where their iron-shod hooves had dug in; and two steaming piles of manure.

AT BREAKFAST, A MAN Grace had not seen before came in, carrying his hat. No one bothered with introductions. "The judge?" the man asked.

"Indisposed, Boyce," said Mr MacFarlane, rising from his chair. "What is it?"

Mr Boyce—the estate manager, Grace remembered—just tipped his head toward the door, with a meaning look: private business, if you please. Mr MacFarlane rose and followed him out of the room, the tap of his stick receding down the corridor. Grace cut her ham; drank her tea; buttered her toast. Agreed with Miss Johnstone to meet in the tearoom at half-past ten.

Fifteen minutes passed before Mr MacFarlane returned to his breakfast, and Grace was beginning to wonder how much longer she could tarry.

He was clearly vexed.

"Well, what is it?" asked Miss Johnstone.

"Two more gone," he said shortly, sitting down to his breakfast again. "Davy and George. And by horseback, so they're probably across the river into Maryland by now. The other stablehands claim they don't know a thing about it, roll their eyes, don't know nothing, massa—pretend they couldn't be more astonished. Well, I've written up their descriptions and sent them on to Mr Hurley in Baltimore and Mr Whitehead in Philadelphia. After breakfast I'll send in the advertisements to the usual newspapers. And that tall bay gelding cast a shoe, confound it, and came in dead lame," added Mr MacFarlane bitterly; and stabbed his ham fiercely, and cut it ferociously, and inserted a very large bite into his mouth.

"Davy? Isn't that the well-grown young one?"

"Well grown, and all too bold."

"And George; which one is George? With the teeth knocked out in front?" said Miss Johnstone.

"Yes, and stammers terrible when spoke to," said Mr MacFarlane, barely intelligible himself, through his mouthful of food. "That's what I put in the description."

"So many of them stammer, though," said Mrs Ambler.

"Neil, dear," said Mrs MacFarlane, objecting.

"Now what?" he said fiercely, turning on her.

"Nothing," she said. "Never mind."

He shoved his chair back and said, "So much for breakfast. I'll be in the business room."

A few minutes later, Grace excused herself too. She strolled through the hall at the center of the house—and under the lofty staircase she noticed an unadorned door cut into the paneling, standing now slightly ajar. She stopped; listened; heard men's voices. Mr MacFarlane and Mr Boyce were there, in a small room under the stair: the business room.

When she passed through the hall again at half-past ten, the plain door to the small room under the stair was shut. She listened, but heard no voices. She looked about, but no one was near. Lightly, she rapped at the door. There was no reply; and after a moment, she tried the doorknob.

Locked.

"WHAT CHURCH DO YOU belong to in Philadelphia, Mrs Pollocke?" Miss Johnstone asked suddenly, from the sitter's chair.

"I have attended various churches, from time to time," said Grace. This was true enough; before Jamie's birth she had on two or three occasions accepted her mother-in-law's urgent invitations to hear highly esteemed preachers preach their sermons to enthusiastic crowds.

"I mean, what church are you a member of?" persisted Miss Johnstone.

"I am not an enrolled member of any church," Grace said.

"No church! That is shocking. It is the duty of us all to worship our Creator, each according to his own conscience, of course—but to worship, nevertheless."

Grace made no reply.

Presently Miss Johnstone said, "Well, what church was you married in, then?"

"My husband and I were married in China, by the missionary Dr Parker."

"In China, among the heathens! What sort of missionary is Dr Parker?"

"His is primarily a—a medical mission, I believe. He has founded an eye hospital at Canton, and cured a great many cases of blindness among the Cantonese."

"No, I mean what church, what fellowship, does he belong to?"

"Presbyterian," said Grace, affecting an unwarranted certitude; it was unlikely that Miss Johnstone could contradict her. "Educated at Yale College, I believe."

"Oh! But you don't go to a Presbyterian church in Philadelphia?"

"No," said Grace.

"And your husband don't either?"

"No," said Grace.

"How extraordinary! You really are next thing to an infidel, then! I could hardly believe it when my girls said so. Depend on it, you haven't thought properly on the subject, which is of the utmost importance to us all. But I hope for the sake of your immortal soul that you've at least made the Holy Bible the subject of your own private study?"

"I think I may say that I am familiar with it," said Grace.

"Familiar with it! I should hope so. Even our slaves are familiar with it. And yet, the Bible is widely misunderstood, especially by those wicked abolitionists; they're the worst of all, twisting holy scripture to their own ends. That's one of the reasons why our slaves ain't taught to read, you know. Well, I'm glad you'll have an opportunity to hear Mr Stringfellow. It's Divine Providence that's brought you here, just when he's coming. For lo, here in our midst is a lost lamb, a prodigal daughter!"

Grace was extremely offended, but she hardly knew how to reply. How was she to repress such remarks as these from Miss Johnstone, while remaining within the bounds of civility herself? At last she said, in a low and serious voice, "I must tell you, Miss Johnstone, that I consider this an entirely personal matter, and I am not accustomed to discussing my religious views with strangers."

"Oh, but only wait until you've heard Mr Stringfellow, Mrs Pollocke. I ask only that you hear him," said Miss Johnstone. "He sets it all out in the proper light. I always feel so much uplifted, so serene and confident, after hearing him! I only wish he could come oftener, and remain longer. I've known him for a very long time—oh, you'd be shocked to hear how long! But he has his own parishes, congregations, his own duties at home. It's a great strain for him to come to us as often as he does. But of the great, great things are demanded, isn't it so? And he is great, Mrs Pollocke. It's just one of the many sacrifices we—we the masters, you know—are always making, are obliged to make, in order to perform our duty, to raise the poor slaves from their savagery, their barbarism. To shed the light of true religion upon them."

"So that they may rise eventually to a level where they may succeed to the blessings of liberty? Is that the ultimate aim?" asked Grace, for she felt quite provoked.

"Oh, no, Mrs Pollocke; the Africans are destined to be servants, bondsmen forever. The Almighty has ordained it thus. But Mr String-fellow will make it all clear to you, if you will only hear him with a humble heart— Oh, William, what is it?" she interrupted herself, when the butler appeared in the doorway. "He's here? He is? Show him in then, straightaway, in here."

She patted her hair, and touched both her eardrops, and licked her lips. In a moment, Mr Stringfellow was with them. He was a tall well-fed man of Miss Johnstone's age, endowed with what Virginians would have called a distinguished head. He had a great deal of brown hair worn rather long and well oiled, and his clerical black was new and unfaded. He made a deep bow to Miss Johnstone.

He's vain, thought Grace.

"Oh, Mr Stringfellow, you catch me at such a disadvantage!" cried Miss Johnstone. "But it's only because my girls persuaded me! This lady is Mrs Pollocke, from Philadelphia, who's come to do all our heads on ivory—and save her soul too, we hope. She has the most terrible heathenist Yankee views, but we don't despair of her, now that *you* are here."

He bowed to Grace, saying, "How do you do, Mrs Pollocke? We are told we must never give way to despair." Then, turning to Miss John-stone again, he said, "I cannot help but remark, Miss Johnstone, on what excellent looks you are in. Quite as blooming as the season."

"Oh, Mr Stringfellow! At our age!"

He bowed again.

"I hope Mrs Stringfellow's health was improving, when you came away?" said Miss Johnstone. "We were so sorry to learn that she couldn't come with you."

"Indifferent, just indifferent, I'm afraid, Miss Johnstone."

But this discouraging report produced only satisfaction on Miss

Johnstone's face. It was clear to Grace—if not to Mr Stringfellow—that Miss Johnstone was not at all sorry that Mrs Stringfellow's health had kept her at home.

Miss Johnstone's eyes glittered now, and Grace worked quickly. Mr Stringfellow's presence animated her as Grace's had not. Her voice took on a new tone: higher, churchly, a good-little-girl tone. "And those Carters have got their favorite in training, so to speak," she was saying, "studying up as hard as he can manage, but he can't possibly come up to the mark *you* have set. . . ."

At length Miss Julia came in and offered to show Mr Stringfellow to his room; and led away the guest.

Miss Johnstone seemed to deflate. Grace had to suspend her work on the eyes, the face, and resorted to stippling in the contours of the dress. Miss Johnstone had nothing to say, but her lips twitched ever so slightly now and again, and Grace had the idea that she was inwardly rehearsing or remembering a scene, a conversation—with someone.

Presently a large elderly black woman wearing a vast homespun apron appeared at the doorway, and ponderously curtsied.

"Well, Harriet, what is it now?" said Miss Johnstone sharply.

"That spiced beef, missus, that I been pickling these three weeks—it's gone," announced the cook in her baritone. "I put it in the fresh water last night to soak out the brine in time for the dinner today, but when I go to get it just now, it ain't there. It's gone."

"Gone! That was ten pounds of flank!" cried Miss Johnstone.

"Yes, missus, it's gone as anything, plumb gone, when I go to get it just now. So I come to ask you, missus, you want me to kill a turkey for the dinner? There's one that's almost fat. Or I go and get that ham from the smokehouse, if you give me the key?"

"Thieves!" cried Miss Johnstone. "Those runaways stole it! Where was it, Harriet? Don't tell me you left it out where anyone could help themselves to it?"

"No, missus, it was soaking in the little pantry next to my room, just on the other side of the wall, where I always puts those things to soak, 'cause it stay so nice and cool in there. But I never heard nothing, all night. Not a thing. Like it just stole itself away," said the cook. There was a dark gleam of satisfaction in the cook's eye, Grace saw; surely even Miss Johnstone must perceive so much as that?

And perhaps she did. "There; now you see what I mean, Mrs Pollocke! What did I tell you?" she snapped.

"That turkey, though, it's not very fat, not yet," said the cook. "Be fatter in three more weeks."

"Here; go and fetch that ham, then," said Miss Johnstone wearily, and she extricated her bunch of keys from the reticule at her waist. "And then you bring those keys straight back to me yourself, Harriet, don't you send them by nobody else, you understand?"

"Yes, missus," said the cook, "I bring them right back my own self." Taking the keys, she made her ponderous curtsy and went out.

"There, you see, Mrs Pollocke?" said Miss Johnstone. "She 'never heard nothing.' A likely story! The entire race is debased. They lie and steal—and fornicate!—" she added in a whisper, "all without a qualm. Their passions are of the basest; mere brutes, even the best of them. And these—these!—are the creatures your abolitionists, your amalgamationists, want to clasp unto their bosoms!"

Grace said, "Chin down just a little, please, Miss Johnstone; and soften the jaw, if you can manage it. That's it; thank you." She resumed painting, in silence.

Presently Harriet returned with the keys. "Where you want these keys, missus?" she asked, jingling the bunch.

"Just set them here, on that table under the window. I can't take them now. It's mighty inconvenient to have to keep disarranging myself. Just set them down. And Harriet!" she called after the cook, who had turned to go. "We'll want jellies with that ham, don't forget. Currant and cranberry . . . no, no, quince; we don't want two of the same color. Currant and quince jellies, Harriet. And the walnut catsup."

"Yes, missus, I got those all ready," said Harriet, and went away.

"And rhubarb and strawberries after, to my own recipe," said Miss Johnstone to Grace, with evident satisfaction. "Mr Stringfellow especially favors rhubarb, and it's a favorite of Judge Grant's too. It was during my sister's second confinement that I came to oversee the housekeeping here. My poor sister was abed for almost two months, and she never was much of a manager. I made myself so useful that she implored me not to think of going away again. Even Judge Grant invited me to stay. So I sacrificed myself: my youth, my independence, my prospects. I did have some splendid prospects in those days, Mrs Pollocke. I was very much admired in the bloom of my youth. And I think I may say that I have an admirer or two, still, after all these years . . ."

Grace noted the cheekbones, the bony orbs of the eyes, the shape of the brows, pale and faded now. Quite possibly she had been handsome once. Her lips were thin and colorless, gathered by pursy wrinkles all around them; but she had kept enough of her teeth so that her mouth had not collapsed. Women who had borne no children were more likely to keep their teeth; everyone knew that. It seemed that a mother's teeth must dissolve to grow her babies, to make their bones. Babies really were made of one's own body: flesh of one's flesh, bone of one's bone.

There was a flurry inside, in the hall, in the library, and Miss Grant, alarmed and breathless, appeared in the doorway. "Oh, Aunt," she cried, "come quick, it's Papa, very bad, terrible bad all of a sudden, we must have the doctor this instant! He's having one of those fits, his eyes are rolled back in his head! Do come quick, Aunt!"

Miss Johnstone burst from her chair and ran from the room.

There were loud voices in the corridor; running; hurrying; a door slammed somewhere.

Miss Johnstone's keys still lay on the little table under the window. No one was near. Grace scooped up the keys and slipped them into the deep pocket sewn into the side seam of her skirt.

GRACE PAUSED FOR ONLY A MOMENT IN THE DESERTED HALL
near the locked door of the business room, listening. She could hear
distant voices from the wing where Judge Grant's rooms were, but no
one was to be seen.

Which key unlocked the business room? Most of Miss Johnstone's
keys were brass or iron, but a few were silver-colored—as was the
escutcheon of this lock. Grace tried one of the silvery keys. It fitted;
turned. Then she was inside, and locking the door again behind her.
She left the key in the keyhole to block it, and to know where it was.
Her heart was thumping against her ribs, and she stilled herself long
enough to draw several deep breaths, and to exhale slowly. She must
not hold her breath; nor breathe anxious hasty songs under her
breath.

It was a small poky room furnished with a desk and several hard
chairs. No rug overlaid the unpainted floorboards, and the ceiling
sloped down under the stair overhead. All the walls were lined with
shelves, and all the shelves were filled with books and ledgers. Nothing had been dusted properly in a long time. A slatted blind covered
the window, but her eyes quickly adjusted to the dim light.

On the desk stood inkwell, blotter, penknife; a gruesome pen cup
made from the varnished hoof of some long-deceased favorite horse;
an oil lamp. Untidy stacks of papers were weighted down by old horse-
shoes. Grace moved aside a horseshoe from one of the stacks. Here was
a letter dated from Philadelphia, last month—addressed to Judge
Grant from his son-in-law MacFarlane. The handwriting was crabbed,
but "D. P. Brown" caught Grace's eye; and she made out enough to see
that it had to do with the recapture of the four runaways, Othello and

his companions. Under this were a couple of folded newspapers: the *Alexandria Advertiser and Commercial Intelligencer*, and the *District of Columbia Daily Advertiser*. Folded uppermost and circled were the advertisements describing the runaways.

There was a crunching on the gravel outside—hooves, wheels—and Grace fell still. She could see a sliver of daylight between the edge of the blind and the window frame: enough to make out a one-horse gig drawing up in the gravel drive before the steps. A negro boy ran up to hold the sweating horse, and an elderly white man climbed out, carrying a satchel very much like the one Grace used for her colors and brushes; surely this was the doctor. He mounted the steps so that Grace lost sight of him, but she heard him ring, and in a moment there were hurried footsteps in the hall outside the locked door of the business room, and the creaking hinges of the big entry door. Hushed voices and footfalls hastened away toward Judge Grant's bedroom.

All was silent again. Grace could see a slice of the horse's haunch between the gig's shafts, hip cocked and tail swishing in the sunshine. From far away, at the opposite end of the house she heard the steady *tink—tink—tink.*

She opened the central drawer of the desk. There was a pistol—an ugly shocking sight! a thing that belonged behind a fig leaf, at the very least—and in the back of the drawer, a pasteboard folder, tied tightly. She untied the knot, and opened it. It was a sheaf of promissory notes, mortgages, demands, renewals. She studied these long enough to see that Judge Grant was the debtor in every case; and the sums were considerable.

But she was not here to investigate her uncle's financial affairs. She returned this folder to the back of the desk drawer, tied as she had found it, and turned instead to the shelved books and journals behind the desk. There were a great many old lawbooks on the bottom shelf, but the more convenient shelves at eye-level lodged half-bound journals, each with a year stamped on its spine, all in chronological order. The earliest was dated 1805, and the latest was for 1838. There was 1814, the year of her own birth; and here was 1822, the year Anibaddh had been taken to Scotland—made her escape—abandoned her infant daughter—and, incidentally, had met Grace. Carefully, so as not to disturb the dust atop its red-edged pages, Grace drew out this volume and laid it open upon the desk.

The first entry was for New Year's Day. A neat handwriting—a Scottish handwriting, her uncle's handwriting—noted the weather: frosty, dry; twenty-six degrees of mercury at sunrise. He noted also the foaling of a bay colt out of the mare Rebecca by the stallion Colonel Blood. Noted the gift of twenty dollars each to his sons James and Charles, and of five dollars each to his daughters Anne, Eliza, Clara, Julia, Charlotte: $65 in all.

On January 2, it was recorded that the weather was a little warmer; that a quantity of books worth $53.93 had been ordered from a Richmond bookseller; and that a slave woman named Hannah had been delivered of twins: "Deld. 1 fem, Celia; 1 male stillborn, her 2nd set of twins." He commented that this was both the first birth and the first death of the year, a poor start, as the previous year had seen "29 births, 19 deaths, and 4 run off. Net increase for 1821: 6 head." None bought, Grace noted, and none sold.

She skipped through the journal, certain entries catching her eye from time to time: Session at Leesburg. Twenty dollars paid to music master. Three-year-old horse bought. Once her eye leapt—but no; it was only a two-year-old home-bred filly named Diana Vernon, who had finished second at the Richmond races.

Method is what you want, Grace told herself. Returning to the beginning, she looked more purposefully—and this time she found, under the entry for January 22: "Annie B., housemaid, deld. 1 fem child, Diana, her 1st." In the column where he sometimes wrote the name of the father—or of the stallion or bull—her uncle had left the space blank.

Miss Johnstone and her slave had arrived in Edinburgh by mid-August that year. When had they sailed from Virginia? Grace paged ahead to June, and there resumed reading each entry. For June 16, about the middle of the page, she read: "Lading wagons for tom'row: 7 hhds tobacco and 60 firlots wheat, all to ship by Pres. Madison for Glasgow; also Miss J & Annie B. Ordered 63 yds osnabrigs on account from McMurtrey & Sons, and sending by Miss J my bill for £20, for outfit & maint. of Elizabeth's Grace." "Elizabeth's Grace" was herself.

The next entry was not until the seventh of July, when Judge Grant had returned to Grantsboro: "Embarked Pres Madison at Alexa. on 20th June and dropped down overnight, ashore at Leonard's Town in Maryd on business but my horse (Athelstane) badly cut going ashore, & ashore at Hampton with view to identify negroes impounded at Norfolk, but none mine. Rode home via Richmd and Frdksbg, 10 days on the road. Found the barrack for the new sawmill near compleated in my absence."

There were hurrying footsteps in the hall, and hushed slave voices. The entry door opened and closed—such creaky hinges!—and Grace heard someone tell the boy holding the doctor's horse to lead it down to the stables and have it put up. The boy led off the horse and gig.

It had been near the end of August when Annie had run away in Scotland, but the news could not have reached Judge Grant in Virginia for four or five weeks at least. Grace skimmed through the entries for late September, until her eye alighted upon his entry for October 3: "Letter from Miss J advises Annie B. has run off in Scotland (abandoning her infant here, I wd not have thought it of her) & no help to be had from Edinb. sheriff. My niece, Elizabeth's girl, declines my invitation." That's myself again, Grace thought. "Burley prices collapsed, to levels not seen in twenty yrs, and wheat down as much, tho' freight and insurance have risen. An expensive venture, my loss incl Annie B in excess of $600."

The tall case clock chimed in the hall: half-past one. How long had she been here in the business room? Would anyone have missed her? Thanks to Judge Grant's crisis, she might not be missed until dinnertime.

Interesting, these events of 1822—but what had become of the infant Diana? She could not pore through each of the sixteen subsequent volumes searching for mentions of her. Replacing the 1822 journal, she took down the 1838 journal, the last one. Why were there no volumes for 1839 or 1840? She opened 1838. How Judge Grant's handwriting had changed in the course of sixteen years! It had still the same distinctive characteristics, but it had grown weak and shaky. And it was not only his writing which had deteriorated; gradually, as she paged through the weeks and months, it was borne in upon Grace that this volume was a record of pecuniary embarrassment, or worse: disaster, catastrophe, an avalanche of debt. When, she wondered, had Judge Grant's deteriorating health forced his retirement from the bench, stopping that salary? Here was recorded his disappointment upon learning that his petition to the legislature for a pension had been denied. Here was parsimony: "told Boyce he will have to pay for carrying his share of the crop to market, and to pay the carriage of all refused tobacco"—punctuated by extravagance: "Pay'd Davies $200 for his grey filly that won the stakes." A Mr Walker—a banker, Grace surmised—cropped up frequently in connection with loans and mortgages, assessors and appraisers. The security for a loan to pay taxes was six negroes. Mortgages were renewed, and eventually a farm—with its "people"—was sold off at a fraction of its value, because bidders there were none, due to the currency crisis. Thirty slaves leased for a year to Mr MacFarlane brought in a promissory note—which was immediately discounted and the funds applied to extinguish an overdue lien. Interspersed were occasional disbursements to James and, to a lesser amount, to Charles.

The last entry for 1838 was this, for December 19: "Davies offers cash down for clean bricks; have set 2 laborers at the icehouse with brickbats & old Walter to clean them."

Grace closed the book and returned it to its place on the shelf. Some eighteen months had passed since that entry, and somehow the Grants remained at Grantsboro, still entertaining guests; still commissioning portraits for which, presumably, they intended to pay; still breeding horses, and farming tobacco and wheat. Still the masters of slaves—who were still cleaning bricks.

Surely, in this desperate state of affairs, a cash offer for a slave must be welcome. But where was the slave? Could Diana have been among the people sold off with the liquidated farm?

Grace's gaze swept along the long row of journals—then sharpened upon a volume at the far end, whose spine was stamped in gold foil: *Stock Book*. She drew it out and opened it.

The first two-page spread was a summary page, headed "Total of Stock on Grantsboro Plantation Commcg. 1st January 1805." The succeeding years, from 1805 down to 1840, were listed down the left edge of the page, and narrow columns were labeled at an oblique angle across the top: Men/Women/Boys/Girls/Total Slaves//Stallions/

Geldings/Mares/Colts/Fillies/Total Horses//Bulls/Steers/Cows/ Heifers/Bullcalves/Total Cattle//Jackasses/Mules//. There was a wide column for remarks down the right side—remarks such as these, for 1816: "6 boys 4 girls born / 2 men 4 wom. died / 4 girls became wom, 2 boys became men/ 1 b drownd/ 2 m, 1 wom. runaway." The handwriting for 1805 through 1835 was Judge Grant's; but a different handwriting recorded the figures since 1836.

Though the journals ceased in 1838, someone had continued the *Stock Book* as recently as January 1 of the present year.

Turning a few pages, Grace found the rosters of the estate's stock— slaves, cattle, and horses—as of the beginning of each year. The annual slave rosters listed each slave by name, age, occupation, and condition. She traced down the heartbreaking list of names for 1822 with her finger: Ketty Venus Rachael Hagar . . . and Annie B. The entire entry for Annie B. was lined through, but Grace could make out what had been written there: her age, fifteen; occupation, "serves Miss J; condition, able & healthy, w/child." In the "Remarks" column at the far right was written, "Jan 22 deld 1 fem Diana." And below that was crammed in another remark, seemingly added later: "runaway, Scotland, Aug."

She turned to the following year's roster, dated January 1823, and skimmed down the long list of names. Near the end she found: "Diana/ age 1/sickly." Under "Remarks" was written, "Annie B's mulatto girl."

Grace turned through the pages, the years, and the fates: drowning; paralysis; snakebite; childbed; occasionally, a runaway. Grace came to the roster for 1830. Some of the names were familiar by now: Prince, mule driver. Harriet, cook. Jacky, bricklayer. And here she was, still: "Diana/age 8/watches infants/recov'd measles."

She turned to the last roster in the book, made in January of this year. Diana, Diana? Where was Diana now? Not listed among the field hands. Not under "About the House." Not among the tradesmen. Not among the children, or the superannuated. The last category—a separate page, in fact—was headed "Arrochar." And there she was: "Diana/18/serves Mrs MacF/able & seeming healthy, but still childless." In the "Remarks" column the entry for her—for all the slaves on this page—was "do." Ditto, supposed Grace, and her eye ran to the top of the column. The notation there was "leased to MacFarlane."

The oblong of midday light slanting against the window blind had slowly contracted and now was gone; the business room was dimmer than ever. Grace listened. All was quiet. The keys still dangled from the lock in the door. She made sure she had put everything back as she had found it, leaving no traces of her trespass. She concentrated for a moment on seeing, as fully as she could—on seeing, and remembering how it all looked: the volumes on the shelves, the messy stacks of papers on the desk, the dust on the blinds. It seemed important to note every detail of what she saw. Then she went to the door and listened again: all still. She unlocked the door; let herself out; and locked the door again behind her. As she ascended the stairs, she found herself breathing the rhythmic *taorluath* movement from an old pipe tune under her breath, in time with her thudding heart.

GRACE WROTE HER LETTERS, using her own pen, ink, and paper, in her bedroom. Two letters: one to Dan; the other to Anibaddh, sealed and enclosed inside Dan's letter. She had black paper for making copies but did not use it, judging it imprudent to keep copies of such letters as these. How she ached for Dan, for Jamie, for home! She made quite sure of the seals and, when she went downstairs, dropped her letter into the mailbag which hung in the hall near the business room.

Emerging from the tearoom onto the lawn, Grace tied the ribbons of her bonnet under her chin and pulled the brow of it well forward to shade her face. This slanting Virginia sunshine could redden and burn her pale Scottish skin in minutes. Passing the old men cleaning the bricks, she nodded to them. *Tink—tink—tink*, replied their hammers on the bricks.

Grace came to the kitchen garden. Through the tall palings she could catch glimpses of the bright kerchiefs of the black women working there. They were dumping barrow-loads of manure; and carrying buckets of water, for the beets, okra, chard, peas, beans. These women's faces gleamed in the sun, in their sweat. Their skin shone, as Grace's never did. They were talking together; someone laughed. They did not know she was there.

She made for the alley of mulberry trees, for the sake of their cool shade; and there she lingered for some time, walking up and down until her agitation should drain away, her equanimity return. Hadn't she a right to feel triumphant? Hadn't she mustered the courage to come here? Hadn't she succeeded, within mere days, in finding what she sought, and without raising suspicion? The rest was up to Anibaddh and that Washington City lawyer. Her responsibility here was done—except for the painting of portraits. She was obliged to see that through, or risk discrediting herself. She was obliged to go to the revival meeting too, and hear Mr Stringfellow preach, though she would much have preferred to bolt.

WHEN THE FAMILY convened in the parlor just before dinner, Grace returned Miss Johnstone's keys.

"Merciful heaven!" cried Miss Johnstone. "So you're the one who's had them all day! I only wish I'd known. I've been like a woman distracted, what with Judge Grant so sorely stricken—and my keys gone astray too."

"I beg your pardon, ma'am. I picked them up for safekeeping this morning when you were called away so suddenly."

"I wish you'd let me know sooner. I've been very much upset, and had the tearoom turned inside out, looking for them. And then I sent Cleo looking for you too, to ask if you'd seen them, but you were nowhere to be found."

"I went outdoors to walk for a time," said Grace. "I had picked up your keys to keep them from falling into other hands, but then I did not like to intrude upon you in your time of trouble. I hope that Judge Grant is resting comfortably by now?"

"No, he's nowhere near comfortable. He's been a martyr to the stone—gravel of the kidneys, you know—for years now, and he suffers untold torments during these crises, when a stone is to be passed." They entered the dining room, Miss Johnstone adding, "Laudanum can do only so much; and even Dr Woodward, the best practitioner in Virginia, Mrs Pollocke, the best—oh, yes, he attended my sister at all her lyings-in—but even he says there's very little to be done. No, poor Judge Grant is nowhere near comfortable—and his terrible agonies drag on sometimes for days. It's enough to try the patience of a saint."

Mr Stringfellow, sitting down beside Miss Johnstone, said, "Nevertheless, dear ladies, we know that an all-powerful and all-merciful Providence oversees us all; and it is not for us to question His ways."

GRACE'S PAINTS WERE thick and ropy this morning; if she had been alone she would have spit into them—just as, when drinking her tea alone, she habitually licked the droplet of cream from the spout of the jug. It was difficult to remember not to do this in the company of others. She was tempted to spit nevertheless, not only because it was convenient and effective, but also for the satisfaction of appalling Miss Johnstone, who was sighing ostentatiously as she settled herself in the sitter's chair. Instead Grace stirred in a few drops of dissolved gum arabic.

"Now, Mrs Pollocke, how are you getting along with that pamphlet of Mr Dew's?" inquired Miss Johnstone. "I do hope you're able to give it some of your attention. There are more important duties in life than gratifying the vanity of those who want their heads painted."

"I finished reading Mr Dew's pamphlet last night," said Grace.

"And what did you make of it?" inquired Miss Johnstone after a pause—just as Grace had hoped. Grace meant to say very fully what she thought of Mr Dew; and she meant for Miss Johnstone first to invite her to do so.

"I think he is very wrong," said Grace, "on nearly every point which he takes up."

"That's mighty positive, from a young person!"

"And I think he is most wrong, and most culpable, in the very foundation of his argument, which is only this: the right and just course need not be followed because it is . . . expensive! That is the ground underlying his entire argument; but as a reason for continuing a grave injustice, it is indefensible, even if true," said Grace. "All his subsequent arguments are an attempt to demonstrate that this grave injustice is not in fact the very worst condition to which any people have ever been reduced. That may be true as well; but as a reason for perpetuating this particular unjustice, it too is indefensible."

"I guess you'd be happy to see us impoverished," said Miss Johnstone. "Grabbing and grubbing for every penny, like Yankees. Who's going to pay you to paint portraits then? It's the distinguished Vir-

ginia families, the good old Carolina families, that can offer real patron-
age, in the grand old style. Not New York tradesmen. Not Philadelphia
merchants. You were eager enough to come to Virginia to ply your
trade, I guess."

Bitter as gall, the taste of the retort that Grace was obliged to swallow. She had not been eager to come; she had not come in order to "ply
her trade"; and this distinguished Virginia family, at least, was already
impoverished; was teetering upon the brink of ruin even now, all wealth
and honor squandered, and Miss Johnstone the last to own it. All this
must remain unsaid.

There were other possible replies, however. Having finished the
last touches to Miss Johnstone's dress, Grace chose another brush for
stippling her lace collar. She said, "You speak scornfully of tradesmen
and merchants, Miss Johnstone, so I will suppose you to be unaware
that my husband is a merchant in the China trade. The profits to be
made in enterprises such as his may seem paltry to the slaveholding
gentry of the southern states, but they are honest gains, got by honest
means. If Yankee tradesmen and merchants live modestly, it is because
they live within the means they are able to come by honestly, and
would be ashamed to mount a display of ill-gotten wealth such as
slaveholders boast of—an opulence obtained by robbing others of their
labor and their liberty! Mr Dew's arguments are, in fact, just such as
a robber might advance in justifying his profession: namely, that he
wants the money! Is the robber permitted on that account to continue
his depredations? No, madam; he is hanged at the crossroads—"

"Oh, shame!" Miss Johnstone interrupted.

"I have not finished," said Grace. "Mr Dew's arguments are no
more than a cold-blooded calculation of the profit which is derived
from this enterprise of robbing others—not only of their labor, but of
their very persons! Of course it is profitable—to the robber! Of course
the robber does not like to give up his profession! Of course he declares
that he cannot possibly afford to do so! And all the while, Mr Dew
pretends to champion the rights of property, and to defend the order
and tranquillity of society!"

"Well; now are you done? I couldn't be expected to know that your
husband was in the China trade," said Miss Johnstone. "And I'm sure I
wasn't referring to any person in particular, so there's no need to get

so huffed, Mrs Pollocke, and call honorable gentlemen robbers, and call for hanging them."

Grace had waxed hotter than she had intended.

"But," continued Miss Johnstone, "even if you stubbornly disregard every practical and worldly consideration that Mr Dew sets forth, there still remains the Ultimate Authority. I mean the holy scriptures, the biblical authorization of slavery, which amounts not just to a divine sanction of the institution—but to a positive commandment, an obligation; a duty, in short! And I'm sure that no decent person could presume to disregard that authority. But we'll talk no more of this just now, Mrs Pollocke, if you please," she added hastily, to head off any reply. "Not until you've heard Mr Stringfellow preach on the subject. He has studied the matter deeply and devoutly, and no one could persist in error, after hearing him."

THE PORTRAIT MINIATURE of Miss Johnstone was finished. Grace marveled at her own accomplishment: here shone Miss Johnstone's pride, her spite, her righteousness.

But when Grace showed it to her, Miss Johnstone said, "Well! You've made me a little too young and handsome after all, despite my express instructions. And what will Mr Stringfellow say?"

ONLY SOME HOURS LATER was Grace able to remember that there were people with whom it was degrading to contend; and that Miss Johnstone was certainly one of these. There was no likelihood of ameliorating her views on any subject; Grace was under no obligation to make the attempt; and it had been imprudent to antagonise her. Leave it to the Americans, Grace reminded herself, to engage in hotheaded and futile dispute.

THAT EVENING, JUDGE GRANT passed his kidney stone. By the next morning, Dr Woodward had been allowed to go home; and Judge Grant, still somewhat yellow and shaky, was at the breakfast table eating eggs and bacon. "Nearly a quarter of an inch in diameter," he reported, "and constituted almost entirely of calcium, or so said Dr Woodward, though I have touched neither milk nor oysters since I was a boy—"

"Merciful heaven!" interrupted Miss Johnstone, who could see out the window from her chair. "Here's a carriage! Why, it's Mr Grimshaw! And our dear Charlotte! And her two little boys, too, after all! What— what a surprise!"

Grace remembered hearing of Mrs Grimshaw; she was another of the Grant sisters, another of Grace's cousins. In a few moments the little family came in. Mrs Ambler, Mrs MacFarlane, and Miss Grant all leapt from their chairs to embrace them, crying, How delightful! and Dearest Charlotte! and so forth. Mr Stringfellow rose to bow at them and shake their hands. Mrs Grimshaw kissed her father while her husband bowed, saying, "I hope I see you well, sir."

"Well enough, now," replied the judge, "but if you had come along night before last, you should have seen me just as bad as could be; the biggest stone I've ever had—"

"And this is Mrs Pollocke, the painter who's been doing all our heads. Maybe she'll have time to do yours, and the little boys too," interrupted Miss Johnstone—just as a platter of bacon crashed to the floor, pulled off the sideboard by the smaller of the two boys. The child set up a howl even before his mother slapped him.

HALF AN HOUR LATER Miss Julia Grant was settling herself into the sitter's chair in the tearoom while Grace laid out her colors. "We all breathed a sigh of relief, if truth be told," said Miss Grant, "when Charlotte wrote that they couldn't come for the revival on account of the measles—but I guess that was only a false alarm. Her Little Responsibilities are always up to some mischief, and so noisy too! Their father talks of discipline—threatens to flog them—but never makes good his threats. Charlotte generally laughs at their monkey tricks, as she calls them, and does nothing at all to check them—until suddenly she loses her temper and slaps them. We'll have no peace until they go away again, I'm afraid." Miss Grant wore a lavender silk dress with a matching pelerine.

"Turn to your right, if you please," suggested Grace. "More. Yes, that is it." She drew the curtains, admitting only a single shaft of light to illuminate Miss Grant's left side, while her right side receded into shadow. "Now let me see you draw yourself up; taller; taller. Can you maintain that posture? Most elegant." Grace began to draw. Even now running footsteps could be heard overhead; then the slamming of a door; a shriek; a yell; then Mrs Grimshaw's voice, followed by another slam, and more thunderous running.

"I hope the weather remains fine, so they can be sent out-of-doors," said Miss Grant. "I think my sister Ambler mentioned that you have a little boy yourself, Mrs Pollocke?"

"So I have, but he has only just learned to walk; I daresay the running will be next," said Grace.

"And do you flog him, to make him mind you?"

"No indeed; I have never flogged him," said Grace.

"But does he mind you, then?"

"Oh, about as well as can be expected, of so young a child," replied Grace, "which is to say, not very well at all!"

"My aunt always says that Obedience is the first duty every child must learn. Is that not your own theory?"

"Oh, theories! I cannot say I ever possessed anything so systematic as a theory, Miss Grant—or if I had, it melted away upon its first confrontation with an actual infant."

"I guess it's generally the spinsters, such as Aunt Bella and myself, who have the most fully formed notions of how children should be brought up," said Miss Grant. "And—since our notions remain untested, they're quite the likeliest to remain intact, hey? There's nothing like a virginal ignorance for breeding assurance."

Startled, Grace paused her brush—and looked again at her sitter. Something showed there now that she had not seen before. Did Miss Grant know what she had just said? Aye, she did; for now a small sly smile turned up the corners of her mouth, wrinkled the corners of her eyes—and one eyebrow lifted, most sardonic.

"Ha!" said Grace, and took up a rag. "Now I shall have to begin all over again!" she declared, and, wiping clean the ivory disk, she did just that.

THE MOUTH AND CHIN OF THE YOUNG MRS GRANT ON THE
dining room wall were shaped just like Miss Julia Grant's. How pleasant, how easy it was to take a likeness without a living sitter, a sitter
who needed to be listened to, flattered, reassured, soothed, cajoled, or
animated! From here, Grace could hear people all over the house: footfalls overhead, upstairs. Voices from the kitchen; and someone passing
along the corridor outside the dining room from time to time. Outside,
tink-tink-tink; and occasional shrieks and howls from the Grimshaw
boys.

Someone entered, and Grace looked up, expecting one of the slaves,
come in to set the table for dinner. But it was Judge Grant, as startled
as herself. "Oh!" he said, and then, "What are you doing?"

"I am making a copy, a miniature on ivory, of this portrait of Mrs
Grant," said Grace.

"And why, pray, are you doing that?"

"Mrs Ambler and Mrs MacFarlane especially desired me to do so,"
Grace said. "As a present for you, sir, I believe. But if your daughters
have not mentioned it to you, I daresay it was to have been a
surprise."

"There is a great deal that my daughters, and their husbands, do
not see fit to mention to me," said Judge Grant. He hobbled across the
room and stood behind her, to look over her shoulder. "It's rather
small," he declared presently, "for an old man's eyes."

"Miniatures are meant to be small," said Grace. "They are for the
hand; the pocket."

"Not for the weak eyes of old men, eh?" He pulled out one of the
dining chairs and sat down near her left side, saying, "You sound like
a Scot, I think, Mrs—Mrs—"

"Pollocke," supplied Grace. "So I am. And so are you, sir, if I can believe my ears," she added, for—in addition to knowing perfectly well that he was—she could hear a faint ghost of the old Lothian pronunciation behind his American words.

"Aye, can you hear it still? But I've been in this country almost fifty years. Since I was fourteen. Well; go on, Mrs Pollocke: talk. It does me good to hear you."

"I can talk, sir, or I can paint. But I cannot do both at the same time."

"Can't you? Mmm. The painter who did those"—he gestured at the big pictures on the wall—"had plenty to say. Chattered away like a mockingbird."

"I daresay he did," said Grace. "Too much talking, and not enough attention to his work."

"Don't you admire them?" he said lightly.

"Who was the painter?" she asked.

"If I were to tell you, you'd change your tune fast enough," he said.

"Of the painter, perhaps; but not of the paintings," replied Grace.

"Well, what is wrong with them, then? To your expert eye?"

"I am not qualified to say whether the likeness is a good one. But the twist in Mrs Grant's shoulder and torso is incorrect, making her chin a little too high, her neck a little too long. The tints used for the skin of her arms and face are muddy and indistinct—overworked, in fact—thus producing a dull and unconvincing opacity. Indeed, the paint in many places has been vexed and tormented beyond all bearing. And the technique of outlining the nose, and shadowing under it, is what I should call primitive. The hands are well done, however, and the overall impression is a pleasant one."

"Hmm! Now, suppose I were to tell you that this picture, which you presume to criticise, is in fact from the brush of the eminent, the Celebrated Mr Gilbert Stuart, the master who painted General Washington on so many occasions? What do you say to that?"

"Do you tell me so, sir?"

He said, "What is your opinion, pray, about the other painting—my likeness, there?"

"Again, as to likeness, I cannot comment; anyone will change a great deal over the course of thirty years. The composition strikingly resembles that used by Mr Stuart for his many full-length portraits of General Washington, certainly. But it is equally like that unauthorised engraving made after them, which everyone has seen—to Mr Stuart's fury. He was a madman on matters of copyright, though I cannot much sympathise with his indignation over that particular breach—as he himself had borrowed the composition from an engraving after a French portrait. Aye, but so he did, sir!—down to the very carving of the furniture, and the folds in the drapes!"

"The dog!"

"It is curious, when one thinks of it—the things one claims to own," said Grace. "A great many things are unamenable to being owned. In Philadelphia I have lately seen a demonstration of a new process by which, if I had it here, I might have produced a perfect replica of this painting of Mrs Grant, in a matter of minutes. By ingenious chemical means and the action of light, anyone may now make an astoundingly faithful replica, of anything. The colors are lost, and the image is reversed, as in a mirror; but in every other respect, the original is replicated with a minute accuracy."

"It seems that you can talk while you paint, after all."

Grace smiled, and fell silent. But she could feel him watching her, watching not the work of her pencil—now on palette, now on ivory—but herself: her neck, her ear, her profile. She felt her ears begin to glow. No wonder her sitters grew so uneasy under her own gaze.

"Do you play chess, by any chance, Mrs Pollocke?" he asked after a few moments.

An odd question. "Aye, sir, I do," said Grace. "When I can get an opponent."

"We shall have to play a game sometime soon, then," he said. Painfully he rose and made his way to the door.

"I beg you will remember to be surprised, sir," said Grace, "when you are presented with the miniature of Mrs Grant."

"MRS POLLOCKE, I'M AFRAID I must inconvenience you, just a little," announced Miss Johnstone with unconcealed satisfaction, as she came into the tearoom where Grace was cleaning her brushes after dinner. "Mr and Mrs Grimshaw's arrival this morning was a complete surprise, I must say—a very pleasant one, of course. But a surprise, because I wasn't expecting them, so I only set aside the Blue Room for Mrs Pratt and her new baby, and gave you the Chinese Room all to yourself. But now that the Grimshaws are here after all—well, I'm at a loss about where to put them, because all my other rooms are already taken up. Reverend Stringfellow and Master Charles have the Bachelors' Hall; Mrs Ambler is with me, in my room, and Mr and Mrs Mac-Farlane are in the Fern Room. So I find that I have no choice but to move you into Miss Julia's room. I hope it will do very well for you both, as the bed is pretty wide."

Grace replied that she had not the slightest objection. By the time she finished her work and went upstairs, someone—Cleo, surely—had carried Grace's belongings to Miss Grant's room at the end of the passage. How fortunate, if share she must, to share with Miss Grant, and not with Miss Johnstone, as Mrs Ambler did! Grace hoped that Miss Grant did not much mind.

A stack of books lay on the table beside Miss Grant's bed, topped by Dr Turner's *Elements of Chemistry*, 1835, Philadelphia. A single window overlooked the lawn. A tea set of old blue Wedgwood jasperware was arranged along the mantel over the dark fireplace: an odd place for an old tea set. Grace picked up the sugar box just as Miss Grant came in.

"I am glad to have a roommate who can appreciate my treasures," said Miss Grant, shrugging off her pelerine and throwing it onto the bed. "Very old-fashioned, Aunt Bella says; and now that most of the pieces are chipped, she don't see why I insist on keeping them. I haven't told her it's because of these priestesses disposed all around. Not wearing much, are they? But I cherish them because they're doing chemistry. Of course they are; look again, Mrs Pollocke. This well-shaped female is pouring oil into the fire on the altar; and there is the burnt offering. They might be changing lead into gold; or maybe cooking up a fresh batch of emeralds. Oh, yes; in those days, you could produce emeralds in a matter of six or eight hours, over a hot fire—if you had the Egyptian recipe, and a pot with a tight-fitting lid. Al-chymy, the black art! Everyone supposes it means the devil's work, but it only means the Egyptian art—when Egypt was called the black land—either for the color of its Nile-ish mud, or for the color of its inhabitants. Is it true that you are a free thinker on religious matters, Mrs Pollocke?"

"Oh, Miss Grant, what a question! Has someone said that I am?"

"My sisters have hinted at it."

"I don't know why they would suppose so; it is not a subject on which I have declared my views to them."

"Well, I am disappointed," said Miss Grant. "I was so looking forward to discussing religion with a free thinker. These matters are so difficult to think through on one's own. I find my mind keeps shying away from such forbidden thoughts—not permitted even to think the unthinkable. But nothing should be unthinkable—should it? Surely one may think about anything?"

"To ponder even the imponderables?" suggested Grace.

"Ha! There is your little joke again," said Miss Grant. "Which side of the bed do you prefer?"

"I do like to see the stars," said Grace, "if you don't mind."

. . .

Passing through the library on her way to the tea-room the next morning, Grace found Miss Grant in her lavender dress, bent over pen, paper, and open books at the big desk. "Oh! Already?" said Miss Grant.

"Half-past ten, by the hall clock," said Grace. "But if it is not convenient—"

"I will be along momentarily. Let me just—just—before I lose my place—"

"What are you doing?"

"Making a table of the elements, in order by weight, from lightest to heaviest."

"By weight! That seems a singular way of ordering anything."

"Not at all; it is far more sensible than Dr Turner's absurd alphabetic table, quite meaningless, based only upon accidents of nomenclature. How would you order them, yourself?"

"I don't know . . . a child's first impulse might be to order things by color."

"Ah, the misleading appeal of color," said Miss Grant. "The alchemists supposed, whenever they succeeded in imparting a golden cast to a metal, that they were making progress in perfecting it, in changing it into gold itself, the noblest of the metals. In fact, they were only tinting it yellowish, by applying a thin film of sulfur." Setting aside her ruler and pen, she came in and sat down to submit to being looked at for the next hour; but she brought her worksheet too, and held it in her lap, outside the scope of the picture. "They had a very high opinion of sulfur on account of its color, and pinned their hopes on it for centuries. Even now, some folks think the water from the sulfur springs in the mountains up west is very nearly the fountain of youth. I have little use for it, myself."

"There are times when the merest whiff of a boiled egg is too much to bear," agreed Grace. "The pelerine a little higher on the shoulder, please; and are those the eardrops you were wearing yesterday? They are? But what is this intriguing notion, Miss Grant, of 'nobility'—in metals? What makes a metal noble?"

"The noble metals are those which are relatively unsusceptible to corruption—"

"Charming irony! And every Scottish title a badge of corruption! But so they are, Miss Grant, I assure you; every dukedom ever conferred was a reward for some betrayal of astounding magnitude, sufficient to rouse not only the notice, but even the gratitude, of the Crown!"

"My aunt would warn you, Mrs Pollocke, that cynicism is unattractive to gentlemen. In a chemical sense, 'corruption' refers to corrosion. And so the alchemists ranked gold, the purest and least susceptible to ordinary corrosion, as the most noble of all—as distinguished from iron and the other base metals, so quickly consumed and destroyed by rust and other forms of corrosion."

"Ah. And silver? Noble or base?"

"Noble."

"I am surprised; I should have guessed that silver could scarcely rank even as aristocratic, much less noble; about minor gentry, I should have said—because it so quickly tarnishes and blackens. Which is heavier, gold or silver?"

"Oh, gold, considerably," said Miss Grant, referring to the paper in her lap. "Near the bottom of my table. Its relative weight is 199.2, and silver only 108—"

"But gold is not the heaviest of the elements?" asked Grace.

"By no means; both mercury and uranium, here, are heavier than gold."

"And lead?"

"Let me see: 103.6. Lighter even than silver. But lead is a base metal, of course—though it is so dignified," said Miss Grant.

"Lead, dignified?" said Grace. "What can you mean?"

"Well, surely an imperturbable aplomb is characteristic of lead— eh? Eh? Ha! *A plomb*, don't you see—the French, for 'lead'—"

"Oh, Miss Grant; that is dreadful!"

"Yes, thank you; isn't it, though?"

IN THE AFTERNOON, Grace returned to the dining room to continue her work on Mrs Grant. She had been there only a short time when Judge Grant came in. He said, "So here you are again, Mrs Pollocke."

"Here I am indeed," said Grace, not in the least surprised to see him.

Again he pulled out a chair and sat where he could see her profile. "Is it a faithful copy you're making?" he said. "Or have you presumed to correct the defects you claim to have discerned in the original?"

"See for yourself, sir."

"My spectacles . . . here they are. It is still dreadfully small, Mrs Pollocke."

"Yes, sir. That is why it is called a miniature."

"Let me see. Ah. . . ." He fell silent for a moment. Then he said, "It is very like her. Very. It is a better likeness than the original. How do you manage that, never having laid eyes on her yourself? Is it mere luck?"

"Luck, sir! No, I beg your pardon; it is skill."

"My bonnie little Anne Johnstone! I remember very well the first time she consented to dance with me. It was at her father's house in Richmond. Her neck does look more natural, more comfortable, the way you've done it."

"Of course it does."

"And you've got the look of her mouth and chin."

"I thought so. Miss Julia Grant has just her mother's mouth and chin, I fancy."

"So she has, the poor bairn; but not her eyes. Well—well. I shall like to carry that in my pocket, whenever it is presented to me. I haven't let on, never fear. I'll be as surprised as anyone could want."

"What did your Virginia bride make of Boston?" said Grace. "And of Yankees?"

"Boston! Yankees! What do you mean? My wife never set foot in Boston in her life," said Judge Grant.

"No? She remained here, then, while you went to Boston without her?" said Grace.

"I've never been to Boston either," said Judge Grant. "What's all this about Boston?"

"Oh! I beg your pardon. I daresay there has been some misapprehension. I was told that these portraits were painted by Mr Gilbert Stuart. And as I knew that Mr Stuart lived and worked in Boston from 1805 onward—and as these portraits were painted sometime after 1807, or, more likely, 1808—I naturally concluded that you and Mrs Grant had gone up to Boston to sit to Mr Stuart there. But of course, someone has misunderstood. These portraits certainly cannot be Mr Stuart's work, regardless of what I was told. Your daughters believe they are by Mr Stuart. But who was it in truth, sir, to whom you and Mrs Grant sat?"

"Indeed, Mrs Pollocke!" he rumbled, very gruff and indignant; but then he erupted into laughter, long and loud, and ended in coughing. At last, wiping his mouth with his pocket handkerchief, he said, "You've got me fair and square, I admit it; and a nicer little snare never was set. What a lawyer you'd have made! Never underestimate a redheaded Scotswoman. But how did you know, exactly?"

"First, sir, tell me who was the painter, if you please."

"A Mr Lawson, in Baltimore, in 1808. My father-in-law had given us money some years before, to have our portraits done. It must have been 1804, when I had a case before the Supreme Court. Mr Stuart was in Washington then, and my father-in-law sent the money—and a nice round sum it was too—for sitting to Mr Stuart, particularly. Most particularly. But—well—I had some unexpected expenses just then. A horse, as I recall; a far better investment than pictures, or so it seemed to me at the time. That was before I bought my stallion Colonel Blood. Colonel Blood! Surely someone has told you about Colonel Blood! And—well, we expected to make up the money soon enough, and sit to Mr Stuart later on, so as to have the pictures to show my father-in-law. . . . But the money didn't come in when expected—money never does—and then, as you seem to know, Mr Stuart left Washington. Boston, was that where he went next? For the rest of his life? Ah. But my wife, not liking to say that we had used the money elsewhere, had told her father that we had indeed sat to Mr Stuart, and that we were only waiting for him to finish the pictures and deliver them. Mr Stuart was notoriously slow at finishing and delivering, Mrs Pollocke; years might elapse before an old bald man might eventually get the picture of himself done years earlier, when he'd still had his hair, and his youth."

Yes, she knew.

"But even that excuse wouldn't last forever," continued the judge. "And we got tired, after a while, of being asked how Mr Stuart was coming along with those pictures. So when we found ourselves in Baltimore for the winter of 1808—a safe distance from my wife's family in Richmond—we sat to Mr Lawson instead. He was quick, and not too expensive—and at last we had something to show my father-in-law, who never suspected anything amiss. Of course, we had to keep the secret about them ever since. Now tell me, Mrs Pollocke; how did you know?"

"By looking at the pictures with my own eyes," said Grace.

"Humbug," said the judge. "Come, now, Mrs Pollocke, I've been frank with you."

"And I am being frank with you, sir. I have already told you my doubts about the muddy tints of the skin tones, the primitive shadowing technique, the unskilled use of outlines. The same faults are evident in the picture of yourself, sir. And although these compositions resemble those favored and often used by Mr Stuart—well, every painter in the world has used them, before and since Mr Stuart."

"And what else? There must be something more than that, to inspire your Scottish skepticism."

"Aye; the reds too. I could not feel quite comfortable about the reds in these two paintings—for I have had opportunities to study numerous of Mr Stuart's portraits, sir, and could not fail to notice how consistently he has favored a certain range of reds—a range which is quite unlike the reds used here. Furthermore, he always touched in a distinctive highlight just inside the lower lid of the eye—and that is missing, from both these portraits."

He went very close to the painting of his young self, and peered at it minutely, at the very brushstrokes. "What else?" he said. "You said they had apparently been painted after 1807. You are quite right, but as these paintings are neither signed nor dated, how could you see that?"

"The books told me that—those five volumes under your hand in the painting, sir. The titles are legible, you see, just barely; actual books are depicted: Mr Marshall's *Life of George Washington*. And when I found the original volumes themselves—aye, in your library—I noted that the fifth volume was not published until 1807; and that your set was inscribed to you by the author, Mr Marshall—"

"Chief Justice Marshall," he corrected her.

"—in 1808. Thus I learned that these books did not exist—not all five volumes—until 1807 at the earliest; and probably came into your possession in 1808. These portraits, therefore, could not have been painted before 1807. And, as I knew already that Mr Stuart lived and worked in Boston from 1805 onwards, I concluded that you and Mrs Grant could only have sat to him at Boston. When you assured me that neither you nor Mrs Grant had ever been to Boston, then I had confirmation—of what I had strongly suspected already, on account of technique and color—that the painter was certainly not Mr Stuart."

"How fortunate, Mrs Pollocke, that my father-in-law lacked your acuity."

Grace made no reply, but she felt him studying her profile again as she bent to her easel.

Presently he said, "You quite put me in mind of someone, a very long time ago . . . my dear little sister . . . I have not thought of her in years."

Grace felt a flush rising through her and, near panic, felt herself quite helpless to stem it. It felt like tears; or shame; or was it love? For a moment, she longed to reveal herself to him, the poor dear old man! But no, he must never guess it; far too much was at stake, for herself, for others. With a great effort she throttled the impulse, and heard her own strangely calm voice say something dismissive. Then she got herself somehow out of the room, and fled to the Mulberry Lane, there to pace up and down in the hot afternoon shade, trying to unwind the tangled skein of her feelings.

She felt shame and love. Shame at being so deceitful, so dishonest:

(But I have stolen nothing, nor told any lies!)

(You have clandestinely sneaked into a locked room and pored through private records.)

(Is that a crime? Under these circumstances?)

(Oh, 'circumstances,' now, is it? What would you not stoop to, given suitable 'circumstances'?)

It was love too. He was so surprisingly dear, unexpectedly mild, vulnerable. So old and weakened, his spotted old face drooping now; so near the end of his life; so weary. He was her own blood kin, nearest in the world, except Jamie; her own mother's own brother. His father had been her own grandfather; she was herself Grant as much as MacDonald—more than she ever would be a Pollocke. They were of the same race and descent, he and she. She had not expected to feel even the scantest liking for this old slaveholder—but what she felt was quite aside from liking or disliking; it was compassion, a deep tenderness. How shameful to feel that! How lovely to feel that! How confusing.

"YOU ARE VASTLY raised in my esteem, Mrs Pollocke, in consequence of your preferring Dr Turner's *Elements of Chemistry* to Mr Dew's abolition pamphlet," said Miss Julia—startling Grace, who, much engrossed, had not heard Miss Julia enter their bedroom.

"I beg your pardon; I borrowed it without asking," said Grace. "I was attracted by the title of this chapter: 'Colouring Matters.' 'So it does, very much!' I said to myself. 'But why?' I had hoped to find some explanation of the—the spiritual attributes, I suppose they might be called, of colors—their occult significance, if you will. Of course, I find nothing of the sort; it is instead a sober discourse on dyestuffs. Still, I am captivated. Here is your litmus lichen, called *Lichen roccella*, from the Canary Islands. Here is turmeric. But I am especially delighted by saffron, for I never suspected that its powers of coloring were so various. Listen: 'The colouring ingredient of saffron (*Crocus sativus*) is soluble in water and alcohol, has a bright yellow colour, is rendered blue and then lilac by sulphuric acid, and receives a green tint on the addition of nitric acid.' Yellow, blue, lilac, and green—all from one stuff! How it would simplify my pigment box to rely on saffron for all these colors! I should then require only red, black, and white to complete my entire palette."

"Those acids wouldn't do your canvas or your brushes much good, I guess. But Mrs Pollocke, since you've engrossed my book, won't you lend me one of yours?"

"What book of mine could interest you, Miss Grant? . . . Ah! But I have it, the very thing. You will be able to understand and appreciate— much better than I—this little pamphlet recently lent to me: *A Practical Description of the Process called the Daguerreotype*."

It was indeed the very thing to delight and engage Miss Grant, who uttered a stream of commentary as she read: "First operation: polish the plate, silver upon copper; nitric acid, yes. . . . Then second operation: vapor of iodine. Iodine, Mrs Pollocke! Such an interesting substance, and very much like my favorite, chlorine."

"What odd interests and favorites you cherish!" said Grace. "Shall I read you what Dr Turner has to say about iodine? 'Discovered in the year 1812 . . . a dark-coloured matter . . . converted by the application of heat into a beautiful violet vapour. . . . All the iodine of commerce is procured from the impure carbonate of soda, called kelp, which is prepared in large quantity on the northern shores of Scotland, by incinerating sea-weeds. . . . Its vapour is of an exceedingly rich violet colour . . . to which it owes the name of iodine, from the—' well, something in Greek letters which, unfortunately, I cannot read."

"And what does Dr Turner say about the action of light upon iodine?"

" 'Not influenced chemically by the imponderables. Exposure to the direct solar rays . . . does not change its nature.' "

"He's wrong there," said Miss Grant.

"But the man who lent me that pamphlet—a practitioner of the daguerrean process—told me that he doesn't use iodine, himself," said Grace. "He uses instead another substance which produces superior results; superior because faster-acting."

"What was it, this other substance?"

"He declined to say, regarding it as a kind of trade secret."

"Just turn a page or two, there, in Dr Turner, if you will, Mrs Pollocke, and tell me: what comes after iodine?"

"Bromine," replied Grace promptly. " 'The term brome or bromine, from—' something in Greek, again, I do wish I had learned Greek— 'signifying a strong or rank odour.' There was a stench in his studio, to be sure; it smelled of a barnyard of the filthiest kind. It reminded me of goats, male goats."

"Billy goats? I wonder . . . ," said Miss Grant. "Go on; what else does Dr Turner say?"

" 'Its odour, which somewhat resembles that of chlorine, is very disagreeable, and its taste powerful.' Do chemists *taste* these substances?"

"I wouldn't," said Miss Grant. "Not bromine. Go on, please."

" '. . . undergoes no chemical change whatever from the agency of the imponderables. . . . To animal life it is highly destructive, one drop of it placed on the beak of a bird having proved fatal. . . . Bromine is usually extracted from bittern . . . it is now produced in considerable quantity, and sold in Paris as an article of commerce.' What is bittern, Miss Grant?"

"A concentrated brine, of ocean water. And the word refers also, I believe, to a group of wading birds resembling herons."

"How erudite you are."

"All for naught. I think bromine would be worth trying. I guess your chemical friend won't be able to keep his trade secret for long. He'll be lucky if someone else doesn't jump in and patent it; then he won't be allowed to use it at all."

"Very odd, this notion of owning ideas and processes, Miss Grant."

"Isn't it?"

"As odd as owning human beings," added Grace.

"So here we are, back to Mr Dew again!" said Miss Grant. "I do like talking in circles. And so few people can manage it. How sorry I will be when you go away; things will be so dull again. Have you seen this daguerrean process with your own eyes?"

"I have had my likeness taken by it; and have extracted a promise that I shall be allowed to perform the process myself."

"Oh, Mrs Pollocke, you are killing me. I am dying of envy! How lucky you are, to live in Philadelphia."

· · ·

THE DINING TABLE WAS LONGER THAN EVER; A LEAF HAD BEEN added, Grace supposed, to accommodate the company, for they were eleven now. Judge Grant occupied his place at the head, hale enough to have exchanged his invalid's chair for a regular chair. Mr Grimshaw had little to say, but drained his wineglass regularly; opposite him, Mr Charles Grant had a great deal to say, but managed nevertheless to require that his glass be filled for a third time by the time the roast chicken arrived at table; and Grace noted that Mr Stringfellow matched him, glass for glass.

". . . Twenty dollars says it was arson," Mr Grant was declaring.

"They'll never bring it in arson," said Mr Grimshaw, and downed a glassful of his father-in-law's wine.

"I don't say they'll prove it—that's another story altogether," said Mr Grant through a mouthful of chicken. "But arson it was, and I'd stake money on it. Brick courthouses don't combust of their own accord, you know."

"And who do you nominate as the arsonist, sir?"

"I'm naming no names, not just yet. But there's always any number of candidates. Who's got a mortgage falling due and can't pay it? Who's got notes outstanding and the interest piling up? Who's trustee for an estate that's years overdue to settle? Who planted acres of mulberry on credit, and saw them all frozen black? Who lost his whole tobacco crop to hornworms—after borrowing to buy the seed in the first place? Whose spiteful harridan of a wife is suing for a separate maintenance, on account of what she calls 'mistreatment'? Who has to pay the value of some hired-out negroes that up and ran off? There's your list of candidates. Now, I don't keep up a familiarity with Loudoun folk, not spending my time here—but I'll lay money that MacFarlane could tell you their names—couldn't you, MacFarlane?"

"I guess I could, if it wasn't slander," said Mr MacFarlane.

"Ain't you the cautious devil, MacFarlane! I think that around the family dinner table, sir, you might make us the compliment of letting down your guard, just a little," observed Mr Grant.

"Slander or gossip, we'll leave it alone," said Mrs MacFarlane stoutly.

"Whoever he was, he was damned incompetent," said Mr Grant.

"Master Charles!" said Miss Johnstone.

"Beg pardon, Aunt," said Mr Grant, without looking toward his aunt's end of the table. "And Reverend Stringfellow. But if I ever decide to burn down a courthouse, I'll make sure it burns good and proper."

"It's not that easy, I guess," said Mrs Ambler. "When was the last time one actually burnt down?"

"It's not that difficult either," said Judge Grant. "Dinwiddie Courthouse burned about six or seven years ago. King and Queen County, in '28, I think it was. Goochland County and Gloucester County a few years before that."

"And everybody knows about that wicked Mr Posey who burnt down the New Kent County courthouse—and hanged for it too."

"Oh, but that was a long time ago."

"Still happens," said Judge Grant. "Twice in Maryland, within just the last twenty years or so. Leonardstown, in St Mary's County. And Snow Hill; that's way out—Worcester County, I think."

"Dreadful," said Aunt Bella. "Very wicked. I'm sure we ought to be very thankful that our Leesburg men are so vigilant. No deeds or records were actually lost, were they?"

"No, all safe," said Mr MacFarlane. "Not even soaked."

CHAPTER

11

THE EVENING WAS A WARM ONE, AND ALL THE PARLOR WIN-
dows stood open to mosquitoes; to the passionate cries of the negro
children and the Grimshaw boys playing outside; and to moths, now
dashing themselves against the glass chimneys of the lamps and can-
dles ranged upon the various tables.

Mr Stringfellow drew up a chair and sat down beside Grace. In
courtesy, Grace set aside the newspaper which she had been reading.
"At last, I find an opportunity to become acquainted with you, Mrs
Pollocke," he said. "You have been very much occupied, as have I. Such
a busy, large, well-blessed family! I hope you have not supposed that it
was my intention to slight you, for that has certainly not been the case.
But now I will avail myself, if I may, of this opportunity to open our
acquaintance a little, before our revival convenes. I always find it helpful to have some knowledge of the individuals who will constitute my
flock, so as to tailor my preaching to their particular needs." He smiled
at her, displaying a fine set of teeth. "Miss Julia Grant tells me that you
have resided long in foreign climes," he added as he bent close, leaning
his elbows on his knees, so that the vanilla scent of his macassar hair
dressing wafted near.

For a moment Grace was not quite certain whether his florid diction was intended as humor; was laughter expected? She decided it
was not, and only replied soberly, "Yes, Mr Stringfellow, so I have; I
passed my girlhood at various cities in India, as well as at Macao on
the China coast, where I met my husband."

"Ah! Is Mr Pollocke engaged in our good work at Cathay, then?"

"I beg your pardon?" asked Grace, unable to guess what he meant.

"Does your husband number among our Lord's missionaries in the
distant Orient?"

"No, sir; he is a partner in a Philadelphia mercantile concern, engaged largely in the China and India trades."

"Ah, a mercantile man! Often it is the merchants who first venture to penetrate those distant realms of darkness, but our missionaries do not lag far behind them. You yourself, then, will have been in a position to observe that some excellent missionary work is being accomplished among the heathens of those distant lands," he said.

"Some missionary efforts in India have met with a certain success, I believe," said Grace. "But the situation in Canton is rather different. There, I am told, Dr Parker's medical skills have won him the esteem of the city's highest officials—but he has not yet gained even a single convert."

"Great courage and persistence are required of those who labor in the fields of the Lord," said Mr Stringfellow. "I pray daily that our missionaries may be strengthened and succored in their efforts to pour the light of the glorious gospel upon those dark empires. And the more resistant the heathens may be, the greater the need, and the greater the merit in the daunting work, don't you agree, Mrs Pollocke?"

No, she did not. "In some cases," said Grace carefully, "the efforts of the missionaries might be better directed, I think. Too many of them have scant understanding or appreciation for those native religious convictions which they hope to supplant."

"Savage superstition and idolatry, Mrs Pollocke, are not to be met with such softnesses as you suggest. The Almighty's soldiers are engaged in a struggle for souls against the devil, a mighty struggle which does not admit of temporizing with savagery and evil."

He so irritated her that she spoke more plainly and more positively than she might otherwise have done: "Oh, sir, I think it is a great mistake to suppose that the religious views and practices of the Hindus—or of the Mohammedans, or Taoists, or Confucians either—constitute anything resembling savagery or evil."

"I guess that you, Mrs Pollocke, in your innocence and youth, were sheltered from any knowledge of the true depths of depravity which surrounded you there, in those dark regions of the earth; and that is as it should be; it is all to the credit of your parents who had charge of you that you should have retained your innocence. But I have read and prayed in pretty considerable depth on these subjects, Mrs Pollocke.

Indeed, I think I may say that I have made it my study. So you may be assured that I know whereof I speak, when I tell you that such savage practices as polygamy, bestiality, infanticide, idolatry—these abominations unto the Lord, these savage and sinful practices—are widespread, quite universal, amongst the heathens. They are too superstitious even to eat meat, you know, those Hindus."

Grace nearly opened her mouth to argue that if certain Hindus were too scrupulous to kill living creatures and devour their flesh, even Christians need not regard this as a sign of depravity—but then thought better of it. Mr Stringfellow, like Miss Johnstone, did not deserve the compliment of rational opposition. She satisfied herself by saying only, "Many Americans share your view, I believe."

"Yes, I thank the Lord daily upon my knees that I live in such a great and godly nation as this," he said, "and in such awakened days as these; in this era when the light of the blessed gospel is spreading so rapidly across the globe—spreading as rapidly as our railroads, our steamships, our Christian merchants can carry it in their bosoms. Still, hundreds of millions of immortal souls languish in darkness, in ignorance! And so it remains our Christian duty, and our privilege, to preach the Christian gospel unto the benighted, unto the hundreds of millions. It is our Christian duty, and our privilege, to rescue those dusky souls from eternal damnation, to baptise them, to wash them clean of sin, to lead them forward, upward, toward their Savior's eternal life and light."

Grace said nothing. She was not about to embark upon a contest with him about that troublesome doctrine of Original Sin.

"You are a resident of Philadelphia, I am told, Mrs Pollocke. May I ask which church enjoys the compliment of your affiliation there?" he inquired.

"I am not a churchgoer, Mr Stringfellow," replied Grace with a smile so faint as to express clear displeasure to any discerning person.

"Not a churchgoer!" He threw up his hands in a theatrical gesture. "Alas! Miss Johnstone intimated some such hint to me, but of course I declined to believe anything so discreditable without firmer foundation. Alas, that you should thus confirm it, Mrs Pollocke! But perhaps you are . . . you are not a daughter of Judea, if I may inquire?"

"What do you mean, sir?" said Grace.

"A Jewess?"

"No, Mr Stringfellow, I am not a Jewess," replied Grace.

"Perhaps, then, reared, as you have been, in pagan lands, you have never had the opportunity to receive instruction in religious matters?"

"No one could complain of any lack of opportunity there for study and for instruction in religion," said Grace, as repressively as she could.

"And yet, apparently incomplete, Mrs Pollocke, if I may say so—as you confess yourself unaffiliated with any church. We shall see what can be done, in the space of the little time allotted to us. Nothing is beyond the might of the Almighty; even the furthest-straying of lost lambs may be found, and saved, and brought into His fold. . . . But you're not a Roman, I hope? Not a Catholic?"

"No, sir, I am not Catholic; and now I must decline to answer any further questions of this kind."

"I see that you are displeased by my persistence, Mrs Pollocke, and while I disparage and regret the necessity of incurring your displeasure, I am borne up nevertheless by the consciousness of performing my appointed duty, in accordance with His divine will. I will pray for your salvation, Mrs Pollocke. Prayer may work miracles."

"Your private devotions are no one's concern but your own, Mr Stringfellow. I cannot prevent your praying for my salvation, nor for any other object you may deem worthy; but you must not expect my gratitude." With this, Grace rose, made him a small stiff curtsy, and went to sit at the piano at the end of the room. She laid her fingers upon the warm ivory and struck a chord. After a moment she found herself playing a tender and pathetic old Highland slow air. She felt exceedingly vexed; as dissatisfied with herself as with him.

She saw Mr Stringfellow rise and cross to where Miss Johnstone presided over the tea tray. Miss Johnstone made room for him on the sofa beside herself. He sat; he spoke quietly for her ear alone; Miss Johnstone's glance flew to Grace at the piano, and swept past her, across her. He spoke for several moments, Miss Johnstone's expression kindling remarkably.

Grace came to the end of the air, and let the resolving chord die away.

"To lead us in family prayers? So gracious of you, Mr Stringfellow, to propose it!" rang out Miss Johnstone's remarkable carrying voice. "There could be no sweeter way of drawing our evening to a close. Just ring the bell there, won't you, Miss Julia? And we'll have the servants in too. Ah, there's William. William, go and tell Master Charles and Mr Grimshaw that we're gathering for family prayers. Has Judge Grant retired? I'm afraid he has. And William, send in all the house servants. Come, Mrs Pollocke, you'll join us in our evening devotions."

Will I? thought Grace. She would have preferred to retire, but after so public an invitation, that might look defiant. It was not very important to her whether she did or did not spend a few quiet minutes hearing someone else pray aloud; and she did not wish, by any pointed refusal, to seem to attach any undue importance to it.

Half a dozen servants gathered in the room, milling just inside the door. After some moments Mr Grimshaw came in, smelling of tobacco smoke, but Master Charles did not appear. Miss Johnstone sent for him again, while the assembled servants fidgeted and jostled. During this waiting, Grace remained at the piano. Word came back a second time that they were to proceed without Master Charles, who was not at liberty to join them just now.

"Why not?" asked Miss Johnstone loudly of Cleo, who had brought this message.

But it was Mr Grimshaw who replied: "Well, ma'am, he'd only just got his cheroot going properly, and he don't much care to stop it now."

"Let us pray," intoned Mr Stringfellow; and everyone fell to their knees. Sliding from the piano bench, Grace followed their example. There was a rug, to cushion her knees a little.

"O heavenly Father, we beseech Thee, look favorably upon Thy dutiful children, assembled here in Thy sight for the purpose of worship," began Mr Stringfellow. "For praise, thanksgiving, and supplication. . . ." He spoke sonorously, fluently; seemly phrases flowed from him without any apparent effort. It was not the style of speech people addressed to one another, searching for the right words to express their meaning. His eyes were closed, his palms pressed together in the gesture of Christian prayer—so much like the Hindu gesture of *namaste*, Grace thought—but his face was turned upward, and tilted to one side, the better to address his deity, presumably located skyward. All other heads were bowed down, eyes closed—or if not closed, then closely shielded by brows, eyelashes, eyelids. Grace gazed upon them all, just as their deity presumably did. This, she supposed, was what the divinities saw; the Golden Calf's vantage point; the gods'-eye view, the idols'-eye view. And was it pleasing? It was.

". . . and endow us with humble and grateful hearts," Mr String-fellow was saying now.

Grateful, grateful; the word thudded in Grace's ears. She had always loathed being told how grateful she ought to feel. In fact she loathed the very word itself: a blend of "grating" and "hateful." Gratitude, platitude.

". . . yea, even the seven that are an abomination unto Thee," Mr Stringfellow said. "A proud look; a lying tongue; hands that shed inno-cent blood; a heart that deviseth wicked imaginations; feet that be swift in running to mischief; a false witness that speaketh lies; and he that soweth discord among brethren. These deadliest of the sins, these abominations, we beg Thy grace and Thy aid, in eradicating from our sinful hearts. Each deadly, each an abomination, each and every one; and the heaviest, the most abominable of them all—because while it persists there is no avenue for piety and faith to enter the spirit, there to wreak their wondrous works—the heaviest of these, we know, is Pride! The prideful heart knows not humility, knows not gratitude; and like a disobedient servant, or a rebellious child, Pride refuses to assume its proper relation unto Thy divine merciful power; refuses even to acknowledge the need for Thy redemptive mercy—and this, this! we know, is the heaviest, the most abominable sin of them all! Lust is hideous; Gluttony is an abomination unto Thee; Greed and Envy are ugly in Thy sight; Sloth and Wrath are to be eradicated in every soul aspiring to salvation. But none of these weighs heavier upon the immortal soul than Pride! Only Pride so burdens the drowning soul that it may sink below the waves, sink into everlasting damnation! O Heavenly Father, Thou hast sent among us for our special care a lost sheep, a strayed lamb. Grant that, by our combined prayers and efforts and exertions in Thy name, this strayed lamb may be brought into the rapture and the safety of Thy fold, into the bliss of piety and salvation, that the weight of this heaviest sin of all may be lifted from her immortal soul. Amen."

"Amen," a dozen voices promptly echoed; and a dozen pairs of eyes flew open and fixed upon Grace.

Through Grace's mind there flashed an adage from her childhood. *Zahir-āsh az shaikh bātin az Shaitān*: Externally he is a saint, but internally a devil.

...

"Can't sleep?" asked Miss Grant, as Grace tried carefully to turn over once more.

"No; I beg your pardon for disturbing you, but it is so very warm," said Grace. Though the windows stood open, the room felt airless. A mosquito kept shrilling around her uppermost ear. And she so longed for Dan!

"You're not disturbing me," said Miss Grant. "It's far too hot for sleeping. I'm just lying here myself, pondering phlogiston. That debacle."

"What is phlogiston, pray, and why is it a debacle?" said Grace.

"You don't know? Oh, Mrs Pollocke! Everyone ought to know about the phlogiston error. It's rather comical—and a good lesson to us all too, as my Aunt Bella would say. Shall I tell you all about it? That should send you off to sleep, if anything could."

"Let us attempt it, then, by all means," said Grace.

"Well!" exclaimed Miss Grant, and sat up in her nightdress to punch the pillows against the headboard. "One of the great puzzles since the beginning of civilization has been—what do you think? You don't want to guess? Of course it's fire, Mrs Pollocke; fire. Obviously some substances are apt to burn—and others are not. Brick courthouses—not particularly. Old ledgers and registers and title deeds—why, yes, indeed! So the question is, why—and how—do substances burn? What is occurring, chemically speaking, when something burns? Just what is fire itself? That has always been one of the—ahem—burning questions in chemistry."

"Oh, Miss Grant!" said Grace.

"The best chemists of Europe eventually arrived at the conclusion that any substance likely to burn must contain 'phlogiston'—and that in the process of burning, this phlogiston was carried off, leaving behind a dephlogisticated residue—a calx; ashes, for example, or quicklime. Though they noticed that air was required for combustion to occur, it was thought to be only the medium which carried away the phlogiston. And though they noticed that 'airs' were given off when substances burned, no one thought of capturing or identifying these 'airs.' Air was air, or so it seemed, Mrs Pollocke, though you may laugh—"

"Indeed, I am not laughing," protested Grace, laughing. "I too have always supposed that air was air, and have taken it entirely for granted. Ought I not to believe in phlogiston? It seems entirely plausible to me."

"Well, it was a very pretty theory, in many respects," continued Miss Grant seriously, "as it explained so much of what had previously been inexplicable. Who could resist so elegant an explanation? Substances which were apt to burn were rich in phlogiston; and phlogiston was the thing given off in the process of burning, in a rapid whirling motion. The residue left after combustion, the calx, was of course devoid of phlogiston. So neat! So mathematical! Everything was explained to everyone's satisfaction, a very pleasant and reassuring and unusual state of affairs."

Grace waved another mosquito away from her ear.

"But then, alas, the apparatuses got better. And a few people—your Mr Cavendish, in particular—got into the habit of weighing things much more carefully than ever before. And a certain disturbing phenomenon was noted. In fact, it happened every time, to the point where it couldn't be ignored or denied. It was found that calxes—the burnt residue of minerals or metals—weighed more after burning than they had before. Now, how could this be? How, in releasing its phlogiston, could a substance get heavier? Explain that, if you please, Mrs Pollocke; shouldn't it get lighter, not heavier?"

"But if phlogiston ranked among the imponderables, having no measurable weight of its own . . . ?" proposed Grace uncertainly.

"Ah! Well thought of, Mrs Pollocke! But wrong; for in that case, the weight would remain unchanged, wouldn't it?"

"Oh, I see," said Grace.

"But anything can be justified, if you only justify cleverly enough. Maybe another, heavier substance was taken up in its place when phlogiston was given off? Maybe even fire particles? Or maybe phlogiston was lighter than the air that took its place? Or maybe phlogiston had true buoyancy, actual negative weight?"

"Ingenious," said Grace.

"Yes—but there were other problems too: Where did phlogiston go, when given up by a burning substance? What about those insignificant drops of dew that appeared in the apparatus? And what were those airs given off during combustion? In an attempt to capture the phlogiston whirling off the substances he burned, Mr Cavendish did some very clever work capturing and examining these airs, and soon it became clear to him, and to others, that air was not just air after all. Apparently there were various airs: fixed air, wounded air, deadly air, mephitic air, nitrous air, fire air, dephlogisticated air, flammable air. Mr Cavendish was particularly fascinated by this flammable air he'd isolated—in fact, he thought it might be phlogiston itself. But when he combined this flammable air—perhaps pure phlogiston—with dephlogisticated air, what did he get? What do you think he got, Mrs Pollocke?"

"Not gold, I suppose?"

"Oh, heavens, Mrs Pollocke, of course not. He got—water!" Miss Grant paused for effect, but Grace, not knowing precisely what a suitable reaction might be, did not react.

"Water, Mrs Pollocke! But brilliant as he was, he didn't understand the significance of what he'd done, though it's so perfectly obvious to us now—"

"Not to me, I'm afraid," said Grace. "Pray explain."

"They had the whole thing backwards, Mrs Pollocke—they'd bridled the wrong end of the horse, don't you see? It was Monsieur and Madame Lavoisier who finished off phlogiston at last, in a paper asserting that burning bodies were not giving off phlogiston—because there was no such thing! Instead, burning bodies were taking up oxygen! Combustion, they showed, was simply the taking-up of oxygen—and heat and light were produced in this taking-up. Monsieur Lavoisier understood what Mr Cavendish did not: water must be a compound of 'flammable air'—now called hydrogen—with oxygen. He recognised that respiration was a form of combustion too. His great treatise appeared in 1789—with illustrations by Madame his wife. Just think of it, Mrs Pollocke: after centuries of investigation, it was only fifty-some years ago that a correct understanding of the nature of air, fire, and water was finally arrived at—all at once, and all by one man! Astonishing. What other mysteries might Monsieur Lavoisier have cleared up for us, if he'd lived? Alas, he was relieved of his incomparable head in the Terror, at the age of fifty. Madame his wife escaped the same fate—but only to marry that horrid Count Rumford. She soon found out her mistake, and threw his clothes out in the street when she evicted him, they say. But it all just goes to show, Mrs Pollocke, that anyone may be wrong, even the most brilliant chemists; and even the cleverest of Frenchwomen."

"Aye; and also that everyone may be wrong together. That an opinion is generally received—even universally received—is no guarantee of its correctness."

"Yes, and error may persist for an indefinite period—perhaps even forever, if there is any such thing," said Miss Grant. "What other fondly held beliefs may yet be torn away from us, I wonder? How are we to know where we may safely repose our faith?"

"We cannot know. That is just why I so distrust persons who are absolutely certain that they are right," said Grace. "It is not being wrong which disgraces us, for, as your account demonstrates, anyone, even everyone, may be wrong. What disgraces us, I think, is our refusal to admit the possibility of being wrong; the refusal to be disencumbered of our errors, to part with our delusions."

"And yet, so many folk consider doubt—even self-doubt—not only a sign of weakness, but even something approaching a sin!"

"And oddly enough, such people win great credit for their earnestness, at least—if not for perspicuity or diffidence," said Grace. "Who is disgraced by earnestness? An honest mistake, if wholeheartedly and energetically persisted in, is for some reason thought to be less disgraceful than a halfhearted or careless mistake—even though it may do a great deal more damage. Diffidence is very much underrated, I think. And assurance carries a great deal more influence than it deserves. Worst of all is a pretended assurance—for it garners undue credit to itself."

"Are we thinking by any chance of the same person, Mrs Pollocke?"

"I daresay that we are," admitted Grace. "Your Mr Stringfellow did succeed in setting a thorn into my paw, and I cannot help but lick my wound. Now, if we were to contrive a table of sins, Miss Grant—arranged by weight from lightest to heaviest, like your table of the elementary substances—which sins would weigh heaviest upon a hypothetical immortal soul, do you suppose? Might not the better-known sins, at least, be ordered thus—by weight, by their gravity?"

"So they might," said Miss Grant. "And as we've just heard a sermon on the subject, we should be able to rank the seven deadliest, at least."

"We have it upon the authority of Mr Stringfellow—who ought to know—that the gravest of them all is Pride," said Grace. "Therefore I feel confident in assigning to it the seventh, the weightiest position. What else?"

"Lust; that's certainly among the seven," said Miss Grant promptly, "and such a favorite among preachers that it must be very terrible, though I'm not allowed to know much about it, on account of my maidenly innocence. Nevertheless, I suspect enough to set Lust just above Pride, in the sixth position—for I have a very vivid imagination, I assure you."

Grace laughed—but wondered fleetingly just what distinguished Lust from that exquisite quick ardor which so beset her when she thought of her amorous husband. When she ached for his embrace, for the strength of his arms, the breadth of his chest—was that lawful ardor? Or was it sinful Lust which ambushed her several times each day, and night? This was not, however, a question to be discussed with Miss Grant; and Grace said, "We have got the two heaviest sins in their places, then; a keel, a steadying ballast, above which to lade our cargo of the lighter ones. Now, against what else have we been put on our guard?"

"Gluttony," said Miss Grant, "and Greed. But it seems to me that Gluttony is actually only a variety of Greed. Isn't Gluttony the greed for food and drink? I don't see why the variety can deserve a separate nomination on its own merits—its demerits, I guess I should say—to deadly status."

"Quite; they are both a matter of grasping, of seizing more than one needs, beyond sufficiency."

"I think we might as well rank them together, then, and assign them a middling weight; numbers three and four, out of seven," said Miss Grant. "Now, your turn."

"Sloth has always puzzled me," admitted Grace. "It means indolence, I suppose; idleness or laziness—"

"And I think there is a creature called a sloth, an extremely slow-moving forest-dwelling creature in South America," added Miss Grant.

"You are a font of obscure facts. I have never heard of it."

"So slow-moving that small plants, mosses at least, take root and grow in its fur, if the reports of travelers are to be believed."

"But in any case, why should Sloth—idleness, indolence—be held as particularly deadly?"

" 'Satan finds some mischief for idle hands to do,' my aunt always says."

"Aye; my mother-in-law says, 'Idle hands are the devil's tools,' and she generally has some piece of plain sewing in hand, destined for the Deserving Poor, as she calls them—who ought to be exceedingly well clothed by now. The Turks say, 'The devil tempts all other men, but idle men tempt the devil.' "

"But it's obvious that busy hands may do the devil's work too—and far more of it," said Miss Grant. "The devil's work is so very attractive—that's the real trouble, I think."

"In India, idleness is rather admired. The holy men—some of them, at least—are much revered on account of their stillness. I knew of one *saddhu*—a holy man—who sat unmoving for more than twelve years atop a particular piling sunk above the shallows of the Ganges at Allahabad. People waded out morning and evening, before their ablutions, to bring him offerings of rice and ghee, and he lived upon those, it seems, until he died, still atop that piling. He had been dead for several days before anyone made sure that he was dead—for there he remained, perfectly still, as always. He did no harm, at least, neither to himself nor to anyone else. No one could accuse him of—of—"

"Of Lust," supplied Miss Grant, and they both laughed.

But upon consideration, Grace said seriously, "Who can know what may have passed through his mind—if indeed he had a mind—during all those years? Perhaps he was entertaining himself constantly with lustful thoughts."

"In any case, he did not act on them."

"No; he did no one any harm through any word or deed."

"Nor did he do anyone any good, though," said Miss Grant. "My aunt would be quick to point out that we have a Christian duty to do good unto others. To make ourselves useful."

"Oh, but he did; by receiving their offerings of rice and ghee, he furnished the good folk of Allahabad with valuable opportunities for winning merit. And Hindus count that as a great good."

"Do they? What a strange place India must be. I don't think my aunt would like it at all, if the objects of her charity took the view that they were doing her a favor in return! But all in all, Sloth must the lightest of the deadly sins, don't you think? Equivalent perhaps to—to hydrogen, in my table?"

"I agree. Let us give it a weight, a rank, of one. What else have we got?"

"There's Wrath," said Miss Grant. "What are your views on Wrath?"

"Wrath as a feeling, unexpressed, not acted-upon? I have often felt wrathful, myself; and sometimes I have had excellent reasons. I felt wrath just this evening, at prayers; and I cannot think that I was much at fault. I was very much provoked, and it seems to me that on the contrary I earned merit by restraining my wrath; by silently bearing such provocation. I am not at all sure that a mere feeling of Wrath belongs among the sins. Indeed, several of these sins—wrath, lust, envy—are mere feelings—"

"States of mind," put in Miss Grant.

"Fleeting, unbidden, and, like all feelings, soon gone," continued Grace, "only to be supplanted by the next, equally fleeting. Is that not the nature of the human mind? Are we not made thus? How can feelings be sinful?"

"But they may lead to sinful acts—that's why they're held to be sinful in themselves."

"But if they do not? If these feelings are allowed to ebb, unacted-upon, where is the sin in a fleeting feeling—or even in a persistent or recurring feeling—of Wrath, of Lust, of Envy?"

"I'm inclined to agree with you about Envy, at least," said Miss Grant. "Envy is essentially a mathematical operation; a comparing; subtraction, in fact. Who could help noticing the relative more-ness and less-ness, in the world? I don't see how it can be a sin to notice."

"We have our seven, I think," said Grace. "Sloth the lightest; Lust and Pride the heaviest; and in between, in no particular order, Envy, Wrath, and our twins, Greed and Gluttony. Can we have got our list of elements right? It seems to me that certain very deadly sins are missing. Cruelty, where is that? Ought not Cruelty to rank heaviest of all, even more deadly than Pride?"

"But isn't cruelty an expression of Wrath, an outcome of Wrath?" suggested Miss Grant.

"No, indeed; it is a different thing entirely. Wrath is only a feeling; one may choose to let it ebb, unacted-upon. Cruelty, however, is act; and at its worst it is cold-blooded, undertaken without even the hasty warmth of Wrath to excuse it." Chattel slavery is an institution made entirely of Cruelty, Pride and Greed, and committed in cold blood, she thought—but only said, "And what of Lying and Deceit—are they not held as sinful?"

"Oh, those come in under the Ten Commandments: 'Thou shalt not bear false witness,'" said Miss Grant. "Number nine, I believe. It's not in this list of sins, though. I wonder why not."

"I have sometimes thought," said Grace, "that there are occasions when speaking the truth is not only unwise, but even wrong. I find it difficult to admire those who prize their own self-respect so extremely high as to refuse to tell a small lie, even if not upon their oath, and even though that small lie might preserve other innocent persons from great and irremediable harm. In their selfish eagerness to avoid the smaller sin, such folk perhaps commit instead the far greater sins of Pride, Selfishness, and Betrayal—or so it seems to me."

"Mm," said Miss Grant. "People usually lie to protect their own selfish interests, though, don't they? It's usually not to protect others, to protect innocence. Such a case as you describe can very seldom arise."

"Not so seldom," said Grace. "One hears of them often enough; and reads of them in the newspapers."

"I guess you mean those Quakers, then, who conceal runaway slaves—but give them up when asked," said Miss Grant.

Grace did not contradict her; for that was just what she meant.

After a moment, Miss Grant said, "And where is Intemperance, in our list of sins? Some folks hold that very grave indeed."

"Oh, but I daresay that comes in as greed—or gluttony—of a sort."

"What about Doubt?" suggested Miss Grant

"Oh, Miss Grant! Doubt? Surely you, of all people, cannot hold that Doubt, Diffidence, knowing that one does not know, is any sin at all! Where would we be without Doubt, without a robust skepticism? Still worshiping at the temple of phlogiston! I should be much more inclined to place Doubt, and its cousin Diffidence, among the virtues; and instead to nominate its opposite, Assurance, as a sin!"

"Well, we are told that Doubt leads to atheism, you know, so it must be a great sin."

"I cannot think so. You have demonstrated how Doubt has led your Monsieur Lavoisier to truth—or at least to oxygen," said Grace. "But if I am not allowed to rank Doubt among the virtues, then I must place it with the imponderables. I cannot conclude that it belongs among the sins."

"I fear we've made a sad muddle of our table of sins," said Miss Grant.

"Well," said Grace, "we have at least succeeded in establishing that a great deal of investigation and study remain to be done."

"And perhaps even . . . experiment!" crowed Miss Grant, throwing her feather bolster at the ceiling.

THE GRANTSBORO CHESS SET IN THE PARLOR WAS OF IVORY and ebony curiously carved, upon a board of dark horn and pale nacre. The faces and figures of the individual pieces were rendered in exquisite detail, each so distinctive, so particular, that they might have been the portraits of actual persons. The ivory pieces had austere Nordic faces, while the ebony pieces had African features. The white queen's bearing put Grace immediately in mind of Lady Macbeth; and her lord and husband the king bore a suitably horror-struck and hag-ridden expression. Grace then examined the countenance of the black queen: Cleopatra, surely! And so this dark smooth-faced king, her co-Pharaoh, must be Ptolemy, her younger brother and consort—for he certainly was not Mark Antony, nor Julius Caesar, nor any other of the Roman lovers of the notorious Egyptian Queen.

Someone who did not know chess had set up the board, for the white square that should have been at the right elbow of each player was at the left instead, and the knights were in the bishops' places. Without turning the board, Grace moved all the pieces onto their proper squares, in their proper ranks. Now it was as though Cleopatra's armies, at Grace's left hand, faced those of the King of Scotland, on Grace's right, across the flat low fields of Flanders, across the regular patchwork of its tidy orchards and pastures. It was as though she, Grace, were poised to send onto a single stage the *dramatis personae* from two of William Shakespeare's great plays; who could predict what might happen? This too was the gods'-eye view; she presided over this board from just that particular angle and elevation she recognised from archaic paintings; and she herself was the god, poised to manipulate her creation spread before her.

"Ah! I think you have promised me a game of chess, Mrs Pollocke," said Judge Grant, at her shoulder.

"I do not remember giving any such promise, sir," said Grace. "But I shall be happy to give you a game. It is an extraordinary chess set."

"Do you like it? It was a present from Mr Jefferson; he had another very like it."

He sat down across from her and, turning the board, took white; laying claim without parley to the forces of Albion, of Scotland, of Macbeth and his redoubtable lady.

Cleopatra and her ebony army, then, were Grace's.

KEEP ALL YOUR PIECES facing forward, looking straight across to the board's far horizon, no matter where their quarry may stand, Grace admonished herself—for she had just caught herself turning her queen's face toward the hapless knight which she intended to capture on her next move. Do not disclose your intent by turning to look at your target. Judge Grant twice committed this error himself, and both times Grace contrived to extricate her endangered piece in time. She was not highly skilled at the game, but she soon recognised that her opponent did not outclass her. Her sight-memory served her well, for it allowed her to recognise positions she had seen in previous games; and to remember how to proceed from them, and what errors to avoid.

Mr MacFarlane came and watched silently for a while, until his wife and Miss Johnstone called him away to explain how four sixes could possibly equal twenty-four.

Grace had to surrender a knight, but captured one of the judge's bishops, the one which traveled on the white diagonals.

"Mr Boyce is in the hall, master," said William, appearing quietly at Judge Grant's shoulder. "He say that you send for him."

"What? Oh—so I did. Tell him—oh—never mind, I'll go. Tell him I'll be there in a minute," said Judge Grant, not looking up from the checkered Waterloo where Grace had pinned his rook. A moment later, he shook his head, saying, "I'm afraid I must request an adjournment, Mrs Pollocke, until this time tomorrow, if you will be so merciful. I did ask Mr Boyce to come and talk over some pressing business matters, and it is very likely that he will take up the rest of my evening."

Of course Grace agreed.

"White to move, then," he said, and, painfully rising, made his slow way out. "Do you come too, Mr MacFarlane, if you will be so good. Boyce and I will be glad of your long head."

GRACE AND MISS GRANT made a habit of walking out together between dinner and tea each day, among the farm fields where they could talk quite freely. One afternoon, Miss Grant, who had been lamenting her lack of laboratory equipment, ended by saying, ". . . though the gods, we're told, want for nothing."

"But that is not because they already *have* everything," said Grace. "I do not imagine them as being encumbered by worldly goods, do you?"

"No; I guess that's why they're called 'worldly' goods, and not 'heavenly' goods."

"One doesn't picture the gods as being freighted with possessions—houses—tables and chairs—plates and forks—"

"No; nor retorts, nor decanting funnels, nor heating apparatus—"

"Nor much even by way of clothes—not the Hindu deities, anyway. All that they need simply comes to hand, instantly, even before it can be wished for. The jeweled cup is brought, brimming with divine nectar, the *amrita*. It is consumed—"

"And the cup, what becomes of the cup?"

"It is no longer seen. . . ."

"I suppose it is carried off, by a servant, to be washed?"

"But the next cupful of nectar?"

"It is brought, brimming, by a servant, just as before."

"Ah! But is it the same jeweled cup, Miss Grant; or a different one?"

"The gods are too magnificent to notice, or to care. Cups simply appear—splendid—bejeweled—and brimming—at the very instant before the wish for them is *quite* formed. There is an infinite supply of cups."

But what of the servants who bring the cups and carry them away again, wondered Grace; and the goldsmiths who make the cups; and the gatherers of the *amrita*; what sort of existence is theirs?

Grace and Miss Grant had wandered on this afternoon down toward the brood mares' enclosure, near the barn. The mares had all crowded toward one side of their pasture, where something beyond the rail fence, obscured by the corner of the big barn, engaged their attention. Behind them, their foals, capering and nipping, were more interested in one another. Grace and Miss Grant encountered no one as they passed through the dark corridor of the barn, between the stalls on either side; where was everyone? Where were the grooms?

But as the stableyard at the far end of the barn came into view, Grace suddenly halted; took Miss Grant's arm as she might have taken Jamie's, protectively. "Perhaps not just now?" she suggested—for she had seen.

But Miss Grant pressed forward another step or two, so that she could see too.

The grey stallion at liberty in the fenced stableyard circled the mare, his strong neck tensely arched at the poll. The deep-pink lining of his flared nostrils fluttered as he sniffed at her flank, then uttered a throaty comment. The mare swung her haunches toward him, and the groom who held the mare's halter lead laughed as he let her pivot. The mare was in full health, full youth and flesh; the hide over her round hindquarters was taut and bloomy, like the skin of a peach about to burst asunder from its own ripeness.

Grace saw Miss Grant's face illuminated by curiosity; avid. After a moment, she met Grace's gaze. "I want to see," she said. "I've never seen it. You can go if you want."

But Grace stayed too, fascinated and appalled as the stallion's male part, black, quickly doubled in length, extending down and forward, like a fifth leg. The stallion was nosing the mare's hind legs now, the strong curve of her haunch. The mare raised her tail, squatted, urinated, and the stallion squealed, threw up his head, and turned his upper lip inside out. His long male part slapped upward against his belly as he sidled behind the mare, who once again swung her haunches against his shoulder. A peal of nervous laughter reached Grace and Miss Grant; unseen grooms must be watching from the stableyard outside. Grace was quite certain that the deep shadow of the corridor concealed Miss Grant and herself; and in any case, the full attention of all spectators was entirely engrossed. Miss Grant gripped Grace's arm as the stallion reared up on his hind legs, his bent forelegs sliding down on either side of the mare's shining back. The mare squatted to receive him, to bear his weight, with her tail arched to one side. Delicately with his teeth the stallion took hold of the mare's withers at the base of her neck; and the muscles of his hindquarters flexed as he thrust. Peals of raucous laughter and shouts, cheers, came from the stableyard. Upon the stallion's sixth thrust, he bit her neck hard, and the mare squealed; then his taut body relaxed over hers. After a moment, he slid off, slid out. Grace was shocked to see that his male organ was still larger now, glistening, springing. The mare appeared unmoved, placid, and after a moment was led off in all her sleek complacency by the groom.

Grace and Miss Grant made their escape before the stablehands should return and discover them. They did not stop nor speak until they had gained the shade of the locust trees near the house. There Miss Grant threw herself onto the wooden bench which overlooked the unstocked stew pond. "It's like *that*?" she demanded of Grace.

"Oh, well . . . ," said Grace. Aye, it was somewhat like that. Her own body shared even now a little of the mare's complacency.

"I had not supposed it was so—so quickly done," said Miss Grant, fanning herself.

"It is not, for people—generally speaking—I believe," said Grace.

"And biting?"

"Oh—not necessarily," said Grace, and felt herself blushing. She looked away, toward the mansion. "If I were to paint the house, I think I should do it from this viewpoint," she said. "It makes a handsome composition from here, doesn't it?"

"Oh, Mrs Pollocke! I will not be turned aside so lightly as that!"

A STACK OF OLD journals and newspapers lay on the round table in the middle of the parlor, under Grace's empty teacup. Her hungry eye caught a word: *Silk*. The topmost journal was titled *The Silk Culturist and Farmers Manual*. Taking the stack onto her lap, Grace leafed idly through the pages; and paused to read an account headed "Silk Culture in India":

> The frame in common use, consists of sixteen shelves, placed in a shed upon vessels filled with water, by way of precaution against ants. After the moths quit their covering, attendance is required to remove the males as soon as their functions have been performed, and the females, when they have produced their eggs. The basket is carefully covered with a cloth, and in a fort-night the worm quits the egg. They are first fed with mulberry leaves, chopped very fine; as they advance in their growth, they are dispersed into more baskets, on the several shelves of the frame, and are supplied with leaves, cut into larger pieces, and latterly with whole leaves, until the period when the insect quits the food. As soon as it recommences eating, branches of mul-berry trees are thrown on with the leaves upon them, and the insects eat with eagerness, and soon fill the baskets on the whole number of shelves; they arrive at their full size in a little more than a month from their birth, and changing their skins for the last time are disposed to begin their cones. They are now removed to baskets, divided into spiral compartments, where they spin their webs, and cover themselves with silk. When the cocoon is completed, a few are set apart for propagation, and the rest are exposed to the heat of the sun, for the purpose of killing the chrysalis.
>
> The peasants sell the cocoons to the filiatures, or winding houses, most of whom are in the employ of the E. India Company.

Yes; just so. Grace closed her eyes, and for a few pleasant moments was transported to Bengal, to the verandah of an airy warm peasant hut, under the deep shade of its thick thatch. Hand-sized patties of cow dung dry in the sun against the mud wall enclosing the yard, each patty bearing a handprint; each patty just the right size to fuel a small cooking fire. A stand of weeds—of castor-plant—luxuriates in the waste ground near the road; rank, but so useful for oil and fuel. Dung smoke perfumes the air, quite like incense. From inside the dim hut wafts that fruity ripe scent of mulberry leaf, and of well-fed silkworms; while palms rustle extravagant fronds overhead—

"Just walking about. I was showing Papa's horses to Mrs Pollocke," said Miss Julia Grant, in reply to her aunt's inquiry; and Grace was recalled once more to a Virginia parlor on a June evening. Miss Grant briefly caught her eye and then seemed to cough, nearly choking for a moment until she succeeded in smothering this untoward outbreak, her hand covering her mouth—though not the laughter in her eyes.

Grace ducked her head, to hide her own smile. She turned a few pages of the archive on her lap, and read some astonishing reports: In America, it appeared, silkworms could be fed on lettuce! On leaves of rose or bramble; of dandelion or hop, hemp or fig! Someone else had written to report that they would eat currant leaves too, in a pinch! Absurd, thought Grace, turning rapidly through the pages. Eventually, in an issue of some months later, she came across a sober correction of these excited and erroneous reports. The worms might eat such unnatural fodder; they might even survive on it, for a time; but they certainly would not spin. They would not pupate; they would not produce a new generation; in short, they would not produce silk.

And here was a report on "*Bombyx Virginiensis*, the native silkworm of Virginia" which was, according to this journal, "found in great numbers on the Plantation of JB Gray, Esq, Stafford Co., and is capable of enduring the most rigorous winter. The cocoons are found suspended upon the Red Cedar, and yield a beautiful white silk of a strong thread." But Grace came across no further references in later issues to this wonderful and promising insect. Perhaps it had proven to be only the chrysalis of what was otherwise a devastating and intolerable caterpillar, some ravenous hornworm or cutworm.

The *Farmers' Register* of 1835 particularly recommended sericulture to its audience of Virginia planters: "If good profits can be there made, in the cold and unfriendly climate of New England . . . how much more profitable would the business be in Virginia, and the more southern states? Our *cheaper* slave-labor would also afford advantages; and many aged or infirm hands could be profitably employed in this business, who are now a useless expense to their owners."

And then there were the hectic calculations: Each mulberry tree makes 6 pounds of leaves; 50 pounds of leaves feed 1,000 worms; 300 cocoons weigh one pound; 3,000 cocoons, or 10 pounds of cocoons, make one pound of silk. And all this yields $3.00 per pound for the silk!

There was advice too on controlling the diseases to which silk-worms fall victim. Someone had written to advise setting out dishes of chloride of lime in any cocooneries where disease threatened, diseases such as uncleanliness or tripes. "Pray, Miss Grant, what is chloride of lime?" asked Grace.

"That is bleaching powder, of course; my darling chlorine, combined with slaked lime," replied Miss Grant, who was showing her eldest Grimshaw nephew how to play cat's cradle.

There was unbridled enthusiasm for the newest and best mulberry of all, the celebrated *Morus multicaulis,* favored for its large soft leaves produced in great abundance upon a low bushy shrub. Seed of this estimable plant was offered for sale at ever-increasing prices. But gradually there appeared dissenting murmurs, voices, and discouraging reports: the *multicaulis* was not hardy; it was ill-suited to northern climes; it did not come true from seed, but only from cuttings. The dissenting voices and disappointing reports were scanty at first. Who, reflected Grace, wants to report his failure? Who, suffering failure, is eager to report it to the world—especially when everyone else is reporting one success atop another? Those who failed no doubt blamed their own bad luck, or faulty technique, or spiders and ants, or the weather, or cutworms, or grasshoppers—as farmers always had done; and so the sober truth about the undeservedly esteemed *multicaulis* was very slow to emerge in the pages of the *Silk Culturist,* the *Silk Record,* the *Silk Growers' Manual,* and the *Farmers' Register.*

Private and common-stock companies published notices announcing their formation: the Connecticut Silk Manufacturing Company; the Atlantic Silk Company of Nantucket; the Poughkeepsie Silk Company; the New York and Northampton Company; the Morodendron Silk Company of Philadelphia; and many others.

Inventors published notices of their machines: devices for reeling silk, for smothering cocoons, for moving worms from one feeding tray to another.

The last few pages of each journal were taken up by advertisements, and Grace studied these with interest. What a frenzy they betrayed! What ignorance, and hope, and ambition! What greed! In 1834, Grace noted, mulberry trees were offered at the moderate rate of $4 for a hundred trees. By the end of 1835, a hundred trees fetched $10. In the summer of '36, they were up to $30. In 1837 and '38, prices got rather exciting, and so did the numbers sold: trees sold at anything from $35 to $60 per hundred, depending on their size—and some for as much as $1.50 each, or $150 per hundred! In a single week, a single grower reported having sold 40,000 trees to be sent to Virginia; and another 20,000 destined for western Pennsylvania. Of course, he did not actually have these thousands of trees; but he agreed to propagate them, for delivery some months hence. What a pity, thought Grace, that this excitement, this speculative frenzy, had not lasted just a little longer—just until Anibaddh had been able to dispose of *her* cargo of mulberry trees.

And then there was the matter of silkworm eggs. In 1837, they had cost $5.50 per ounce. By the spring of '38, they fetched $10 per ounce. By the spring of '39, they were offered at $20 to $25 per ounce.

But the summer of 1838 had been blazing hot, and droughty. Many of those expensive silkworm eggs failed to hatch.

And then the spring of 1839 proved unusually cold. Many of those expensive mulberry saplings were blackened and then killed by recurring late frosts.

The inevitable collapse followed.

The editors of the *Farmers' Register* in 1839 disclaimed all responsibility, either for insufficient support of the enterprise, on the one hand, or for feeding the irrational frenzy, on the other: "It is true that our zeal, and estimates of profits, are still much in the rear of the most sanguine—that we have insisted that the *dealing in mulberry plants is not silk-culture*—and that, unless turned to silk-culture, the mulberry speculation would be but a bubble, not only worthless, but injurious to the country."

And so it had proven, thought Grace. The next article in the *Farmers' Register* was a caution against using potatoes as a winter food for sheep.

How had Americans achieved so spectacular a failure? How could all this flurry—this bustle—this enterprise—this "zeal, energy, intelligence, and the investment of sufficient capital," as the *Farmers' Register* put it, have resulted only in ruin for all involved? Journals—prizes offered by legislatures—the American spirit of enterprise—all this had been insufficient to establish a viable silk industry in America. Yet the most ignorant peasants of China and India had been profitably carrying on this selfsame industry for untold generations.

It seemed to Grace that perhaps it was precisely this characteristic flurry—this bustling spirit of enterprise—which had prevented American success. Some undertakings did not thrive under such a style of husbandry. Some undertakings required other qualities instead: meticulous skill, care, patience, sustained effort over time, discipline, individual seeking after mastery. In short, thought Grace, it was *gong fu* which was required; that was the Chinese term for it. There was a *gong fu* style of preparing and drinking tea. Grace knew it well: the stillness; the quiet deliberate rinsing; boiling; pouring; steeping; waiting; sniffing; and then, at last, the sipping. It was a style quite opposite to Miss Johnstone's officious bustle over the Grantsboro tea tray. *Gong fu* was in some respects a spiritual practice. The Indian monk who had brought this discipline to China had been able to bore a hole through a brick wall by only gazing at it with sufficient intent, skill, and patience.

Or so it was asserted. Grace had always been dubious of this particular claim.

Nevertheless, it was clear that Americans, impatient as children, sought profit, not mastery. Skill and patience were lacking; were not even sought; were held of no account. She remembered the beguiling little model she had seen under glass at the Patent Office in Washington: a steam-powered silk-winding machine. Even now her retentive mind's eye could see it; could see even the little pasteboard card bearing the name of its inventor: Obadiah Hale. No doubt the machine had been a marvel of ingenuity and cleverness, a miracle of technology. But perhaps ingenuity, enterprise, cleverness, and miracles of technology—those American specialities—were not the qualities required to establish a silk industry. Machines had never before been necessary for the winding of silk; until now, skillful patient people—peasants—had always performed that task.

Setting aside the stack of dreary journals, Grace rose and went to the piano. What of her own painstakingly acquired skill, her mastery of portraiture? Might new and ingenious chemical techniques—Mr Daguerre's process—supplant her care and expertise? It seemed quite possible, if not inevitable, in America at least.

Grace was picking out the melody of a Bengali song when, from the corner of her eye, she saw Mr MacFarlane saunter over to the chessboard. He paused to study the game suspended there, the combatants frozen in their positions until such time as the gods—Judge Grant and herself—should deign to animate them once more. Having studied the board at length, he then glanced quickly around the room—as Grace, concealed behind the piano, dropped her gaze to her hands on the keyboard. He shifted so as to shield the chessboard behind his body; remained there for just a moment, and then strolled off. He threw himself into an easy chair and, taking up a newspaper from a table, rattled it open in front of his face, a study in nonchalance.

Twenty minutes passed before Judge Grant came in, breathless from having toiled the length of the corridor. Miss Johnstone poured his tea from off the lees in the pot, and he drank it without complaint though it must have been strong and stewed.

Presently Mr MacFarlane said, "Won't you and Mrs Pollocke finish your game, sir?" and nodded toward the chessboard.

"I will," said Judge Grant, "if Mrs Pollocke likes to resume the drubbing she was giving me. What do you say, Mrs Pollocke? Shall we finish what we have so fairly begun?"

"Whenever you please, sir," said Grace, and rose from the piano.

As soon as they had both sat down to the board, Grace saw that something was wrong. "But this is not right," she blurted. "Something has changed."

"Has it?" said Judge Grant. "How can you be sure?"

"It does not look right," said Grace, aware that Mr MacFarlane was now crossing the room to join them. She looked upon the board, eyes narrowed. What had changed? She closed her eyes; called upon her mind's eye; and knew. "Your bishop is on a white square," she said. "It ought to be one square back—aye, there, upon that black square. That is where it stood when we adjourned. Perhaps someone accidentally moved it—while doing the dusting." As she said this, she let herself look long and hard at Mr MacFarlane, leaning now upon his walking stick with both hands, looming over them. He blinked once, slowly.

"But how can you remember?" said Judge Grant.

"I can see it with perfect clarity if I shut my eyes," said Grace. "Your bishop which I have already captured is the one which travels upon the white diagonals; I have a very clear image, in my mind's eye, of taking it." So she had: she could see even now the creamy yellow-netted carved ivory, swept up from its faintly rainbowed mother-of-pearl square—and replaced there by the close-grained brown-black ebony column of her rook which had captured it. "That left you, sir, with only the bishop which travels on the black diagonals. And it stood right there, last evening, when we adjourned our game." She tapped the black square where it belonged.

He shrugged; moved the bishop to its proper square; said, "If you say so, Mrs Pollocke; though I don't know how you can speak so very positively."

"A lady of my acquaintance can remember perfectly any melody, having heard it only once," said Grace. "I cannot do that; but my mind's eye can recall what I have seen with a vivid clarity—even to the very print on the pages of the books I have read. White to move, sir."

He soon succumbed to her pin; and Mr MacFarlane then lost interest and wandered off. Grace noted that the bishop, in its wrong place, could have saved his rook—could in fact have turned the tables on her. Judge Grant struggled on manfully for a while before resigning the game at last. "I am compelled to surrender to your superior force, Mrs Pollocke," he said. "Shall we make it two games out of three?"

"If you like, sir."

"But not this evening," he said.

GRACE SET UP HER EASEL near the stew pond the next afternoon, after dinner. There would be no walk today with Miss Grant, who was engaged instead in welcoming the latest of her sisters to arrive: Mrs Pratt at last, with her little baby and nurse. The sound of a hammer rang as usual across the wide lawn from the brick pile below the piazza; but old Walter cleaned bricks alone today. Grace had completed her preliminary sketch of the house in its setting and had begun to lay in the shadows when she saw Judge Grant approaching. He attained the bench set in the shade just behind her, and let himself down upon it, breathless.

When he had regained his breath, he said, "You paint landskips, then, as well as heads, do you, Mrs Pollocke?"

"From time to time, I do."

"And horses? Do you paint horses?"

"Ah, no! I am not competent to paint horses—nor bulls, nor any other prize livestock, though I have sometimes succeeded at portraying a dog with its mistress or master. Horses are a special case, requiring particular knowledge. It would seem that exceedingly long arching thin necks are much prized in horses, and so are tiny hooves—if I am to judge by the paintings I have seen. Painters of horses are obliged to exaggerate these to an absurd degree, quite beyond what any unknowledgeable painter would consider reasonable. I—being no judge of horseflesh, and knowing no better than to paint the creature before me—might make the mistake of painting the horse's actual stout short neck, or his actual large round hooves."

"Ha! Well, that's a pity. I might have asked you to paint my horse Lochinvar—you'll have seen my Lochinvar?—not so young anymore! But still peremptory as ever, in the breeding shed! Ahem. He is a great-grandson of Diomed, through my Colonel Blood—and a grandson of Sir Archy too, who sired my excellent mare Rowena. The very best blood of the finest lines in the country flows through the veins of my horses, Mrs Pollocke. But to think that I missed the greatest opportunity of all! I could have owned Sir Archy himself, imagine that! Ochone, that I missed such an opportunity! That was long ago, when Mr Wormely was trying to sell him, a sickly three-year-old. But I was newly married then, and I had recently laid out a round sum for another horse—using the money that was supposed to have paid Mr Stuart, as you have so cannily found out—and so—and so I turned him down, alas! How different my present situation would be, if only I had bought Sir Archy, all those years ago! But he was just a plain bay colt then; no one could have foreseen his future successes. It wasn't just the purses either—though he won plenty of them—but it's said that his earnings at stud amounted to over seventy thousand dollars by the time he died, at the age of twenty-eight. Seventy thousand, Mrs Pollocke! My situation would be very different indeed. Still, it is a superior stock I have bred here; the Grantsboro bloodline is very well thought of, and fetches good prices—or did, until this universal crash, which has brought down the whole country—indeed, the world. It is all the fault of that scoundrel Jackson—and his creature Van Buren has been worse than useless. I see nothing but melancholy prospects ahead, for us all. Now, what is that? What are you doing?" he asked, interrupting himself—for, turning her back to the house and her canvas, Grace now held up a small black plate.

"This? It is my Claude glass," she said. "It is useful for evaluating lights and shadows." She gave it to him. "It is only a black mirror—a pane of glass with a smooth black backing. Here, turn your back to the house, and then hold up the mirror, and view the house in it; there, you see? The entire composition is simplified; the small unnecessary details are lost altogether; the masses of light and dark are heightened; the composition simplifies itself. They were all the rage among landscape tourists of a few generations ago—entire troupes of ladies and gentlemen were to be seen at well-known beauty spots, with their backs to the view, squinting instead at the reflection in their Claude glasses! I daresay it must have been very comical."

"Oh, aye, comical—but it is still with us, this determination to see only what we like, while turning a blind eye to all else," said Judge Grant. "Now, that new invention for making scientific drawings—that Frenchman's invention—where will that leave us? The horses of the world—and the ladies—will suddenly be revealed as having short stout necks and large feet! How will we preserve our cherished illusions?"

"Well . . . I daresay that even a daguerreotype might be used to deceive," said Grace.

"You would be skeptical even of a daguerreotype?"

"I think I might," said Grace, after a moment's thought.

"You are a skeptic by nature, then, Mrs Pollocke," he said. "A doubter. Well, you are just in the fine old Scotch tradition, then."

"Am I? I had supposed that staunch faith was more in the Scotch line."

"Going to kirk and taking the sacrament? No, I mean our

independent-mindedness, our skepticism and defiance of authority. My old friend Sir Walter Scott had a low opinion of the Scotch Verdict—the Third Verdict—except when it benefited his client, I daresay. The Bastard Verdict, *he* called it, when complaining because an evil old lady who, he felt morally certain, had poisoned her servant got off nevertheless with a verdict of Not Proven."

"Was Sir Walter Scott indeed your friend, sir?"

"He—well—I will not attempt a misrepresentation to *you*, Mrs Pollocke, as you should probably find me out. But I did know him by sight, if he did not know me. I even had speech of him, on several occasions; and once we drank a glass, or six, of punch at the same table, at a reception in honor of someone or other, whose name has slipped by now into obscurity. He was a senior student at the University of Edinburgh—he must have been eighteen or so—when I was just a callant of thirteen there. Aye, my early education was Scottish; that was shortly before I left Scotland to seek my fortune in this brave new world of Virginia. It was a sad day when I heard that my old schoolmate had died, a few years ago. It often seemed to me that we had followed similar lines in our lives, he only a few years ahead of me—he married his little half Frenchwoman, and I my Anne Johnstone. I bested him on the score of children, though: my seven to his five. He was a horseman and a huntsman after my own heart; and a judge too: sheriff of Selkirk, you know, like a district court judge here. He suffered his financial reverses too, as we all must, it would seem. And now I have outlived him, though no doubt my time approaches. I have outlived a great many. Still I get a pleasant shock when my glance falls across that yard-long expanse of books on my bookshelf, each bearing my Auld Acquaintance's name in gilt upon the spine. . . . Now, what have you painted, there? Old Walter, on his brick pile! Why have you put *him* into your handsome picture? What a pity, ma'am! The entire picture is spoilt; quite spoilt."

A DARK SEAL-BROWN, WITH RUSSET AND BLUE HIGHLIGHTS. Burnt sienna, thought Grace, of a quite strong value, with glints of vermilion and lapis for the highlights; that would do for the horse ridden by Mr Charles Grant. He reined up alongside the old carriage which was carrying the Grantsboro ladies to the revival meeting, and addressed some remark to his sisters, who sat on the foremost seat just behind the coachman. To Grace, seated beyond Miss Grant and Miss Johnstone at the far end of the rear seat, his words were unintelligible.

"Give up my Diana!" cried Mrs MacFarlane. "But Charley, I've had her for years! What did my husband say? I guess he wouldn't go for that at all, would he?"

"MacFarlane always says no to everything to begin with, but then he comes around eventually, I've noticed," said Mr Grant. "I guess you could bring him around. And think how pleased his father would be."

"Why should I care about that? He don't try to please me," said Mrs MacFarlane. "I swow! This road's rough as a washboard, and what this cushion's filled with I can't guess, but it feels like it might be acorns, it's that hard and lumpish."

"Here, Miss Clara, you try this one," said Miss Johnstone, handing along her own cushion.

Taking it and placing it under herself, Mrs MacFarlane continued, "And don't it strike you as a funny business, though, Charley? This Mr Biggles, who's he? If that's even his real name."

"Not Biggles; Bigelow. Your husband says he's a lawyer up in Washington City; says he does the dirty work of some of the worst of those abolitionists."

"Well, I don't know of any reason to believe a word of it, then!"

"The offer's probably on the up-and-up, MacFarlane says. And Bigelow offers whatever she's appraised at, plus a ten percent premium, the funds to be deposited with a neutral party until she's delivered to an agent of his in Washington City, with a bill of sale—or a recorded deed of emancipation, whichever we prefer."

"But how could some abolitionist lawyer up in Washington City ever come to hear of our Diana to begin with? And why in the world would he write and offer to buy her freedom, of all the hands on the place?"

"His letter says he's acting for some relations of hers."

"That can't be true. She hasn't got a relation in the world."

Mrs Ambler said, "What do you think she'd appraise at, Charley?"

"Well, she's never had a baby yet, has she? No; I thought not, and that don't help," he said. "These days, maybe a hundred and forty, or thereabouts, depending on the appraiser. We'd want to get Lowry up from Alexandria for this."

"With the premium, then, that would be—ah—a hundred and . . . what would it be, Charley?"

"A hundred and fifty-four," said Mr Grant.

"It's something," said Mrs Ambler thoughtfully. "What did Papa say?"

"We didn't mention it to him yet. I want MacFarlane to think it over first, since he's got the lease on her. We could send up another girl for you instead, I told him, for the rest of the lease term."

"And he said no?"

"He always says no, to begin with."

"I just can't quite believe in it, though," said Mrs MacFarlane. "This Yankee, Biggles—Bigelow—whatever he says his name is—offering out of the blue, for Diana? I smell a rat. And how could I possibly manage without her, after all these years? I've had her with me practically all my life."

"I think you might consider your own father's interests too, just a little, Miss Clara," said Miss Johnstone.

"Well, I always do, Aunt Bella, don't I?" retorted Mrs MacFarlane. "And besides, aren't we taught to leave our father and mother, and cleave unto our husband?"

"You're not required to place your husband's interest above your own father's, though," said Miss Johnstone.

"Well, I'm not; I never do," said Mrs MacFarlane sulkily.

"Actually, it's the husband who's instructed to cleave unto the wife," said Miss Julia Grant faintly. "If anyone wishes to be literal about it."

THE CHURCH HAD burnt down some two or three years earlier and, due to a perennial scarcity of money, was not yet rebuilt. The site was now only a pleasant clearing in a park of oak trees; a rectangular stone foundation; an old picket-fenced graveyard. Sheep had recently been pastured here, so the grass under the trees was green and close-cropped—but it was essential to watch where one stepped. By midmorning, when the Grantsboro carriage arrived, a rectangle of tents for the Grantsboro party had already been pitched by the Grantsboro slaves who had come earlier. Inside the tents were arranged beds and tables, washstands and chairs, candlesticks and plates—everything needed for gracious living during the revival meeting.

"Oh, heavens; not there!" exclaimed Miss Johnstone upon catching sight of the tents. "That's much too close to the well. We'll be plagued night and day by other people's servants coming and going, passing right by!"

But her nieces assured her that this was a very good place indeed for the Grantsboro tents, and dissuaded her from ordering them moved.

Wagons, carts, carriages, riders, and walkers poured into the park-like clearing all day, a steady stream of God's faithful, both white and black. Sometimes the Grants remembered to introduce Mrs Pollocke to their neighbors—Carters, Whites, Graysons, Taylors, Lees—but just as often they forgot. By evening, scores of tents had popped up under the trees around the perimeter of the clearing, quick and thick as forest mushrooms after a rain. They were pitched very close together, Grace thought. The tent which she was to share with Miss Grant and Mrs Ambler was not five feet from the Grimshaws' tent on one side, and three feet from the MacFarlanes' on the other.

———

"WELL, NEIL, HERE you are, at last! What took you so long?" sounded Mrs MacFarlane's voice from the next tent, as dusk fell. "We've been waiting for you all day, and I know Charley wants to talk to you about that 'xtraordinary offer for Diana."

"Sssh! Can't you be discreet? All you Grants will say anything, singing it out, no matter who can hear you."

"Oh, don't be so mysterious. Nobody's listening. She's here?"

"Of course. They're all here, just as I agreed—for all the good it's likely to do. All except the hands that can't be spared from looking after the stock. They're supposed to be setting up camp down by the picket line."

"Well, how about it? Charley talked to Boyce, and I guess I wouldn't mind having Dorrie or Cleo instead, for the rest of the lease term."

"No."

"Well, I swan! just like that? Well, why not, Neil? I've been think-ing it over all afternoon, and I've come to the conclusion that we should agree to it—and after all, I'm the one who's most nearly concerned, because I'm the one who has to give her up and get used to somebody new. Charley says that sum of money would mean a great deal right now. Any ready money means a great deal just now to Papa, you know, and if I'm willing to give her up, after all these years, what difference can it make to you, so long as they send me Dorrie or Cleo instead?"

"No. And that's all I intend to say about it."

"Well—but Neil—why, I'm just dumbstruck! Why won't you?"

"I only wish you was dumbstruck. Nothing would please me better. And I don't intend to hear any more about it neither, Clara."

"But Neil—" she said again; and then there was a flesh sound, a gasping, unvoiced. Another; two blows. Then silence.

"Your own damn fault," he said, quietly, distinctly. "You bring it on yourself, every time."

"DO COME ON, MRS POLLOCKE, it's time for the invocation," said Mrs Ambler, suddenly looming up out of the dusk. "You'll want a good place for that. Clara? Clara, ain't you ready?" she called through the closed flap of her sister's tent. Grace was perched on a folding stool just outside their tent, and she was sketching the dark scene laid out before her. Bright straw had been strewn thickly upon an acre of grass in a semicircle before a pulpit raised up on a board platform, and benches had been set out in rows. Off to one side was a low canvas partition hung from rails to separate the slaves' section from the masters' benches. Someone had laid a spill to the dry limbs piled across a pit in the center of the old church foundation, and now orange flames licked up, throwing macabre shadows across the circle of tents under the oaks, and illuminating the undersides of the heavy oak limbs and foliage.

"You all just go on without me," called Mrs MacFarlane from inside her tent.

"Ain't you coming?" called Mrs Ambler. "Is everything all right?"

"I'm just tired, awful tired. I'm going to lie down for a while yet," called Mrs MacFarlane.

"You want me to send Diana along to set with you? I saw her over on the other side, just a few minutes ago."

"No, don't send nobody, I just want to lie down by myself for a while. You all just go on ahead."

"Well, all right, then. Come on, Mrs Pollocke, let's go on and get our places before those Carters take all the good ones. They always think they're entitled to the best place, everywhere they go." Grace put away her sketchbook and followed Mrs Ambler to the second bench from the front, over which Mrs Ambler had previously spread her shawl, to reserve her place.

"I'd rather be over on the other side, near the bonfire, but those Carter girls think it's all for them, over there," said Mrs Ambler. "Did you bring plenty of handkerchiefs? Oh, Mrs Pollocke—you'll need every handkerchief you own. Well, I should say so. It's very—very moving, you understand, when the preachers get warmed up. They really do let loose, you'll find out. I brought—let's see—three, four, five. I guess I could probably spare you one; here. Oh, good, here comes Miss Julia, and Aunt Bella. Julia, where's Charley? And the Grimshaws? They better hurry up."

The front benches remained empty, both here and on the Carter side.

Hugging her shawl around her, Grace made a point of remaining near the end of the bench, making way for latecomers to cross in front of her. The low canvas barrier separating the negroes from the whites was a dozen feet away, on her left. Beyond it, the black people brought from all over the county by their masters were gathering. They had no benches to sit on; they were to stand, it seemed. Grace watched them as they milled about. She saw a middle-aged work-worn woman tearfully kiss and embrace four youngsters—two boys, two girls—like stairsteps in height, who were so much alike they must surely be siblings, surely the woman's own children. She embraced them as though she had not seen them in months—so tightly that they complained.

Your own morbid imagination, Grace rebuked herself. Do not leap to conclusions.

Then there was a push and a shuffle behind the barrier, and some of the black folk there formed themselves into ranks. Their choir leader, a grey-haired man, took his place facing them; he hummed them their pitch; and then they launched into a hymn—or something that somewhat resembled a hymn, of sorts:

Sanctify me, sanctify me, sanctify me,
sanctify me, sanctify me,
Just now, just now, just now,
Sanctify me just now. . . .

Then the next verse: Good religion, good religion, good religion. Even in this open night air, the voices were vast and resonant, low and high. The hymn was in three-quarter time; and yet the fabric of it was stretched, subdivided, ornamented, transformed into something far more complex and far more interesting. No choir of Welshmen, thought Grace, could have beat them for pure music.

Come to Jesus was the next verse. The white people talked, chattering among themselves as the negroes sang. "There you are, at last! What took you so long?" whispered Mrs Ambler to her brother Charles when he came and settled onto the bench behind her. "What's wrong?" she added.

"Nothing. Later," said her brother shortly.

"Where's the MacFarlanes?"

"How should I know?" he replied; then he rose and went away again without explanation.

"Well, I don't like the look of that," murmured Mrs Ambler into Grace's ear, as though Grace were her confidante. "What's that all about?"

Now a horn sounded; and a collared preacher appeared at the pulpit. It was not Mr Stringfellow. "This little fellow must be the Carters' preacher," whispered Mrs Ambler. "I don't much care for the rickety look of him, do you? Mr Stringfellow has a far better countenance."

The Carter preacher had an unfortunate voice for his line of work, a high-pitched smallish voice, and could scarcely make himself heard. A hat was passed around to collect donations for the church rebuilding fund, but Grace had not provided herself with money, and the hat passed by her none the richer.

After a while, the Carter preacher finished, and all joined in singing a hymn. "Hmph! That was nothing!" said Mrs Ambler to Grace. "But just you wait, Mrs Pollocke, until Mr Stringfellow begins to preach, you'll see the difference. Look, here he comes; ah!" For now Mr Stringfellow bounded onto the stage (for so Grace thought of the raised platform where he stood; it was more theatrical than exalted). He appeared especially tall and broad-shouldered after the meager Carter preacher; and the dozens of lanterns hanging from the tree limbs all around the platform flattered his Byronic profile and his luxuriant hair. He stood, quite silent and still, while all eyes devoured him, and he let his gaze rake the congregation slowly, from west to east, and back again—giving to each quadrant in turn, Grace could not help but notice, a long look at the noble profile. An expression of unspeakable disgust animated his face; the nostrils flared as though a stench offended them; the lip curled into a sneer. Slowly a hush fell over the rustling crowd.

Grace felt her stomach turning over. Possibly the plate of fricassee that had been brought to her earlier did not agree with her.

At last Mr Stringfellow gave tongue: "Sinners!" he thundered, with stentorian power. "What could be more foul in the sight of the Almighty, what more loathsome, than to see His vile disobedient depraved children, all gathered together in their pride, their folly, their sinful depravity? Presuming to lavish praise upon what is so far above them? Do you patriarchs crave the praise, the admiration of your low-liest and blackest field hands? Do you mothers melt under the approval of your handmaidens? Of course you do not! You would be insulted at their presumption in offering to comment upon your conduct! What could be more offensive? It is just thus that the Almighty scorns your attempts to flatter His glory! For it is not your praises and flatteries, your empty words that the Almighty requires of you! These will never buy you eternal salvation! What is it, then? Oh, it is no mystery, no hidden Romish mystery. It is very simple; it is only this: only the utmost—instant—complete—Obedience!"

"Jesus, oh, Jesus," a woman's voice was declaiming faintly from somewhere in the congregation, over and over again, very rapidly. "Jesus, oh, Jesus."

"Obedience to His law, which He has set out for you with the most—perfect—clarity! You are to submit to His every command, instantly, with the most complete submission! Does it injure your pride, to come when you are called? To drop your worldly doings and answer—instantly answer—to His summons? Does it injure your self-respect, to bow down before the Lord of All? Does it not become you, to abase yourself before your Master? Are you diminished in His sight, think you, in your sinful pride?"

"Jesus, oh, Jesus! Jesus, oh, Jesus!"

"What becomes of His bad servant? Of His disobedient and care-less servant? What becomes of His ungrateful child? Have you brought your black servants here, to hear His divine word—only to disregard His word yourself? Too high and mighty to bow down before Him yourself? When he calls you, sends for you, do you humble yourself to the earth which He has made for you, and answer Him: Here am I, Lord, your obedient humble servant? Do you not hear His mighty call? Can you pretend that you do not hear His summons? Can you refuse to hear His summons? Refuse to do His perfect bidding?"

"Jesus, oh, Jesus! Jesus, oh, Jesus!" By this time, the middle-aged woman who had been uttering this refrain had worked herself into a blubbering hysteria. "Jesus, oh, Jesus!" she cried, never varying in tone or inflection, while her face and neck became grotesquely swollen, and all her veins stood out as in an apoplexy.

"And what is the lot of the disobedient servant?" demanded Mr

Stringfellow of his congregation. "When your servant runs away, do you not go after him and fetch him back again? Yea, for he suffereth in his disobedience. And is our Lord not the mightiest of shepherds? Doth the mighty shepherd suffer even the blackest of His sheep to be lost unto Him? Reflect, then, upon thy unworthiness, yea, reflect, then, I say, upon thy sinful nature, depraved from the instant of thy birth until the blessed moment when thou dost surrender thy own will, until thou dost open thy innermost soul to receive there, welcome there, thy Divine Master—as Master!"

The sobs of a young girl two rows back had now escalated to shrieks; and the Carter preacher had gone to her, to whisper into her ear and stroke her fair disheveled hair. He was whispering prayers and consolations, Grace hoped—but the whispers had none of the calming effect that prayers and consolations ought to have had.

"For thus has the Almighty designed all things!" thundered Mr Stringfellow. "Regard the orderliness of His creation, all in train, all in order, each subservient to each: As the servant owes obedience to his earthly master, as the child owes obedience to his father and mother, as the wife owes obedience to her husband—so do we all—all sinners, all!—owe instant and complete obedience to our Divine Master in heaven."

Mrs Ambler had deployed the first of her handkerchiefs; and Miss Johnstone beyond her was rocking from side to side, shaking her head, her eyes closed prayerfully and her hands twisting her handkerchief into a string.

"When He calls, who dares disregard His summons? Reflect, sinner, upon thy peril! What are twenty lashes upon thy bare back—compared to an eternity of lashings, and no release to be hoped for by a merciful death? Feelest thou, sinner, the lash upon thy back? Each—word—is—a—stripe!—Each—word—a—fresh—cut!—Writhe—thee—then—in—pain—unto—eternity! Thy flesh laid open afresh with each cut, thy blood a-flying, cut to the bone, the flesh cut to a jelly—"

Overcome by nausea, Grace slid to the end of the bench, and there managed to rise, turn, and stumble toward the Grant tents in the half darkness at the distant edge of the clearing.

"Wilt thou flee the Lord? Thou mayest flee, now, from the mere anticipation of His justice, His judgment!" she heard his voice pursuing her. "Thinkest thou, sinner, to flee death itself? To escape judgment itself? Art thou not mortal? Death and judgment thou shalt never escape! Thy pride cannot save thee—riches cannot save thee—motherhood cannot save thee! Upon the Day of Judgment, when thou shalt stand in thy nakedness before Him, awaiting His perfect justice, be it mercy or be it eternal punishment—" His declamation seemed to hunt her into the darkness, but as Grace collapsed onto the canvas stool in front of her tent where she had sat earlier to sketch the scene, his words were no longer intelligible. She was panting and swallowing as saliva flooded her mouth. Waves of heat and chill ran up her arms and neck as she held her forehead in her two hands, elbows on knees. She fervently hoped she would not vomit, and concentrated for some moments on preventing only that.

After a few minutes the tide of nausea ebbed, and Grace was able to sit upright again as her breathing eased. At Calcutta she had once witnessed the Churuk Puja in honor of the goddess Kali, where intoxicated devotees passed large steel hooks suspended from long ropes into the flesh and muscle of their chests and backs—then had themselves raised up by these steel hooks in their flesh, and swung about for half an hour at a time, while they chanted holy verses and threw sweetmeats to the crowds of spectators. That had been horrible and shocking; but the sight had not made her sick.

Whence this nausea, then?

The meat in the fricassee had been unidentifiable, but it had smelled and tasted wholesome enough, though somewhat metallic—the tingle of iron on the tongue, raw as blood, due, she had supposed, to the steel fork. But who had prepared it? Were the servants, even here at camp, all catering separately to their own masters, as at home? Or was a central communal kitchen set up to feed everyone? Grace slipped the collar of her fancy, turned it loose: such a peerless opportunity, if all the white folk were served the same food, from a single source! She pictured it: three stealthy handfuls of spotted castor beans scattered by a quick black hand—the winking of the pink palm—into a kettle of shell beans over the fire; then stirred in; all spotted alike, so who would see the different shape? The finished dish would kill anyone who tasted it.

Grace imagined the sheriff's men coming upon the scene a day or two hence, to find all the white folk lying dead; all the black folk flown. All the Flower of the Chivalry felled, in one stealthy swoop (all of that Flower which belonged to Loudoun County, and to the Lord, at least— excepting of course the Quakers, who did not go in for this sort of thing)—and the coroner left to conclude, perhaps, that their Maker had stooped to gather them all, in their perfect Rapture, unto Himself!

What a perverse fancy you have got, she rebuked herself. But she understood now why slaveholders might sometimes wonder if their coffee tasted more bitter than usual; and if the cabbage hadn't an odd coppery tang.

In any case, she had eaten no beans, castor or otherwise; and others, who had eaten the same fricassee, were not sick. It was not the food which sickened her.

What could it be, then, but Mr Stringfellow's preaching? The visions Mr Stringfellow evoked with his words were disgusting. But most sickening was his own obvious relish as he evoked these visions of suffering—of torture, in fact. He reveled in it. And he deployed his depravity so artfully; like a master angler casting his fly out upon the waters—teasing, testing, to find out who might rise to this, who might be fascinated by this particular disturbance. Was it possible that he did this all unknowing? Possible; but equally likely that he did it very knowingly indeed.

That is an evil man, she thought. From childhood she had always been able to sense evil quite clearly. How could others fail to perceive it?—so frank, hideous, and shameless, before their very faces?

His particular style of depravity was not rare. There were artists, painters, who catered to such tastes. Not the lush classical nudes; nor even those harmless scenes of wholesome sexual congress—cabinet scenes meant for private viewing—produced by painters everywhere, in India and China, and by European painters too. No, she was thinking of specialist pictures—often, oddly enough, of ostensibly religious subjects. These were sometimes so veiled in their appeal that they might make their way into the collections of naïfs who quite innocently admired the composition, the brushwork, the masterful chiaroscuro; who possibly did not even sense the underlying depravity conveyed to initiates by the sight of this suffering St Agatha grasping her mutilated but still virginal breast; nor the allure of that naked boyish St Sebastian so fatally and fascinatingly penetrated by arrows.

There was a different voice ringing from the pulpit now; perhaps the preacher backed by the Lees had taken over for the present. He started a hymn. At first just a few voices joined his, then gradually more voices joined in, tremulous to begin with, but gradually gaining strength and substance as the effect of Mr Stringfellow's words wore off, Grace supposed.

Slaves fed more branches to the distant bonfire and it leapt up afresh, throwing sparks upward. Silhouetted figures passed forward and back in front of the licking flames, creating a remarkably diabolical effect. If she were to paint hell, she would paint it just thus. But then one of those backlighted figures rose up, and seemed to enlarge. Someone was advancing toward her; approaching, out of the fire. It was a man, a well-made broad-shouldered man; but his hair was disheveled in just such a way, on either side of his head, as to resemble in silhouette two short curving horns—the devil's horns? a satyr's horns?—and she knew very well who it was even before he came near enough to speak: "Jonah thought to flee his Lord's summons too, Mrs Pollocke," said Mr Stringfellow, in his deepest tone.

How was one to reply to such a remark as that? She could smell him: a strong odor of sour sweat, the nervous kind, not the outdoor-labor kind. His broad brow was glittering wet.

He fell upon his knees before her low canvas stool, saying hoarsely, "Let us pray, Mrs Pollocke! Let us pray together to our Heavenly Father. Come, sister, kneel by my side, and I shall lead thee along the narrow way, I shall plead for thee, I shall intercede on thy behalf. Thou hast not prostrated thy prideful soul before thy Heavenly Father for lo, these many years, I can see very well—but it is not too late. Come," he said, and seized her two hands, as though to draw her by force to her knees close beside him.

Instead, Grace leapt to her feet and pulled free. "I beg your pardon, sir," she said loudly, in a tone which expressed neither begging nor pardon.

"Who's that? That you, Mrs Pollocke?" called a woman's voice from inside the tent at her back, and Grace remembered that Mrs MacFarlane had remained here, to rest.

"Yes, Mrs MacFarlane; may I come in?" she called, and slid inside, into the darkness behind the loose tent flap, without waiting for any answer. "Have you no light?"

"I didn't dare doze off with my candle a-burning, not with all this dry straw strewn about, so I blown it out," said Mrs MacFarlane's voice from the corner. "But there's a paper of locofocos here somewhere."

By feel in the darkness, Grace found the packet of lucifers on the candlestand; unwrapped them; broke one free; struck a light against the brass base of the candlestick, and lit the candle.

The flame flared up, throwing deep shadows into the corners. But that was no shadow—that angry bruise all red and black—across Mrs MacFarlane's left cheekbone and the outside corner of her mouth. Grace stared, and Mrs MacFarlane's hand flew to her face, fingertips gently outlining the bruise. "Oh!" she faltered. "I fell, in the dark, when I tried to get up to use the convenience. Right there, against the corner of the stand. . . . Is it bad? Does it show up?"

Grace picked up a little looking glass from the folding washstand and held it up before Mrs MacFarlane's face. "Oh, my," Mrs MacFarlane said, and gingerly touched her split lip. "It is bad. I guess I should get something onto that right away. No, I don't want Aunt Bella—and not my husband, no! My Diana would know just what to do. She must be here by now, but you don't know her, do you? Could you find Cleo out there, Mrs Pollocke? Cleo would find her—or you could just send any of the Grantsboro servants for my Diana."

Grace screwed her courage up to the necessary pitch before slipping outside again, but Mr Stringfellow had gone.

A PANDEMONIUM; a bedlam. From every point there mingled the sounds of praying, singing, preaching, and lamentation: Amen, amen! Jesus! Oh, sweet Jesus! And from the negro quarter there rang out wildest singing and shriekings, mixed with laughter. Now two of the three preachers were bent over the penitents who had made their way to the front benches, empty hitherto, while the third preached from the pulpit. Other figures lay writhing on the straw before the benches, just below the preachers' platform. "Mercy, mercy," shrieked someone without cease. "Mercy, mercy!" All these frantic penitents were women, noted Grace. She identified Mr Stringfellow's form, now kneeling beside a blubbering girl of sixteen or so, whose face was shiny with tears and snot. As the girl hysterically declaimed over and over again, "Oh, Lord, how I have backslided, oh, Lord forgive me, for I have back-slided—" the preacher stroked her loosened hair and whispered in her ear. Another woman was uttering an incomprehensible stream of bab-ble, while a woman who might have been her sister tried to hold her hands, which were clawing at the kerchief at her throat, trying to tear it away. Even the mud-smeared, self-mutilating, bhang-intoxicated religious fanatics of India were not more frightening, not more mad-dened, than these Christians in their pious frenzy.

Where was Cleo? Grace scanned the shining black faces behind the canvas fence. Those faces shone with the same savage ardor. Some were singing, and Grace could make out these words:

Oh, Satan, he tole me not to pray.
He want my soul at judgment day.

"Oh Satan! Oh Satan! Let go me, Satan!" howled one boy, in convul-sions in the dirt. Was that Cleo, near the front there, swaying back and forth, a handkerchief over her face? No, certainly not Cleo. . . .

But there she was, sitting on a barrel near the back, cradling her little daughter on her lap, crooning to her, it seemed. Grace made her way around the end of the canvas curtain and approached. Cleo did not see Grace until Grace was quite near; but then she rose, still holding Cordie on her hip. Even by firelight Grace could make out the yellow-ness in the whites of her eyes; the red veins there.

"Mrs MacFarlane wants her maid Diana," said Grace.

Cleo said nothing.

"She's hurt," added Grace.

Cleo set down her little daughter. "Cordie, you go on and fetch Dinah here," she instructed her, and the little girl ran off into the dark teeming crowd. Grace lost sight of her immediately. "Miz MacFarlane always getting hurt," said Cleo after a moment. "She tell you she fall down?"

Grace nodded yes.

"Mmm-hm," said Cleo. "She the most falling-down lady I ever know of."

Hypocrite and the concubine
Livin' among the swine,
They run to God with the lips and tongue
And leavin' all the heart behind

sang half a dozen baritone field hands nearby in march time. It limped oddly against the hymn shouted by another group of field hands on the other side of where Grace waited:

Halleluia, hallaloo,
Halleluia, hallaloo.

"I brung Dinah," announced Cordie, reappearing suddenly and dragging a tall young woman along behind her by the hand.

"Your missus send for you," Cleo said to her. "Come on, I show you where." They went, Cordie following. Grace watched their backs until she lost them in the darkness.

So that was Diana.

The men were singing:

Wrestle with Satan and wrestle with sin,
Stepped over hell and come back again.

One of them had the deepest bass voice Grace had ever heard. He was not a big man, but his voice was as deep as the ocean. But then her nausea came again, saliva welling up in the most alarming way; and Grace fled. By the time she got inside her tent, the nausea had receded. Without a light, she undressed down to her shift, draping her bodice, skirt, and corset over a nearby chair by feel, and put herself to bed.

———

GRACE COULD HEAR women's voices inside the next tent. "Got no arnica," said Cleo's voice, "but I reckon missus has got some of that laudanum. You want I should go and ask her for it?"

"No," said Mrs MacFarlane.

"Just have to make do with cold water, then," said a voice uncannily like Anibaddh's: Diana's voice.

Mrs MacFarlane whimpered.

"That's ugly," said Diana. "That's a bad one."

"Diana, I want you to sleep in here with me tonight," said Mrs MacFarlane.

"Yes, missus," said Diana. "If you think that do any good."

BUT IT DID NO GOOD. "No, Neil," Grace heard, some time later— through her dream of the tidal surge on the Delaware River. It was Mrs MacFarlane's voice: "No, Neil, please don't. . . ." Had her husband come back to the tent? It seemed to Grace that it was very late; and the firelight and the hymn-singing were somewhat subdued. "But I've got Diana sleeping in here with me."

"Diana, you can go on out," said Mr MacFarlane's voice, heavy and slurred. "Your mistress don't need you again until the morning. You come on back then." He or some other gentleman must have brought special liquid provisions to the revival meeting.

"I'm feeling so very unwell, though, Neil, with headache, and the baby—" pleaded Mrs MacFarlane.

"I've heard that one before. Never a damn thing to show for it."

"But Neil, I want Diana with me," tried Mrs MacFarlane.

"I don't care if she stays or goes," said her husband. "Makes no difference to me. You're the one who always wants her sent out."

There was a silence. "Diana, you go on, just outside the doorway, then," said Mrs MacFarlane after a moment. "Stay there in case I need you."

Grace tried to sleep again, but she could not help hearing what was happening in the next tent. Certainly Diana, sent to lie on the ground outside the tent flap, must be hearing too.

———

BEFORE DAWN, GRACE awakened to nausea. She arose, and retched into the pot behind a screen in the corner. Her tentmates did not awaken; only Miss Grant turned over. After wiping her mouth, Grace eased herself back onto her cot, mentally counting over the days and weeks since Daniel's return.

She had felt just this wretched before. It had been a couple of years ago, when she and Daniel had been about to return to China; but instead she had been obliged to remain behind in Philadelphia, because she was pregnant.

CHAPTER
14

Diana's ear, Grace saw, was neatly curled, flat to the head, and had scarcely any lobe.

Hazy morning sunlight streamed beneath the dapple-green oak limbs, falling in shafts here and there upon the congregation (brushed and hatted, or bonneted and shawled this morning; exhibiting no hint of last night's excesses, except for a certain scrubbed pallor); and upon Mr Stringfellow, who, from his pulpit, was delivering a learned lecture upon the history of slavery. From the rearmost bench, near the canvas divider, Grace drew in her sketchbook. Her nausea had abated, and she drew rapidly. She had been sketching the scene before her: Mr String-fellow's white audience lined up in rows upon their benches; the canvas barrier; the colored people beyond. Those benches ought certainly to have backs to them, Grace had been thinking; for what was so absurd as the view from behind of human posteriors being sat upon? The bouffant skirts of the women puffed outward, exaggerating the bulg-ing squashing effect, like pumpkins in the field; worse still were the trousers of the men, stretched tight wherever their coattails were askew. But when one of the slaves had come and sat upon a stump not ten feet away, just beyond the canvas curtain—posed in perfect profile, and unconscious of Grace's scrutiny—Grace had turned instantly to a fresh page and begun to draw, as quickly as she could: Diana.

"Some would have it that slavery is a great sin," Mr Stringfellow was saying, "the greatest individual and national sin that is among us. But before we conclude slavery to be a thing hateful to God, and a sin in His sight, it is proper that we should search with great care the instructions He has given us, to consider in what light He has in fact looked upon it, yesterday, today, and forever. Now, I propose to show, from the scriptures, that slavery—far from being any sin—was sanctioned by the Almighty in the patriarchal age, and that this merciful and philanthropic institution was incorporated in the only national constitution which ever emanated from the Almighty. And I will demonstrate furthermore that the legality of slavery was recognised, and its relative duties regulated, by Jesus Christ in His Kingdom."

Diana was shelling peas into a bowl on her lap, and dropping the emptied pods in a pile at her feet. She was tall, well above the common height, and very slim. In feature and in bearing, she resembled her mother, though her jaw was perhaps finer-boned, and her neck even longer than her mother's. Her fingers were blunt, her nails square.

Grace had got the profile, the head and neck, quite accurate and complete; and had proceeded to outline the overall sweep of Diana's figure: the relaxed bend of the back, the graceful attenuated wrists. She was sketching the drapery of the skirt when she felt someone approach from behind and linger near her shoulder. Grace turned back a page in her sketchbook to hide the drawing of Diana and applied her pencil instead to the half-completed sketch of the congregation, adding some shadow beneath the benches on which the Grant women sat.

"The very first recorded language regarding slavery is Noah's, in Genesis, ninth chapter," Mr Stringfellow was saying. "Noah is speaking for the Almighty when he curses the Canaanites: 'Cursed be Canaan'; 'a servant of servants shall he be to his brethren;' and 'Blessed be the Lord God of Shem; and Canaan shall be his servant.' It is well worth remembering that Noah's famous curse was occasioned by Ham's disrespectful mocking of his own father in that father's moment of weakness. Be this as it may, it is clear that God decreed slavery, and He shows in this, His decree, tokens of goodwill to the master."

"Humbug," said a low voice just behind Grace's shoulder. "The curse is Noah's, not God's; it is quite plain that Noah was speaking for himself, wreaking his own little revenge at having been caught out in his disgraceful drunkenness. A fit of pique."

The speaker was a respectably dressed grey-haired man, rather small and neat of build. His voice had carried no further than her own ear, and to judge by his speech, he was most certainly a Scot.

"And in any case," he added quietly, "it hardly seems a model of justice—not even of Divine Justice, which has its enigmas—to punish the descendants for the sin of the father. I daresay that even Virginia courts would see the absurdity of imprisoning, of enslaving, a man and all his descendants forever and ever in punishment of—let us say, a murder committed by his father—much less for a disrespectful peal of laughter produced by his father! There may be a certain logic in holding a father responsible for the misdeeds of his own minor children; and perhaps even for the misdeeds of his adult children, on the grounds that the father has been responsible for their training and their education. But how can a child be held responsible—liable to be punished—for the misdeeds of his ancestors? It is absurd, patently absurd—Genesis or not."

"I wonder, sir, at hearing such a sentiment expressed here," replied Grace, equally quietly. *"Cò às a tha sibh fhèin?"* she ventured in Gaelic: Where are you from, yourself?

"Tha mi à Arrochar," he replied promptly, but then switched back to English: "From Arrochar on the shore of Loch Long; and Arrochar plantation here too, a few miles beyond Leesburg."

"I daresay, then, that you must be Mr MacFarlane," said Grace. "The elder."

"So I am," he said, and made his bow. "And I will venture to suppose that you are the free-thinking lady painter who is staying at Grantsboro. How do you do? Mrs . . . Mrs—"

"Pollocke," supplied Grace.

"A lowlands name," he said.

"But I was born a MacDonald, from Skye," said Grace, and immediately regretted having divulged so much.

"An t-Eilean Sgitheanach," said Mr MacFarlane; and Grace's heart leapt, to hear the old name, in the old speech: The Winged Isle.

Mr Stringfellow was now praising the patriarch Abraham: "A man of high distinction wherever he went," he was saying. "Not merely for his sterling moral qualities, but also for his magnificent wealth, and its inseparable concomitant power. 'He had sheep, and oxen, and he-asses, and men-servants, and maid-servants, and she-asses, and camels.' Genesis, chapter twelve, verse sixteen. This verse tells us that servants are inventoried just as other classes of property are inventoried—are enumerated as property, as patrimony; they are not to be considered as voluntary servants, but as properly belonging to Abraham, given him by God." Mr Stringfellow then discussed at some length the travels, the financial standing, and the political career of the patriarch Abraham. "Now, any man as rich and powerful as Abraham requires an heir as a matter of course; and in fact God had promised him one. But when the requisite heir had failed to put in his appearance by the time Abraham was eighty-five and his dutiful wife Sarah seventy-five, the wife proposed to her husband that he get that heir upon a secondary wife: a female slave of the black Egyptian stock," Mr Stringfellow said matter-of-factly.

"The shameless old procuress that she was, that Sarah!" murmured the elder Mr MacFarlane, to Grace's ear. "Still, Ishmael didn't inherit, you will have noticed."

Mr Stringfellow said, "But this female slave, identified as 'Hagar, Sarah's maid,' became, predictably, puffed up by the new importance thus conferred on her, and presumed to resent the authority still exercised over her by her mistress—an authority exercised even unto severity, it may seem to some, an authority which some might even call an abuse of the rightful relation between mistress and slave. Whereupon Hagar took it upon herself to run away—to abscond, in fact. Now, here we have a perfect test case—got up expressly for our instruction, it may seem—even unto the aggravating circumstance of the harshly severe mistress, provoked perhaps by a quite understandable feminine jealousy."

Jealousy, though understandable, was no virtue; and Grace could never approve Sarah's conduct: to offer her maid to her husband, expressly to get a child; then to punish both the maid and the child! And how base of Abraham, to accede to it all! A poltroon.

"Now, what is the doctrine taught us, in this perfect test case?" Mr Stringfellow was saying. "What happens next? God proceeds to send His angel unto Hagar, to seek her in the wilderness where she has fled her mistress's harsh discipline. And, upon finding Hagar there, God's angel addresses the fugitive thusly: 'Whither wilt thou go?' asks the angel; and the fugitive replies, 'I flee from the face of my mistress.' Now, what does the Lord's angel say to this? Does the angel commiserate with the poor harshly treated servant, and lead her out of bondage—as the abolitionists, who claim to have more mercy than God Himself, would no doubt have recommended? Judge the angel's answer for yourself, as recorded in Genesis, chapter sixteen, verse nine: 'The angel of the Lord said unto her, Return unto thy mistress, and submit thyself under her hands.' Submit thyself," repeated Mr Stringfellow, now pointing at the black slaves behind the curtain; "under her hands!" he finished, indicating with a bow and a flourish the white ladies seated on the benches before him.

Grace became aware of her uneasy stomach; but this, she thought, might be due merely to Mr Stringfellow's style of discourse.

"The mountebank!" murmured Mr MacFarlane. "What blether! But all too plausible; that is the worst of it."

Mr Stringfellow continued: "Thus far we have seen that God Himself first of all decreed this state of involuntary bondage. We have seen that those whom God blessed with the greatest marks of His favor—Abraham, Isaac, Jacob—were most certainly the owners of involuntary and hereditary bondsmen, purchased with money and treated as property. And we have seen that severity on the part of the master—or mistress—does nothing to nullify the absolute obligation of the slave to submit, completely and abjectly.

"Now let us consider those instructions in Mosaic law which treat of the severity which the master may use in governing his own property. These instructions, given us in the twenty-first chapter of the book of Exodus, explicitly authorise chastisement, even with the rod, and even with a severity that terminates in death."

It seemed to Grace that Mr Stringfellow particularly relished the very feel of these words in his mouth.

"And in that same chapter," continued Mr Stringfellow, "we find the divine sanction of those practices which may result in the separation of man and wife, or of parent and child, who are held in bondage. . . ."

Diana had now finished shelling her bowl of peas; she gathered the emptied pods into her apron, and rose and went away. Her back was like her mother's, observed Grace; and so was her lithe gait.

"Our self-righteous abolitionists harbor a marked hatred against such laws," declared Mr Stringfellow dryly. "Nevertheless, Almighty God has given these laws His sanction; therefore they must be in harmony with His moral character. All who believe the Bible to be of divine authority must believe also that these laws were given by the Holy Ghost unto Moses. Here is the authority, from God Himself, to hold men and women, and their increase, in slavery, and to transmit them as property forever. Here is the plenary power to govern them, whatever measure of severity it may require. Here is power given unto the master, to separate man from wife, parent from child. Under every view that we are allowed to take of the subject, the conviction is forced upon the mind, that from Abraham's day, until at least the coming of Christ—a period of two thousand years—this institution found favor with God. No marks of His displeasure are found resting upon it.

"And yet the abolitionists would assert that during the two thousand years that elapsed between the time of the patriarchs and the coming of Christ, God came to take a different view of the subject— their own view of the matter, to be precise—and that God, in short, upon second thought, came to see the error of His ways, and decided that the institution He had Himself decreed ought now to be abolished.

"Is there any evidence to support such a view? Once again, let us carefully examine God's own book to discover His revealed truth. We read that during those two thousand years, God raised up a succession of prophets to reprove His chosen people for the various sins and errors into which they had fallen, as any people are wont to do; yet not a single reproof is uttered against the institution of involuntary slavery; nor for any species of abuse that ever grew out of it. Let us now ascertain whether Jesus Christ, upon His coming among us, has abolished slavery—or whether He has, to the contrary, recognised it as a lawful relation existing among men, and prescribed duties which belong to it, as He has for the other relative duties, such as those between husband and wife, parent and child, magistrate and subject.

"First, we may take it as granted that Jesus has not abolished slavery by commandment—for no one pretends that He ever did. And it is worth remark that Jesus, come among us as lawgiver and preceptor, for the express purpose of putting into place a system of measures whose object is to subjugate all men—kings, legislators, and private citizens in all nations throughout the earth—to the Almighty—it is remarkable, I say, that under such circumstances, Jesus should have failed to prohibit the continuance of slavery, if it was indeed His intention to abolish it. To pretend that He has introduced new moral principles which must extinguish it as an institution—yet have failed to make any direct prohibitory command requiring such extinction—undermines any profession of faith in our Lord's competence and fitness as legislator. We Virginians would be pretty quick to vote out of his office any legislator of ours who did so careless a job of work as that!"

This wry sally evoked a little appreciative laughter from the more politically astute members of the congregation; but only a snort from the elder Mr MacFarlane.

Mr Stringfellow got off another little sarcasm: "And to say the least, it makes Jesus rely largely upon the intellect of His disciples, to expect them to spy out a discrepancy in the law of Moses, which God Himself never saw. . . ."

More members of the congregation appreciated this broader hint.

"Nevertheless," continued Mr Stringfellow sternly, "we are increasingly afflicted by those who pretend to have found out that this institution, though it was expressly ordained by God, and regulated by God, is now secretly frowned upon by God—for even they do not pretend that God has ever openly prohibited or abolished His institution which is so abhorrent to themselves. Perhaps they suppose this has merely been an oversight on God's part, one which it is their duty to rectify. Or perhaps they consider that they are called upon to set God a good example in this matter, an example which He would do well to follow—"

Again there were guffaws of appreciation.

Mr Stringfellow paused to swallow a few sips of water and to wipe his broad brow with a large handkerchief. Then he lifted up his voice once again, proposing to demonstrate, he said, "that the institution of slavery is full of mercy. Authentic history warrants this conclusion," he declared.

"What sort of pretended history, then, has he been citing hitherto?" Mr MacFarlane murmured.

"For a long period of time, it was this institution alone which furnished a motive for sparing the prisoner's life," said Mr Stringfellow. "The institution of slavery has saved from the sword more lives, including their increase, than all the souls who now inhabit this globe. And it has brought within the range of gospel influence millions of Ham's descendants among ourselves, who, but for this institution, would have sunk down to eternal ruin; knowing not God, and strangers to the gospel. In their bondage here on earth, they have been well provided for, and great multitudes of them have been made the freemen of the Lord Jesus Christ.

"Nevertheless, there is now abroad on the land a spirit of intrusive, presumpuous, busybodied officiousness and interference. Our citizens have been murdered; our property has been stolen; our lives have been put in jeopardy; our characters traduced; and attempts have been made to force a political slavery upon us, in place of our benign and divinely sanctioned domestic slavery—by strangers, who have no right to meddle with our affairs. We have had to put ourselves upon our mettle to suppress among our slaves a rebellious spirit, engendered by false doctrine, propagated by men of corrupt minds, and destitute of the truth. Such wrongdoing and wrong-speaking we are obliged to rebuke with all the authority which the words of our Lord Jesus Christ confer; and if we fail, we shall have failed in our duty to Him—to ourselves—and to the world!"

It was finished. Mr Stringfellow fell to his knees; the Taylor preacher mounted the platform and led the congregants in a prayer and a hymn, before dismissing them at last to their dinner.

The Grants gathered up Mrs Pollocke and the elder Mr MacFarlane as they made their way back to their quarter of the encampment. Dinner could be smelled by now, and everyone was hungry. They were congratulating one another on Mr Stringfellow's eloquence, and repeating the especially good bits as they took their places around the table that had been set up by their slaves in the clearing in front of their tents. "I do admire that knack of his for witty understatement . . . our elected legislators, did you get that? Ha ha!" laughed Mr Grimshaw.

"And so vastly well informed on every subject! So learned, so thorough," said Miss Johnstone. "I do wish Master James would come and hear him sometime."

"Surely you must now see, Mrs Pollocke, how entirely wrong those abolitionists are," said Mrs Ambler. "Mr Stringfellow has proven them wrong, and even dangerous, beyond all argument."

"Entirely unanswerable," agreed Miss Johnstone. "If only they could be made to hear him. They'd be left speechless—mouths agape but blessedly silent, for once, I guess! Now, Mrs Pollocke, you'll have to admit that Mr Stringfellow has removed every possible objection to our institution of domestic slavery."

"So it may be, as regards scripture," said Grace. "But an objection to slavery may be based not upon scripture; nor indeed upon any idea of what conduct Christian principles may require—for that, apparently, remains open to argument. But it may be based instead upon the guarantees given in your national declarations of first principles: your declaration of independence, your Constitution, your Bill of Rights. Surely those—not the Bible—are the governing documents of your republic."

"Merciful heaven, Mrs Pollocke! You misunderstand entirely!" exclaimed Miss Johnstone. "That's what comes of being a foreigner. If you was American, you'd understand it all very well. Of course God's law is the highest law of all—no one could deny that—"

"It may be the highest moral law for Christians," said Grace. "But others of us, who may not profess Christianity—"

"Heaven preserve us! Not profess Christianity!"

"You see, Charley; didn't I tell you she was an infidel!" said Mrs MacFarlane. Her veil somewhat hindered her eating, and seemed oddly incongruous here, in her own family circle, but no one commented upon it.

"Oh, Mrs Pollocke! How can you persist so in mortal error?" pleaded Mrs Ambler. "And after hearing Mr Stringfellow's impassioned eloquence too!"

"Will you send along that dish of turkey sallet, if you please, Miss Johnstone?" interposed the elder Mr MacFarlane. "As soon as you have been served, yourself. And is it only water we are drinking? No, not for me, I thank you; I have always considered that this well is too near the burying ground. The Carters have brought their best preacher, I see—he is not as tall as Mr Stringfellow, is he? But those Carter carriage horses are tall—perhaps even taller than Judge Grant's. And who will tell me what I missed, last evening? Any especially picturesque conversions, at all?"

Mr Charles Grant asserted that the Grant carriage horses were most certainly taller, by at least half a hand—and far better formed too—than the Carter specimens; and Mrs MacFarlane hastened to assure him that the churchyard well produced the most wholesome

water to be found this side of Goose Creek; and Miss Johnstone gave
a detailed account of the previous night's spectacular coming-to-grace
of a widow of spotty reputation, who had confessed not only her own
iniquities, but also the names of her fellow sinners.

Deftly done; and *tapadh leibh*—thank you!—thought Grace toward
this elder Mr MacFarlane. But it was too soon to let down her guard,
despite the recommendations of his Scottish origins, speech, and cleverness. His son was loathsome; and how could the father of such a son
be blameless? Hadn't he himself conceded that a father might bear
some blame for the misdeeds of his offspring—even adult offspring—
as having failed in their training and education?

"But sir, what a pity that you missed seeing it for yourself—the
saving, I mean, last night. It was deeply—deeply affecting," said Mrs
Ambler.

"Ah, well," he said. "I had business that could not be put off."

"And a greater pity still, sir, that you missed Mr Stringfellow's lecture just now," said Miss Johnstone. "It was superb in every respect;
and it would have done you a great deal of good to have heard him, for
he was really unanswerable."

"Oh, but I did hear him, Miss Johnstone," replied the elder Mr
MacFarlane. "I arrived in time to hear every word. But as no one was
offered the opportunity to make any answer, it is hardly fair, I think, to
call it unanswerable. I, for one, should have been happy to make Mr
Stringfellow his answer."

"How can you? What argument can you possibly make?"

"First of all, ma'am, I will not grant his first premise: that sin may
be inherited; and with it, punishment. I deny that these are valid
notions which ought to govern our civic institutions."

"Do you deny that Noah was speaking from divine inspiration when
he pronounced his curse upon Ham and his offspring, and placed them
under the control of and in the service of Shem and Japheth?"

"I do deny it. There is no warrant for regarding Noah's curse as
divinely inspired—nor indeed as anything more than the malice of a
tyrannical old man who, having disgraced himself by his own intemperance, desires afterward to silence anyone who witnessed it. Not
only drunk, but power-drunk as well. Very often tyrants do blame
their victims, you know. In practice, the first thing anyone does, when

contemplating inflicting some cruelty or injustice upon another, is to contrive some excuse, some trumped-up proof of the victim's deserving such vile treatment."

Grace did not permit herself to glance at the veiled Mrs MacFarlane, whose husband had told her that his cruelty to her was her own damn fault; that she brought it on herself every time.

"And yet you cannot deny that the Almighty has sanctioned the institution from that day to this! And Mr Stringfellow has demonstrated this sanction beyond all argument!"

" 'Whatever is, is right'? I cannot approve so lazy and careless a line of thought as that, ma'am. And I think it a great shame that any One with the power to put a stop to Noah's tyranny has instead tolerated it—indeed, indulged it so far. Furthermore, I deny the identification of the black peoples of Egypt and Africa with the descendants of Ham. What scientific or historical justification can Mr Stringfellow show for that?"

"Oh, well, sir; as for that, it has been conclusively proven, you know," said Mr Charles Grant. "Proven by the soundest scholars and historians and—and natural philosophers."

"Nonsense; nothing of the sort has ever been proven. And the arguments set forth in support of that absurd notion are nothing more than expedient—self-serving—wishful thinking! Nor has it ever been established that the Virginia slaveholders, whose representatives are gathered here together in this churchyard, are the descendants of Shem or Japheth; for I have never yet heard even a single scion of one of these proud old families boast of his Hebrew ancestry. Quite the contrary; if I am to believe what I am told, they are all the descendants of King Charles's cavaliers! How, then, can they represent themselves simultaneously as the legitimate descendants and heirs of Shem and Japheth, pray?"

"Oh, but Mr MacFarlane—" Mrs Ambler exclaimed; ready, perhaps, to explain this paradox.

"But in any case," continued the elder Mr MacFarlane, "I return to my first assertion, that neither sin nor honor can be inherited."

"Sin cannot be inherited! But it is the inheritance of us all, sir! Surely you won't deny the doctrine of Original Sin!" cried Miss Johnstone.

"Aye, that First Sin—and such a petty little misdemeanor it was too—the raiding of an orchard! Well, ma'am; I do deny it. No evidence has ever been laid before us as to whether Adam did indeed partake in said raid; nor as to whether his wife and consort Eve may have done likewise. We have only rumors, only unsworn hearsay—mere gossip, in fact!—about the alleged event. As to whether there may have been extenuating circumstances, having to do with entrapment, by serpent, or by Eve—and mighty dishonorable on Adam's part, I think, to blame his wife for his own conduct, and entirely inconsonant with our understanding of the limitions of liability and autonomy in a *femme couverte*—well, we have likewise been shown no actual evidence. Whether the prohibition was clearly published, properly noticed, and based upon a reasonable foundation, again, I have been shown no evidence; nor on the question of whether Adam and Eve were competent to understand the prohibition, nor the consequences of transgression. If I were sitting as judge, or jury, in a court of law, then I should be obliged, on the basis of the deficiencies in the evidence actually presented—or rather, in this case, not presented—I should be obliged in all good conscience to find both Adam and Eve not guilty—or at utmost, if I were in a bloody frame of mind, I might be able to bring in that fine old Scots verdict of Not Proven."

"That is no verdict in law, sir," objected Mr Charles Grant.

"Not in English or American law, alas; and one of their sorry shortcomings too. It is a very useful alternative to the excessively simple-minded and clear-cut guilty or not guilty. Nevertheless, Mr Grant, even if we grant that shocking miscarriages of justice do sometimes occur, and that Adam and Eve might somehow have been found guilty—how, upon proceeding to the penalty phase of the trial—how can there be any possible justification for entailing the penalty incurred by these two unhappy individuals—for entailing it instead, sir, forever and ever, in perpetuity, upon individuals who not only did not commit the alleged offense, but who had not yet even been conceived at the time when the offense was allegedly committed?"

"Well! That is just rankest heresy, Mr MacFarlane!" said Miss Johnstone.

"Aye, so I have been warned. And 'rankest' too; why is heresy always credited with this quality of rankness, I wonder? And yet it is such an attractive thing, 'heresy.' Oh, but so it is, ma'am! From the Greek *haire-sis*, you know; meaning, the act of choosing; the exercise of the free will. Now, there is a dignified notion, fit for thinking men! And so I had rather maintain my heresy than collude in a miscarriage of justice, by pretending to subscribe to so absurd a doctrine as this Original Sin. It is fit, I think, for pusillanimous, toadying sycophants—but not for rational men. If that is what is required of believers, I had rather remain an infidel. I had rather be *heretic*, ma'am—than the *inheritor* of such a doctrine."

"You are very flippant, sir, with your puns and your Greek verbs—but I will pray for you," said Miss Johnstone. "Mr Stringfellow tells us there is nothing under heaven more effectual than sincere and disinterested prayer."

"Madam," he said, and made her a little bow from his chair.

"At table, still!" exclaimed the younger Mr MacFarlane, breaking in upon them all.

"Well, where have you been all morning, MacFarlane?" asked Mr Charles Grant.

"Diana, fetch another chair, and a plate," said Miss Johnstone. "We didn't expect you back already, Mr MacFarlane. I hope you left Judge Grant quite well?"

"Well enough. Is there nothing but water to drink?"

"Cleo will fetch you coffee, if you want it. And Diana, bring that dish of peas and the frizzled beef. And so, Mr MacFarlane, did you and the judge reach an agreement?"

"Oh, the judge and I always manage to agree, sooner or later," said Mr MacFarlane.

"But I mean, as to that—that extraordinary business of the offer that was made by that letter from—from the person in Washington City," said Miss Johnstone.

"That business is settled," said Mr MacFarlane, and spooned a quantity of frizzled beef onto his plate from the dish which Diana held before him.

"Settled how?" asked Miss Johnstone.

He did not reply, only gesturing toward his mouth, now full of beef and peas. But Miss Johnstone waited until he swallowed; and then she asked again: "What has been decided, Mr MacFarlane? I guess we'd all like to know."

"The extraordinary offer has been declined, Miss Johnstone, and I posted Judge Grant's reply myself as I drove past the post office just now," said Mr MacFarlane.

"Oh!" said Miss Johnstone, and Grace saw her glance fall upon Diana, who was pouring coffee for Mr MacFarlane. "But why?"

"Well; because it don't suit me to change the present arrangement," said Mr MacFarlane.

Diana and Cleo rounded the table once again, now clearing away the used plates. Here was a black hand snaking between Grace and Mrs Ambler; Diana's hand. The hand grasped the edge of Grace's messy plate (a smear of butter; some crumbs of bread; a rind of gristle), thumb uppermost. Diana's thumbnail was broken off short, and not entirely clean; the creased joint bore a half-healed scrape, whitish. The pink palm (brighter, pinker than Grace's own, she thought) turned up; and then the plate was whisked away. To be washed, somewhere, Grace supposed; perhaps in the stream near where the horses were picketed—upstream of them, she hoped.

Home, Grace thought; now it is time to go home. There was no reason to remain among these selfish complacent people—her own kin—any longer. She had failed. She had found Diana; had told where Diana was; the offer for Diana's freedom had been made. Despite Grace's painstaking careful discretion, despite her success at each step along the way, despite the lawyerly intercession of Mr Bigelow, their plan had ended in failure. Their offer had been turned down—for no better reason, perhaps, than Mr MacFarlane's resolve to rule his wife and thwart his father-in-law. What more could be done?

Grace was free to leave whenever she pleased. And Diana was not.

BUT EVEN FOR GRACE, LEAVING WAS NOT SO EASY.

"It is time I made my arrangements for returning to Philadelphia," she said over tea in the parlor on the evening after the Grants had all returned to Grantsboro in a magnificent thunderstorm, and the Mac-Farlanes to Arrochar. "The last of the portraits will be finished in a few days, and I have been away from my husband and my baby for too long."

"Oh, Mrs Pollocke! Are you tired of us so soon?" protested Miss Julia Grant. "What'll I do without you?"

"And you haven't gotten the chance yet to paint my dear little boys!" said Mrs Grimshaw.

Mrs Ambler said, "We're so disappointed that you haven't been saved. I thought Mr Stringfellow would succeed for certain."

"But how do you expect to travel, Mrs Pollocke?" asked Miss Johnstone.

"A wagon from Leesburg to Alexandria, I suppose; and from there, the cars to Philadelphia."

"A wagon! Whose wagon?"

"Don't farm wagons pass very frequently, on the Leesburg Pike to Alexandria?"

"Heavens, Mrs Pollocke, you can't just ride along on any old farm wagon, with strangers," said Miss Johnstone. "'Tisn't genteel. I'll ask Mr Boyce when he's sending a wagon next, if you're so determined to go. It would be far more convenient, certainly, if you would wait until Mrs Ambler returns home, in a fortnight, or so. Then the two of you could travel together all the way to Philadelphia. That's a far better plan."

———

IT HAPPENED THAT Mr Boyce did not intend to send a wagon to Alexandria for at least ten days, because the oats would not be ready any sooner. "So you and Mrs Ambler can go to Alexandria together then; and then ride in the cars from Washington City to Philadelphia," announced Miss Johnstone, upon finding Grace alone in the tearoom after breakfast the next morning. "I don't know of any better plan, Mrs Pollocke; and I'd advise you to possess your soul in patience until then. Unless you feel a repugnance to patience, on account of it being one of the *Christian* virtues."

Grace chose not to take this up.

Miss Johnstone seemed determined to goad her to speech, however, for she now said, "And when you do go north again, Mrs Pollocke, you must be sure to tell the truth about us. You've seen the kindness and indulgence our negroes are treated to here, and never the slightest hint of harshness or cruelty."

"It is true," said Grace slowly, "that I have never seen a negro struck, whipped, beaten, starved, ill-clothed. But I have seen families torn apart, a husband sold away from his wife and his child. And my conviction remains unshaken that the institution itself is fundamentally unjust, because it denies to humans that greatest treasure, liberty—the right to seek to live as they think best—the exercise of the free and individual human will—"

"Oh, pshaw!" interrupted Miss Johnstone.

But Grace went on: "Even without harsh excesses, without overt cruelty, which—as you say—I have not witnessed here, the practice is abhorrent. It is not because excesses and abuses may occur at some times or places—but in the very nature of the institution itself."

"Now, that is completely unreasonable, Mrs Pollocke. You might as well say that the institution of marriage is wicked, on the grounds that a few husbands mistreat their wives. I throw up my hands. You see how enlightened and gentle we are; you see how well our negroes are looked after, here, from infancy to their useless old age—and still you want us to cast them out to fend for themselves, all in the name of 'liberty'—as your starving laborers and naked children are, in England—"

"I am not from England," said Grace.

"Scotland, then; worse still. I throw up my hands. Mr Stringfellow warned me about you."

Did he! thought Grace. But she would not give Miss Johnstone the satisfaction of biting this gaudy bait.

"Don't you want to know what he said?" demanded Miss Johnstone.

"No, indeed, ma'am. Mr Stringfellow's views weigh very little with me," said Grace.

"Well, I think you should know. He said he hoped we would not regret taking up a viper into the bosom of our family."

FROM THE REVIVAL, Mrs MacFarlane had gone home to Arrochar with her husband, her father-in-law, and her maid Diana; and there, within a week of her return, she suffered a miscarriage.

"I tried to convince her to stay here, didn't I?" said Miss Johnstone, throwing down the letter which brought this news. "It wouldn't have happened if she'd stayed here. I always say what an unhealthy situation it is at Arrochar! Well, don't I?"

"Of course you do, Aunt Bella," said Mrs Ambler, mopping her red nose with a handkerchief, for she had a heavy cold. "Oh, poor Clara! Again! Who'll go to her? I'd go myself, if it wasn't for the chance of passing her this dreadful cold."

"And I can't go," said Miss Johnstone. "Not while your father's doing so poorly again."

"I could go," said Mrs Grimshaw, "but I don't think I'd best take my boys there just now, as Clara will be needing peace and quiet. I guess I could leave my boys here with you?"

"Who would look after them here? They can't be left here, Charlotte," said Miss Johnstone.

"I could go," said Miss Grant.

"No, you can't, Julia; it should be a married woman," said Miss Johnstone.

"You're not married yourself, Aunt Bella," pointed out Miss Grant.

"Heavens, I'm old enough, though," said Miss Johnstone. "I'm not a girl. I wonder if Mrs Pollocke is willing to make herself useful, since time is hanging so heavy on her hands. If you, Mrs Pollocke, would take charge of the little boys, Mrs Grimshaw could go and nurse her sister at Arrochar."

"Suppose I went instead to Arrochar, to nurse Mrs MacFarlane myself," said Grace, who wanted nothing to do with Mrs Grimshaw's little boys. "I am an experienced nurse."

And despite the objections of various members of the family on the ground that she was no kin, it was Grace who went to Arrochar.

ARROCHAR WAS A LARGE new white house in the Greek style, with a high portico across its front, and absurdly slender columns with plain Doric capitals. The broad steps underfoot were limestone, but Grace tapped one of the columns in passing, and found it only whitewashed timber.

Grace followed Diana upstairs, and there found Mrs MacFarlane abed in her room.

"I swow, if it isn't Mrs Pollocke! My sisters couldn't none of them be bothered, I guess?" The bruises and cuts on Mrs MacFarlane's mouth had all but healed and, though she looked sallow and miserable as expected, no fresh injuries were apparent. "My husband was off pretty quick too, in my time of sickness and tribulation. I begged him to stay; but no, off he went, just as though his business in Leesburg couldn't wait, not even for a day or two! And there's no knowing when he might be disposed to come home again. So here I am, all alone in my suffering, the only white lady on the place, surrounded by black faces on every side, except for my father-in-law over there in the old house, and certainly no comfort to be expected from him."

While Mrs MacFarlane aired her grievances, Grace opened the windows, for the room needed airing too. She was relieved that the younger Mr MacFarlane had absented himself, for her only misgiving about coming to Arrochar had been her dislike of him. This room faced south, the windows overlooking a pond just below the house, apparently man-made, for its banks had a raw new look; there were no rushes growing around its margins, no willows or cottonwoods, and the further shore was curiously straight and narrow: an earthen dam, in fact. How many hours of slave labor had been required to make that, Grace wondered; and why? Did Mr MacFarlane aspire to make a park, a country gentleman's estate, of his farm? Another house—older, smaller, brick-built—stood off to the west, in a grove of locust trees. And to the east the slave cabins could just be seen, their rough garden plots outlined by palings, beehives nearby, along a ribbon of trees that must mark a streambed.

"Fever? No, I don't think so—I don't feel 'specially feverish, anyhow—" said Mrs MacFarlane, putting her palm to her own forehead, in response to Grace's inquiry. "Here, feel for yourself. What do you think? No; but I'm weak as a kitten; look, I can scarce so much as lift my arm. I've lost a dreadful lot of blood this time, more than before, but Dr Woodward said it was nothing out of the way, though I've suffered dreadfully," she said, her lip trembling now, and tears welling up in her eyes. "Oh, Mrs Pollocke, it's so unfair! Why should I be punished so? I know my aunt thinks it must be the judgment of the Almighty, for some sin of mine, or my husband's—well, yes, she has said so—and she's recommended that I examine my conscience, though I don't see how I'm to examine Mr MacFarlane's for him. But Dr Woodward says it's just a matter of—of—circumstance, and nothing to do with—sin."

She took the fresh handkerchief which Grace offered, her lament and her tears in full spate: "And no one even sends to inquire as to how I do!—Oh, well, yes, my father-in-law has sent across—but I think he might call himself, don't you? It's not five minutes' walk from his house across to here. I think he might call."

Grace hinted that natural feelings of delicacy might have prevented his calling, under the unhappy circumstances.

"Feelings of delicacy? Him? Do you think so? Well . . . I guess. But he's never shown me much courtesy or consideration, and that's the mark of a true gentleman, don't you think? Oh, no; it's just that I've never quite felt that he held me in very high regard. A lady can always tell when a gentleman holds her in high regard, don't you think? I guess he'd be kinder to me if there was any grandchildren . . . ," she choked out, and the freshet of tears renewed itself.

Grace smoothed her hair back from her forehead, giving comfort: and Mrs MacFarlane's sobs subsided a little. "This has nearly healed," said Grace, letting her fingertips graze over the cut lip. Mrs MacFarlane's fingers flew to her lip too, and her glance met Grace's. A moment passed; she volunteered nothing; but Grace thought she read entreaty there—but entreating what? Was it invitation: Ask me! Or was it fear: Don't ask me! Which was it? Grace chose the bolder course. She said, "Have you any other injuries? That is a thing your nurse ought to know."

Mrs MacFarlane looked away, out the window, and Grace could see the rise and fall of her rapid shallow breaths. Presently, still looking out, she whispered, "It's nothing to do with that. With him."

Grace waited; and just as it seemed that Mrs MacFarlane might speak again, they were interrupted by Diana, who entered carrying a large tray.

"What a deal of food!" exclaimed Mrs MacFarlane. "How on earth am I to eat all that? Oh, for Mrs Pollocke too. Well, I hope her appetite's better than mine."

But it seemed to Grace, as they both dined off the tray, that nothing was wrong with Mrs MacFarlane's appetite.

And when Diana returned a short time later to remove the tray, she brought a note. "What's this?" said Mrs MacFarlane. "From my father-in-law! Let's see . . . hm! He says he's very sorry, and hopes I'm improving. Well, I guess he could call and see for himself, couldn't he? Oh, he brought this himself? But he wouldn't be troubled to walk upstairs, I guess? Well, if he comes again, Diana, tell him he can walk upstairs, at least. And I want my book. Oh, here it is. But the print only swims before my eyes, and my head aches so! Besides, I'm far too fretful to read. I'd take it most kindly, if only someone would read to me. . . ."

Grace took this broad hint. Mrs MacFarlane's bookmark was about midway through *The Heart of Midlothian*, to the chapters in which Jeanie Deans takes leave of her betrothed and sets out to walk from Edinburgh to London, there to seek a pardon for her poor sister, sentenced to hang for infanticide. Grace read aloud for about half an hour. " 'With a strong heart, and a frame patient of fatigue, Jeanie Deans, travelling at the rate of twenty miles a day, and sometimes farther, traversed the southern part of Scotland, and advanced as far as Durham,' " she was reading, when a small snore made her look up, and she saw that Mrs MacFarlane's eyes had fallen closed and her mouth open.

Diana had been listening too, from her station near the door. "Is that true, ma'am, that story?" she asked.

"Oh, it is only a novel—but it is supposed to have been based upon a true incident, if memory serves; about a real woman," said Grace, and she turned back to the author's introduction and skimmed through it. "Aye; Helen Walker was her name, or so Sir Walter claims here, in his roundabout way. But she never would talk about the incident, he says, for 'the natural dignity of her character, and a high sense of family respectability, made her so indissolubly connect her sister's disgrace with her own exertions, that none of her neighbours durst ever question her upon the subject.' And here he says that 'Helen Walker died about the end of the year 1791, and her remains are interred in the churchyard of her native parish of Irongray . . . distinguished for her undaunted love of virtue . . . lived and died in poverty, if not want.' Well, that much has the ring of truth, surely."

LEAVING DIANA TO sit with the sleeping Mrs MacFarlane, Grace went out for her walk and, not quite by accident, made a circuit that passed near the slave quarters. The cabins stood all in a row above the steep bank of a creek, and the little gardens outside the cabins were well tended and neat. The bees hummed in the locusts, whose sweet blossoms scented the afternoon sunshine, but there was no other sound, and the little settlement felt oddly deserted. During the days at Grantsboro while the laborers were in the fields, the slave quarters teemed nevertheless with old folks and children; but not here. Of course, she ought not to expect to see any elderly unproductive slaves at Arrochar—because Mr MacFarlane was sharp enough not to lease any. But where the entire slave force was in its young and lusty prime, ought not there to be children?

Upstream, a little further along the footpath, Grace came upon another cabin in a clearing on the opposite bank of the creek. The cabin was nearly concealed by a tall blooming hedge, a rampant thicket growing as tall as the eaves, and bearing spidery lily-like orange flowers. Grace stopped to look, and after a moment she became aware that a stocky woman, very old and very black, her head wrapped in a dark red turban, was standing in the shadowy doorway of the cabin and watching her in return. "Hello," called Grace, and nodded to her, but the woman only blinked. She was knitting as she stood, her hands moving automatically; no need to watch what she did.

"What is your flowering hedge, growing up so high?" Grace called, for it seemed familiar, though she could not remember where she had seen it before.

The old woman gave no sign of having understood Grace's words. Her hands did not falter. Perhaps deaf, thought Grace; or perhaps not. There had been a period in Grace's childhood when she had refrained from speaking for more than a year. And why? Just because she had not felt like it, then. It had seemed unworth the trouble. There was nothing she had wanted to say to anyone, nor to hear from anyone.

A log lay across the creek, a narrow footbridge, its top surface worn. Durst I? thought Grace—amused that the old word came to mind. Aye, she durst; and she crossed, carefully, for the wood was polished smooth, treacherous under her leather soles. Still the inscrutable old woman watched her, knitting, silent. Grace approached the tall blooming thicket. Now, close, she could see that the flowers, offered in clusters, were not orange; they were in fact crimson, with egg-yolk-yellow edges, so that from a distance they seemed to blend to orange in the eye. They had very long curved stamens arching outward from the center, as long and curved as an elephant's eyelashes. The lacy foliage was a pleasing bluish green, pealike, acacialike; and there were long sharp spines disposed here and there along the stems. It was very like the foliage of the gum arabic tree. A few of the blooms, darkened and spent, had already set seed, and Grace could see that they made long flat pods, like large pea pods. Someone had manured the ground around the base of these shrubs; someone cherished them, cultivated them. Was it a food plant, then? She found a large seedpod in which the seeds had plumped, and picked it. She peeled open the sticky pod, to expose the peas inside, still green and soft.

Turning, she found the old woman watching her intently. "Good to eat?" Grace asked, and pantomimed placing them in her mouth.

But what was that gleam that flashed in the old woman's black eyes (the whites not white at all, but yellow, jaundiced), as she mustered a voice (long unused, apparently), to croak, "Oh, yes, ma'am, Barbados flower beans good, good to eat, mm-mm!"

Are they indeed? Eat them yourself, then, thought Grace, and she held them out to the old woman, who dropped her knitting into the pocket of her apron and took them. And of the seven seeds in the pod, the old woman ate one. She made an exaggerated face of delight, sounds and show of deliciousness; and handed the other six seeds back to Grace, nodding and smiling graciously.

What a sudden eagerness there, thought Grace. Behind the show of graciousness was something else; something that might be malice. Then Grace was thinking of India, seeing the luxuriant sunlight there, and before her mind's eye there came an image of the ornament on Krishna's turban: Krishna Chura. Ah! And now she knew; she remembered from India this beautiful shrub—and its name, one of its several Indian names: Krishna Chura, for the flower's resemblance to Krishna's turban ornament. Its other names came back to her too: *ratnagundhi; guletura; shankasura.* And with the names, there came also the knowledge that it was most assuredly not good to eat; not unless by young women who did not want to remain pregnant.

Feeling absurdly like a girl in a fairy tale, Grace smiled, shook her head no; and indicated that the old woman should keep the seeds for herself. And then she passed on, turning up toward the big white house.

You must not leap to conclusions, she reminded herself.

"OH, THAT OLD OBEAH woman from Jamaica or Barbados or somewhere? Such a troublemaker!" said Mrs MacFarlane. "I swan, she gives me the shivers—why, look at my arm! The thought of her is enough to make the hairs rise up on end! But my father-in-law insists on letting her stay there in that old cob cabin, and I don't think he charges her more than a few dollars' rent, and since that piece of land belongs to him alone, there's not a thing that can be done to make her go away."

Diana carried in the tea, and Grace poured it out for Mrs MacFarlane, who had been complaining of feeling sometimes very hot. Grace had felt her forehead again, but found it still cool. "These heated spells are not unexpected, after the loss you have suffered, I believe," she said. "And I am sure there is no fever. But perhaps it would be best if I slept in your room tonight, in case assistance is wanted beyond what Diana can provide."

"Oh, I'd take that very kindly of you, Mrs Pollocke, and I'd sleep so much easier, knowing you was right here with me. You hear that, Diana? You move your mat on out to the hall and sleep out there tonight, and make up a bed for Mrs Pollocke in here with me."

At early candle-lighting, there came from outside Mrs MacFarlane's still-open window a rough honking, as though a gigantic hoarse goose were dying on the pond below. Then another; and then a piercing wail went up. To Grace, it was a delight, and entirely unexpected: that familiar powerful night music!

"Preserve us!" said Mrs MacFarlane. "I think he might spare me that, at least!"

Grace looked out. On the far edge of the pond, she could just make out the silhouette of a bagpiper standing at one end of the dam, apparently serenading the crescent moon with its attendant star slipping down the western steep of the dark sky. The piper was the elder Mr MacFarlane; she recognised the profile of his head, and his deep barrel chest, expanded now to fill the pipes. He played a melodic phrase, then played it again. A third time.

Of course his pipes were out of tune; pipes always are. He played for a few moments to awaken the dense thin wood of the conical-bore chanter, to awaken the thicker turned wood of the three tall drones resting against his left shoulder, and to settle the reeds inside them to their work. Four reeds in all: a double reed inside the chanter, and three single long tongue-shaped reeds, one inside each of the three drones. And as the wood fibers awakened, and the reed fibers settled to their work, vibrating to the warm damp air blown through them— yet embraced outside by the cool damp evening air rising off the black surface of the pond—the sound changed, each moment. The pitches, the timbre—the voice of the instrument soon opened, warmed—and then it was time to tune.

While holding a steady note on the chanter, Mr MacFarlane reached up to the two inside drones and touched their tops, to silence them. Now only one drone sounded alongside the steady note he played on the chanter. He tuned that drone, shortening it to raise its pitch—

until the two pitches were exactly matched. One at a time, then, he quickly restarted and tuned each of the other two drones, until all was tuned—or very nearly tuned.

It still was not exactly true . . . but good enough, it seemed; or perhaps his ear was not very exacting, not as exacting as Grace's, whose ear had been trained by hearing *raga* all through the velvety nights of her Indian childhood.

He played a few phrases, the main notes heavily embellished by a certain rapid ornament of the kind much esteemed by pipers, perhaps for its rhythmic thrumming thrill. Then he launched at last into the long opening phrase of a slow march—no; a stately walk; a considered and dignified processional—from that old-fashioned traditional body of pipe music known as *piobaireachd*.

"Now, isn't that more than any mortal can be expected to bear?" said Mrs MacFarlane. "I'd rather hear cats squalling. He does it most every night, seems like, and even when I'm well, it grates painfully on my nerves. I've complained more than once, but that don't do much good, not for long. Still, I don't think I should have to put up with it now, not in my condition."

What was the tune he was playing? It was familiar, but Grace couldn't think of its name. She had always liked the sound of pipes, and had heard a great deal of them. But some people, she knew, could not bear the sound of piping; could not hear the music that was in it. The fascinating and exhilarating play of the melody against the background of the fixed drones was, to some, an excruciating assault by various harsh dissonances, relieved only occasionally by an all-too-brief assonance. "Well, it is not an easy, pretty sound, I grant you," Grace said. "Shall I go down and try to persuade your father-in-law to abbreviate his concert, for once?"

She went downstairs, out into the cool evening.

He was stalking slowly back and forth across the dam as he played. Grace waited in darkness at the west end for his return. He stopped a few yards away from her, and stood stock-still there, to deliver the last two of the prescribed variations: the *crunluath*, and then the *crunluath* doubling. He was playing them to her, Grace felt; for her. Exultant, always, these ultimate movements; triumphant. She could feel the mosquitoes settling upon her face and neck, and brushed them away, repeatedly. Surely they were tormenting him too? But he stood like a pillar of salt, delivering now, at the end, the first long phrase once more, finishing as he had begun; but this time that long phrase was a summing-up of the entire composition, enriched now by all its developments, explorations, and complexities.

Gradually there welled up in Grace some words in Gaelic, from very far away, very long ago; surely the name of this tune?

Mr MacFarlane played the last falling notes, valedictory, drawn out—and then abruptly let off the pressure from the bag. Silence fell: heavy and soft as a sack of flour dropped and split on a stone floor. He removed the mouthpiece from between his lips and made her a little bow.

"*Is fhada mar so tha sinn?*" asked Grace, for that was the phrase which had come into her head as she listened.

" 'Too Long in This Condition'?" he said. "No, Mrs Pollocke, not quite; but you are very nearly right. We MacFarlanes play our own MacFarlane version, you know; and it is very like 'Too Long in This Condition.' Everyone else calls our version 'The MacFarlanes' Gathering'—for that is just what it is: our gathering tune, our *cruinneachadh*. But its true name is *Thogail nam Bo theid sinn*—'To Lift the Cows We Shall Go'—the cattle of our neighbors, of course; what else would the moonlight be for? What else would the neighbors, and their cows, be for? But they are very similar, the two tunes. Have you indeed come out just to admire my piping? Somehow I doubt it."

"I do admire your piping," said Grace. "But that is not why I have come out. Your daughter-in-law is unwell and exhausted, and needs nothing so much as to sleep. So I have come out to ask if you will be so kind as to forbear, just for this evening?"

"Certainly. I am very sorry; please convey her my apology." He slung the pipes under his arm and turned to walk with her back up to the house, saying, "In any case, the mosquitoes are a torment at this season. I did warn my son about digging the pond so very near to the house, but he maintains stoutly that they are no more numerous than ever they were. It is very good of you, Mrs Pollocke, to come and nurse my daughter-in-law."

"It would mean a great deal to her, sir, if you were to call upon her tomorrow morning, and come upstairs to ask her how she does."

"Would it? I did not like to intrude. But if you tell me that it will do her good. . . well, I will come, then."

How could this likable man be the father of his loathsome son? As they walked up toward the white house in darkness, Grace said, "I have been thinking, sir, about some of your remarks at the revival meeting."

"Have you? I did air some unconventional views. Was it anything in particular?"

"Well, yes: in particular, your repudiation of the doctrine of Original Sin. You said, I think, that neither sin nor its punishment can be inherited."

"Aye; that neither disgrace nor honor can be inherited. I think that we are answerable in law and in conscience for only our own conduct, not for that of others, even if those others are our ancestors. I was a little heated, when I spoke, but I do maintain the justice of the position. It is not a popular view, however, here in Virginia."

"But sir, what of the gains—the profits or proceeds gained by wrongdoing? Those gains may be passed along to the next generation in the form of money, is it not so?"

"It is so, indisputably."

"But not the disgrace attached to the methods of acquiring that money?"

"Now, that is a very interesting question, Mrs Pollocke. Is there such a thing as tainted money—dirty money? And if so, what is to be done with it?"

"Are the inheritors of such money bound to make reparations, amends?"

"And if those who were originally wronged, to whom the debt is owed, can no longer be found—to whom, then, ought reparation be made?" he said.

"Well, to the descendants of the wronged ones, perhaps?" Grace proposed.

"But they themselves were not wronged; why should they receive any amends, for a wrong which they did not suffer? Is grievance to be considered any more heritable than disgrace, or honor?"

"And if there is no money—if it has all been lost or squandered—

what then? Is the debt extinguished? Or is something else due? An apology, even? And if I receive payment for my labor here—for the paintings I have made—with money which is wrung from the sweat of slaves, am I defiled too, by receiving that tainted money? Do I join thereby in the robbing of those slaves?"

"Ah—but *have* you been paid?" he asked, stopping at the foot of the limestone stairs. "No; I thought not. And I shall be most surprised, Mrs Pollocke, if your tender scruples confront that problem of conscience at any early day. I hope it will cause no material inconvenience to you if any sums due you should be delayed—perhaps indefinitely."

DESPITE THE DISCOMFORT of the cot which had been set up for her in Mrs MacFarlane's bedroom, Grace had nearly dropped off to sleep, when Mrs MacFarlane's voice out of the darkness jolted her: "For better or for worse. Richer or poorer. In sickness and in health. That's the vow I took, didn't I? Little did I know."

"Little do any of us know," Grace said patiently, rolling over and addressing the shadowy ceiling. "None of us, when we marry, truly anticipates the worse; the poverty; the sickness." For some patients, laudanum was at first stimulating, and only later soporific; perhaps Mrs MacFarlane's bedtime dose had taken her this way.

"I guess not. But somehow I expected it'd be like when he was courting me—only better! A house of my own, and an end to my aunt's interfering ways, and him bringing me pretty presents, and begging for kisses, just like he did then! Well, wasn't I in for a rude shock! But I don't know that I was any more foolish than most girls."

On this question Grace offered no comment.

Presently Mrs MacFarlane said, "Sometimes I think he only married me for the sake of tightening his hold over Papa. He'd already lent Papa money—oh, years ago—even before he ever started coming to court me. But I thought he wouldn't be so pressing about it, after we was married."

Grace said, "Money is a remarkably complicated thing."

"If Diana was sold, Papa could maybe even pay off that note at last, though it's got a tremendous high interest rate, I guess. So why don't my husband allow it? I don't understand it. It's as though he don't even want Papa to pay it off! But it's all between him and Papa, and it's not my fault, is it?"

"No, it's not your fault."

"He gets so wrathy—over nothing at all, sometimes! And I do my best to calm him—but—but it only makes him wrathier. Do you find me terribly provoking, yourself, Mrs Pollocke?" Fortunately she did not pause for a reply, speaking quite rapidly now: "He says I provoke him past all bearing, and that I've got only myself to blame if I make him lose his temper."

"That cannot be right," said Grace. "We are each of us responsible for governing our own temper. No one can do it for us."

But Mrs MacFarlane seemed not to hear. "Examine my conscience— that's my aunt's only advice! Examine my conscience! Well, she's never been married, has she? What could she know about it? And my sisters . . ."

Silence fell, and Grace hoped that Mrs MacFarlane had fallen asleep. But no; after a few minutes, there came several smothered sobs, and a great sniff; and Mrs MacFarlane said, "I remember when I was a girl, and I used to pity the young widows. Pitied them! And now . . . now—" For a moment she choked on a sob, but then blurted, "Oh, heaven help me, I know very well what my great sin is, that's caused my five miscarriages! I used to pity those young widows, didn't I? But now, oh, how I wish I was one! Oh, God forgive me! But I do! Like now, when he's away—I imagine that his horse would run away with him, I imagine that his shay would overturn and throw him out! Or that he'd fight a duel, and . . . be shot. And everyone would feel so sorry for me, in my mourning, just like I used to! But I can't see no other way out! And it's all my own fault! And that's my great sin, that's why I can't have babies: it's my wicked wishing, my hoping that he'd die!"

"No, dear, that is not so," said Grace. "Calm yourself, do try. Thoughts cannot cause miscarriages. Not even the wickedest thoughts, far more wicked than your wish to be free of your husband, can do that. If it were so, there would be far fewer babies in the world."

"And my aunt suspecting me all along, and Dr Woodward don't know, nobody knows except you! There, I've said it: I wish he was dead, the wicked sinner that I am. And I don't see no other way out of my misery."

"There are other ways out," said Grace. "You are not the only wife to have found that she cannot live with her husband. In cases of—of cruelty, such as you have suffered, wives have sometimes found it necessary to obtain a separation, an allowance to live by themselves. A separate maintenance. A petition; an agreement. Their brothers or their fathers intercede, insist upon it. Lawyers are consulted. It can be done."

"Not my father, or my brothers. They must see the bruises! But Charley wouldn't dare interfere, and James hardly ever comes here. Everyone pretends there's nothing wrong."

"Of course they do. You have been pretending that yourself."

"They all pretend they don't know. Where am I to turn? You're the only one who's ever asked me—you, Mrs Pollocke, a stranger!"

"Tell them the truth. Ask them to help you."

"I couldn't. My husband would never agree to a separation. Never. He'd kill me first. He'd kill me even for asking."

"This—this most recent miscarriage; was it—did he—"

"No. He hasn't raised his hand against me since—well, down at the revival."

"But the ones before this?"

Mrs MacFarlane did not answer.

"NO, NO!" CRIED OUT Mrs MacFarlane during the night. "Oh, no! Too late!" Her words were oddly distinct up to this point, but then her cries became inarticulate. Grace rose from her cot and felt her way across the room in the darkness. She laid her hands on Mrs MacFarlane's shoulders and felt that her arms and legs were twitching, thrashing, though she lay with her head on her pillow.

"A dream, a dream, my dear," she said, quite loudly, to pierce Mrs MacFarlane's bad sleep; and with one hand she felt across the top of the bedside table, feeling for a packet of lucifers.

But Mrs MacFarlane's dream had a strong grip on her. "No, no!" she cried out again. "So much blood! Too much blood!"

"Wake up! Clara! Clara, wake up!" cried Grace sharply, shaking her, but she moaned, and went limp, and did not wake up. It's that laudanum at bedtime, thought Grace. Might she really be bleeding? Might she be hemorrhaging, there in her bed, in the dark? Grace felt the mattress around Mrs MacFarlane's hips, shoved her hand under the heavy flesh to feel the sheets for a sticky wetness. No, surely not. Well, perhaps just a little dampness, but nothing more than perspiration . . . surely? Grace went to the door; Diana's bed was on the hall floor just outside, in case she was wanted during the night. The hall was dark too, but Grace could make out the shape of the straw mattress laid down opposite. It had a still quiet look, an air of emptiness; no sleeping breathing body seemed to occupy it; where was Diana? "Diana?" she called out, without much conviction. "Diana, are you there? I need a light—bring a light, will you?" Did anyone hear? Would she wake the household? Ought she to wake the household?

In her bed, Mrs MacFarlane groaned again, and then cried out, quite horribly.

"Diana!" shouted Grace. "Someone! Bring a light, this instant!" and she hastened to Mrs MacFarlane's bedside, just in time to catch her as she heaved violently over. "Clara! Clara! Wake up!" Grace cried sharply, and thought that she could feel the tone of the body under her hands start to change, and perhaps her eyes were open now? But did she see from those eyes? Oh, for a light!

And then someone came in at the door, bringing a light—a candle, in a brass candlestick. Grace laid her cool hand against Mrs MacFarlane's cheek, hoping to rouse her more thoroughly; and fumbled at the ribbon drawstring of her nightdress, trying to loosen it so that the night air upon her neck and chest might recall her. "Bring that light here," she said sharply; and the light approached. Grace glanced back over her shoulder—

But this is not Diana.

Not just chiaroscuro, but murkier than that: tenebroso. That's how Grace would paint it: In the style of Caravaggio, yet more dramatic still—the light more dazzling, the shadows entirely black—and the flame at the very center of the composition, before the very face, obscuring the face entirely. In the center burns a brilliant tongue of flame, so brilliant as to eradicate the face behind, a black blankness, as nonexistent as the stars behind the midday sun. Only the edge of the cap at the perimeter can be faintly discerned, like a dim halo. No matter how Grace moves aside to see the face behind the flame, the holder of the candle moves it too, so that the brilliant flame remains between their two faces. Some light is cast down over the arm, and over the hand which holds out the candlestick at arm's length, well away from the face—but only a little, for the wide bobeche shades it. The arm wears a darkish linsey-woolsey uncuffed sleeve, bottle-green perhaps; the wrist is strong and rectangular, the color of night on top, pale dawn underneath, with dark creases; and Grace can make out dark fingers wrapped around the brass candlestick. And she can almost see—can be nearly certain—that on the third finger there is a gold ring set with a tremendous rectangular green stone.

The light is set down upon the small table at bedside. The bringer of the light turns away into darkness and silently leaves the room.

"Ah . . . ," moaned Mrs MacFarlane; and then she awakened quite suddenly, and came to herself. "What? I'm bleeding. Oh, Mrs Pollocke, it's you. Am I bleeding? I dreamt there was blood all over my bed."

"No, no, it was only a bad dream," said Grace, holding the candle close over the bed to inspect it. "Look; there is only a little dampness of perspiration, which is quite to be expected, but no blood to speak of. Only a dream, Mrs MacFarlane. Now you must just rest, and go back to sleep."

"Do stay here with me, Mrs Pollocke," said Mrs MacFarlane. "You'll stay, won't you? Oh, it was terrible, I was so scared."

"Of course I will stay," said Grace. "I have been here all night. But there is nothing to fear."

Soon Mrs MacFarlane fell asleep again; that laudanum at bedtime was perhaps a boon after all. But Grace lay awake for a long time, considering and wondering about what she had seen—or had imagined she had seen (a tremendous, a memorable emerald ring); and what was missing (Diana from her bed); and what the coming daylight might reveal.

"WELL, WHERE'S MY DIANA? I've rang for her three times now!" demanded Mrs MacFarlane in the morning, as Grace drew back her bedroom curtains. "I'm feeling a little stronger than yesterday, but I'm awful thirsty, and she knows I always want my tea first thing, soon as I wake up in the morning. Where could she have gotten to? Mrs Pollocke, won't you kindly send down and find out why she hasn't brung up my breakfast?"

Grace, who had already been downstairs, and outside, and through the dairy and smokehouse and icehouse and barns and stable and woodshed and washhouse, knew very well that Diana was not in the kitchen, nor anywhere else about the place. But she went down to the kitchen and asked the cook to take up Mrs MacFarlane's breakfast. "And leave my stove?" objected the cook. "Where's Dinah when she's wanted?" she grumbled; but she did as Grace requested.

Nor was Diana to be found when Mrs MacFarlane had finished her breakfast and wanted her hair combed and a fresh nightdress. A boy was sent down to the cabins to ask for her there; to the river; someone checked to see if she had drowned in the pond; or was sleeping in the hayloft; or shirking about the granary; or filching eggs from the henhouse; or holed up in the obeah woman's cabin.

But Diana was not to be found; and when questions actually were asked, no one could recall having seen her since last night.

"Can you remember when you saw her last, Mrs Pollocke?"

"I think it was last night, just at bedtime," said Grace, with perfect truth; but dreading that someone might ask if it was Diana who had brought the light, during the night. But no one did think to ask that.

AT LAST, MRS MACFARLANE reached the inescapable conclusion: "Run off! Run off! But I can hardly think it, not of my Diana! Why, I've had her ever since I was just a girl! I practically brought her up myself, ever since she was just a little pickaninny, my little negro doll baby! Do you suppose she might have overheard a whisper about that offer that was made for her? If she heard about that, it might have gave her ideas, might have made her discontented enough to—oh, run off to the Quakers. Oh, my husband will be so angry! Well, she can't have gotten far, though, can she? Not just since last night. She's probably asleep under a tree somewhere. Or, or—gone off to meet some boy, do you guess, Mrs Pollocke? I never thought she was a wicked girl, or not more wicked than most, but she is getting to be that age, now. . . . Oh, what should I do? And my husband away at Leesburg, so inconvenient! My father-in-law? Well, I guess so, Mrs Pollocke, I guess I'd better ask him what I should do, though he will gloat so. Will you go and ask him, Mrs Pollocke, since I'm not allowed to get up yet?"

So Grace went and reported to the elder Mr MacFarlane that Diana could not be found.

"Good for Diana," said Mr MacFarlane. "I always suspected her of pluck. But surely my daughter-in-law does not expect me to get up a search party, or anything of that sort?"

"No, sir, I daresay she does not. She only asks your advice."

"Has she sent word to her husband?"

"Not yet."

"Or to her father? Who pretends to own the individual in question, after all?"

"BUT I CAN'T FIGURE out just exactly how to get started, though," said Mrs MacFarlane, when Grace, reluctantly, and with qualms of conscience, had gathered pen, ink, paper, and lap desk for her, and placed them all within her reach. "I shouldn't have to be bothered with this sort of business in my condition, and it's awful ungrateful of her to run off now, just when I'm so poorly and so miserable. And my husband will be so angry! Sometimes it's all just too much to bear!" And she burst into tears; and let fall the pen, smearing ink on the bedsheet, none too clean to begin with. "Oh, Mrs Pollocke, won't you write the letters for me? I'm helpless as a kitten this morning, and now I'm all but blinded by this headache."

Grace consulted her conscience. But no; that she could not do; she would not. "I am very sorry, Mrs MacFarlane," said Grace, "but I cannot comply. It is a thing you ought not to ask of me. I would much prefer that Diana were free—Diana and all the others; and if she has indeed mustered the courage and the resolve to take her own freedom, then in all good conscience I may do nothing that might aid in her recapture, not even though you ask it of me. I am afraid I must leave you to write your own letters."

"You won't help me, when I ask it? You won't! Well, I swow! I never guessed anyone would be so disobliging! I guess you might as well go straight back to Grantsboro, Mrs Pollocke, if that's the kind of tender care and nursing I'm to expect from you in my hour of need. My aunt warned me about false friends. Ain't that just like a abolitionist! Here, give me that pen. Though it kill me, with my last dying gasp, I'll do my duty." She dipped the pen again, and began furiously scratching away at her paper. "What's all that hallooing out there? Won't you just lean out the window and tell them to be quiet, Mrs Pollocke—always assuming it don't offend your tender principles, of course?"

Indeed, what was that galloping commotion in the drive before the house? It was a boy on horseback, a half-grown slave boy whom Grace recognised from Grantsboro, just pulling up a lathered blowing horse and leaping to the ground, brandishing a paper, a letter. Within moments, his news was known; and the new catastrophe utterly swamped the minor calamity of Diana's disappearance: Just after dinner, the previous evening, Judge Grant had been suddenly taken ill—suddenly, excruciatingly ill—the most severe attack ever—and during the night, he had—had—actually—died!

Had passed on to his eternal reward, as Miss Johnstone's letter put it.

"INEVER SAW HIM TOOK SO, NEVER," SAID MISS JOHNSTONE. "That sudden, and that severe. He had I don't know how much laudanum—but it wouldn't stay down, not for long, so I guess it can't have done him much good. All the gum arabic in the house went the same way, and now there's none left, just when it's needed. Gallons of soda water too, and not all of it by mouth, if I understand Dr Woodward aright. All you children had better take your marshmallow root every morning if you don't want to suffer like your father did. Dr Woodward says it runs in families, especially father to son. High living don't help, of course—bibulous living, such as so many young men of even the best families are liable to—"

"Oh, but Aunt, I've read that the stone is thought to be a consequence of ill-made blood, from badly conducted digestion," said Miss Grant.

"Nothing so disorders the digestion as bibulous living and intemperate habits," declared Miss Johnstone. "Now, I have plenty of spirits of ammonia, and Mr Boyce says he'll bring up some turpentine—but where will I get gum arabic?"

"I can furnish gum arabic, Miss Johnstone," said Grace. "And turpentine too, for that matter."

"There, thank you, Mrs Pollocke," said Miss Grant. "But what for, Aunt?"

"Well, just look at my black silk," said Miss Johnstone, holding up a mourning dress whose enormous puffed and padded sleeves marked it as ten years out of fashion. She sternly shook it. "It's a disgrace, though I'm sure I paid a tremendous sum for the stuff when your mother died, far more than I could easily afford at the time, and I've had very little wear out of it."

"Oh, Aunt, those sleeves!" exclaimed Mrs Pratt.

"Never mind the sleeves; look at the stuff. Here, at the cuff, and the neckline; and the gathers along the waist—all fraying, and falling to shreds. Black always is the worst. I paid a very considerable price for it, and on the bolt the silk was heavy and thick, but look at it now: it's just the nature of blackness, you see. Here's an excellent demonstration by which you might profit, Mrs Pollocke—a demonstration that blackness is inferior in every species—in the silkworm as in the man."

"The greedy heart of the dyer may be at fault," said Grace tactfully, "but I think we must exonerate the silkworm. All silk begins white or a pale tan; and light-colored silks which never visit the dye vat remain pure and strong. But I have heard that unscrupulous manufacturers sometimes weight their silks in the dyeing process, especially their dark-colored silks, using certain weighty substances in the dye vats— oh, iron filings and copperas, I don't know what, I am no chemist—so as to make the reeled silk appear more solid, and thicker, and stronger than it actually is. I have made the mistake myself of buying weighted silk."

"Well, I never did," said Miss Johnstone. "I'm never taken in by spurious goods. I'm a remarkable judge of stuffs, and my dry-goods man would never dare pass off inferior goods, not on me, anyhow. No, Mrs Pollocke, I know what I'm talking about when I tell you that black silk is always inferior simply because it is black. That's why it always needs freshening, and that's why there's so many receipts for freshening and renewing it. I use an excellent receipt given me by Mrs Taylor. Now, if you'll let me have that gum arabic?"

"How could we have worn sleeves like those?" said Mrs Pratt.

Grace let her have the gum arabic, a large spoonful of amber teardrops. Miss Johnstone ground them in a mortar, talking all the while. "Dr Laurie, up in Leesburg, takes quite an opposite approach to Dr Woodward's. He says that during an attack of the stone, the sufferer should take as little liquid as possible. The medicines administered by mouth may then be as concentrated as possible, so that the urine—"

"Oh, Aunt," remonstrated Mrs Ambler.

"There's no need to be squeamish and dainty, here among ourselves, Miss Anne," said Miss Johnstone. "In medical matters, there's no place for mincing words, and I'm only quoting Dr Laurie himself. So that the *urine* may be the more strongly *impregnated* with the medicines—and the longer retained in the kidneys and bladder too, where it does the most good. But Dr Woodward takes the opposite view. He recommends washing the gravel out, you see, so he has the sufferer take as much liquid as he can hold, or more. And, if I understand aright, he even used a flushing device in your father's case, injecting soda water—into the bladder—by—by a catheter arrangement. . . ."

"Oh, Aunt!" cried Mrs Ambler.

"Your poor father; and all to no avail," said Miss Johnstone. "Miss Anne, just ring for Cook, won't you? And tell her I want a pint of boiling water and a basin. Yes; well, by that time your poor father was vomiting, and purging too, even more violently and continuously than usual. . . . Oh, Harriet, there you are. I want a basin and a pint of boiling water, straightaway. And you might as well put the irons to the fire too, I'll need them shortly. . . . Where was I? He'd eaten a good dinner, and enjoyed it too; it was turkey and okra, and his special dish of his own early spotty beans, just for him. And then about candle-lighting was when the crisis came on with hardly any warning, bad as I've ever seen it. At first I wasn't much alarmed, because by now I know just what to do—Dr Woodward says I'm a remarkably capable nurse, and why shouldn't I be by this time, I always tell him, after all these years of looking after others, always putting others before myself? So I just gave him his laudanum, fifteen drops in a glass of wine, and at first it seemed like the attack might pass off altogether. But then the pain got worse, and not just in his back, but in his belly too. That's what I told Dr Woodward, who thought the bladder might be affected—and then the vomiting began, always so unpleasant—oh, Harriet; wait, while I put this ground-up gum arabic in the basin; now pour the hot water over it, and give it a stir—didn't you bring a spoon? Well, of course we'll need a spoon! Go and fetch one. Heavens, these people have to be told *everything*, don't they? And Mr Boyce hasn't brought up the turpentine either. What can he be doing? I'm afraid I'll have to trouble you, Mrs Pollocke, for yours, if you don't mind. Here's Harriet now, with a spoon; why don't you send her on upstairs for the turpentine—but you'll have to explain just exactly where it is."

"I shall fetch it myself," said Grace, and went out, just ahead of the cook. At the end of the passage, she paused and waited for Harriet to catch up to her. "Judge Grant always appreciated his dish of spotted beans, did he?" asked Grace.

"Oh, yes, ma'am," said Harriet. "When the first spotty beans plump out in June, he always have a sallet of them, the very first ones. He always like how I serve them up so sweet and young, with some fat bacon and some parsley and celery, and the old best vinegar. He call it his own spotty-bean sallet."

"Delicious, I'm sure. The beans don't require much boiling, I suppose, when they are so fresh and young?"

"Oh, well, ma'am, some folks likes them raw, I guess, but me, I always boil 'em good so's to make 'em digestible. Master always have that tender stomach, so I boil 'em good, for him."

"And was it only for himself, this special dish? No one else eats it?"

"They's never very much of 'em, when they first comes to table, not enough for all the family. I send in a dish of okra too, and salsify greens, for the rest of the family so Master, he can have his spotty-bean sallet to his self."

"How busy it must keep you, to put so many dishes on the table. Have you a clever girl or two, to help you in the kitchen? Someone to beat the biscuits, and shell the peas and the beans, while you attend to the pie and the roast?"

"Oh, I have that Sukey to help me, but she's the stupidest creature in the world, and the laziest. She lose the water bucket in the well; she let the fire go out overnight. And I never let her touch a knife, she like to cut her hand off just to get out of work, so I has to do all the slicing and the chopping myself."

"Not too stupid to shell beans, though, is she?"

"I guess she's just about 'cute enough for that," agreed Harriet, but still Grace did not know who had shelled the spotty beans for Judge Grant's Last Supper.

Curb your fantastical imagination, she rebuked herself; and carried her bottle of turpentine downstairs again, where Miss Johnstone was saying, "Though why I should trust Boyce to get the oats to market to any advantage, when he can't even manage to bring me a measure of turpentine when it's asked for, I don't know. . . . Well, there, Mrs Pollocke. This will do." Into the basin in which she had already dissolved the powdered gum arabic in hot water, she now poured equal measures of ammonia and turpentine, and stirred well. What a smell! But she proceeded then, noisily, busily, bossily, to sponge her black silk dress with this mixture; to press the dress hard on the wrong side with very hot irons, making steam and mess and fuss, talking and bossing all the while. Miss Johnstone's black silk mourning dress did look fresher and blacker after this treatment, though its sleeves remained irredeemably enormous. Mrs Ambler and Mrs Pratt and Mrs MacFarlane and Miss Julia Grant then submitted their own mourning dresses to the same treatment; and touched up their bonnets and caps and veils too, and several pairs of gloves; until, by evening, they all were decorously outfitted in deepest black.

Grace, being no kin of the family but only a visitor—insofar as the Grants knew—did not don mourning, but only changed her calico pelerine for a plain one of deepest indigo.

BY THE THIRD MORNING after their father's death, the Grant daughters had begun to fear that their eldest brother James Grant might not arrive from Richmond in time for the funeral—which, in such hot June weather, could not be deferred beyond the following morning. However, he arrived just before dinner, to their vast relief; and after dinner, Grace retired by herself discreetly to the tearoom, leaving the parlor to the grieving family.

Later, Mrs Ambler and Mrs Grimshaw came seeking Grace, to beg a great favor of her: "We've talked it all over among us, Mrs Pollocke, and we're hoping to prevail so far upon your generosity as to ask you to paint one last likeness for us to cherish," said Mrs Ambler.

"Though the circumstances are so very sad," said Mrs Grimshaw.

"But as it's so unlikely that the opportunity would ever arise again," said Mrs Ambler.

Many painters acceded to such requests, Grace knew very well; but she had never painted a posthumous portrait, and would have preferred to decline. Her reluctance must have shown, because Mrs Ambler said, "Of course, if you can't bring yourself—"

"It's only that we don't have no pictures at all of him," said Mrs Grimshaw. "And you're so good at getting a likeness. Your pictures of my sisters turned out so like, and my aunt's too, no matter what she says about it; even Charley admits they're ever so much more accomplished than he expected—"

Mrs Ambler said, "We've spoke with him about it already, and got him to agree, starting the day after tomorrow, if only you'll be so good . . ."

And now Grace was perplexed: surely it was neither necessary nor possible to obtain the consent of the deceased, for a posthumous portrait?

"He never has cared much for the notion of sitting," continued Mrs Ambler, "but we've prevailed at last, I think, by telling him he really has to have his likeness taken—a miniature at the very least—now that he's head of the family. It's only right."

Grace hoped that her relief did not show. "Of course I will be quite happy to take your brother's likeness," she said.

IN THE MORNING, the Grant brothers and brothers-in-law, and all the neighboring gentlemen—Taylors, Carters, Lees, as well as others of less ancient, eminent, and respectable name—accompanied the coffin to the churchyard to pay their last respects; but ladies stayed home, as was the custom here. Grace found herself thinking very much of her uncle that morning. She had liked him much better than she had expected—and much better than any dispassionate weighing of his virtues and his failings could warrant. Her heart had gone out to him. Was that only because he was her own kin? Or because she had a compassionate heart?

Her nearest living blood relative—except for Jamie—was now extinguished. How she missed Dan, and Jamie! She settled herself at the writing table in the library, and began a letter to Dan.

My dearest Dan, wrote Grace, thinking: my song; my poem. She had been away from home for far too long. My dearest Dan: dearest fate; dearest destiny.

My dearest Dan—
I have been away from you—from home, from Jamie—for far
too long already—so imagine my distress (as I imagine yours, dear)

at the sad news that Judge Grant, a sufferer from the stone for
many years, passed from this life four nights ago, quite suddenly.
The family are naturally distraught, and Mrs Ambler now proposes
to remain here for some indefinite period. I must therefore arrange
my own return to Philada., just as soon as I may. If I can contrive
to get to Alexandria, I shall easily return from there on the cars; but
it seems that it is not so easy to get myself to Alexa.

Runaway slaves generally got themselves to the safety of Pennsylvania and points north upon their own two legs. On the face of it, it would seem that she, a free white woman, might do at least as much for herself. But she was not merely a free white woman; she was a gentlewoman, a lady; and any lady would disgrace herself—would cast away her very gentility—if she were known to have walked alone to Alexandria upon her own two legs—or limbs, as the Americans so genteelly referred to them. She would lose caste, as shamefully and irrevocably as any brahmin would lose caste by selling flesh, salt, or lac. By such walking she would disgrace not only herself, but all her kin as well. She imagined her mother-in-law's mortification, should such an exploit become known (but why must it?)—and caught herself smiling at the thought.

How absurd! Grace's eye ranged across the books on the shelves, across the matching sets of green-calf volumes—and came to rest upon *The Heart of Midlothian.* Hadn't Sir Walter Scott's Jeanie Deans walked on her sister's behalf from Scotland to London—and back—to see the Queen? She had; but Jeanie Deans had been no lady to begin with; had no caste to lose, no mother-in-law to mortify; and was a mere fiction besides. Still, Grace felt herself strongly disposed to emulate Sir Walter's plucky heroine, if no Alexandria-bound wagons hove into view very soon.

But if a letter, this letter (all unwilling and unconscious, a mere
folded sheet of inked paper) may make its way to you, in a matter
of two or three days, it ought to be possible for me, endowed with
volition and consciousness—and moreover with two sound limbs—
to do at least as well. And as soon as anything has been decided,

I shall be sure to let you know when you may expect to enfold yr affecte. wife once more against yr warm heart—

Ever thine—

G

She sanded her letter; folded it; sealed it with wax. But letters were not so very secure, for all that. Letters sometimes went astray, sometimes were opened and read by eyes other than those for whom they were intended—so she referred to "Judge Grant," not "my Uncle Grant," and to "Mrs Ambler," not "my cousin Ambler." And while no one who had suffered so long and so grievously from the stone as Judge Grant could be said to have died suddenly or unexpectedly— still, it was just a little sudden and unexpected. She did not say so. She did not mention that a certain young slave woman had disappeared the same night; nor did she mention the bringer of the candle in the night, that astounding apparition.

How lucky for Diana, to have disappeared just when no effective pursuit might be undertaken! What felicitous timing! If some clever planner had wished to create a distraction, a red herring, nothing could have been more effectual than this.

And so Judge Grant had succumbed to the stone at last.

Or had he? Was she the only one to wonder that? Her unruly imagination careened about like a galloping two-year-old colt eyeing the fences, gauging them for leaping.

ONCE AGAIN GRACE set up her studio in the tearoom off the library; and before many days had passed, Mr James Grant came and sat to her, wearing his mourning clothes. How remarkably yellow he was, quite jaundiced, like an old Indian campaigner! On the first morning, his sister Mrs Pratt came in to talk with him and make the time pass; but on the second morning, she did not appear. He seemed disinclined to talk and Grace soon gave up the attempt to draw him out. He had the same name as her own father, and her son, but Grace saw no other resemblance between this taciturn cousin and those beloved Jameses.

"WHY ARE THE BIRDS thronging the mulberries so?" said Miss Grant, coming in to the tearoom, where Grace cleaned her brushes. "It's like an Independence Day parade down there." She and Grace walked down to see.

Mulberry Lane was a melee of birds, a Kumbh Mela of the birds. Their voices in the distance made a shrill cacophony; and as Grace and Miss Grant approached the avenue, Grace could see that the trees seemed to teem with birds, crawl with birds. Occasionally from one spot or another there would erupt an explosion of birds; they would circle a few times, and then settle back into the trees again. Grace and Miss Grant walked under the shelter of the avenue and looked up. The birds took little notice of them, not interrupting their delirous feeding—for that was what they were doing: for them it was indeed the Festival of the Pot of Nectar.

"Mockingbirds; jays. Those are chickadees . . . nuthatches. And those are orioles, of course," said Miss Grant, who knew her birds as well as her halogens.

Something soft struck Grace's head, atop her bonnet—something unpleasant, she feared, of the sort one must expect when walking beneath flocks of feeding birds—and she did not like to put her hand up to touch it. Something fell onto Miss Grant's shoulder too, a whitish splotch—but no, it was not what Grace had supposed; it was a largish white soft-bodied caterpillar.

"Oh—look—here is another. And another." In fact, caterpillars—and fragments of caterpillars—were showering down all around them; and there were more caterpillars squirming or walking among the litter of leaves that covered the walk underfoot.

"So that's what's brought the birds: a tremendous hatch of caterpillars," said Miss Grant. "How peculiar. I wonder what kind they are. And how'd they come here? I don't recognise them—not that I'm an entomologist, much."

But Grace thought she did recognise them. How could she not recognise those fat soft white bodies, nearly the size of her small finger, with black spots along their sides; a single upright spike atop the tail, like a shark's fin; the ardent prayerful way they clutched a mulberry leaf and devoured it, chewing repeated edgewise passes along it, devouring an arc from high to low, up to down, bowing over and over again, in devoted submission to the sacred task of eating. Surely these caterpillars feasting on mulberry leaves were fifth-instar silkworms.

She turned about, looking upward in wonder—and in tingling suspicion. How could these possibly have come here? Silkworms, she knew very well, were so unfitted for natural conditions after two millennia of domestication that they were unlikely to survive even a single complete generation in the wild. They had not suddenly appeared here by mere chance—had not been unwittingly carried here as unsuspected stowaways in a sack of wheat, a barrel of flour, a bolt of fabric, a ream of paper. She felt quite certain that they had been brought here on purpose, and the certainty filled her with a tingling of apprehension, as though she had just tasted something poisonous.

THE EVENING WAS WARM, the windows open. In the drawing room, the lamps were mobbed by large sooty-colored moths. They battered themselves against the glass chimneys which shielded the flames. Mr Charles Grant took up the body of one of them and turned it over, examining it in the light. "Darts," he said. "That's a bad sign, and so early too. Has anyone checked the wheat?" No one replied.

Grace went out to the piazza. The jasmine growing up the pillars was fragrant, near-luminous in the dusk. Grace looked northward, homeward. Who was putting Jamie to bed? Did Daniel feel her longing for him, at this moment? A heavy fluttering in the air at ear-level distracted her: what was this? It was like a hummingbird, but hummingbirds do not frequent flowers after sunset. It was hard to see, in the gloaming—but it was a moth, Grace could just make out: a very large moth, as large as a hummingbird, and hovering as hummingbirds do, to feed upon the nectar of a flower; and then another. And then away. Grace had never seen so large and beautiful and birdlike a moth.

But there was another; and after a moment, two more, further along the piazza. One alighted upon a flower, and Grace crept near, to see it. Its wingspan at rest was broader than the palm of her hand, some four inches from one wingtip to the other, and the grey wings were marvelously merled, marled, marbled, mottled; like watered silk; like Jawhar steel. The thick body was shaped like a rattlesnake's rattle, and banded with gold; the long velvety antennae swept back like a gazelle's horns. The moth took wing again, and Grace jumped back.

AFTER MR JAMES GRANT's third sitting, Grace walked out alone, to the Mulberry Lane. Several jays and mockingbirds still fed there, but it was far quieter today; were the birds already sated? Or had they found something better to eat, elsewhere? Grace stood quite still under the trees, looking upward, and listening. It seemed to her that the leafy canopy was already lighter, lacier; already the ravenous caterpillars had devoured bushels of leaves. There was frass underfoot, and fallen worms; there was that rich fermented fruity smell of silkworms; and if she held her breath, she could hear the tiny sound of a myriad of worms chewing. Not worms, she reminded herself: Caterpillars. Larvae.

Emerging at the far end of the avenue, she made her way past the barn and out toward the nearest of the wheat fields. The young wheat was intensely green: a peculiar green of its own, juicy and perfectly balanced, it seemed to her, between yellow and blue, a definitive greenest green. From a distance, it seemed that all was well, all was as it ought to be; but as she drew nearer, she saw better. For one thing, the birds were here; a knot of them flew up as she approached. They circled, and settled back down onto a further part of the field.

And what brought the birds here? Not grain; it was far too early for grain.

Up close, she could see that the formerly uniform field looked patchy now; there were places where the long green stems seemed shredded, and many had been decapitated. They would never make seed now. They might be mowed for the sake of straw—of some use as bedding, or as fodder, perhaps, for cattle, never too particular.

Could it be caterpillars, here too? Not silkworms, surely; for those, Grace knew, would condescend to eat nothing but mulberry leaves. What, then? Grace investigated the leaf whorls, where leaves grew off the stems, and found that several of them harbored slender greenish brown caterpillars an inch or more in length, festooned with a pair of orange stripes along each side, and mottled brown heads. But how could these few caterpillars account for such extensive damage? With the tip of a stick, Grace raked aside the leaf litter, brushed aside dirt clods—and saw that the soil was riddled with caterpillars, curled, resting, digesting. She brushed her stick across the tops of the green stems, and dozens of dusky moths flew up, like those that had been mobbing the lamps the previous evening.

Darts, Mr Charles Grant had called the moths. Presumably he knew all about them; presumably wheat fields were often infested by darts. It might happen spontaneously, as these things often happened. There was no need to imagine exotic sources for an infestation of caterpillars such as these.

Grace walked out toward the field where the precious tobacco plants were growing. The stout young plants stood nearly five feet high by now, in their deeply tilled, richly manured, closely fenced two acres, the most painstakingly and lovingly cultivated field in all of Grantsboro's broad acres. But as she drew near, her sense of unease welled up; and overflowed. On this plant—that one too—and all these, along here—the broad leaves were chewed to lace, to mere ribs, to skeletons. Here and there, something had chewed entirely through the thick stems, so that the heads of the plants had toppled, wilted.

Grace lifted up leaves, examining under them. At a quick glance, it seemed there was nothing, only shade and stems. But several huge mottled moths fluttered up as she disturbed the damaged foliage, as large as hummingbirds; and then she found an enormous green caterpillar on the underside of a leaf. It was more than three inches long, and thick-bodied, with a row of chevron markings along each side, like those on a sergeant's sleeve; and had a long sharp red spike to its tail, like a shark's fin; like a rhinoceros's horn. Hornworms. And now that her eyes knew what to seek, Grace saw another; and another; and several, there. Some were marked differently, yellow slashes instead of chevrons along their sides—or black spikes instead of red on their tails. But all were feeding voraciously, greedily, their big knob-heads swaying and jaws milling steadily as they devoured green tobacco leaves, stems, buds, everything. As she watched, one caterpillar slowly emitted a large corrugated pellet of excrement, never pausing or even slowing in its chewing, as unconscious of dunging as a horse.

Judge Grant's beans grew here too, clambering up the stout tobacco stems; but they also had been plundered. No leaves remained to them, and only a few swollen pods. Grace picked one, peeled it back; shook into her palm the mottled tender beans inside. They were indeed spotted—like castor beans—but bean-shaped; curled like an embryo. Not tick-shaped.

Raking lightly with her stick in the soil under the plants, she found what she expected: shiny pupa capsules, pointed on one end, a loop on the other, and the body ribbed. This field—plants, soil, and all— was infested, riddled with hornworms, in every stage of their development.

How had the Egyptians accounted for that series of plagues which had afflicted them? Pharoah's experts had insisted that they were only natural phenomena; only vicissitudes which must be expected and endured from time to time; had denied that any divine fury was at work. Had some fury, divine or otherwise, been at work here at Grantsboro?

It was another blazing hot day, and Grace pulled the brim of her bonnet forward to keep the sun from her face as she turned again toward the house. From somewhere, Grace could hear voices. It was Monday, laundry day; and the slave laundresses were hauling firewood to fire the big wash kettles. But what was that distant crackling noise, like timber breaking—but steadier, sustained? It seemed to come from over the slope of the hill, where the stream ran down to the sawmill. And why was there a plume of mist? Wasn't it rather late in the day for rising plumes of mist? And in so singular a form, rising from only the one spot? Then the crackling sound seemed less like cracking branches, and more like something else. Grace hastened across a pumpkin field in the furrow between two rows, trying not to trample the spreading shoots. That rising plume of mist was not so very pure; it was mixed with darker grey, and even before she had arrived at the edge of the pumpkin field, Grace knew what that grey plume was, and what she would see.

Flames were licking up a tall stack of logs piled just inside one corner of the shed roof sheltering the mill.

"Fire!" shouted Grace, turning and waving in the direction of the laundresses, waving to catch their attention. "Fire, fire!"

The laundresses heard her, and raised the cry, and then Grace could see them running toward the big house. She herself plunged down the slope toward the sawmill. The millstream was small and sluggish at this season, choked by algae. There was no pump, no fire engine such as was the pride of any ship, or of any Philadelphia fire company, but there was a large wooden bucket. She snatched it up, filled it in the stream, and dragged it, full, as close as she could get to the flames. When she threw the water at the stack of logs, there was a hissing—an explosion of steam—and she leapt back, shielding her eyes—then ran back to the murky stream for more.

She had been doing this for—how long? hours?—perhaps six or seven minutes before other people came: the laundresses, the old men who chipped mortar, Mr Charles Grant, Mr Boyce—all carrying buckets or wash kettles or earthenware jars or canvas pails—and in a few moments more, the fire was extinguished. Grace was panting, and noticed that she had somehow grazed the knuckles of her right hand. It did not hurt at all. She used her handkerchief to stanch the blood, and noticed, as her breathing slowed, that she was breathing a tune, quite inaudible to anyone but herself; it was Mr Frank Johnson's tune: "The Philadelphia Firemen's Cotillion."

Might a furious, an implacable person who had brought a plague of caterpillars also commit an arson? No; impossible; absurd! thought Grace. Nine days had passed since Diana's disappearance; and the damage wrought by those caterpillars—three kinds, now!—had been at least nine days in the making. How could anyone commit a delayed arson?

It had been nine days too since Judge Grant had died in agonies. But from that thought, Grace shied violently.

MR CHARLES GRANT dumped a small pile of sooty glass shards onto the round table in the drawing room. "That's what started the fire," he said. "An old broken bottle, left in the bright sun, in the dry leaves next to the log pile."

"Oh, Master Charles, dear, so dirty," objected Miss Johnstone.

"I don't see how broken glass could start a fire," said Mrs MacFarlane.

"Haven't you ever heard of a burning glass?" he said.

"No," said Mrs MacFarlane.

"Educating girls wouldn't be a bad thing," he said. "I'll bet Mrs Pollocke knows a thing or two about lenses."

Did he mean to imply suspicion; accusation? Grace said, "I do, certainly. There is quite a good large magnifying lens in my kit. It is useful for painting miniatures."

"Every boy knows how to burn up an anthill using a glass," said Mr Charles Grant.

"And I guess that's your notion of an education?" retorted Mrs MacFarlane wittily.

Grace picked up the largest of the sooty shards of glass, a fragment some three inches across, curved, jagged-edged, with a few small air bubbles trapped inside the solid glass. It might function as a crude lens, she supposed. If the sun, on this particular day near the solstice, were to strike this shard just so, the curve of the glass might focus the intense sunlight sufficiently—in the brief time before the sun passed on—just sufficiently to ignite dry leaves; and then the smoldering leaves might ignite seasoned wood. It might. Undeniably fire had occurred; it might have occurred thus.

It was a method—a most uncertain method—of perhaps committing an arson at nine days' sight. Was she obliged to suspect any particular person of placing that broken glass?

"It looks like those bottles that Boyce brings back from Alexandria," remarked Miss Johnstone, fingering the piece that had been the neck.

"Well, a bottle's a bottle, Aunt," said Mr Charles.

"You would know, I guess," said his sister.

GRACE WAS DETERMINED to finish Mr James Grant's portrait during this, his fourth sitting. "There you are!" cried his younger brother, bursting in to the tearoom. "Having your ugly phys painted, while MacFarlane and I attend to business. We've been looking all over the place for you."

Mr MacFarlane came in too. "What a cravat, Grant!" said Mr Mac-Farlane. "Is that how they're worn in Richmond?"

"Did you tell him?" said Miss Johnstone as she and Mrs Ambler arrived in the doorway, Miss Julia Grant behind them.

"Tell me what?" said Mr James Grant.

"About that trust," said Miss Johnstone. "Tell him."

"What trust?" said Mr James Grant.

"See, nobody knew about it," said Mrs Ambler. "None of us. It wasn't just me."

"I knew," said Miss Johnstone. "I knew, all along."

"Later might be better . . . ," said Mr MacFarlane. He inclined his head just a little, to indicate Grace: the presence of an outsider.

"Oh, that don't matter," said Mr Charles Grant. "And we haven't got all day; we've got to get back up to Leesburg this afternoon to see the contents of all those deed boxes properly inventoried. Well, it's like this: our father—well, no; I mean, his sister—oh, you tell him, Mac-Farlane; you've got the head for this sort of thing. Go on and explain it all; he's got to know all about it, and the sooner the better."

Mr MacFarlane turned around a chair and sat down astride it, saying, "Well, here's the gist of it, then, as far as anyone can tell. It turns out that your father was the sole trustee of a certain sum held in trust for his niece. Apparently his sister in Scotland married, and bore a daughter, and then died soon afterward; but her marriage articles provided that her estate, instead of going to her husband, was instead to be held in trust for the issue of her body. She bore just the one child; and her brother, your father, was the sole trustee."

Miss Johnstone said, "That was the ungrateful little Scottish orphan girl—maybe you remember, Master James—that I traveled all the way to Scotland to fetch and bring her home, here. But nothing came of it, because she wouldn't come."

"I guess I remember that, a little. It was a long time ago," said Mr James Grant.

"Well, that's the niece, you see," said Miss Johnstone. "I'd have preferred to have brung her up here, since a considerable sum of money was involved, but things don't always turn out just the way we might like; a valuable lesson to us all."

"But the point is," said Mr MacFarlane, "that your father was trustee of his sister's estate—of the assets held in trust for that niece. It seems that some attempts were made to find the niece a few years ago, about the time when she would have come of age—but to no avail."

Grace felt an intense heat radiating from her face, but no one was looking at her.

"Well, what of it? I hope it don't mean any delays in settling up my father's estate," said Mr James Grant.

"Well, that's just the problem," said Mr MacFarlane. "Ordinarily, a substantial effort would have to be made first of all, to find the niece."

"Heavens; how absurd!" said Miss Johnstone. "After all these years! And after she refused to profit by her uncle's kind invitation, all those years ago! And, meanwhile, seems to have disappeared entirely! Why, she may very well have died, for all anyone can find out now! I don't see why she'd still be entitled now, after all this time, and after all the trouble that's already been taken for her. Can't a trust be canceled, MacFarlane? There must be some way to do that."

"To dissolve the trust would require petitioning the court," said Mr MacFarlane. "It would take some time, at least a year; and it would cost some money. And it looks rather complicated, unfortunately, by—by . . . because . . ." He fell silent.

Miss Johnstone said, "Well, how much money is in this trust? I guess it must be worth quite a bit by now? I did have the impression that it was a nice round sum, years ago."

"Well, yes; it was pretty round, I guess; it amounted to just about two thousand dollars, back in 1818, originally."

Grace's hand trembled; she smudged Mr Grant's inner eye. Taking the point of a rag, she blotted away her misstroke.

"Two thousand dollars! My, my! And what'll it be worth by now?" said Miss Johnstone.

"According to the executors," said Mr MacFarlane, "the trust seems to have been bankrupt for the past six years."

"Bankrupt! Now, how could that happen?" demanded Miss Johnstone.

Her hand steady now, Grace touched in the dark shadow at the tear duct of Mr Grant's right eye. For a moment she had been an heiress; but it had passed off quickly. Easy come, easy go, as the Americans said.

"Well . . . it seems to have been invested rather . . . unluckily," said Mr MacFarlane.

"I guess so! In what? Mulberry trees?" demanded Mr James Grant.

"No, it was invested in, oh, livestock and chattels, and so on. But the livestock all seems to have died; and the slaves all to have run away or died."

"Well, that's pretty remarkable, ain't it?" said Mr James Grant.

"I guess it is," said Mr MacFarlane. "It does strike the fancy, somewhat. But let me be perfectly accurate: not quite all have died or run away. Your old Walter, out there, chipping mortar off those bricks, was sold to the trust about four years ago. And, as it happens, the sale was recorded just a few weeks before he had that accident in the sawmill that crippled him, when, you may remember, he didn't look likely to live. But live he did; and here he is still, chipping mortar off bricks— and he's the only remaining chattel belonging to that little girl's estate. I guess an appraiser would put him at just about twenty-five dollars— and that's all that's left of that two thousand dollars. But to return to your question: yes, all the others soon died or ran away—"

"Every single one?" asked Mr James Grant.

"So the executors tell me," said Mr MacFarlane, "though I haven't seen the books for myself. And that's just why it would be so awkward to have to petition the court, you see, and place all the records and deeds in front of them for their inspection. It is so very striking, so astounding, to see that *all* the colts and calves owned by the trust were sold by Judge Grant to the trust shortly before they died; and *all* the slaves owned by the trust were sold by Judge Grant to the trust shortly before they ran away; or in their useless old age, shortly before they died; or shortly before they became injured or sick—and useless. With Walter the solitary exception."

Everyone thought about this. "That might be devilish awkward to explain," declared Mr Charles Grant presently.

"Worse still, not *every* runaway slave was sold to the trust," Mr MacFarlane said. "How prescient your father the judge must have been! The very ones that were successfully recovered—Shandy and Simon in Boston, Lucy in New York—they all happened still to belong to Grantsboro. It was only the ones who actually succeeded in getting off—and staying off!—those were the ones that, it turns out, had been just recently sold to the trust."

"Huh," said Mr James Grant.

"Furthermore, the executors tell me they've had a look at the deed books at the courthouse," said Mr MacFarlane. "And it just so happens that the records of all these transactions fall—just happen to fall—at the top or at the bottom of the page they're recorded on. Where someone might have fit them in, just squeezed them in, you know, just a little bit late . . . someone who might have been willing to do a favor, or need a favor, from so influential and well-respected a magistrate as—your father, the judge . . ."

Silence fell.

Presently Mrs Ambler said, "No one must know. What a scandal, what a disgrace, for Papa's reputation, and him unable now to clear his name, to explain the misunderstanding!"

"But every penny will have to be made up and restored to—to—I guess she'd be our cousin?—out of Papa's estate," said Miss Julia Grant.

"That would be very difficult indeed," said Mr MacFarlane. "Because it seems pretty clear that your father's estate is in no condition to make up any such shortfalls. In fact, you'd better start getting used to the sound of the word 'bankrupt.' "

"What! Papa?" cried Mrs Ambler. "Impossible! No, no, Mr MacFarlane, I'm sure you're mistaken."

"I wish I was. The extent of the shortfall won't be entirely clear until all the claims and notes and mortgages and leases and bills come in, which could take several months. But it's obvious already that the mortgages secured by the livestock and the hands, and the notes held by Mr Walker, are just the froth on the top, so to speak. It appears already that your father was in a lot deeper than he ever let on to any of us, and had been for quite a long time."

"But when the wheat goes to market, everything'll come right," said Mr James Grant.

"Your wheat don't look likely to get to market. Boyce tells me you've got an infestation of cutworms and army worms in the wheat, the worst he's ever seen. And hornworms in the tobacco and everywhere else, and some kind of new caterpillars in the mulberries even, which ordinarily nothing'll touch. Instead of having the boys chase the birds out of the fields, he should be grateful for all the birds he can get. You'll be lucky to reap anything at all this year; but even then, if word gets out about these plagues you've got, the markets are likely to refuse anything from here, for fear of transporting the infestation."

"Oh, but can't loans be arranged, for next year?" suggested Mrs Ambler. "I can't believe that Papa, always so well respected by everyone, could possibly have let things go so far amiss as to deserve anything like the word 'bankrupt,' Mr MacFarlane."

"Why, it's impossible!" said Miss Johnstone. "Imagine the disgrace! What a mercy that my poor sister is not here to see it."

"Honest bankruptcy is no disgrace," said Miss Julia Grant. "But embezzlement is another story altogether, and not just a disgrace; it's a crime. First of all, that cousin's inheritance has to be restored to her—honor requires that much. A search must be made, and—and—"

"Well, I don't see that at all," said Mr Charles Grant. "Not under the circumstances."

"Me neither," said Miss Johnstone. "Not now. The less said or done about that old business, the better. If only she'd been brought up here, among us! I did my best; no one could have done more, and at great inconvenience to myself. But no; she refused to profit by the generous offer made her. And now that the child has disappeared—well, she couldn't be found, you say, MacFarlane, when Judge Grant made the effort. It seems to me that everything that could reasonably be done, has been done. No good could come of making a public scandal; nothing but harm could follow, for everyone concerned."

"I agree," said Mr Charles Grant. "Why should another attempt be made now—at great expense, and publicity? Why should she be any easier to find now than she was then? And even if she was found, it would only be to tell her—what? That she can get in line with the other creditors? I don't see it at all."

"She most likely departed this life years ago," said Miss Johnstone. "She didn't look wholesome at all, when I saw her as a child, so puny and undergrown. I'm sure that dreadful climate was the cause. I could have nursed her into good health here. Didn't I bring you all up safe and sound? She would have thrived here, with us, and grown up to make a good match too. But no, she refused to come. It wouldn't surprise me in the least if she died years ago, and that's why your father couldn't find her. For all we know, he then privately dissolved the trust, and converted the funds with perfect correctness."

"Oh, but on this point at least," said Grace, setting down her brush and wiping her palms over her hips, "permit me to set your mind at ease. As fortune would have it, I have not died. Here I am."

CHAPTER
17

ALL EYES UPON HER. THOSE FACES! IF SHE COULD PAINT THOSE!
Miss Johnstone was the first to break the astonished silence. "Liar!"
she cried. "And base opportunist, to take advantage of us here, *en
famille*, in our bereavement!"

"I am no liar," said Grace. "And I remember you very well, Miss
Johnstone, though I was only eight years old then. You insulted my
Uncle MacDonald in his own house. Oh, aye; I heard you from the stair
landing. 'A low sort,' you called him, and my aunt a 'cheat.' And then
you . . . actually abducted me! You kidnapped me, by force! Have you
told my cousins of that? Did my Uncle Grant know of that?"

" 'Kidnapped' indeed! Nothing of the sort! But that is just the scan-
dalous way abolitionists talk! They are always accusing us of 'kidnap-
ping' when we attempt to recover our own property. It is a perfectly
legal and proper manner of proceeding; I had it on the best legal
authority."

"I was not your property to recover."

"Imposter!" cried Miss Johnstone, changing tack abruptly. "Everyone knows that wicked opportunists always do come teeming up out
of their dung heaps, trying what false claims might do, whenever an
eminent family suffers a bereavement. And after what we, in our trusting innocence, and in our unguarded grief, might have mentioned in
your hearing . . . it is too, too bad of you, whoever you may be, or pretend to be. . . . 'Mrs Pollocke' is just a false name that you've been passing under, I guess?"

"Oh, Miss Johnstone, you know very well that I am no imposter.
Let us have a test: Think back, all of you, on what was said in my hearing just now—and most indiscreet of you too. Did anyone mention the
name of your Scottish cousin?"

They all looked about them, trying to remember if any name had been mentioned. No; no one had mentioned any names. . . . "I don't think I ever even knew her name," offered Mrs Ambler helpfully.

Grace said, "I will tell you some names, then. My mother was Elizabeth Grant, and she was your Aunt Elizabeth, your father's own sister. I scarcely remember her, as she died even before I could walk. My father, her husband, was Mr James MacDonald; and he, to my lasting sorrow, died in a driving accident when I was seven years of age. In maidenhood I was Miss Grace MacDonald; and now that I am married to Mr Daniel Pollocke of Philadelphia, I am Mrs Pollocke."

Mr MacFarlane gave one quick unwilling nod. "That's all right," he admitted; "all in line with the family documents." Everyone stared at her still, a little differently than before; now they were seeking family resemblance, thought Grace; looking for something of themselves in her face and bearing.

"It was you who brought this viper into the bosom of our family, Miss Anne," cried Miss Johnstone, turning fiercely on Mrs Ambler. "Into the innermost sanctum of our family! You and Clara!"

"I guess you tried pretty hard to get her here yourself, Aunt, all those years ago!" cried Mrs Ambler.

"Couldn't you see what she was?"

"Couldn't you?" retorted Mrs Ambler.

"I did always have a bad uncomfortable feeling about her, didn't I?" cried Miss Johnstone. "Why'd she come here, sneaking and spying among us like this? So sneaking, so deceitful and secretive! Hunting us into our own house, even! Why did you? What do you want from us?" she demanded, turning back to Grace.

There was no reply to be made; Grace remained silent.

"Left speechless, I see," said Miss Johnstone. "Well, it's criminal, that's what it is; criminal! Come, MacFarlane, why don't you do something? I'm sure it's against the law, her coming here to spy and eavesdrop like this, under false pretenses, inside our own house. Why don't you arrest her? I insist, MacFarlane: arrest her, this instant."

"Aunt, Aunt, do take just a minute, now, and collect yourself," urged Mr Charles Grant.

"Why . . . we can't even be sure she had nothing to do with your poor father's unhappy decease!" cried Miss Johnstone. "It wasn't natural, the way the stone took him, this time. And he always lived through it before, it never proved fatal until she—"

"Aunt, she wasn't even here in the house when he—" said Mrs Pratt.

"Now, Aunt—" said Mrs Ambler, and, taking her aunt's arm, turned her away, to remove from her field of view the source of irritation: Grace herself.

"Aunt, no illness ever does prove fatal more than just the once, you know," pointed out Mr James Grant.

To Grace, Mr Charles Grant said, "Never mind any of that, Mrs Pollocke. She don't mean any of it. But I can't say I like the—the extreme awkwardness of the situation. I—you—I mean to say, it is awkward, ain't it? I never knew anything like it, for awkwardness."

"I had best return immediately to Philadelphia, I think," said Grace. "Under the circumstances, could a carriage be made available, to carry me as far as Alexandria?"

"Well, now, I'm not sure that'd be the best plan, though, Mrs Pollocke," said Mr MacFarlane. "Nobody thinks you had anything to do with Judge Grant's death, of course—how preposterous, absurd! But there will be other matters requiring arranging and—and negotiating, I guess, and maybe it might be best—discreetest, you know—if you was to remain here with us, and engage a Virginia lawyer to, ah, to represent your interests in untangling this—this unfortunate situation, eh? Of course, a Virginia lawyer would be quickest and best, any way you like to look at it, and I'd be happy to refer you to some good men, as I know 'em all, and could just tip you off, you know, as to who's worth his money and who's best avoided, eh?" He was blinking hard as he spoke. "And meanwhile, we're most happy for you to continue here as our guest. I hope we've always made you comfortable? And after all, we're all kin, aren't we . . . cousins, it turns out!"

"Do I understand you, sir? Do you say that no Grantsboro carriage will take me to Alexandria?"

"It'd be better, I'm sure, for you to stay here with us, for the time being," he said. "Just until we get this business sorted out."

———

HOW MUCH COULD SHE CARRY? What would she have to leave behind? All her paints and brushes would have to remain; she would carry only some of her clothes. She would take no food from here, but buy some along the road. It was less than forty miles to Alexandria; an active man might even walk it in one very long day. It would probably take her at least two days, and perhaps part of a third, with a night or two spent somewhere on the road. This day was half spent already, and blazing hot again too. She put on her bonnet; she would carry her cloak, for nights. Here was her purse, with some money in it; enough. But the soles of her boots were thin, and how her legs and back did ache! She shut the two trunks she would leave behind, the one containing her clothes, the other her painting kit, just as Miss Julia Grant came into their shared room.

"But Mrs Pollocke—what are you doing? You can't blame us for being shocked, all of us—but what are you doing?" said Miss Grant, when she saw Grace cinching the trunk straps as tight as possible.

"Here is some money, Miss Grant, for sending my trunks along to Philadelphia, just as soon as you can manage it, if you please," said Grace, and held out several dollars to her. "I have written the direction on the top of each."

"But where are you going?"

"I am going home, Miss Grant."

"But how?"

"On foot, it seems," said Grace.

"You can't intend to—to walk, Mrs Pollocke! Not set out on foot— and all alone!"

"That is just what I am doing, though, Miss Grant. Goodbye. Pray bid all my cousins goodbye from me, and your aunt too." Grace went out to the landing, and down the stairs, with Miss Grant coming after.

"But Mrs Pollocke! Dear Mrs Pollocke! Don't go!" cried Miss Julia Grant. "Pay no attention to what Aunt Bella says. She speaks for no one but herself, and she don't mean it, not when she comes to think about it! You mustn't pay her any attention; none of us do," she added as she followed Grace across the wide hall. "I feel certain that—that

all this has been only a most unhappy accident. Surely you didn't realise when you came among us that we were kin; I'm sure it must have
just gradually dawned upon you, a sort of mounting conviction as time
passed; isn't that so, Mrs Pollocke?"

"No, Miss Grant, that is not so. I knew before I accepted your sisters' invitation to come to Grantsboro that you were my cousins, and
Judge Grant my uncle."

"I can't believe it! I just can't believe it of you, Mrs Pollocke, that
you would have kept such a secret!"

Grace stopped, with her hand on the door handle. Her poor cousin!
In her distress, Miss Julia Grant's right eye had slid off to the apogee
of its orbit. Grace said, "I cannot tell you how I learned of our kinship,
without compromising another person's safety; and for the same reason, I have been obliged to maintain silence on the subject all these
weeks. I ought not to have said anything today; I wish I had not. You
have a generous kind heart, Miss Grant—Cousin Julia!—and we have
been something like friends. It pierced my heart to keep this secret
from you, and I am very sorry for it. Perhaps someday you will know
the reasons it had to be thus; and perhaps you will then forgive me—or
more likely not. Now, goodbye, cousin. Thank you for your kind hos-
pitality, but I find I must be drawing my very pleasant visit to a close.
Goodbye, Cousin Julia," said Grace; and letting herself out, she shut
the heavy door behind her.

SHE STRODE DOWN the long drive, in the shade of the beeches. There
was her uncle's devastated tobacco, and the mottled beans; all dying.
Already weeds were pushing up between the wrecked stems. What a
great many weeds! Arrested by their regularity, their familiarity, Grace
paused to look.

They were not ordinary weeds at all, but castor bean seedlings, at
perfect eight-inch intervals, just as though they had been sown with a
Bengali peasant's seed drill. As she passed down the long avenue and
out to the public road, Grace saw more of them; against the fence, in
the damp ground down in the creek crossing, in among the wheat
stalks . . . castor bean, Palma Christi, errindy: "The Friend of Down-

trodden Wives." To what other cruelly treated, harshly subjugated persons might castor bean be useful?

And how did it happen that they appeared here, now? Pushing up so stoutly—here, now—eleven days after her uncle's death? All the suspicions which Grace had taken pains to push away came crowding upon her again.

WALKING FAST, she soon left behind the Grantsboro fields, and passed along uninfested Taylor wheat fields, where the swelling green heads of grain rose upon uniform stems to a particular height, flat as a table, and very beautiful. The wild grasses along the roadside were more beautiful still, in their motley: heads like plumes, like spires, like rattles, feathery, spiky, pink, golden, tall, and short, interlaced with flowers, graced by butterflies. Curtsying, nodding, bowing, like dancers. In the hedgerows flourished roses and their hips. Now shade, now sun; now breeze, now still.

She thought: And to learn that I have been an owner of slaves! Am even now the owner of a slave: of old Walter, this minute sitting and chipping mortar off the bricks he made in his youth. Against my will, without my knowledge, they have made me an abomination, an owner of human property! And their excellent reason for doing so? Why, only so that they might rob me of my rightful inheritance.

Her fury gave her fresh vigor, carried her along for another mile.

Lambs looked up as she passed; they were the most charming children's toys, running high-kneed to their dams. Calves, braver, stood and stared as she passed by. Horses grazed in belly-deep grass, their tails swishing steadily; Grace could hear the *swish-swish-swish.* They had no heads, only necks extended downward into the grass. Bird voices trilled in the fields and the hedgerows: what were they, these Virginia singers? All were unfamiliar to Grace. Who made that cascade, that limpid waterfall of notes? Who warbled overhead, like a piper's ornament? That was a mockingbird; this she knew by its characteristic changeableness, instantaneous and unceasing invention, a brilliant and never-ending stream of improvisation, never itself but no one else either—and so, itself. A flock of small brown birds erupted from deep grasses nearly under her feet—her footfalls were muted, in this soft bottomland here—exploded, whirred off to low trees overhanging a fence. Three crows caught sight of her as she emerged from a wood; they followed her for a furlong or two, leapfrogging each other, rasping, *Caw-caw-caw*, until more crows arrived, curious; and soon Grace was running a gauntlet of crows, all guffawing; ridiculing her appearance, her gait, her earthboundedness. But when a large thick-bodied hawk slid down the slope of the sky toward them, they dispersed, joking coarsely. There were slim hawks too, sharp quick falcons fit for the sport of Indian princes, and Grace took their presence as a favor.

WITHIN AN HOUR, she was footsore; and feeling a little foolish. Sir Walter Scott had made his Jeanie Deans walk to London at a rate of twenty miles a day—but Jeanie Deans hadn't been pregnant—had been indeed only a fiction! Aye; but a fiction based upon the real exploit of a real woman, or so Sir Walter had claimed; a real woman named Helen Walker. Walker! Now that Grace thought about it, this sounded suspiciously like one of Sir Walter's jokes.

Her right foot fell near a small pink naked embryo, shriveled—a hatchling stolen from a nest, perhaps, then dropped by the marauder when the parents attacked in return—or, sadder still, dashed out of its egg even before hatching, stolen, and dropped here. How pitiable! How wasteful! The pink naked wrinkled body was curled; thin grey membrane still covered the large purple patches that would have been eyes. In another day this unborn one would be dry, shriveled, black, invisible. A day after that it would be indistinguishable from dirt; it would be dirt. Grace imagined the tiny curled pink creature under her heart, cradled, rocked there, in the safe deep bucket, the rocking walking cradle of her hips, carried safe. She thought: Nothing shall harm you. Not if I can help it.

Unpaid, for all those paintings! She tallied them up in her head. Left behind; not yet dry; not yet varnished. Good work too. She thought: I suppose I may send in my account with all the others, to the executors. And when the estate is settled, a year hence, I suppose I may expect then to be paid, in line with the other creditors.

———

SHE HAD BROUGHT NO FOOD. But these were walnut trees, surely? And under last year's leaves, these dry round black husks covered last year's fallen nuts, the ones no one had troubled to pick up. They were very small, and the shells black and thick under the peeling husks. She tried to crack one open between the heels of her two hands, but it would not yield. Nearby was a farmer's stone wall, topped by flattish stones; and there was a stray rock that would do as a pestle. She used too much force on the first walnut, smashing the meat into the fragments of shell. The second nut had no meat, only mummified worms tangled in silk; the meat of the third was shriveled to nothing. The fourth had a small meat, very small, but uninfested, and Grace picked it free of the thin woody crust and ate it. The empty shell resembled the face of an owl.

She thought: When I get back to Philadelphia, I suppose I had best consult a lawyer. Mr Brown?—if he does this sort of work? He will know who does, in any case. And I will have to consult him as to what can be done about this slave I have unwittingly owned: a sin entailed upon me, like Original Sin. Old Walter could not simply be given his freedom, not turned out, at his age; where would he go? What would he eat? I will have to pension him.

Using what money?

What will Dan say about that?

Oh, Dan, my Dan! Oh, Jamie!

HERE WAS A LONG wide field to cross in the sun, its distant edge curving a little, like the curvature of the earth, like the curvature of the sea from the deck of a ship, when there is nothing but water in every direction, as far as the eye can see. She walked, and walked, gradually approaching the gallery of tall forest trees at the far boundary, very far, but eventually closer; closer still. At last she entered shade; the ground fell away steeply; there was the gracious smell of water, and shiny poison oak thrusting up along both sides of the narrow track. Grace drank of this water, cupping handfuls, and hoped that sheep were not pastured upstream nearby.

In the next field, she could hear voices. Voices carry far.

She came suddenly upon a crew of field hands, men and women, negroes, lying under trees at the edge of a field. They had eaten their midday food and now were resting, their hoes lying nearby. Some were sleeping; the eyes of others followed her. "Hello," said Grace, and nodded in their direction; but no one replied, and she felt foolish, and felt their eyes on her back for a long ways.

Later, when she could feel the bones in her feet, she passed a house built very near the road. Dogs barked, and Grace picked up a stick lying on the verge, a stick half as long as her arm. The dogs immediately fell silent. Grace carried the stick until she found another, better one, as long as Mr MacFarlane's walking stick. One could not help swaggering a little, she noticed.

She passed through Leesburg and, inquiring of a woman loitering outside the courthouse, was directed to the turnpike that led toward Alexandria. It was thirty-three miles, the woman said, and though she'd never gone so far herself, she'd heard the road was a good one.

About two miles further, where the road passed between broad wheat fields, Grace heard a fast-moving vehicle coming up behind her. This could be no farm wagon, for those went at a plodding pace. It was a carriage very like the Grantsboro carriage, moving at a good clip behind a pair of brisk high-headed greys very like the Grantsboro greys. Her first impulse was to hide; but the wheat, only two feet high, afforded no hiding place. And why should she hide? She was a free white woman with a right to walk on the turnpike if she pleased. She moved aside to let the carriage pass, but the old coachman drew up the horses just abreast of her, and it was Mr MacFarlane, riding just behind him, who hailed her: "Well, we catch up to you at last! We had no idea of you being such a great walker, Mrs Pollocke. Now, ma'am, better late than never, you know; none of us realised you was so determined to go away upon the very minute—or we'd have put the carriage at your disposal instantly. You'll accept this apology, I hope; do, Mrs Pollocke." He opened the door and descended to the dusty ground with the help of his stick; and Grace saw that Mrs MacFarlane under her parasol was in the carriage too, with tear tracks on her face. "Come," he said, and bowed; "no grudges, no hard feelings; you really must accept my apology, you know. Do shake hands, now, Mrs Pollocke; we're all cousins, after all, and it don't answer to quarrel, not at a time like this. Here we are—better late than never—to apologise, and put the carriage at your disposal, to take you wherever you like, wherever it is you're so determined to get to. Straight through to Alexandria, if you like." He blinked, twice.

"Come and sit down beside me, cousin," called Mrs MacFarlane, and patted the seat beside her. "You must be dreadful tired! I was sure we must have missed you, or mistooken your road—or that you must have mistooken your road, for I never dreamed you'd walk so far. I was just begging Mr MacFarlane to turn around and go back, so as to look for you on another road. I was quite distraught, I was indeed, Mrs Pollocke. I swow, you're dusty as a miller! Come, here's some watermelon ice that my aunt put up for you, and I'm sure you must be perished of thirst. You'll be carried in comfort wherever you say—all the way to Alexandria, if you only say the word."

"Shake hands, now; do, Mrs Pollocke," said Mr MacFarlane again, proffering his own. "Don't bear a grudge; you only caught me unawares, you know, and unprepared. All of us. But here we are, to make you all the amends within our power. And the carriage, to command just as you like."

But as Mr MacFarlane stepped forward, Grace stepped back. Fury flared for an instant behind his eyes; he blinked hard; the vein in his forehead swelled; and she knew that her instinct had been correct. He said, "Oh, come, now, Mrs Pollocke. You make yourself ridiculous; you make us all ridiculous. If you won't shake hands, at least don't make a scene in the road, but get in at once; enough of this foolishness. It's a long ways to Alexandria; and my guess is, it's fixing to rain; let's don't waste any more time."

Grace curtsied, her best Diwani curtsy; and, still wordless, turned and set off again toward Alexandria on her own two feet.

"Oh, Mrs Pollocke!" cried Mrs MacFarlane from inside the carriage. "Well, I swan!" Mr MacFarlane caught up to her after a moment, walking beside her, half a pace back; and the carriage followed too, all at her walking pace now.

Mr MacFarlane at her elbow said, "But what's all this, Mrs Pollocke? I didn't expect rudeness from you; and I'm sure I don't deserve insult."

When she was eight years old Grace had been kidnapped—for several brief terrifying hours—by Miss Johnstone, in Edinburgh, in a carriage. She stepped up her pace a bit, and so did he; but his gait was not so good as hers; he favored his right leg a little, and the snake-headed walking stick tapped an uneven cadence. Grace was glad of her own rustic stick.

"Haven't I offered you our apologies? Haven't I given you my sacred word of honor?" he said. "Isn't that good enough for you? Surely you can't suspect us of—of anything mean or underhanded? Come, Mrs Pollocke, if you suspect some kind of deceit, have the common honesty to say so."

Still Grace did not reply; and after a minute he said, "Well; nothing at all to say?"

"Pray turn around and go home," said Grace at last, without breaking stride. "I will never get in that carriage; and there is no use in your following me."

"What a mean opinion you must have formed of us, ma'am! Did any of us ever give you the slightest cause for doubting our good faith?"

Grace stopped suddenly; turned to face him. He was slightly out of breath, and the vein in his forehead throbbed. Grace said, "Why did you not bring my trunks, then?" She nodded toward the empty luggage rack at the back of the carriage.

He turned to look; but the luggage rack was indisputably empty. "Clara!" he snapped at his wife. "I told you to have Mrs Pollocke's trunks loaded—didn't I! I did," he said, turning back to Grace, "but she foolishly forgot, I see, in the rush. Is that what's troubling you? I'm very sorry for it; and of course we'll have them sent along after you by the first possible conveyance. Now, do get in, Mrs Pollocke, and let's get on for Alexandria. It's infernally hot for quarreling in the road."

But Grace turned and walked off once more; and this time, no one followed.

SHE PASSED ANOTHER slave field crew at some distance; men and women, they were bent over their hoes, but singing nevertheless:

Bendin' knees a-achin',
Body racked wit' pain.
I wish I was a child of God,
I'd git home by & by.

Grace's own knees ached, and the muscles in her thighs and calves complained with what now began to amount to pain. Nevertheless, she too expected to get home by and by. For the past half hour, tall clouds had been piling up ahead to the east, and now a distant rumbling foretold rain. The slaves sang:

O hear dat lumberin' thunder
A-roll from door to door,
A-callin' de people home to God;
They'll git home by & by.

When they sang of thunder, the men's bass voices rumbled out their deepest and most thrilling tones.

O see dat forked lightnin'
A-jump from cloud to cloud,
A-pickin' up God's children;
They'll git home by & by.

And then it did rain. Grace gained the shelter of a wood—some farmer's woodlot, perhaps—just as the drops started pelting heavily.

In the shelter of the woods, there was a rustling—a snorting—then pigs dashed away; impossible to see how many in the dappled light under the tall trees. But Grace noted where they had been rooting in the deep crackling mast. These were beech trees; so there might be beechnuts to be picked up. She found a dozen of them, carried them to the next stream, and sat down there upon a rock. Removing her shoes, she inspected the soles and found them woefully thin; and getting thinner. She removed her damp coarse hose too. The water was only cool on her hot feet, not cold enough; but it was some comfort.

Both ends of her corset busk were chafing painfully—the top at her breastbone, and the bottom below her navel. She would have liked to remove it, discard it; but that would mean undressing. The negro field hands, the women among them, did not wear corsets; their bodies were sufficiently strong to hold themselves without corsets, without stays, without busks.

With her fingernails, she peeled open the old beechnuts. They were dry, shrunken, a bit rancid, but she found a few edible small meats.

The wild mulberry fruits were mostly seeds. The poison oak had small green berries, but she knew better than to touch those; nor did they look tempting. She resumed her walk.

THE SOLES OF HER FEET were hot and painful. Each step burnt upon the ball of her foot. There was a particularly tender place, and she tried to shift her weight to another part of the foot; but this warped her gait, and made her calf and thigh muscles burn painfully. The sun had set; dusk was falling, and she was still walking, not very briskly now. She came to a downslope, where it was painful to feel the muscles in her legs braking her at each step. She could not walk much further. How far had she gone? Not far; not far enough. Not twenty miles—but Jeanie Deans had been a work-hardened milkmaid, a stout country lass; and even she, Grace now remembered, had ended up riding in a carriage for much of her journey to London—and for the entire journey back to Scotland again.

There was a smooth stone topping a low fieldstone wall, a perfect seat. She could not resist: a brief rest, no more. The leather sole was worn very thin under the ball of her right foot; that boot would not last much longer. The left was not much better. Her legs did not hurt when she was sitting. The sky was mauve, lavender, cobalt; and there just above the dark humpbacked hill glimmered bright Venus, about to set.

A wagon came down the slope she had just descended. It was drawn by a mismatched team, horse and mule, and driven by a farmer. There were barrels upright at the rear of the wagon's cargo deck, and a canvas covered the rest of the lumpy load, tied snugly at the corners.

"Good evening, mistress," said the man, "where are thee bound, afoot, and so late?" A Quaker, to judge by his language and his hat. Grace kindled at the kind tenderness of the familiar "thee." To her, it felt humane; it expressed much deeper fellow feeling than the formal "you." Gaelic, her cradle language, used *thu*, the equivalent, and so did Hindi—*tum*—and Bengali—*tumi.* In English, "thee" was seldom heard now, except among Quakers, and some Border Scots—and among American preachers, who generally thee'd the Almighty Himself. But on the whole, the English language had drawn back from familiarity; stood now upon its sore and inflamed dignity.

"To Alexandria," Grace said. "Do you know of any farmhouse nearby, where I might get a meal and a bed for the night?"

"It's four miles to my farm," he said. "My wife will give thee a supper and a clean bed under the stair. Come, here's room for another," he said, sliding to the far side of the seat.

It was not in Grace to decline this offer from an angel. She rose—attempted to rise—but her legs would not bear her weight, and she caught at the stone wall and pushed herself upright. Then she willed her legs to straighten—she balanced over her painful feet—and tottered to the wagon, catching at the rail to keep her balance and falling against the canvas cover over the load, which shifted away under her weight; soft, perhaps a sack of grain. Embarrassed by her debility, she tried to laugh, saying, "I fear I cannot climb up, though. Perhaps I had best ride in the back? Upon your grain sacks?"

"No!" said the man sharply. "Thee must ride up here." Looping the reins around the whip socket, he got down and helped lift her onto the seat. Once they both were seated, he slapped the lines on the rumps of the horse and mule, which set off again at a walk. "Thee has walked far this day," he observed.

"I am not sure how far," said Grace. "But I have been walking for some seven or eight hours, I believe. How far is this from Leesburg?"

"Twelve miles, at the creek crossing just ahead," he said. "I am called Gideon Janney. What is thy name?"

"Helen Walker," said Grace.

THE FARMER HALTED his wagon in front of his house and shouted, "Susan? Susan! Come out, prithee!" A farmwife in homespun emerged, and at his bidding she helped Grace down from the wagon seat. Grace could not even have stood, unaided. "This is Helen Walker," said Mr

Janney, "who is walking to Alexandria, and she needs supper and a bed this night. Do thee help her to the spare bed, Susan, while I get the wagon and my consignments put safe away into the barn." Then he drove his team and wagon directly into his barn. Two half-grown boys appeared—his sons, doubtless, about the same ages as Anibaddh's— and shut the wide barn doors behind the wagon, while Grace made her way painfully into the house, leaning heavily upon sturdy Mrs Janney.

Susan had a substantial supper ready for her husband; remarkably substantial. In the vast fireplace was a large iron pot brim-full of boiled salt pork and greens. On the table lay two large baked cakes of corn-bread, and a rye loaf, with something else set to rise under a cloth in the tray of the dough trough. A twelve-year-old daughter stoked the fire. It was food enough for a dozen, Grace thought; but Mrs Janney helped Grace directly to a tiny room sectioned off under the stairs that ascended from one corner of the large kitchen. The little compartment held nothing but a bed, and had only a narrow opening for a window. The bed had a well-washed homespun counterpane over a wool blanket. "Thee must lie down and rest thy limbs," instructed Mrs Janney, and Grace was glad to do as she was told. In a few moments Mrs Janney returned with a basin of hot water in which Grace was ordered to soak her feet. Mrs Janney took away Grace's boots, tsk-tsking at the state of the soles.

A short time later, the daughter brought a plate of food: pork, greens, baked beans, rye bread, and cornbread. Grace devoured this greedily; it was fortunate that she was alone. The fork was of crude steel, and the tines left a metallic tingling on her tongue. There seemed to be a great deal of coming and going in the kitchen on the far side of the thin board wall, low voices; and then there was silence. Grace was too exhausted to wonder much; her tiny chamber was dark and quiet; she loosened her stays, and slept.

"CHICK-CHICK-CHICK-CHICKEEEE!" cried a woman's voice some distance away, awakening Grace. Full daylight poured through the small slit of window high up under the stair; and Mrs Janney was feeding her hens. In another moment, Grace heard someone come into the kitchen. Grace remembered now some nocturnal impression of tap-pings and stirrings, of creakings of hinges or cartwheels or floorboards or stair treads overhead during the night. Now, carefully deploying herself, Grace found that she was able to stand. She arranged her clothing as best she could, concealed her untidy hair under her bonnet, and emerged stiffly from her tiny sleeping nook, to be greeted by Mrs Janney. The house was quite still, and all signs of the vast meal of the previous evening had disappeared.

"No, my children are at school, and my husband drove out again, very early, before light," said Mrs Janney, in answer to Grace's polite inquiry.

"Drove out again so soon! Back to Leesburg already?" asked Grace, surprised.

"No, on toward Maryland," said Mrs Janney.

"Did he! Alas, I might have gone with him, then, if I had known!" exclaimed Grace. "It would have saved me miles upon my own two feet."

"He has mended thy boots for thee, though, Helen Walker," said Mrs Janney, and she set them before Grace. Thick new soles had been neatly nailed onto both boots, incongruous against the ribbon laces and the soft leather of the uppers—but perfectly serviceable.

Mrs Janney set a plate of flat griddle cakes on the table and invited Grace to eat. But as Grace sat down, there came the sound of hooves and wheels on gravel; and from the window, the women saw two riders and a light buggy carrying two men wheel into the yard, and draw up before Mrs Janney's door. She betrayed no surprise, but only said quietly, "Thee had best remain inside, Helen Walker," and went out to her front porch, closing the door behind her. Grace watched and lis-tened from behind a half-shuttered window.

"Where is your husband?" demanded one of the riders, a white man with a pistol at his belt and a rifle in a scabbard at his horse's shoulder. He seemed to be their leader, though his horse was remarkably ugly, thought Grace, for its entire face was all broad white blaze, coarse and ill-bred; and its four feet were all touched with white too. In India, where horses were supposed to be bay—brown with inky black legs—this would have been a very inauspicious sort of horse.

"He is not here," said Mrs Janney slowly.

"Well, where is he?"

After a moment's pause, Mrs Janney said, "He drove out this morning . . . early," as though this were a great intellectual effort.

"He was here last night, then?"

Mrs Janney the dullard gave the question some painstaking thought; and then allowed as how she guessed that he had been.

"Mr Preston, here, from Winchester, is the owner of five fugitives—two men, two women, and a child—run away three days ago, and known to be headed this way. Now, Mrs Janney, I guess you won't tell me a lie. Tell me, did your husband bring any strangers here last night?"

"Well, I guess he did," said Mrs Janney slowly, after some ponderous reflection. "He did bring a poor exhausted woman he found walking all alone on the turnpike."

"About how old, this woman?"

"Oh . . ."

"Older than yourself, or younger?"

"Maybe younger, I guess," said Mrs Janney.

"And complected how? Dark? Light?"

"Oh, not dark," said Mrs Janney. "Reddish."

"Could be Molly," remarked the man to his companions. Then, to Mrs Janney, he said, "And I guess this woman slept here last night?"

"Well, she did," admitted Mrs Janney.

"And your husband took her off again this morning?"

"No," said Mrs Janney.

"No? How did she go, then?" demanded the man.

Mrs Janney was silent.

"Is she here still?"

Mrs Janney remained silent.

"Ha!" exclaimed the man. "No answer? You was ready enough before. I guess we know well enough what to think of that. In the barn, is she, Mrs Janney?" When she maintained her silence, he turned to the other rider and said, "Cole, you go and search the barn first, then, while I keep an eye on the house. Mr Preston, you might just go around behind and watch the back door. If there's nothing in the barn, we'll search the house next. Davis, you go and stick a pitchfork into the corncribs, and any haystacks you find. And don't forget the hedges and the woodpile!"

It took Cole and Davis nearly half an hour to determine that the barn, the haystacks, the corncribs, the woodpile, and the hedgerows concealed no fugitives. The other two men sat on their horses outside the front and back doors of the house. During this time, Mrs Janney sat on a rocking chair on her front porch and combed flax while Grace remained concealed inside.

I would lie, thought Grace. Much simpler; much safer; and neither sin nor crime, under the circumstances. But perhaps, she thought, that is only because I am so vain; too vain to let even such men as these think me stupid.

"Now, Mrs Janney, we want to come and have a look inside your house," called the lead man at last. "You won't make no objection, I guess? It won't take long."

"Well, I guess," said Mrs Janney the half-wit.

Grace retreated silently to the tiny sleeping compartment and closed the board door. She heard them entering the kitchen on the other side of the wall of boards—and then the board door opened, not two feet from her knees—and four men peered at her. As she pointed to Grace, Mrs Janney was saying to the men, "There she is, the poor woman walking by herself on the turnpike last night, that my husband brought here."

"But that's a white woman!" exclaimed one of the men in disgust. "We're looking for negroes. Didn't your husband bring no negroes here last night?"

Confusion spread over the simpleton countenance of Mrs Janney, and she did not reply.

The man turned to Grace. "Did you see or hear any negroes here last night? Coming or going?" he demanded.

"No, sir," said Grace. "I saw no one but the family." This was truth; she had neither seen nor heard any fugitives—the fugitives who must have been concealed in Mr Janney's wagon under the canvas cover, where he had not permitted her to sit.

The man spat tobacco juice on Mrs Janney's floor. "Damn me if we ain't just wasted nigh an hour," he said. "Come on, let's go."

"Shouldn't we search the house anyhow?" said another.

"Waste of time," snapped the leader. "Can't see how Janney puts up with it. Quaker honesty, my hat. It ain't honesty, it's downright stupidity." So the house went unsearched.

"AND PLEASE CONVEY my deepest gratitude to Mr Janney too," said Grace as she took her leave of Mrs Janney. "I am all the more grateful for his kindness, now that I know how much was at stake." He could not have been certain, when he took pity on her, that she would no more betray him—or the five fugitives—than she would betray her own husband and child. He had no reason to suppose that she, a stranger, might abhor slavery rather than uphold it. "And he may rely entirely upon my discretion."

Mrs Janney smiled and shook her head. "A firm reliance may always be placed upon the protection of a Divine Providence," she said.

Grace neither assented nor demurred. She said, "Still, I am sorry that your husband drove off so early without me."

"There was no time to be lost. He knew that pursuers were coming. But, as Providence would have it, thy presence here, Helen Walker, has been the means of turning aside the suspicions of wicked men, and delaying them in their designs."

GRACE SET OFF AFOOT, laden by Mrs Janney with a jar of buttermilk, four boiled eggs, and two thick slices of bread slathered with yellow butter. The new-soled boots felt stiff and slick to begin with, but Grace soon became accustomed to them; and her tender feet were much better protected now from the sharp rocks and ruts of the road. The painful muscles of her legs loosened and eased considerably within the first ten minutes of walking, and then she was able to marvel at the beauty of this new-world Eden. The chestnut trees were in bloom, and the fragrance of their tufts of bloom—like mango trees in bloom—wafted far. The elders were blooming too; and wild grapes; and wild roses, perfumed. The morning was not yet hot. Blackbirds harassed a hawk; crows rose flapping from a field of watermelons. Meadowlarks caroled from the dubious safety of their ground nests in a hay field. Riding in a carriage, Grace reflected, was all comfort and ease—one glided along, seated upon upholstered cushions, perhaps with the side curtains fastened down to keep out the dust and glare—but how much one missed! And how much more still, speeding along inside an enclosed railway carriage, all metallic goblin shriekings, foul smoke, and smuts! She was glad to be afoot—a little.

She did not stop at the busy tavern at Dranesville; but took comfort from the thought that only fourteen miles remained to Alexandria.

It was slow and laborious walking, however, she admitted to herself an hour later.

At a junction in the road, she was unsure of her way. There were no signs, and both forks seemed equally heavily trafficked, to judge by their dust and ruts. She chose the fork which seemed to lead more nearly southeast, where she knew Alexandria lay, and walked more than half a mile in some doubt before coming across schoolchildren in the play yard outside their school, who set her straight; she had chosen wrong, alas! and was forced to retrace her steps, a heartbreaking affair! Her right hip was beginning to ache too.

Rest, then, she told herself; and accordingly, at the next stream crossing, she made her way a little distance along the bank—careful to avoid the shiny beautiful poison oak growing lushly there—and sat upon a log in the shade, and ate two of her eggs. Mrs Janney had told her that the miles to Alexandria were easy ones without cruel hills, and the last part of the turnpike lay near the broad river. She walked on, through the afternoon, not so cool or comfortable or lovely and fresh as the morning. The sun beat hot on her back. A farmer driving his wagon toward Leesburg told her she was eight miles from Alexandria. Eight miles, still! Her hip hurt. She stopped to remove a pebble from her shoe, and walked on. She ate the remaining two eggs, and the bread. She had finished the buttermilk hours earlier, and was thirsty again. She passed a pair of negro men sawing massive branches from an old hollow oak that had toppled into a field.

Had fugitives ever used that hollow tree as a hiding place? A dramatic and well-composed scene sprang to her mind's eye: a brave but desperate family of negro fugitives, sheltering there from storm, and from mounted patrollers. It would make a very appealing subject for a romantic and sentimental kind of artist, she mused; engraved, it might sell thousands of copies, spectacularly popular with all but southern slaveholders. For a while as she walked, Grace amused herself by evaluating every haystack, every corncrib, every isolated farmhouse with its barn, every passing canvas-covered wagon—as hiding places for fugitives. Now the Virginia countryside seemed more interesting than before.

Mrs Janney had said that her husband knew he was pursued. Grace supposed that they, and other men and women like them, had somehow found safe ways of passing secret knowledge and news among themselves. Among Friends.

She was stumbling a little. Pick up your feet and walk, she warned herself. Her fingers had swelled, sausagelike. Instead of letting her hands hang downwards by her sides swinging with each step, she held them upwards for a while, until the puffiness receded a little from around her now-snug gold wedding ring.

A rhythmic tune was circling through her head, in cadence with her pace. Her breath came in time to it. What was it? She could not name it, and could not banish it. At last she succeeded in eradicating it by humming "The Philadelphia Firemen's Cotillion" instead. But after a while, she noticed that the first tune had come back again. At once she knew what it was, for this time an old Gaelic phrase came with it. *Is fhada mar so tha sinn*: "Too Long in this Condition." It was the bagpipe tune which old Mr MacFarlane had played, that evening on the dam. He had said it was the MacFarlanes' gathering tune, their *cruinneachadh*; and called it *Thogail nam Bo theid sinn*: "To Lift the Cows We Shall Go." The MacFarlanes had always been notorious cateran; cattle-lifters.

To free the cattle of our neighbors.

To free the people whom our neighbors insist upon viewing as cattle.

That was the night Diana had gone away.

A particular tune played upon a bagpipe would make an excellent signal, a message, Grace mused, carrying across great distances of open country. The instrument had been devised for just that.

HER SHADOW ELONGATED before her on the dusty road; and eventually the sun set, and she was glad of the cool. The farms were smaller here, the houses closer together. Surely she was approaching Alexandria? Here the road undulated along the edge of a long narrow valley and from some bends she could see far ahead, perhaps a mile. From other places, she could see only as far as the next bend, a few hundred yards. Evening sounds—a girl calling in the cow for the night: *Suuuu-key*; a cow lowing to her calf; a cowbell—carried far in the cooling dusk. Grace was so sorely tempted to stop—oh, to rest! To lie down! No; keep walking, she told herself. If you stop now, you will be too sore to resume. The thought of comfortable beds, in the comfortable inns which surely awaited her at Alexandria, kept her moving: to sleep in a bed! Between smooth sheets! Not here, in a wheat field. Not here, on a stream bank.

From a bend she could see across the next field, to where the road curved around a wooded bluff—and in the gathering dusk she heard rapid hoofbeats, several horses approaching; and could just make out a carriage drawn by two horses and escorted by two outriders—one of them mounted on an ugly beast with a broad white blaze splashed crudely across its entire face, quite unmistakable even in this gathering darkness.

Would these men recognise her? Perhaps not; they had seen her for only a few moments this morning. But Grace was loath to risk any encounter with them. The pumpkin field to her right offered no concealment. There was no hedge or stone wall or tall corn to shelter her. To her left loomed tall trees over a dense understory of—what? Elderberry? Dogwood? Wild rose? Poison oak? The four horses were fast approaching, to judge by the sound of their hoofbeats, and Grace stepped into the shelter of the dark bushes under the trees. Thorns grabbed at her sleeves as she pushed deeper into the shadows. Ducking under a low-hanging branch, she found good cover behind a thicket. She could see out; she heard their approach, then saw them trot past, only fleeting black silhouettes against the last light of the darkening cobalt sky. There was no sign of any captives with them. The hoofbeats receded westward, then faded out of hearing when they had rounded the next bend in the road.

Grace made her way out of the trees with her arms held up before her face to ward off twigs she could no longer clearly see; nevertheless, a leafy branch rudely slapped the right side of her face; and then she was out on the open road again.

All was still. She resumed walking, comforted to see the familiar summer constellations gradually becoming visible overhead: the Swan; the Harp. Soon there were houses; then warehouses, brick pavements, and gas lamps: the outskirts of Alexandria. She walked on; the hotels, she surmised, were probably near the bridge at the far edge of the town.

So they were. Grace chose the Hotel Cincinnatus, and there, despite her lack of male escort, of female attendant, her lack even of "plunder"— the baggage which accompanied any respectable traveler—the desk clerk was sufficiently impressed by her accent and her banknotes to cede her a small, ill-lit, and ill-furnished room. Grace rang three times for warm wash water and a towel, but none was forthcoming; and at last she took to the bed like a fox to its den, though neither the dingy linens nor the wretched mattress resembled those of her imaginings. It was not until she awakened in the morning that she became aware of the swelling itchy rash already disfiguring the right side of her face.

"My, oh, my! look, Jamie, dear, it's your mamma, come home at last," said old Mrs Pollocke to Jamie, in her arms. "And you must tell her never to leave you again. Come, now, dear, can you say it, just as we practiced: 'Never leave me, Mamma'?" Jamie's nose had run horribly down his upper lip, but he ducked away from his grandmother's attempt to wipe it, and instead left a streak of slime on her collar.

Grace had arrived in Philadelphia by the railroad cars from Washington City, and a hack cab delivered her at last to her own marble doorstep. Home! To her dearly beloved ones!

But Daniel was not at home; and Jamie was in the arms of old Mrs Pollocke. Grace was surprised to see Anibaddh's young protégée too: Miss Babcock, in Grace's chair by the parlor window. Mrs Pollocke and Miss Babcock declared themselves delighted and astonished to see Grace, but expressed scant interest in the details of her journey—and Jamie, once his first transports were over, refused even to look at Grace, and certainly would not say the words his grandmother had rehearsed with him.

"Why, we've been here all day," said the elder Mrs Pollocke. "Since right after breakfast, when we hurried down to take charge of poor Jamie, I and Miss Babcock, so Danny could go out looking for your colored girl. Of course we did, even though it was very inconvenient for us, as it's our day for sewing. Oh, yes, Miss Babcock has been staying with me, paying me a visit—didn't you know? Well! I am surprised; I thought Danny would surely have mentioned that, when he wrote to you."

"But Rawley?" said Grace. "What has happened to Rawley?"

"That's just what we'd all like to know. Danny said she stepped out this morning, first thing," explained Mrs Pollocke, "just around the corner to go and buy eggs at the New Market, and—well—she never came back. So after an hour Danny went out looking for her. Nobody remembered having seen her, but somebody told him that some slave-catcher had been hanging about. So then he sent for me, to come and take charge of Jamie, and Miss Babcock too—and here we've been all day long, while poor Danny has been turning the town upside down and shaking it. First he called on Mr Forten, who advised him to go to the mayor's office; and then the mayor sent out a couple of his men to search. But I've been saying all day it's no business of the mayor's, haven't I, Miss Babcock?"

"Yes, ma'am, you have," said Miss Babcock.

"That girl is lazy, that's the trouble," said old Mrs Pollocke. "I reckon she's just shirking, and that's just what I told Danny. Cat's away, mice will play. Depend on it, she'll come sauntering back of her own accord soon enough. And when she does come back, Grace, dear, I hope you'll give her the sack. My new Irish cook is turning out to be as steady as you like. Well, now, what in heaven's name happened to your face?"

Grace had drawn back the veil which had covered her face all day. Her fingertips brushed the blazing oozing rash on her swollen right cheek. The left was nearly as bad, and the crease under her chin was maddening. "Oh, it is nothing," she said. "I only—"

"After a while I thought I'd better get along with the dinner," said old Mrs Pollocke. "There wasn't much, but I did manage some nice cutlets and dumplings. By the way, I thought your flour was looking mothy, so I took the time to sift it, and was shocked to find it full of worms. I don't know who you've been buying flour from, but you're being robbed blind, and I'd sure say something about it, if it was up to me. But we'd only just sat down to eat when a messenger came a-pounding on the door for poor Danny—yes, he was here, to wait for any word from the mayor's men. And they sent word they'd found a girl down there—in Southwark, at one of those squalid boardinghouses—just like his description of your colored girl, and they wanted poor Danny to leave his dinner at once and go and see if it was her or not. That was—how long ago, do you think, Miss Babcock? A couple of hours?"

"Perhaps an hour ago, I should say," said Miss Babcock.

"I guess he should be back by now, don't you, even if it was just a wild goose chase? I hoped it was him coming in just now—we sure didn't reckon on seeing you, Grace, dear. Have you had your dinner? There's some dumplings left, but it'll be getting on to teatime before we know it."

Though Grace had had no dinner, she declined the dumplings. At dusk, she took Jamie upstairs to put him to bed. He was less sulky now, happy to cling to her, and she sat in the rocking chair and held him on her lap. She wiped his nose, rocked him, kissed him, sang to him. She sang "The Fishermen's Song to the Seals" until he fell asleep in her arms, warm and heavy as treasure—heavier than when she had left him—until he could at last be gently disentangled and laid in his cot.

ON HER WAY DOWNSTAIRS, Grace startled Miss Babcock, who was trimming the lamps in the spare bedroom. "A word," Grace whispered. "Tell me this much: are they safe away—the Rani and all her family?"

"They are not," replied Miss Babcock in a low voice. "They are still in this city, but they have left the house in Christian Street, and they are well concealed—in another house, in another district of the city. But I am bound to say no more than that, not even to you."

"Still here!" whispered Grace. "But this is dreadful news, dreadful! Why have they not gone away?"

"Passport," said Miss Babcock. "They cannot get a passport for Diana."

"And this difficulty was not forseen, not provided for?"

"Oh, we had thought to use mine, for her—yes, I have mine, issued in Calcutta—and so have we all—but it will not do for Diana, after all—"

"Miss Babcock? Miss Babcock!" called old Mrs Pollocke up the stairwell; and they both went downstairs. "My, oh, my, look at that: dark already!" said old Mrs Pollocke. "I think that I and Miss Babcock might as well stay to tea, under the circumstances. Besides, I've got that spare room aired and the bed made up, since there was no knowing when you—or that Rawley—might come back. It certainly needed a good airing. Don't you think Danny should be back by now, even if it really was Rawley that they found down there? We didn't bring our own sewing with us, but I found *your* mending basket, dear, and plenty of work for three, I'm sure."

Reluctantly, Grace threaded a needle and took up a worn stocking, for she could not sit idly by while others bent over her mending under the parlor lamp. Darning occupied her hands, and kept her from touching the blazing itchy rash on her face.

BEFORE NINE O'CLOCK, Dan returned, and Rawley with him. Grace was struck by the fatigue in his face—and when his gaze alighted, kindled, on her, she read from his expression that she herself was perhaps not quite at her best either. He took her in his arms and kissed her, in front of his mother.

"So, Danny, you caught up with your lost sheep after all!" cried his mother. "Your black sheep! Now, do tell, all about it, from beginning to end!"

Rawley looked frightened and exhausted, and Grace thought she had been crying. Drawing her by the hand into the kitchen, Grace whispered, "Oh, Rawley! Are you all right?"

"Yes, I'm all right, missus, but I'm so glad to get safe home again— and see you home again too!" she said, and burst into tears. "I was so scared! And—oh—I didn't know if anyone would even come and look for me!"

"How good of you, Mamma, to drop everything and come to help," came Dan's voice from the parlor. "I don't know how I'd have managed today without you. But I'll walk you and Miss Babcock home straightaway. I'm sure you'd both like to sleep under your own roof, in your own comfortable beds."

"Oh, but Danny, you've been out all day long and half the night too; I'm sure you'd rather not set out again," said his mother. "And we don't mind staying the night; I've got the bed in the spare room aired and ready. We'll just stay until morning."

But even while Grace comforted Rawley, holding her hand, she also had one ear tuned to hear what Dan was saying to his mother. "No, Mamma, I'll walk you home directly," Grace heard him say—and gratitude bloomed in her heart. "Come, here is your cloak," he added cheerfully. "Miss Babcock has hers already, I see. It won't take us twenty minutes, and it's a fine evening, with plenty of moon."

Grace fetched Rawley a duster for a handkerchief—and from the kitchen doorway she called out, "Good night, then, Mrs Pollocke, and Miss Babcock; and thank you so very much!" as Dan ushered the two visitors outside. Then Grace sat down with Rawley, and held her hand until she had stopped crying.

"Oh, missus! I thought I never would see you again, or Jamie, or Mr Pollocke!"

"But what happened, Rawley?" asked Grace.

"Well—I—I went out early to the market, to get eggs and butter, I went real early while Mr Pollocke was eating his breakfast, so he could look after Jamie for just a few minutes. I didn't like to take Jamie out because he's had that terrible heavy cold. But the woman who I usually buys the eggs from, she wasn't there yet, so I went to another one, a stranger; and then—then two white men grabs me, just lays onto my both arms, like this, and one of them, he says, that's her, grab her. And I hollered, of course I did, but they just bundled me down around the corner, and nobody said nothing to stop them, even though I was hollering and trying to get away from them, nobody helped me, and they pushed me into a wagon. And it drives off, I can feel it going maybe down into Southwark, it seemed like. And they made me get out and go inside a house, a dark shabby bad house; and there's a white woman there, the woman who run the house, but when I call for her to help me, she just turn away, and they locked me down in the coal cellar—and oh, Mrs Pollocke, I feared the worst, the worst! But they just left me locked up there all day long, and nobody come near, except that white woman who brung some beans with some fat pork in it after a while, and I told her I was free, but she wouldn't say nothing to me . . . and then at last there's a noise and a fuss, and she come and unlock the door again, and lets two other white men come in—oh, Mrs Pollocke, I was so afraid, I was trying not to cry. And they said, what is your name? And I said my name is Rawley Tanner, and I am free, and I have my paper to prove it, and I live at Mr Pollocke's house in Lombard Street. Well, show us your paper, then, they said. But I said, no, sir, no, sir, I'm not showing my free paper unless I show it to the judge, sir. A real judge in a real court, I said, or you can ask Mr Pollocke."

"Have you a free paper, Rawley?" asked Grace.

"Of course, missus, I always have my free paper, every minute I have it, that's my most precious thing in all the world. I never set it aside, ever since I got it at the courthouse when I was seven years old."

"Do you mean to say that you carry this precious paper on your person at all times?"

"Every minute, missus, I never stir without it."

"And you are required to produce this paper, whenever any white man pleases to demand it of you?"

"Oh, no, you want to be real careful about that, missus, 'cause that's how they get it away from you, and throw it in the fire, and next thing you know, they carries you down to Alexandria and sell you, or pretend you belong to them, and ran away, and they just getting their property back. So I always plan to say, I won't give up my paper except to the judge, you have to bring me before the judge. 'Cause that's the law, you know—oh, yes, it is, Mrs Pollocke, don't you know that? They have to go to the judge, and prove you're not free, before they can take you down across the line. Well, they supposed to, of course they *supposed* to, but they don't sometimes, not if they can just do it quiet and never mind all that botheration about a judge and a courtroom. So I always ready to make a noise, and yell and holler and kick up a fuss, not just go along quiet, not if I can help it. So I said, no, sir, I won't show it except to the judge, or you can ask Mr Pollocke who lives in Lombard Street. And so then they locked me up and leave me there in the dark again . . . and . . . I was afraid they might come and—and take my clothes, and steal my paper, and I wished I didn't tell them after all. . . ."

"Oh, Rawley," said Grace.

"But then, after a long time, they come back—and oh, missus, I was so glad to see Mr Pollocke with them, you can't imagine! Yes, that's our Rawley, he told them; and so after a while, a long time, they let me come home with him."

"Oh, Rawley," said Grace again. "What a dreadful time you have had!" At this moment she hated Americans. "I daresay—wouldn't it be prudent, though, Rawley—to get another copy of your paper; another copy, properly made out, from the courthouse where yours was issued, to be kept in a safe place here, or at Mr Pollocke's offices, or even at the bank?"

"Oh, but missus, I can't; and that's because that courthouse done burned down. Yes, missus, it did. It was Leonardstown Courthouse in St Mary's County, in Maryland. Maryland, that's where I was born. And that's where my paper is from; but I can't never get a copy made, 'cause that courthouse done burned down to ashes one night. It was . . . let's see . . . just about nine or ten years ago. Yes, when I was eight years old, so it must of been in '31, that's nine years ago. The whole courthouse gone and burned down, and all the deeds and papers and records and record books, everything. So I can't get no copy of my free paper, and this one has to last me my whole life."

What a great deal of burning-down these courthouses, these Temples of Property, seemed to do! Remarkable.

"And I guess there's still no eggs or butter in the house!" wailed Rawley.

WHEN DAN RETURNED, Grace was in bed.

During that warm summer night, Grace and Dan slept little; talked little. The windows stood open, and the night air stirred through the room, across their skin. If Grace closed her eyes, it was like those first nights, those summer nights they had spent on the rooftop terrace of the old house in Calcutta, under a wafting canopy of netting, under the dome of wheeling stars, in the unseen, unheard company (on other rooftops, of other old houses) of other couples—each absorbed in their own raptures, their own delights; and overlooked only by the devas and devis, the Shining Ones, who approved wholeheartedly—for those Hindu divinities were doubtless likewise engaged.

From time to time, Grace heard Jamie coughing, but he did not awaken; and Grace was very glad that Mrs Pollocke and Miss Babcock were not occupying the bed in the spare room.

"There is a piece of an old Sanskrit poem in my head," she told him at one point. "Not a very decent one."

"Tell it to me," he said.

She did, in Sanskrit.

"Well . . . what does it mean?"

"Something like:

The drawstring of my skirt was already loosened;
it scarcely stayed on my hips.
And when my man came to bed
the knot came untied all by itself.
That's the last thing I knew."

"A nice education you've had!" he said. "I have a poem running through my head too; and it goes like this:

You, you;
you you you.
You,
you."

Tomorrow I will tell him that I am pregnant, Grace thought. Toward morning, they slept at last; and when she awakened, in broad daylight, he had gone. Yesterday's shirt lay across the back of a chair and, still hungry, Grace pressed her face to the linen, to the smell of him. The rash on her face began to itch again.

. . .

"AND IF YOU DO EMANCIPATE AND PENSION THIS ELDERLY PER-son," explained Mr David Paul Brown in his chambers to the red-haired Scottish woman who had consulted him once before on a different matter, "he must remove from Virginia within twelve months, or else risk re-enslavement, in accordance with the statute of that commonwealth. Has he a wife? Or children, do you know? These former slaves are sometimes reluctant to leave their relations, especially in their old age."

The young woman—a flaming red rash disfiguring her face—admitted that she had no idea.

"Are you by any chance a married woman, ma'am?" he asked; for she wore a gold ring.

"I am, sir," she said, after a moment's hesitation.

"And has your husband consented to this proposal to emancipate this slave, and make this settlement?"

"I have not yet discussed it with my husband. But the trust which acquired this slave without my knowledge or consent is my own property, left me by my mother; and the money with which I propose to fund his pension is my own, earned by my own work."

"Do you understand, ma'am, that in law, there is no such thing as a married woman's own property, unless it has been left to her explicitly as her own, by her husband's consent, by settlement concluded prior to her marriage?"

"Is it so? Well, I have still a small sum which I laid aside during the period before I was married," said the red-haired lady.

"Unless explicitly retained to yourself by prior settlement, ma'am, any such funds became your husband's property at the time of your marriage."

"Can this be possible, sir?"

"It is law. I am sorry to tell you that, although I should personally be quite willing—most happy—to oblige you by drawing up the deeds to enact this emancipation, it can have no legal effect without your husband's signature. Every married woman is *femme couverte* in the eyes of the law—excepting, of course, for those unfortunate cases in which it has been found necessary to obtain a legal separation. I hope, however, that this exception does not apply to your particular situation?"

"No, indeed," she said.

• • •

"WILL YOU SHOW ME YOUR FREE PAPER, RAWLEY?" SAID Grace. "I have had an idea about it." Rawley was feeding Jamie his porridge in the kitchen.

"Oh, missus!" exclaimed Rawley; and Grace saw an instant's hesitation, a moment's fear before Rawley masked her unease. Then, turning her back for modesty's sake, Rawley reached into the recesses of her clothing and drew out a small packet folded in an old piece of tabby homespun. The packet was curved to the shape of a body.

Rawley held it close, and instead of reaching to take it, Grace nodded at the table. "There," she said. "Just lay it there, Rawley, and unwrap it, so I can see it. I won't touch it."

"Don't touch, Mamma!" Jamie commanded.

Rawley carefully laid back the cloth, unfolded the paper inside, and delicately smoothed it open. The folds in the paper were worn and frayed, and an amber stain like tea or ale on one edge had bled, blurring the ink a little. Grace approached, just near enough to make out the rustic unpracticed handwriting:

To all to whom these presents shall come be known ye, that I Mildred Beale of the County of Saint Mary in the State of Maryland for divers good causes & considerations have emancipated and set free, & by these presents do for me and my heirs, & all claiming or to claim by, from, through, or under me or them, fully freely & absolutely liberate, emancipate & set free one negroe girl Slave called & known by the name of Rawley, now seven years of age, of medium coffee color & without scar's or particular marks. Witness my hand and seal this 6th day of May in the year of our Lord 1830

> *Mildred Beale*
> *Signed Sealed, acknowledged & delivered in presence of*
> *Philip Weems*
> *James F. Payne Jun.*

So this was a "free paper." It had never occurred to Grace that Rawley might not have been born free.

"I can make you a copy of your paper, Rawley," said Grace. "I can make you as many copies as you want."

"But no copies won't do, missus," said Rawley. "Not no copies that we can make."

"Yes, I think it might, though," said Grace. "I will make a daguerreotype replica of your paper."

"Like that picture of you, on that mirror that you showed me?"

"Just so," said Grace. "Such a replica will satisfy any idle inquiry, I daresay; and it is not so easy to destroy such a thing, by tearing it to pieces, or throwing it in the fire. You could carry that replica about with you, ready to present to any ruffians who may demand it, while keeping your original paper safely put away, to be presented only to a judge in a courtroom. Or vice versa, if you prefer."

Rawley folded up her precious packet again, thoughtfully. "We could try that," she agreed.

GRACE'S BAGGAGE ARRIVED by rail at Philadelphia several days after her return. A messenger from the stationmaster brought notice that two trunks awaited her at the station; and that a storage fee would accrue unless fetched within twenty-four hours. Daniel had again left the house early under a press of business, so Grace herself had arranged for a carter to go and fetch them; and now they were here, on the floor of her studio. It was a relief to have her painting kit safe under her wing again: her paints, brushes, linseed oil, turpentine, sketchbooks, canvases, ivory blanks—and even the unpaid-for paintings. Grace looked at them, one by one: Mrs Ambler, half-sized. Mrs MacFarlane, in miniature. Miss Johnstone, in miniature. The late Mrs Grant, in miniature, copied from (and an improvement upon) the full-length by the painter who was not Mr Stuart. Miss Julia Grant. Mr James Grant. And the view she had painted for herself of the mansion house— "spoilt" by the figure of old Walter over his bricks.

In the larger trunk containing her clothes she found a plump well-sealed paper packet tucked into her nightdress; and a letter folded around it.

My Dear Cousin,

Enclosed is a half-pound of Tennant's Bleaching Powder, this quantity to be placed in a wooden pail with one pound of sal-soda, and boiling water to be poured on until the pail is full, and stirred with a wooden spoon to dissolve the soda. Let it remain over night, and the next day let the liquor be strained through a cloth into glass bottles or stone jugs, to be tightly corked and stored in the dark. One

*tea-cup full of this liquor—which is the genuine Javelle water—
may be added to your wash kettle, and you will be satisfied, I think,
with the results. You must on no account make a stronger solution,
nor add more than one cup of the Javelle water to the wash kettle,
or you risk injuring your linen; but if a stronger bleaching action
is required, let the stained linen remain for a longer period in the
wash kettle, up to a day and a night if you please. Let the linen
then be thoroughly rinsed in clear water, and wrung out as usual,
before being hung to dry in the sun.*

*All this by way of honoring my promise, which I remember,
though you may not. As for other matters of honor—we are all
pretty grum hereabouts, as my brothers would say. Both of them
remain here, consulting daily with my father's executors and my
brother MacFarlane and another lawyer, who shake their heads
and make long faces. The flood of notes and demands for repay-
ment of loans continues unstaunched, and the newest blow is, that
although my father had insured his life some years ago as collateral
for several loans, he had not, it seems, paid the entire sum necessary
to continue the insurance in force. But I think you may expect before
long to hear some proposal for settling the debt of honor which
is owed to you, at least. You will be happy to know that my sister
MacFarlane does better, and though she speaks from time of time
of returning to Arrochar with her husband, they seem in no hurry
to go. My aunt professes herself unwell, and remains in her room
until dinner time each day. This is a novelty in one who has always
boasted of her robust constitution, and has regarded ill-health as
a moral failing, but I may say that under the circumstances it is
rather a relief than otherwise. I myself am well enough. I long to
visit Philadelphia with my brother MacFarlane when he goes there,
but such an indulgence is the unlikeliest thing going, so I am schooling myself to accept such disappointment as may be my lot and to
possess my soul in patience, just as my aunt would advise.*

The letter ended there, unsigned.

But as she unpacked her belongings and put them away, Grace realised that the book which set forth M. Daguerre's process—lent her by

Mr Cornelius, then lent again to Miss Grant—was not in the trunk. She felt exceedingly vexed at this; unreasonably vexed.

"YOU ARE TO SIT in that chair, Rawley, and hold your paper up to the camera's lens in your two hands; better let them rest upon your lap, I think, for you must hold it perfectly still," said Grace. It would have been simpler to borrow Rawley's free paper to make a daguerreotype of it—but Rawley could not bear to be parted from it; not even to Grace, not even for an hour or two. Rawley had to accompany her paper.

"I hope that Jamie don't wake up too cross for Mr Pollocke," said Rawley. Jamie, still suffering from his cold, had been left asleep at home, where his father proposed to spend this Sunday afternoon catching up with the correspondence which had accrued alarmingly during a three-day absence in New York to meet with prospective buyers of *Rebecca Rolfe*. Sunday was the only day when the daguerreotype studio was closed to sitters, and generous Mr Cornelius had made it available to Grace. Though he had shown her just what to do, and assured her that the process, if correctly executed, must infallibly succeed, Grace did not feel entirely confident.

She chalked the camera stand's original position on the floor, and then pushed it forward, nearer to Rawley. "About there," she muttered to herself. "Now extend the lens . . . ah, an image that is both large *and* sharp! You must hold your paper perfectly flat, Rawley, for my plane of focus is not much deeper than the paper itself." The image would be at just about half size, for the largest plate the camera could accommodate was less than four inches by three—and Rawley's paper was about twice that, about six-by-eight inches. "The image of your paper just fills the plate," said Grace, "and your fingertips are showing too, your fingers holding it at the edges. It should be just legible, I think; and any old judge who has forgotten his spectacles can call for a magnifying glass—or better yet, his shaving mirror, for of course it will be backwards."

As her subject was only a sheet of paper, and not likely to squint or blink in the glare, she tied back the pane of blue glass. The exposure could be as long as she pleased; as long as necessary. She covered the lens; removed the glass focusing screen; and inserted in its place one of Mr Cornelius's prepared plates, in its apparatus. "Now, you must hold perfectly still, Rawley, perfectly. How long can you hold your breath? No, just a joke; of course you may breathe; but no deep sighs, if you please. Let us try one minute, and see what we get. Sixty seconds. But where is Mr Cornelius's pocket watch?" He had promised to leave it for her, as its seconds hand was indispensable for timing the exposure. "Wait here, Rawley, don't move, while I look in the other rooms." Grace searched the reception room, the darkroom, all the tables and desks; but at last sorrowfully concluded that Mr Cornelius had forgotten to leave his pocket watch for her; had slipped it into his pocket and taken it away with him.

"I shall simply have to try to judge the time myself," said Grace. "Are you ready, Rawley? Quite still, please. Now." Grace removed the lens cover. Rawley sat perfectly still, her hands holding the paper resting in her lap; and perfectly quiet, as though noise were movement.

How difficult it was to judge the passage of time! The large increments were simple enough; the years, the months, the days—for the heavenly bodies, the devas and devis, the Shining Ones, marked those; indeed, defined those. But the smaller increments, the made-up human increments, the fractions of those natural rhythms of light and dark, were much harder to judge. How long was a second? How long was a minute? How long was an hour? And why were days divided into twenty-four segments, come to think of it? Who had decreed the number and length of "hours"? Very inconvenient, mathematically speaking!—like pounds divided into shillings and pence, so irritating—compared to dollars, divided into cents. Why were days not divided into decimal segments—to be called "graces," perhaps?—for they must be called something! Ten (or a hundred) of them in the cycle of the sun's day and night?

How many seconds had passed, now? How was one to judge, without the guidance of a change of light—or of a seconds hand? Once could count—but count what? Heartbeats? Breaths? Too variable. Count the changes of thought, the passages of ideas and perceptions through the mind? Worse still; her own mind, at least, was deplorably irregular; now stupid, stalled; now exhaustingly, frantically active. But until now, who actually needed to measure the passage of these tiny increments of time? No one. Until now, watches needed only hour and minute hands. But now time was become so precious that the minutes had to be fractured into seconds.

Surely a minute had passed by now?

Grace replaced the cover over the lens. "There, you may breathe, Rawley," she said. "You might come with me into the darkroom if you like."

But no; after her frightening day locked in a coal cellar, Rawley did not like the idea of a small dark room. Grace went alone into that dark stifling closet—that camera obscura—filled with fumes of mercury.

"TOO LONG," SHE SAID, when she emerged. "We'll try forty-five seconds."

So they did, all over again; and once more, Grace took the exposed plate into the dark room. At the end of the fourth operation, as she was removing the plate from the mercury box, she heard a knocking at the street door; and heard Rawley passing through to the front; and voices: Daniel's voice! Grace proceeded to the fifth operation: bathed the plate in salt water, then rinsed it in hot clear water. She heard Jamie's voice too, as they all passed through the corridor and into the studio.

Grace emerged with the finished daguerreotype. "Look," she said, and showed it to them. By skill or by luck, this second attempt was a success. This mirror image of the unpracticed handwriting was small but sharp. The old stain along the edge showed plainly, and even the whorls and swirls on Rawley's fingertips were exquisitely clear.

Reading upside down was easy enough; anyone could do it, over a clerk's desk. But for most people, reading backwards was another matter. To Grace—able to read backwards ever since a childhood accident—the plate was perfectly legible. Taking the little mirrored plate gingerly between her fingertips, she held it up to the looking glass mounted opposite the sitter's chair, mounted there for the convenience of sitters wishing to arrange hair or countenance; to practice their expressions. Daniel and Rawley looked over her shoulder at the reflected image—now intelligible to them too.

Rawley, who could read nothing but her own name, immediately spotted it, touched its image in the looking glass. "Rawley," she whispered.

It was a perfect half-sized replica—transferred to robust metal now, not perishable paper. Rawley gazed upon it. "Don't touch it," said Grace. "It must be sealed yet, behind glass."

Jamie, squirming in Daniel's arms, reached for Rawley.

"Here, Mr Pollocke, I take him," said Rawley.

"You can take him home," said Daniel. "Mrs Pollocke will come later."

"Yes, sir, I do that," said Rawley.

As soon as Rawley and Jamie had gone, Grace turned to Dan, query in her face.

"You'd better see this," said Dan, and handed Grace a letter. "And explain it to me, if you will be so good."

LEESBURG, JULY 5TH.

MR DANIEL POLLOCKE:

Dear Sir:—

Please accept my solemn condolences upon the recent decease of your wife's estimable uncle, the late Judge Andrew Grant. I myself had also the honor of a personal connexion with Judge Grant, in my case through marriage, as he was my wife's revered father.

It happens that certain business affairs call me to Philadelphia immediately; and while I am there, I have the authorisation and consent of Messrs R. Lee and J. Taylor, Judge Grant's executors, to call upon you at such time and place as you may please to name, for the purpose of placing before you a very generous proposal for the private settlement of any claim you might have contemplated lodging against the estate of Mrs Pollocke's late uncle.

If you will kindly direct your reply to the address below, I will receive it upon my arrival in your city.

I beg you will convey to Mrs Pollocke the best compliments of her cousins. We have not ceased to regret that she declined to avail herself of our offer to send her home by carriage, and we hope to be assured that she has suffered no ill effects from her long walk.

> *Yours, &c.,*
> *Neil MacFarlane, Esq.*
> *256 Arch St., Philada.*

Grace looked up from this awkward letter. Where was she to begin her explanations?

"You walked?" he asked at last.

"Aye," admitted Grace.

"Why?"

"Well . . . ," said Grace.

"And why would I be contemplating lodging a claim against your uncle's estate?"

"Oh, aye, there's that too," said Grace. "I was only waiting for an opportunity to tell you all about it—but you've been so much occupied with business, and then away, up to New York—and I did not like to oppress you with still more difficulties to be solved, upon the very minute of your returning home—and it did seem as though all this could wait, until your business affairs should have sorted themselves out somewhat . . . until you were at liberty to devote your attention to it."

"You have my attention," he said. "You might have had it at any time, for the asking." Crossing his arms, he sat down in the sitter's chair. He crossed his legs also, one ankle on the opposite knee. The bright light from the mirrors outside the window fell across his face, and his brow furrowed as he frowned against the glare. Here was the man who had refused a shipment of expensive tea because it had not measured up to his expectations; here was the husband who, though willing to tolerate a wife who painted heads, was by no means to be kept in the dark and made a fool of.

Where was she to begin? Probably he did not know, even now, of Diana's existence. As Grace explained Anibaddh's true reason for coming to America, she moved the camera on its stand back to the chalk mark on the floor, where it belonged.

Then, explaining her own true reason for going to Grantsboro, she released the pane of blue glass from the hook which held it aside and let it return to its proper place. The dazzling sunshine on his face turned to cool blue light, and his brow unknotted, his frown faded.

She replaced the glass focusing screen in the back of the camera and focused on his countenance—while explaining how she had ascertained Diana's whereabouts; how the anonymous offer to buy Diana's freedom had been received, and how declined.

Then she replaced the lens cover, and, removing the glass focusing screen, inserted in its place yet another of Mr Cornelius's prepared silver plates. Diana had taken her freedom nevertheless, she told him; and after Judge Grant's death the careless indiscreet talk of her cousins had revealed to her that she had formerly been a small sort of heiress, but was now, through her uncle's perfidy, only the owner of an old slave named Walter. Upon the unbearable provocation of hearing herself presumed dead, she had impulsively revealed her identity—had judged it advisable to promptly absent herself—had done so on foot for want of any other means.

Through all this, he listened without comment or reproach, asking questions only occasionally.

"... And the next morning," finished Grace at last, "I limped across the Long Bridge to Washington City, and there secured a place on the cars to Philadelphia."

He said nothing, only looked at her. This was his business face; his appraising, weighing, considering, mercantile countenance, which she had not seen before. She said, "Has your pocket watch a seconds hand to it, by any chance?"

"Yes," he said.

"Might I borrow it, please, for a few moments?"

He extricated it from his watch pocket and handed it to her. At last he spoke: "I am dumbfounded, and dismayed too. My own wife! I am astonished, Gracie. Here I've been trotting along, engrossed in my own affairs from morning to night, never suspecting, never dreaming of all that was going on under my very nose. Weren't you ever going to tell me?"

"I did try; I very nearly told you before I went ... but it was a very grave secret, and time was so short, and I could not find the right moment for confiding in you . . . and when I came back—well, there was that trouble of Rawley's, and then you were out, all day, every day, from morning till night; and then you went up to New York, and—"

"I've been at home each night, except the last two."

"Oh—but the nights!—" said Grace; and saw a small knowing quirk at one corner of his mouth. Their nights had been very much occupied too, though not with talk.

"Well," he said. "Anything else I ought to know? Any other trivial little matters of life and death that you haven't yet found the right moment to confide in me?"

"Oh, aye; now that you mention it, there is another wee matter," said Grace from behind the camera. "Now, will you sit perfectly still, my dear; because I am just about to uncover the lens and take your likeness. Perfectly still, pray, for three-quarters of a minute, until I give you permission to move. Are you ready? You must not think of moving a muscle; nor must you so much as blink, not if you can help it. Well then, the wee matter is just this, Daniel—Dan, my darling; my fate; my song—" She broke off for a moment, to glance at the watch; then she reached up to remove the lens cover, saying, "We are going to have— another—baby. And though I hope you are very glad of it, you must not think of moving!"

She saw that he was glad of it, very glad indeed; and he did not move until—after forty-five seconds of *darshan*—she re-covered the lens, and gave permission.

CHAPTER
19

Grace's poison oak rash by now oozed a vile yellow fluid, and itched to distraction, sorely trying her temper. During her waking moments she was unable to forget about it for longer than two or three minutes at a time. How could so fleeting, so superficial an affliction—only skin-deep!—cause such torment? No genuine threat to health, it was nevertheless a virulent assault upon her vanity, temper, and comfort. It was humbling to acknowledge that—unhinged as she was by this trivial affliction—she would probably disgrace herself utterly under any genuine suffering of any grave nature.

It had rained a little, overnight. Grace walked down to Southwark and strolled along Christian Street, past the house which had housed Anibaddh and her family; had harbored the short-lived Palma Christi Silk Company. The house had an abandoned air. The shutters at the windows were latched shut; fallen leaves and damp discarded broadsheets littered the front steps and the padlocked coal hatch.

Passing around to the alley behind, Grace counted her way past the gates set into brick walls and wooden fences behind each house, until she came to the gate which opened into the long yard behind Anibaddh's house. It was unlocked; Grace drew it open; and found herself—here, in bricky Philadelphia!—at the edge of a leafy forest, a patch of jungly India.

Butterflies fluttered in the sunshine above a mass of foliage. The castor plants—errindy—had been only tidy knee-high rows when she had seen them last; now they had burgeoned into thriving little trees, as high as her head. Their glistening leaves were like innumerable broad-palmed hands reaching upward, outward, everywhere, some flopped over others. Grace plunged into the lush garden, and as she pushed into the thicket, the wet leaves soaked her with the remaining droplets of last night's rain, and a cloud of moths and butterflies flew up where she passed.

The mulberry saplings too had sent out exuberant long shoots covered in heavy mitten-shaped foliage, heavy-headed now, still weighed down by last night's rain. Given only sunshine, rain, and good rich manured soil, Anibaddh's plantation had become a small Eden inside this brick-walled enclosure, this *hortus conclusus*: overflowing, exuberant, luxuriant, abundant, damp, sweet, and green. The gravel walks were untended, and untrodden by human feet. Grace felt herself suddenly child-sized, dwarfed in this wilderness.

Yet it was a ragged Eden, a frayed paradise. The hand-shaped leaves were tattered, gnawed; nearly all had been damaged by insects, and some were reduced to mere skeletons. Grasses and weeds had burgeoned too, overtaking the gravel path.

The door to the wormery stood open. The shelves remained in their places, their feet in dishes—but those small moats were dry now. The shelves were empty, the trays of ravenous caterpillars gone. Surely Anibaddh had not taken the trays of caterpillars with her, to her place of concealment? Grace turned again, scanned the jungly plantation. That was a tray, surely? She went to look. So it was. Indeed, here was an array of trays, laid out in the furrows between the rows. Someone had removed the trays from the wormery and had set them out between the rows of fodder plants. Goodbye, dear worms; now feed yourselves; here is your own Eden, which has been prepared for you.

The errindy plants had been blooming, were blooming still; the blooms were little tufts of stamens, pollen-dusted. At one or two days of age, the blooms began to transform into spikys, like soft pink chestnut burrs; like small pinkish rubber balls covered by long rubbery spikes. These were the ripening seed capsules. Lower on the same plant were fully ripe seed capsules, mature, dry, and splitting open. Grace picked one of these and, peeling away the shriveled husk, uncovered a cluster of three spotted seeds inside. She spread them in the palm of her left hand, turning them with the index finger of her right. Each hard tick-shaped seed was shiny, mottled, distended as a full-fed dog tick. They were tan, with spots and stripes of coffee-brown or maroon. These three seeds in her palm amounted to death; these three would suffice to kill a grown man.

She squatted down in the shade of the mulberry and Palma Christi forest, as children did, as Hindus did. It was time to think; to bravely contemplate the private doubts and suspicions from which she had been shying; had been averting her mind.

Anibaddh. Who was that Anibaddh, the creator of this paradise? A dauntless mother, determined to rescue her daughter? Or a vengeful fury, wreaking retribution? Who was that woman, formerly so well known to her, so well loved—and Grace's own rescuer, so many years ago? Was she a vengeful goddess, a Kali, a bringer of destruction, thirsty for vengeance? An executioner? Grace thought of Ani as she had last seen her here, wearing that necklace: a handsome strand of dark irregular pearls. Now, in her mind's eye, her perfect memory, that necklace resembled Kali's necklace of severed heads; and Ani's little ruby eardrops might have been Kali's: a pair of children's corpses.

Anibaddh had said she would not be deterred by unrighteous laws. Deterred from what? Only from redeeming her daughter? Or from having her revenge, as well? To what heights, or depths, might her revenge have reached?

Grace had once noticed various green worms at this wormery: American caterpillars, Ani had explained, collected because they might prove of some use. To what use had she put them? Had Anibaddh brought to Grantsboro not only the silkworms in the mulberries—but also the cutworms in the wheat, the hornworms in the tobacco?

She had brought castor beans too; how else had all those seedlings suddenly sprouted, eleven days later, between the ruined row crops, everywhere, at perfect eight-inch intervals? Anibaddh had told Grace plainly that she intended to establish errindy in America—and someone had made a fine start of it at Grantsboro. Grace rose and made a desultory search for the small single-wheeled seed drill she had once noticed here, but did not find it.

That proved nothing. Still, Grace could not shake her conviction that it was Anibaddh who, upon coming to Arrochar to redeem her Diana, had also loosed a series of plagues at Grantsboro, some miles off.

But the most awful question, the one Grace would have liked to shirk—had shirked until now—was this: Had Judge Grant died of the stone that night, as everyone supposed? Or had he died of his favorite dish of spotty beans? Spotty beans, with a handful of castor beans stirred in, somehow, by someone?

Impossible, she would have liked to assure herself. The beans were not toxic when thoroughly cooked; and Harriet had said that she always cooked Judge Grant's special dish of spotty beans very thoroughly indeed. Even if someone had contrived to add a handful of castor beans to Judge Grant's dish (and it is only your own unruly imagination that conjures such a vision, Grace reproached herself) they would have been rendered harmless by Harriet's long cooking of them. It was a simple matter of chemistry.

Grace might reasonably conclude, therefore, that her uncle had indeed died of the stone.

Probably.

How wicked it felt, even to consider this possibility! Even to entertain such a suspicion, of such a beloved friend!

But no thoughts are forbidden; there are no unthinkable thoughts; only forbidden acts, impermissible acts. And when a thing lies plain before you, it is cowardice to avert your gaze; you must behold it.

A fat white worm fell to the ground before her. It was one of the mulberry silkworms. It squirmed, ineffectual; and Grace, looking closer, saw that it had no legs, and a black ant clung to it. Looking up, she saw a flock of the smooth mulberry silkworms, quite conspicuous in their whiteness, devouring mulberry foliage overhead: fat soft white worms grazing, chewing, placid and unhurried as brood mares; nearly all of them oblivious to the teeming black string of ants streaming up and down the mulberry stem. The ants were assaulting the worms at the perimeter. Some thirty black ants had seized a fat soft worm and were tearing away bits of its body. Feebly, ineffectually, the worm squirmed and writhed, but the ants covered its white softness with their glassy hard black bodies, lean and wiry, and tore away still. Could a worm feel agonies? So it seemed; it writhed in death throes, helpless to fight off assault—having never dreamed of assault hitherto. Within a few minutes—while Grace watched, fascinated, horrified—it was dead, dismembered, its substance being carried off in portable morsels, by the black ants. And now several more pale fat helpless caterpillars had come under attack.

There was nothing Grace could do to stop this mayhem, this genocide. She could not say, Shoo! shoo! as she might attempt to chase ravening dogs from a helpless lamb. Nor could she bear to watch.

Not proven, thought Grace, walking home: the third verdict, the Scotch Verdict, the Bastard Verdict—the preferred verdict of those who, like herself, were skeptical by nature and temperament; perhaps even too inclined to skepticism. There was room for doubt; a little; enough.

Grace posed the question to herself: Could I, would I, wreak death, if it were necessary to save Jamie? Of course she would; right or wrong, she would, certainly, instantly. But in Diana's case, it had been unnecessary. If Anibaddh had indeed administered poison, it had been a gratuitous act of vengeance.

Was vengeance ever defensible?

Vengeance is mine, I will repay, saith the Lord. Was vengeance by nature, then, godly, after all?

And what was that to her? *Mānte to deo nahīn to bhūt kā leo*: If you are a believer, it is a God; but if not, it is only a shard of plaster fallen from the wall.

Since the age of eight, Grace had loved and admired Anibaddh unreservedly; but now she hoped that Anibaddh and her retinue would succeed very soon in leaving the country, and not only for their own sake.

DANIEL HAD ENGAGED his usual lawyer, a Mr Ogden, to represent Grace's interests—identical, of course, with his own—with regard to Grace's embezzled trust. Mr Ogden had not only replied to Mr Mac-Farlane's ingratiating letter, but had also written to Judge Grant's executors Mr Lee and Mr Taylor, requiring that they should relinquish immediately all ledgers, letters, deeds, titles, conveyances, together with any and all other records whatsoever, which documented or had any bearing upon the trust which Mrs Pollocke's mother had made in Mrs Pollocke's favor. As for this business of old Walter, Mr Ogden had advised Mr Pollocke that no such emancipation ought to be prematurely and hastily undertaken; that it might in due course be commenced upon conclusion of his investigation of this larger matter of the embezzled trust.

When Daniel reported to Grace this lawful and liesurely approach to old Walter's freedom, she had objected, on the grounds that his emancipation could not benefit him if it did not occur within his lifetime.

"Well, Gracie," Daniel had said, "I will raise the question again, next time I speak with Ogden, if you think it is so very urgent. Just as soon as I get an opportunity."

Grace had to content herself with that. In law, she was only a married woman—*femme couverte*—and had no legal identity separate from her husband's. *Femme couverte!* Grace found the phrase objectionable in every respect; and indeed, obscene. A covered woman! Did no mind but her own conjure, quite unbidden, a vision of stallion covering mare?

"LOOK WHAT JAMIE FOUND!" panted Rawley, having trudged up the steep stairs to Grace's studio, carrying heavy Jamie on her hip. "Out in the bean patch, under the straw!"

"Mine!" declared Jamie, but Rawley held it out of his reach, handed it to Grace.

A key, not an inch long; a small tarnished brass key, with a narrow soiled ribbon tied to it. Grace took it, turned it over. The metal had ripened to green-black, and the ribbon was stained dark by the rotted manure that had been dug into the garden patch. "What sharp eyes you have, my jo!" said Grace. "You have found Mamma's lost key! What a clever boy! Thank you, my darling."

"Mine," repeated Jamie.

"No, it is Mamma's," said Grace. "Look, I'll trade you. You can have your cent." She held out to him the penny given him by Anibaddh (or one identical to it), while slipping the key out of sight into her pocket; and by this deft sleight of hand he was satisfied.

"I guess it must of gone out after all in the straw from that big crate that Mr Pollocke brung home from China," said Rawley, "and the straw got spread on the beans, but nobody spot this little key until Jamie, playing there just now while I hang out the washing. I use that new

Javelle water you brewed up, missus, and those bedsheets and shirts turn out fresh and white as can be, white as snow."

GRACE, ENGAGED IN TINTING daguerreotypes for Mr Cornelius, resumed her task. He had set aside half a dozen plates for her to minister to; and had even made careful notes as to the correct colors. But he had confessed himself unfamiliar with painters' names for colors, unable to distinguish between carmine and crimson, scarlet and vermilion, ruby and ochre; it was all red to him. For this gentleman's waistcoat, for example, he had written, "Red, but tending slightly toward the orangish side." By this, Grace supposed he meant scarlet; and did the best she could.

But when at last she was at liberty, she went to her bedroom, knelt at the chest at the foot of the bed, and opened it. She laid aside the woolen blankets that were stored there, and the spare bed linens. At the bottom of the chest was the lacquered inlaid writing slope, the beautiful but locked present from her stepmother, inset with flowers and foliage, caterpillars and butterflies, and her initials. She set it on her bed.

Wiping the tarnished key on her apron, she inserted it into the little ivory escutcheon. It fit—and turned, smoothly, with the faintest click.

She lifted and folded back the hinged top of the box. So simple and so elegant, the geometry of these writing boxes: when closed, only a box; but when opened, the angled top folded back—and the thing was transformed, becoming an elongated sloped writing surface, with compartments below.

The green leather writing surface had a plain gold fillet along its perimeter, and a crease across the middle at the hinge where the two halves of the box joined. Along the top edge of the writing surface were the usual wells, for ink bottle, pens, and pounce pot. There was no ink in the bottle, a reasonable precaution; but the little pounce pot had made a mess. Grace swept the loose grains of fine white silt into the palm of her hand: India sand, or China sand! From what riverbank? What green water, along what sun-drenched shore? What luxuriant trees bloomed and fruited overhead? She sniffed the sand, but could smell only the turpentine in the pores of her own skin. She dusted the sand from her palm, into the pot under the bed.

Laying aside the ink bottle and the pounce pot, she pressed the spring lever which operated the release to open the "secret" compartment underneath. Most writing slopes had just such a "secret" compartment, opening in just this way. And in the "secret" compartment was a letter from Grace's beloved stepmother; an affectionate letter wishing Grace a long, happy, and fruitful marriage with the good man she had taken as her busband. Grace read it with tears in her eyes.

Mrs Fleming's own writing slope, so very like this one, had had another, truly secret compartment under and behind the usual obvious one. When Grace had been very young, Mrs Fleming had shown it to her; had shared the secret with her. Grace remembered very well being shown how to press the back of the obvious and well-known "secret" compartment—to access the truly secret compartment hidden behind.

Had this writing slope—made to Mrs Fleming's order for Grace—such a compartment? Grace pressed the back panel. Nothing happened. She pressed again, a little harder; perhaps this box had no such compartment? Or perhaps it had, but the wood underlying the lacquer might have absorbed moisture while at sea, might have swelled and stuck. Still nothing budged. Grace pressed her fingertips against the inside and the outside surfaces, and looked from the side, trying to judge whether there was indeed a space unaccounted for. How far apart were her fingertips? It was hard to tell; and if there was a hidden space, it must be a very shallow one. It did seem to her that the ends of the inside board were not quite joined to the inside walls of the box. And she tried once more to release the spring latch which might be there.

Something gave under her fingertips, just a little. Was she breaking this fragile present? Or was she opening it?

It opened, a tight fit. And there, in the truly secret shallow compartment behind and below the usual "secret" compartment, were several sheets of paper; folded, sealed.

A letter, folded around another, thicker letter. There was a brittle old wax seal, but it had been breached. The old linen paper was of a superior quality: smooth, thick, opaque.

Grace unfolded and read. Both the letters were addressed to Grace's stepmother, and dated 1822—eighteen years ago. The outer note was from Miss Johnstone, and remarkably ill-spelled. The inner letter was from her now-deceased uncle; and the handwriting—the distinctive tails of the *y*'s; the shape of the *s*'s; the *o*'s and *a*'s left disjoined from the letter that followed—was immediately familiar to Grace. "I have the honor to be, your obdt. Humble servt. A. Grant" was the signature at the bottom of the sheet. These were the letters in which those Virginia relatives had first proposed to assume custody of Grace herself. Of course, that had not come to pass . . . but how extraordinary that these letters had been preserved, all these years! And how extraordinary that they fell under her hand, *now*!

EVEN BEFORE SHE had finished reading them, a plan—The Plan— had taken form, had assembled itself in her mind. She had not thought it up; the plan had simply appeared, entire and fully formed: naked, bold, and full-grown as Venus.

Oh, rash! Oh, dangerous!

And wrong: deceitful, fraudulent. Criminal.

But in the cause of justice and right.

And here, now, was everything she needed. She saw how each element might work.

This was as bad as being obliged to go to Grantsboro.

I could just make the thing, thought Grace. Just to find out if it is possible. Making the thing does not oblige me to do anything with it. I can make it; and then destroy it. There is nothing deceitful, fraudulent, or criminal in just *making* the thing, merely as an experiment; a test of materials and skills.

. . .

NEWS SOON CAME FROM MR OGDEN THAT MR MACFARLANE— duly bonded and appointed administrator by the executors of Judge Grant's estate—had arrived in Philadelphia; and had proposed a meeting between Mr Pollocke and himself, at Mr Ogden's chambers, for the purpose of tendering an offer of settlement.

"I want to be there too," said Grace, when Daniel told her that a time had been set for this interview. In truth, Grace abhorred the prospect of meeting Mr MacFarlane again—of being in the same room with him—of feeling his reptilian speculative gaze, like an actual touch. Why did he not tender his offer in writing? But if there must be a meeting, it ought not to take place without her, she explained to Daniel. And he—fond, indulgent husband!—let himself be convinced of her right to accompany him.

They arrived punctually, but Mr MacFarlane was there ahead of them in Mr Ogden's anteroom. He seemed entirely at his ease. "Ah, cousin!" he said, bowing with exaggerated poise over his walking stick. "I hope I see you very well, Mrs Pollocke—and—Mr Pollocke, no doubt? How do you do, sir? Mrs MacFarlane asks me to carry you her best and warmest greetings, Mrs Pollocke—the affectionate greetings of one cousin to another."

Grace would not pretend to the same friendly feeling; she did not inquire after her cousins, or the family at Grantsboro, but only wondered whether her cousin Julia had succeeded in coming to Philadelphia.

The clerk ushered them into Mr Ogden's chamber. After the preliminaries between the lawyers (how cordial they were to each other! Grace did not like that) Mr MacFarlane began: "Well. Yes. As Mrs Pollocke is already aware, her mother's marriage articles settled her property upon her issue; and that sole issue is of course Mrs Pollocke herself. And those articles furthermore appointed her brother the Honorable Andrew Grant as trustee during the minority of any such child. Now—as I have disclosed to you, Mr Ogden, and as Mrs Pollocke has become aware—it is apparent that very little remains of the sum originally settled. The executors advise that sole remaining asset of the trust in question is at present vested in an elderly slave called Walter, valued at about twenty-five dollars, and now residing at Grantsboro Plantation."

"I hope you have brought all the documentary evidence which I have required of the executors?" said Mr Ogden. "All ledgers, letters, deeds, titles, conveyances, together with any and all other records whatsoever, which documented or had any bearing upon the trust which Mrs Pollocke's mother had made?"

"Unfortunately, Mr Ogden, those documents remain at present in the hands of the clerks who are copying them, but they will be sent as soon as possible."

Mr Ogden said, "Might it not then be most prudent, Mr MacFarlane, to defer any such discussion as you now propose until those documents are at hand?"

"If you desire it, sir, I shall of course be content to defer the presentation of my offer until such time as the documents can be laid before you. But the executors and I had particularly desired to tender this offer to your client with all possible promptitude, as a gesture of our sincere good faith and goodwill. Naturally your client is under no obligation to arrive at any decision until you have subjected the relevant documents to your diligent scrutiny."

"Naturally, sir," said Mr Ogden, and considered for a moment. Then he said, "Well then, under the express stipulation that my client may take as much time as he likes to accept or reject your proposal, I think that there can be no harm in your setting it forth, even in the absence of the documents in question."

Mr MacFarlane then delivered a dense preamble in which he emphasised that the offer was not to be construed as admission of wrongdoing on anyone's part; that Judge Grant's heirs were under no legal obligation to make up any deficit in the trust of which their father had been trustee; and that his estate was in any case all but bankrupt. "Under even such deeply unfortunate circumstances as these, however, the heirs, always preserving, even now in their suffering and bereavement, a magnanimity and a most delicate sense of honor, would wish to do all in their limited power to preserve their father's reputation. And therefore I am authorised by them to come to you today and present to you a proposal which ought to satisfy your client. In short, gentlemen—"

Was she transformed into a gentleman, Grace wondered; or was she beneath notice?

"—I am authorised by Judge Grant's heirs-at-law to offer to your client—in exchange for a duly executed deed of quitclaim and agreement of confidentiality—to offer to convey to him the sole unmortgaged objects of value which remain to the deceased's estate; to wit: The full-length portrait of the late Judge Grant, together with the

pendant portrait of his wife, which hang in the dining room at Grantsboro, and whose value Mrs Pollocke may well estimate, as they are
both from the brush of—"

Would he say it? He did:

"—the celebrated Mr Stuart."

If only they had indeed been the work of Mr Stuart! If only she
were able to believe that they were! In that case, she might have passed
them off and sold them as Stuarts—and as Stuarts, they would fetch
more than enough money to pension old Walter. Alas, they were not;
and she could not. What a terrible old cheat and fraud he had been, her
uncle! How could she have so liked him; even loved him a little? Now,
even in death, he succeeded in cheating her again—and in cheating his
children too.

Grace shook her head, smiling ruefully, and said, "It is a generous
offer, Mr MacFarlane, and you may thank my cousins from me, but it
will not do. No; because those venerable paintings, of the estimable
judge and his lady wife, are not in fact from the brush of Mr Stuart at
all. No, sir, they are not. I knew it as soon as I laid eyes on them; and
so I said to Judge Grant one afternoon; and he admitted as much. He
told me that he had instead used the money given by Mrs Grant's
father to buy a horse. You do not believe it! Well; it matters little
whether you believe me or not; but my point is this: I decline your
proposal of settlement. And," she finished, "I am sorry you have had
the trouble of a trip to Philadelphia for nothing."

He blinked—oh, those hooded eyes! Grace knew by now that,
snakelike, he seldom blinked; but when he did, he was concealing some
malice.

He had not come for nothing, then. What other business had he
here? She tried not to think of Anibaddh and Diana, Jeebon and Bajubon, fearing how much he might read from her countenance, all too
transparent. She was glad that she did not know where they were.

"THEY'RE NOT WORTH fifty dollars," Grace told Dan afterward, as
they walked together down toward the waterfront to see something he
wanted to show her. "As Stuarts, they might have been worth twelve
or fifteen hundred, together. The Virginia legislature might buy them;

or Loudoun County, to hang in their courthouse. Someone would pay that for them—*if* they were Stuarts. But it is very interesting, I think, that my cousins are willing to give up to me something they had imagined to be so valuable as that."

"Maybe they have some sense of fair play after all," suggested Daniel.

"I suspect they are only anxious that their father's infamy should remain a secret," said Grace. Had all families their secrets? What but their secrets-in-common made a family? Made a family, a lineage; a race; a stirpes? It could not be merely their descent from a common ancestor—for, though she had that much in common with them, they were not her family. She preferred to think of them as a decayed branch of the true line which she herself represented. She herself; and now Jamie . . . and the next one.

"Here she is—here's what I wanted to show you," said Daniel, coming to a halt halfway along the dock. "Isn't she the comeliest little vessel you ever saw? Come, my darling, climb in, and I'll take you out for a pull. There's no finer place to be, on a sunny summer afternoon, especially after a stiff bout with a comprador—or a lawyer." He clambered down into the pretty little skiff tied against the dock; then reached up to help Grace jump down too, and seated her upon a cushion on the thwart nearest the stern. The little boat, some twelve or fifteen feet long, had fresh varnish over handsomely grained wood; a pair of new unscuffed long oars; and bright brass oarlocks. "How do you like her? She's a little longer than the skiff I had at Canton, but not so broad, and rows far better; a capital little sailer too. I am thinking of calling her *Wind Lass*—ha! Don't you get it? Well, a windlass, you know, is a sort of—of marine winch." The oarlocks shrieked horribly with each stroke. "A little tallow will fix that," he declared. "You may think her an unwarranted luxury, my dear, an indulgence—and she *is* a pretty toy. But Gracie, here's the thing. You won't let on to anyone; but I must share my happiness with you, or burst." Lowering his voice—for voices may carry far over water—he said, "It's very unfortunate that your uncle should have been so dishonest, but my dear, do not be too downcast by it, for—it really does seem—there is every likelihood of—in short, my dear, thanks to the singularly felicitous combination of circumstance surrounding this latest voyage—I find that we are on the very brink of—of actual riches!—of a competency—of sufficiency, and more than sufficiency—of real prosperity! Now, what do you think of that?" He stopped rowing; the little boat glided, oars dripping. The voices of hilarious holidaymakers on Smith's Island rang over the water.

"Again!" exclaimed Grace. "We have been frequenting this particular precinct a great deal lately, treading upon this brink of riches! But does this newest prospect hold any truer promise than when I was very nearly an heiress? Or very nearly the owner of two valuable paintings from the hand of the celebrated Mr Stuart?"

"Oh, Gracie, for shame! You cynic, you skeptic! My own wife! Will you doubt even me? Come, for that you must kiss me, and beg my forgiveness. Careful—careful—she is a little tippy." When Grace had done as he required of her, and retreated safely to her seat in the stern, he explained: "I had feared that the present distress would reduce demand for my goods—feared that the ships arriving before us might glut what little market remained; and so, my dear, I chose my cargo with particular care; and made sure to arrange sufficiently long terms so that I wouldn't be forced to part with my goods prematurely, into a depressed market. And now I am repaid for my pains! All the costs of the voyage have been covered already; the tea, the china wares, and the lacquer wares have all sold at far greater multiples than I had dared to hope; in short, my dear, I have been able, during these two years, to clear, to set aside a sum—a sum in excess of forty thousand dollars; and still hold out a strong prospect of having near eighteen thousand more, if the New Yorkers' offer to buy *Rebecca Rolfe* herself holds good—if my expectations as to that arrangement do indeed conclude as they are in train of doing. In short, my dear, the sacrifice we have made—I mean our long and painful separation—has rendered us a fortune!—a fortune sufficient to support us comfortably—if we continue to live prudently, but well—so that we need never separate again. Now, don't you think I have earned another kiss?"

Grace did think so; and acted upon her conviction. This time she did not retreat to her seat in the stern.

"What present will you ask of me, Gracie? I long to give you anything your heart desires. I can and will give you anything your heart desires—what will it be?"

Grace disowned any unmet desires whatsoever, except his promise never to cross the sea without her again. He made the promise; but still, he insisted, "There must be something you want; I have bought myself this pretty toy, and you must let me give you a present too."

At once, Grace knew what to ask of him. "There is something, though, after all," she said. "I wonder if you will give it to me."

"You need only ask, and it is yours," he said.

She asked; he assented. Old Walter was to be emancipated and pensioned—not in the full ripeness of lawyerly time—but now, immediately.

ON THEIR WAY HOME, Daniel bought several papers from a news vendor. But it was not until the next day that he showed her the *Alexandria Advertiser*, folded to the inside page where the runaway notices filled half a column:

> RAN AWAY—On Saturday night, 20th ulto., from the subscriber, near Leesburg, Loudoun County, a Negro wench, DIANA, copper-colored, about 5 feet 5 or 6 inches high, of a pleasant and intelligent countenance, erect bearing and well made, pleasant when spoken to, 18 years old. I will give one hundred dollars if taken in the State and returned to me, or secured so that I get her again; or two hundred dollars, if taken out of the State, and secured so that I get her again.
>
> N. MACFARLANE, ESQ.

"Oh, an 'intelligent countenance'!" said Grace, reading. "And 'well made' too! Well, so she is. I should like to place an advertisement, myself. Let me think; how would it read? 'ARRIVED—in Philada. On or about Fri, 10th inst, a white man, NEIL MACFARLANE, red-nosed, sandy-haired, thin-made, about 5 feet 9 or 10 inches high, eyes narrow-set, blinks when lying, his right leg shorter than the left, so that he limps, and generally affects a walking stick; about thirty or thirty-five years old. Of an unctuous and ingratiating manner, and copious speech, though ill-tempered in private and prone to the exercise of a violent tyranny upon helpless females. The undersigned will give one hundred dollars if he is taken in this state and made to go out of it; and two hundred to prevent his ever returning to trouble good folk again!' "

"I HOPE THAT OUR friends have got safely away by now?" whispered Grace to Miss Babcock, upon next meeting her when old Mrs Pollocke had come to call one afternoon. All hinged upon the reply.

But Miss Babcock looked grave and shook her head: no.

"Will a letter reach them, through your hand?" Grace whispered.

Yes; Miss Babcock nodded.

Grace had dearly hoped to hear that they had succeeded in getting away; but she was prepared to hear that they had not. Her decision was made. Already she had wrestled with her conscience; already conducted her experiment; already prepared her letter. Her experiment, her test of materials and skills, had been far more successful, far more convincing than she had dared to hope. She slipped her prepared letter, with its convincing enclosure, from her pocket to Miss Babcock, who then concealed it in her own pocket.

TWO MORNINGS LATER, at breakfast time, Miss Babcock burst in—startling Jamie so that he cried.

"Oh, Mr Pollocke!" gasped Miss Babcock. "Pray, come at once! As quickly as you can! They've come with a warrant, to arrest them all!"

"What? Who?" demanded Dan, leaping up from his breakfast.

"The sheriff's constables, and those dreadful men from Virginia! They say they have a warrant to search the house, and arrest the Rani, and all her family!"

"What house? Where?"

"Your mother's house, of course! Come quickly!"

"To arrest the Rani Lyngdoh? At my mother's house?"

"Yes, yes. They have all been concealed in the attic these three weeks. Oh, do come at once, hurry!"

CHAPTER
20

DANIEL DASHED OUT, CRUSHING HIS HAT ONTO HIS HEAD AS he went, leaving Grace with Jamie. Rawley was out at the market. Grace waited some ten minutes for her return; then, unable to wait any longer, she was just setting off with Jamie on her hip when Rawley came around the corner. Grace transferred Jamie to Rawley's arms with the scantest of explanations—and then she too set off northward, running up Third Street. She ran in rhythm with the word echoing through her head: Impossible; impossible; impossible! At old Mrs Pollocke's house! How could it be? Concealed there, of all places, for all these weeks!

A stitch in her side forced her to a walk before she crossed Chesnut. When she got up to Race Street and turned the corner, the street in front of Mrs Pollocke's house was empty, though several fresh piles of horse manure testified to the recent presence of several horses; and the neighbors, if she was to judge by the twitching of the curtains at the windows, had recently had plenty to look at. Still-wet tobacco spittle stained old Mrs Pollocke's marble doorstep.

Old Mrs Pollocke threw open her door. "What could I do?" she said plaintively. "There wasn't a thing to be done, no way to stop them! It wouldn't do no good to call the police, Danny said, because it was the police here with them, and they had a warrant, all made out proper and signed by a judge. Well, Danny said so; I didn't see it for myself, but he said it was. And they seemed to know just where to look! Straight up to the attic they went, straightaway! You'd better come in, Grace, dear." She led the way to her parlor. "And I've told a lie, heaven forgive me, and all for naught too. Well, of course I turned to the Good Book, in my extremity; I just let it fall open, asking for divine guidance. And where do you suppose it fell open? I'll show you; it was the most extraordinary thing." Her Bible lay, as always, atop the closed cover of her old piano, which served as another table. "Just here, these verses here: 'My soul melteth for heaviness: strengthen thou me according unto thy word. Remove from me the way of lying: and grant me thy law graciously. I have chosen the way of truth: thy judgments have I laid before me. I have stuck unto thy testimonies: O Lord, put me not to shame.' Psalms, number one-nineteen."

This struck Grace as being of scant comfort, under the circumstances.

"'And take not the word of truth utterly out of my mouth,'" the widow continued. "That's just what I was reading, when one of those policemen came down to ask for the key to the attic. How was I to answer, and just on the very moment of reading those verses? Well, Grace, dear, may heaven forgive me—but I couldn't betray them who reposed their trust in me. So I told him the key to the attic was lost. I told him I never could find it after Mr Pollocke was buried, ten years ago, and I supposed the key must have been buried with him, in the pocket of his waistcoat, where he always carried it while he was alive. I said, 'Tell your captain that I have not been able to open the attic hatch for more than ten years.' May the good Lord forgive me!

"I'm sure he didn't believe me—and the next thing I knew, there was a terrible smashing, from the top of the house—and as Danny and Miss Babcock had come in by then, we all three went running upstairs—just as the attic hatch gave way, which the young constable had took a crowbar to, the housebreakers as they are, and so I said! But it was no use at all, because there they were—'just like four shiny blackbirds a-settin' on the fence,' that lame man from Virginia said. I cannot like the look of that man, even though he may be some sort of cousin of yours, Grace, dear, or so Danny told me. He looks like a scoundrel to me, even if he is a lawyer. What's his name? MacPherson?"

"MacFarlane," said Grace.

"Yes, so this scoundrel MacFarlane identified them, said they was just the four in the warrant, and they made them come down from the attic, the poor dears. How terrified they must have been, though they didn't show it, what perfect self-command! I was most impressed at how they kept their heads, even when the police captain said to them,

'Now, here's your master, come all the way up from Virginia after you, and caught you fair and square, ain't that so?' And when your cousin MacFarlane tried to talk to Diana—why, she just looked at him, not a flicker of fear, like she'd never seen him before in her life. Then the Rani, she said, 'No, indeed, that man is no master of mine.' And can't she talk just like the Queen of England, when she wants to! I guess she must have picked that up in India. She said, 'I have never seen him before. No man is my master. I am Anibaddh Lyngdoh, Rani of Nungklow, a free woman, and my children are free too.'

"That scoundrel still insisted they were his four fugitives, so the captain tried to get them to admit it, by telling them they could go home with their kind master right now or else go and rot in jail for weeks, or months even, and no bail to be posted. 'You'll just have to sit there, sit and wait, until your master can bring his witnesses north to prove his claim in front of the judge. Or you can just say, yes, massa, beg pardon, massa—get it over with right now—and you'll be on your way home again by tonight. Eh? How's that? Back home again, with Mr MacFarlane, kind treatment and no more trouble? Or jail,' he said to them.

"But the Rani, she said, 'Take us to jail, then, and a judge.' So the police arrested the four of them, as being fugitives from labor, and carried them off to the jail! And Danny went to follow them, and make sure they really were taken there, not just handed over to MacFarlane once they got around the corner. And Danny said that once he'd seen them safely lodged, he'd go straight along and find out what Mr David Paul Brown could do for them. Oh, there's no better man than Mr David Paul Brown for this sort of thing; he's famous for it."

"And Miss Babcock?" asked Grace.

"She insisted on going along too, with Danny, to speak with Mr Brown, despite all I could say. She seemed to think it was specially required of her. She's a nice enough girl, that Miss Babcock, but a little too fond of her own opinions, I'm afraid; and not to be guided by older and wiser heads."

"But—but I am utterly astounded, ma'am," said Grace, now following her mother-in-law up the stairs to the top of the house, "astounded to learn that they have been lying in concealment here! With you! For all these weeks! I did not—I had never dreamed of supposing that your—your sympathies lay in this direction—the last place I should have guessed—"

"Oh, but that's just the point—that no one should suspect," said old Mrs Pollocke. "Come, dear, if you don't mind climbing up this ladder with me. We might as well sort through their things and see what to send along to them at the jail. It might take weeks for MacFarlane to get his witnesses here, and I guess they'll need their things, or some of them, at least. But of course I spoke as I did! That's the best way of turning aside suspicion, you know: to talk like other people. What good is it to shelter fugitives, if your house is the first one searched by slave catchers with warrants, because you've been making a public show of your sympathies, eh? I've had more than a hundred fugitives pass under my roof, during these ten years—ever since Danny's father passed away. He wouldn't never allow it while he lived, but since he passed, I've been able to do what I like. And every one passed safely along to the next place of refuge. Never a warrant served on me— never my house searched—never any poor fugitive snatched away and returned to slavery from *my* house! Not a single one! Until now! Do you think they'll need all their neckcloths, in jail?"

"Perhaps just their shirts. And their books."

"And that's why I couldn't invite you to live here with me, Grace, dear, when Danny sailed for China again. I was that sorry—but it wasn't a thing I dared to explain, not to anyone, not even to Danny and you. You'll understand, now, that I couldn't have a portrait studio in the house, sitters coming and going at all hours, one never knows who, or what they might notice, or who they might mention their suspicions to; I couldn't run the risk of that. Maybe this shawl? Handsome! Yes. But it grieved me, Grace, dear, to see that you felt me inhospitable. And then, when Jamie was born, what I wouldn't have given, to have you all living with me, if only! But there; I couldn't see my way to it, not without risking the safety of those poor folks fleeing here for refuge. And there was nothing I dared say, to correct your impression. I couldn't really know your personal views, even, could I? Not until I seen you openly welcoming negroes into your own house. And then, it seemed—well, pretty excessive, and you was so outspoken, dangerously outspoken, about your abolitionist sympathies that I feared to associate too close, lest suspicion spread to me as well, and endanger the refugees at *my* house."

To Grace, delving through Anibaddh's belongings felt like trespass; like paging through the daybooks in her uncle's business room. In the bottom of Anibaddh's trunk, Grace came across a tiny box upholstered in silk, exquisitely embroidered and decorated with appliquéd iridescent butterfly wings: a betel-nut box. As Grace recognised it, she felt time falling away beneath her; felt herself a child of eight years old—seeing Prince Teerut present this box to Anibaddh, a betrothal gift. Grace opened it. Inside was a small rock, a smooth rounded pebble, jasper-green with reddish speckles. She had no way of knowing what this might mean; how or why this pebble ranked among the Rani's cherished treasures. Grace supposed it was a memento of something—someone—some event in the life of the Rani and her Rajah; quite private, a personal treasure whose significance was known only to the two of them.

"Oh, well—we have our ways," old Mrs Pollocke was saying now. "Ways to know when to be looking out, and where, and for how many— and ways to notify who's to expect them next, after they leave here. There's ways of signaling, of sending messages, some of them pretty clever! Merchants may send 'bills of lading' describing 'parcels' to be expected on this or that train. Ladies may propose picnics to be held at such and such a crossroads, with food for so many. Once I even heard tell of a fiddler—or a piper, maybe?—down South somewhere, who plays a certain tune whenever he has passengers wanting tickets on the Underground Railroad! No, Grace, dear, those three trunks are mine, not the Rani's. A trunkful each of men's, women's and children's clothing, for any of my needy travelers. Very often the masters' advertisements describe the fugitives' clothes, to identify them by, so I'm prepared to give them a change of clothes. The rags they arrive in, you can't imagine. I sell to three ragpickers—to ward off suspicion about how one old lady can discard such a quantity of worn-out old homespun! They generally need decent new linen too—the women in particular are sadly unsupplied in that article, sometimes with nothing on under their dresses but their own flesh. I send them on their way decently clothed, at least—thanks to my sewing circle. Oh, no, the dear old biddies; they haven't the faintest idea! My friends all imagine we're sewing and mending for the sake of the poor Irish. They'd never guess it's the backs of runaway negroes we're covering! Well, no one else wanted the job of distributing the garments we make—so I offered to take that over. Oh, years ago, years. And never a breath of suspicion— until now! What went wrong, this time? I've been racking my brain, and it's terrible to entertain suspicion where no proof can be had . . . but I think I mentioned to you, dear, that I gave my new Irish cook the sack, three days ago? Didn't I mention it? Well, yes; her habits were uncurably slatternly, and she had no more idea of the consideration due a nice cutlet than—than your Jamie has—and—it's only suspicion, you understand. But I feel somehow quite certain, quite miserably certain, that it was she who gave them up, for the sake of having her revenge on me, and on them—and for the reward too, I expect."

BRISKLY MR DAVID PAUL BROWN ascended the wide steps; eagerly he passed under the massive Egyptian porch of the Debtors' Apartment at Moyamensing Prison, for this new case was uncommonly interesting to him. He had closely questioned Mr Pollocke about the arrest: Had he himself seen the warrant? Did it name all four of the prisoners? By Christian name only? Signed by what judge? Had the prisoners said anything when arrested? Had they admitted any past, present, or future obligations of servitude to Mr MacFarlane or to the Grant family? None at all? Very good; they had kept their wits about them, then.

Mr Brown relished the prospect of a rematch against his old foe Mr MacFarlane. What a remarkable case had fallen into his hands on this occasion, and attended by what extraordinarily fascinating circumstances! Mr Brown followed the warden down the long hall of the women's wing. Here in the Debtors' Apartment, where untried prisoners, witnesses, women, and insolvents were confined, imprisonment held a less repellent aspect than in the city's older prisons.

But he was not the first caller to be admitted to the cell of this tall black prisoner. Here already was the red-haired Scottish lady—the very one who had come twice to his chambers to consult him, without ever giving her name. He was not at all surprised, but he derived an instant's hot satisfaction from *her* unconcealed surprise. He was delighted, triumphant, to find all his suppositions borne out; and now he knew her name.

"Ah! The Rani Anibaddh Lyngdoh," he said, bowing first to the prisoner; for he always made of point of according to his negro clients a courtly politesse. "Under the unfortunate circumstance in which we find ourselves at present, I beg you will excuse me for intruding upon you without introduction: Mr David Paul Brown at your service, your lawyer and advocate, engaged by your friends acting on your behalf, to represent and defend you to the best of my ability, with the aid of the Almighty, in the tribulation which now besets you." Making his next bow to the red-haired lady, he said, "You and I have spoken before, Mrs Pollocke, and more than once. You *are* Mrs Pollocke, surely? Of course. I have just had the pleasure of making Mr Pollocke's acquaintance—I come directly from an exceedingly interesting interview with him, and with your young friend Miss Babcock. Allow me first of all, Mrs Lyngdoh," he said, turning back to the prisoner, "to reassure you as to the probable outcome of this distressing event. I beg you will not be discouraged or cast down, for I venture to assure you, ma'am, that this case bears a most promising aspect; indeed, it is one of the most promising that has ever come in my way; and you are not to despair. I hope you find yourself tolerably comfortable? Yes; the cells in this building are airy and well lit. The food is held to be of acceptable quality, and your friends are permitted to send in any such comestibles as can't be furnished by the landlord. But I daresay you'd like to know the probable duration of your sojourn here, nevertheless? Yes. As brief as possible, to be sure; but it will depend upon Mr MacFarlane's witnesses. If they happen to be in the city already, the hearing may take place within a day or two—but if they are not, Mr MacFarlane may plead the necessity of sufficient time to send for them. It may be put off for some weeks, as long as two or even three weeks. Bail? I'm afraid not; bail is never granted in such cases. But your friends may send whatever may be required for your comfort—your clothes, or books, or any such personal belongings as you may require." Indeed, books and clothes were here already; perhaps this Mrs Pollocke had brought them.

"I beg your pardon, Mrs Pollocke? Yes; Judge Lewis will conduct the hearing. It was he who signed the warrant—so your husband has informed me—and the hearing will take place in Judge Lewis's courtroom—barring some indisposition on his part."

Mrs Pollocke said, "I daresay the temper of the jury—their sympathies, their views—will be of the greatest importance in a trial of this kind. How is the jury selected?"

"Oh, but this is not a jury matter, ma'am; it does not go to trial," he was obliged to explain; indeed, it was one of the many points that the lay public generally failed to understand. "It is only a hearing. The law stipulates that a judge must hear and decide the matter; no mere alderman or justice of the peace may decide it. But it is only a hearing, not a trial, and it is Judge Lewis himself who will decide whether or not Mrs Lyngdoh and her children are indeed to be—to be free—or not."

"Is it reduced to a question, then, of whether Judge Lewis chooses to believe the Grants, rather than the Rani?"

"It is not quite so bad as that. The oath of the master—the claimant—is not admissible in these cases; the master, or in this case his representative, must produce other, disinterested witnesses. Who? Oh, they are usually the claimant's neighbors, or overseers, or others such as those."

"And if this Judge Lewis's decision is unfavorable?" asked the prisoner. "One appeals, then, to a higher court? One may then demand a trial by jury?" She was better-spoken than he expected. Her voice and diction were cultivated; rather foreign-sounding, and she wore a ring set with an emerald of quite remarkable size and color.

"I am afraid not, Mrs Lyngdoh. Judge Lewis's decision in this matter will be final. He may decide either to issue a certificate—a warrant for your removal, authorizing your re-enslavement—or not. And from his decision there can be no appeal."

"No appeal! I am astounded!" cried Mrs Pollocke. "Can this be American justice? Where any white man or woman, accused of any crime, no matter how trivial—risking perhaps no more than a fine—may demand and receive a trial by jury! Aye, sir, it is in your Bill of Rights, I have read it there! Yet the liberty of these four persons—their lives, their right to their own bodies—is to be determined solely by a single judge, without review, and without recourse?"

"I am quite of your own view, Mrs Pollocke," said Mr Brown with a bow. Red-haired persons were, in his experience, apt to be excitable. "I do not defend the law, you understand; I defend persons at risk under the law."

"What can you tell me of this Judge Lewis?" asked the prisoner. "Can impartial justice be expected of him?"

"Ah," said Mr Brown. "Well; Judge Lewis is somewhat irascible; both his temper and his health are uncertain." Indeed, members of the bar who pled before him disputed among themselves whether it was gout, sciatica, or piles which so irritated him. His domestic life too was turbulent; he and his wife had lived apart from one another for many years, and his children, now grown, had not turned out satisfactorily. In short, Mr Brown would have preferred to plead before any other judge in Pennsylvania, and he felt certain that Mr MacFarlane had taken his initial claim before Judge Lewis designedly. Judge Lewis was known to issue these warrants without demanding as high a standard of cause as certain other magistrates did. And Mr MacFarlane had prevailed in his most recent case before this judge; it was Judge Lewis who had returned Othello and his three fellow fugitives to servitude. But that had been a very different case from this one; very different indeed! Mr Brown said, "I feel very fortunate in this matter to have an unusually complete defense. Very complete indeed, remarkably so— considering that it extends over the entire globe, and over such a period of years! I will, as a matter of course, cast doubt on what will probably be very positive identifications of the respondents by Mr MacFarlane's witnesses, but that certainly is not our main line of defense, especially not as regards your daughter, ma'am. First of all, ladies, you must understand that if a slave is brought—*with* the master's knowledge and consent—into a state where the institution of chattel slavery is not admitted, and if the slave there of her own free will claims her freedom, the slave is *not* deemed in law a 'fugitive from labor' liable to recovery and re-enslavement, but instead is deemed free in law. I believe I shall be able to establish without difficulty the master's knowledge and consent. And I consider that we are very fortunate in this matter to have you, Mrs Pollocke, to testify as to Mrs Lyngdoh's free will in the matter. I am counting upon your testimony as to the circumstances of Mrs Lyngdoh's taking of her freedom, all those years ago in Scotland, to which you were an eyewitness. Your

testimony will be most valuable as establishing that she took her freedom of her own volition, and without interference, influence, or coercion from others. You were very young at the time, I believe—only
eight years old, I understand? Yes; and Mr MacFarlane may try to
challenge you on that account; he may attempt to challenge the clarity
of your recall after so many years, or the completeness of the understanding of so young a child. If he asks you something you do *not*
remember, you must be sure to admit it without argument or rancor.
But do not let such questions shake your confidence as to those essential matters which you do indeed remember very well. Your testimony
will be of critical importance, of course, as the necessary corroboration
of that of Mrs Lyngdoh. Hers would not stand alone, I am afraid—a
negro's testimony, you know, is held of little account. But once we have
established that you, Mrs Lyngdoh, became irrevocably free in
Scotland—why, then we have simultaneously proven that your sons,
born subsequently, are free as well.

"Now, the case is of course entirely different for your daughter,
ma'am, born while you were still in bonds—born, therefore, a slave for
life. There, we must rely upon the deed of delayed manumission executed by Judge Grant in Maryland in 1822, and taking force this year,
upon the young woman's eighteenth birthday. Imagine my delight,
Mrs Pollocke, upon learning from the documents in Miss Babcock's
custody that it was you yourself who found the missing deed! After all
these years, stored away in a writing slope sent you by your stepmother! It is a tremendously helpful circumstance to have your testimony about that. I greatly look forward to eliciting your testimony
about your finding of the deed, and about the occasion when you passed
it to Mrs Lyngdoh. Thus I shall establish as complete a chain of evidence as possible, with regard to that deed of manumission—and I
don't mind telling you that your testimony on these points will be
exceedingly valuable. I am relying heavily upon it, particularly as the
deed books for St Mary's County no longer exist—no, alas! the county
courthouse burned down some years ago, *very* unfortunate for us, that
it should have been that particular courthouse! Consequently, we are
unable to present any independent proof to confirm the validity of the
manumission deed. Well, yes; the deed *is* slightly irregular, in that it
bears no witnesses' signatures, but that need not invalidate it. On the

whole, I am not pessimistic; no, not at all pessimistic as to the likely outcome! I dare to hope that with the aid of a merciful heaven, a just Providence, we may indeed prevail.

"Now, ladies, with your kind permission I will take my leave—well, yes, ma'am; while I am here I shall go and look up your daughter, and then I'll just go across to the men's ward and introduce myself to your sons too, and tell them what I have told you. Is there any message you would like me to convey? Oh, their books? Of course; glad to be of use. Very well, then; I will take my leave. I am fully sensible of the burden of troubles which must weigh upon you, but we know that we may faithfully repose our trust in our Heavenly Father, who has in His mercy supported us to this day; let your faith be in Him, with prayers for His continued goodness to us, who are nothing without Him. I beg you will possess your souls in patience, and never admit despair into your thoughts."

He noticed, as he crossed to the adjacent wing, what books he was carrying: three medical texts; and a lawbook, the prolix and impenetrable old Blackstone. Quite out of the ordinary run, these particular prisoners.

WHEN THE WARDEN had let out Mr Brown, and locked the door again behind him, a silence fell over the two women in the little cell. Presently Anibaddh said, "Last evening, I had desired Miss Babcock to return your letter to you, at her earliest opportunity—with its enclosure, and with my grateful thanks, and my regret that it could not serve the purpose for which you so generously intended it."

"Did you indeed?" said Grace. "Well; she has disobeyed you, it would seem. Has exercised her own judgment in the matter."

"Obedience has never been strongly marked in her character," said Anibaddh. "But I have until now always found her judgment to be remarkably sound, for one so young." After a moment, she added, "What happened to your face?"

"Poison oak," said Grace. "It's much better now, nearly healed. You should have seen me a week ago."

"I've never had a rash from it, myself," said Anibaddh. "Though I've had ample opportunity."

Again silence fell, until presently Grace said, "Ochone, ochone; what a fix we have gotten ourselves into—as the Americans would say. . . . Well; but just how was it unserviceable, then, my little work of artifice, Rani? So unserviceable that you attempted, at least, to send it back to me?"

"Oh, it was handsome enough, and most convincing. But no free paper could have got Diana a passport; not the most authentic free paper in the world. No, because your state constitution, here in Pennsylvania—"

"Pardon me, Rani; it is neither *my* state, nor *my* constitution," interrupted Grace.

"—has been recently amended," continued Anibaddh, "and improved; so as now to provide that no colored persons, whether emancipated or freeborn, are to be deemed genuine citizens of Pennsylvania, nor of the United States of America. Passports therefore are not to be issued to colored persons."

"Not citizens!" exclaimed Grace, rising. "Colored folk cannot be citizens! And is this one of their Self-Evident Truths, pray? Here in the Land of Liberty, in the Age of Discovery? Discovery indeed! Who but the Americans could *discover* that a man or a woman born in a country was not a citizen of it?"

"It seems that black men and women have no business embarking upon ocean voyages," said Anibaddh. "It is presumptuous and insulting of us to be able to afford the expense of passage; too provoking of us to behave with such freedom and independence. There is not the slightest use in your waxing indignant, Miss Grace. This is America. So we had just retired to the modest seclusion of your mother-in-law's attic, until we could safely get out of Philadelphia and go up to New York or Boston, where, I am given to understand, even black people are still allowed to be citizens of their native land—permitted even to sail away from it, if they so desire."

"All for naught, then, my skill and patience, exercised on that interesting old paper—not to mention the suffering I endured from the very painful reproaches of my conscience."

"I thank you for all of it; but no free paper would do," said Anibaddh. "It could not get Diana a passport, and it will not do for Judge

Lewis's courtroom either. One of us had best tell Mr Brown that he must devise some other line of defense, and the sooner, the better."

"But why must he devise some other defense?" said Grace, after a moment's reflection. "He is quite satisfied with this one. Indeed, I think he is perfectly delighted with it."

"That deed cannot stand up in court—not for a minute! It will be denounced instantly as a forgery—and where shall we find ourselves then?"

"Who can denounce it?" demanded Grace. "Who can disown it?"

"Why, Judge Grant himself, of course, who knows perfectly well that he never wrote any deed of manumission for my baby!"

"Judge Grant!" cried Grace. "Not from the place where he is now."

"Why, where has he gone?"

"But Anibaddh, can you not know? Can you not know that he is dead?"

"What!" cried Anibaddh. "Judge Grant is dead? No! When?"

"Dead and buried. He died that night . . . that very same night . . . when Diana went away from Arrochar. Surely you knew that?"

But Anibaddh appeared not to have known that. "Died of what?" she asked.

This looked like innocence too—if not the very deepest cunning. "Of the stone, it is supposed," said Grace. "He had been a martyr to the stone, a great sufferer, for a great many years, it seems."

"No more than he deserved," said Ani. "I hope they all suffer from the stone, all those Grants. Dead and buried, you're sure of it? Well, you're quite right, then; not even he can testify from that hot place where he is now." She walked two lengths of the cell; then asked, "But if I knew perfectly well that Diana was entitled to her freedom upon her eighteenth birthday, why would I have offered to *buy* her freedom instead?"

Grace said, "Because you were unable to present the deed of manumission. No doubt you had given it to Mrs Fleming for safekeeping, all those long years ago; and now, here, when so many years and so many thousands of miles separated you from her—and from it—you had supposed it lost, beyond recovery. Therefore you had resolved to buy Diana's freedom instead."

"Hmm!" said Anibaddh, and searched Grace's countenance for a moment. Presently she said, "But wouldn't I have gone to that courthouse—where was it? in Maryland?—and secured another certificate, a copy of the deed?"

"But you knew that you could not get one, because the Leonardstown Courthouse burnt down in 1831, and all the title deeds with it. . . ."

"Ah; burnt down. And I knew that?" asked Anibaddh dryly.

"Aye, you did," replied Grace.

"So no one can prove whether or not this—this deed of emancipation—has ever been recorded there?" said Anibaddh.

"No one—"

"Except Judge Grant—"

"Who is dead," finished Grace.

Anibaddh said, "Could it be shown whether he ever in his life went near this Leonardstown? Wherever it is?"

"He did go there, though, Rani. Aye, he did; I saw his daybook for 1822. Think back, my dear; didn't he accompany you and Miss Johnstone down the Potomac from Alexandria, when you were on your way to Scotland, all those years ago? Down as far as Norfolk?"

"Yes . . . he did," said Anibaddh, after a moment.

"And didn't he go ashore at Leonardstown in St Mary's County on business of some kind?" If Grace closed her eyes, she could see even now his handwriting, his entry on that page: *ashore at Leonard's Town in Maryd on business but my horse (Athelstane) badly cut going ashore.*

"Did he? I don't remember that. He might have done."

"And didn't he, at that same time, grant to you his promise to emancipate your baby daughter Diana on her eighteenth birthday? And didn't he write up the very deed himself, and go and have it recorded at the Leonardstown Courthouse; and upon his return to the ship, didn't he give this very deed into your hand? Isn't that the way it happened?"

"Why would he have made *me* any promises?" said Anibaddh.

Why indeed? Grace mustered her courage, and dared: "In recognition of . . . of Diana's paternity, perhaps?"

Anibaddh rounded on Grace: "Do you suppose that you know something about that?"

"No," said Grace. "I don't know anything about that."

Anibaddh paced three lengths of the cell before saying, "He never in his life emancipated any slave of his, and he made sure no other masters did either, if he could hinder them."

"Well, that would explain why he waited, then, in this exceptional case of yours, to do it in Maryland, where none of his usual associates would get to hear of it."

"Haven't you become the sly one," said Anibaddh, and added, "Don't scratch that rash, that poison oak. Leave it alone."

"It's driving me to distraction. Why must poison oak exist? If it were of some use, like lacquer trees in China, I could forgive it. But it's not. There are no lacquerers in America. The plant is of no earthly use here."

"Oh . . . ," said Anibaddh. "It was useful to me, on one occasion. Indeed, I cherish a certain fondness for it—bordering on gratitude. Shall I tell you . . . ? A bullying young gentleman who had presumed once already to insult me—the grossest insult that can be offered a woman—surprised me one evening near the creek, and offered to repeat that insult. I defended myself with the only weapon that came to hand—which was a bough of most luxuriant poison oak. I believe he regretted his presumption, for he suffered in consequence a terrible and long-lasting rash over his entire person, and never approached me again. And that, though I give it to you without names, is the true story of Diana's paternity, which you have been speculating about." She sat down on the cot and studied Grace. "Do you intend to offer up your fable about this free paper in court, as testimony? Under oath?" She did not ask Grace to do it; did not beg the favor.

Grace wrapped her arms around herself, chilled. She looked away, unable to meet the Rani's gaze. She felt ashamed of having wondered if Anibaddh had poisoned Judge Grant—though Anibaddh need never know of the suspicions she had harbored.

Was there no other way to save Diana? Grace doubted whether she could even sufficiently command herself so as to give convincing testimony.

"Don't touch it, dear," said Anibaddh, and she reached out and gently took Grace's hand away from the rash on her face. "Let it heal."

GRACE RAN HOME through a thunderstorm, and found old Mrs Pollocke and Miss Babcock just leaving. They had been talking over the whole sensational matter with Daniel.

"Well, we must repose our faith in Providence," were Mrs Pollocke's parting words. "I trust—I must trust—that justice will be done."

You may trust, thought Grace. But Providence so often fails to provide! And justice so often is manifestly outraged!

"DANIEL," SAID GRACE, AT BEDTIME.

"What?" he said, drawing back the tarpaulin which had been laid over their bed to keep it dry. "This mattress begins to remind me of a wet dog. I've got another slater's promise to come and have a look at the roof—for as much as any slater's promise may be worth. Did you ever imagine, Gracie! My own mother! I never dreamed for a moment of her concealing fugitives, did you?"

"Never," admitted Grace.

"My esteem for her is vastly increased, vastly. All these years! I never thought of her as much for discretion—to be trusted with secrets or anything of that sort—and to find that she's been carrying such a secret as this about, under her cap, all these years! I am astonished. Come to bed, Gracie; a good night's sleep is what you'll need, if you're to testify tomorrow. Come, Gracie; one kiss, that's all."

Grace lay awake, sick with dread, and deeply shaken. Her errors and misjudgments paraded themselves before her. How could she have been so wrong, her judgment so faulty, with regard to her mother-in-law? How, despite reminding herself not to leap to unwarranted conclusions, had she leapt to the faulty conclusion that a free paper would secure a passport for Diana? How could she have been so wrong, about so much? What else was she wrong about? Here in America, she had been assuring herself that it was the Americans who were wrong; but suppose it was herself, after all, who was wrong—wrong—wrong?

Anyone may be wrong, she thought; even I—especially I!—may be wrong.

How was she to testify about that free paper? Was there no other way to save Diana? Might not this cup pass from her lips?

"We'd better get some sleep, Gracie," said Daniel, when she had turned over a score of times. "You'll be fine tomorrow, never fear. Come, rest your head on my shoulder," he said, and stroked her hair back from her forehead; and she had very nearly resolved to confide in him—to share her trouble with him—when his hand stopped stroking, fell away; and his breathing deepened, slowed, in sleep.

My soul melteth for heaviness.
Take not the word of truth utterly out of my mouth.

CHAPTER
21

W HEN SHE AWAKENED, GRACE HAD AN INSTANT'S EASE, ONE
breath's worth—until, in the second breath after waking, the full tide
of her sick dread came flooding over her and closed over her head,
shutting out all light, all air. Her mouth was dry as the Benares crema-
tion ground, dry as bone ash.

GRACE WAS GLAD of Daniel's arm as they entered the courtroom and
took their seats near old Mrs Pollocke and Miss Babcock. Though she
had steeled herself, she felt an unpleasant shock upon first catching
sight of Mr MacFarlane, lounging easily at a table within the railing
which separated the public seats from the enclosure for the parties and
the counsel and the judge's bench. Mr MacFarlane did not avoid her
glance; indeed, he stared for a long moment. Grace would not be first
to look away; after a moment more, Mr MacFarlane addressed some
remark to Mr James Grant seated beside him, and laughed.

Mr Brown was seated at another table. He was busily writing something; after a moment he folded up his paper, and, gesturing for a messenger, sent it off. The jury box stood empty.

Grace's other cousins came in, wearing their dark mourning
clothes: Mr Charles Grant; Mrs Ambler; Mrs MacFarlane, looking
ill; Miss Julia Grant. With them were Miss Johnstone and the farm
manager Mr Boyce. They all looked past Grace, pretending that she
was invisible, except for Miss Julia Grant, who shyly smiled in her
direction, then ducked her head in embarrassment. There was considerable bustle over the question of where they ought to sit. Eventually
the bailiff evicted them all from within the railed precinct below the
bench itself, except for the two Mr Grants, and instead they found

seats as distant as possible from the Pollockes, on the far side of the courtroom.

Presently a side door opened, and Anibaddh, wearing a plain green silk dress, was escorted into the courtroom by the bailiff, followed by Diana—in grey—and then Bajubon and Jeebon. The bailiff led them to Mr Brown's table, where chairs awaited them.

After a few moments, Anibaddh turned her head to scan the public seats. For a moment, her glance met Grace's. Anibaddh's expression did not change; and Grace tried to put reassurance into her own glance. But in truth she felt sick with dread, felt her entrails convulsing, and she could not help thinking, *Jiskī lāthi us kī bhains*: He who has the stick, his is the buffalo. Mr MacFarlane tap-tapped his stick on the floor and then laid it aside.

"Come to order, and all rise," cried the bailiff. "Judge Lewis presiding. Court is in session." With a great sigh and rustling, everyone rose as Judge Lewis entered and settled upon his seat behind the high bench, and adjusted his spectacles. "All be seated," cried the bailiff, and with another great sigh and rustling, everyone sat down again.

Mr MacFarlane arose, and after a few preliminary remarks in which he quietly presented to the judge his credentials for appearing before the Pennsylvania bar, he raised his voice so as to be heard by all, and opened his case thus: "It is my duty and my privilege today, may it please Your Honor, to represent the plaintiffs in this case, the recently bereaved heirs of Your Honor's lamented colleague, the Honorable Andrew Grant, in this proceeding. I stand here before you—I appear before you, Your Honor, to undertake the task of proving—of *proving*, I say—that the respondent, known as Annie"—and he used his stick to point at Anibaddh, seated on the far side of Mr Brown—"to prove that Annie, sometimes called Annie Bad, or Annie Bad Lyngdoh, is a slave for life of the late Honorable Andrew Grant, of Grantsboro Plantation in Loudoun County in Virginia, and that said slave Annie is, and has been, a fugitive from labor since the year 1822. And that her daughter, Diana"—and here Mr MacFarlane pointed his stick at Diana, who looked down at the table in front of her—"is likewise a slave for life, born and bred upon Grantsboro Plantation of the aforesaid Judge Grant, and abandoned by her mother there as an infant, and lived there all her life until her absconsion, a fugitive from labor, some weeks ago. I will prove furthermore that the two boys subsequently born to the respondent, while she was a fugitive from labor, known as John Lyngdoh and Benjamin Lyngdoh, or sometimes called—called Jeebon and Bajubon—being the offspring of a fugitive slave mother who is lawfully a slave for life, held to labor, and owing service or labor under and according to the laws of the Commonwealth of Virginia, are also slaves for life, and the lawful property of the heirs at law of the aforesaid, the late Judge Grant."

Daniel squeezed Grace's hand.

Then Mr MacFarlane called his first witness: Miss Arabella Johnstone. Seated in the witness box and sworn to tell the truth, Miss Johnstone answered Mr MacFarlane's preliminary questions, allowing that she was indeed Miss Arabella Johnstone, but she objected to being asked her age: "Oh, Mr MacFarlane, it cannot be right for you to ask a lady her age!"

"You must answer the questions put to you, unless I instruct you otherwise," said Judge Lewis.

Miss Johnstone bridled, but then answered, "I am fifty-six years old."

Was this true? Grace wondered. Was this what she usually admitted to?

Miss Johnstone replied docilely enough to the questions which followed: "I have never married; I live at Grantsboro Plantation; I have lived there for more than thirty years; I make no claim of any ownership, in whole or in part, of any of the four negro respondents; my deceased sister Anne was the dearly beloved wife of the late Judge Grant."

"Now, Miss Johnstone," said Mr MacFarlane, "cast your mind back, if you will, to the year 1822. That was the year of the slave revolt in Charleston; and *that*, I am sure, is a period which remains vividly engraved in the memories of all who were then living. Now; were you living at Grantsboro Plantation at that time?"

"I certainly was. I went to live there in aught-five when Miss Anne was born, and I've lived there ever after. My sister always said she couldn't have done without me, not with such a numerous young family to be brought up, and such an extensive household to be managed."

"Did you live at Grantsboro as a member of the family?"

"Well, yes, of course."

"Not as a housekeeper, or a paid companion or servant?"

"Merciful heaven! Certainly not!"

"Do you, or have you ever, owned any slaves as your own property?"

"Well, no," said Miss Johnstone. "Not to say as my *own* property, no."

"Who waited upon you, then? Did you wait upon yourself?"

"Of course not. The negro girl Annie was assigned to wait upon me. It was entirely understood that she was my maid."

"The girl Annie belonged to Grantsboro, then? Or to you?"

"To Grantsboro; to Judge Grant. But it was her duty to wait on me. I think Judge Grant hoped I could train her to be a more tractable servant, though she was awfully mule-headed by nature, and that's why the children generally called her Annie *Bad.*"

"Ah!" and he lightly tapped his walking stick on the floor—tap; tap. "Now; how old was this mule-headed slave girl Annie Bad at that time, Miss Johnstone? In, let us say, January of 1822?"

"Well, I think she was must have been about fifteen years old, then. Yes, she was; because she's nearly as old as Miss Eliza, and I know that Miss Eliza turned sixteen on New Year's Day."

"And aside from being somewhat intractable, what sort of servant was she, this Annie Bad? Was she a good, decent girl? Well behaved? Modest and virtuous?"

"I am sorry to say she was not."

"And why do you say that she was not?"

"Well, she—she had already got in a family way by that time. Got in the condition of a married woman."

"*Was* she a married woman?"

"No."

"Ah," said Mr MacFarlane—tap; tap.

Grace saw Mr James Grant sigh; uncross his legs, and recross them the other way. Anibaddh had named no names when telling Grace how Diana had been conceived—and why she cherished poison oak. But Grace had heard from Mrs MacFarlane of James's mishap with poison oak. It was he who had, at the bold and ardent age of eighteen, 'somehow got himself into the poison oak one night,' in his sister's words; had got it everywhere, as though 'he'd gone diving into a thicket of it without his clothes on.' While this did not amount to proof, Grace felt nearly certain that Diana—so somber there, in grey—was her own cousin at one remove.

"And in the fullness of time did this servant girl, this Annie Bad, give birth?"

"Yes, she had a baby girl."

"And the name of this baby girl?"

"She was called Diana."

"So the fifteen-year-old maid called Annie gave birth early in 1822 to a fatherless baby girl called Diana. Is that right?"

"That's right," said Miss Johnstone.

"Now, in that same year—that is to say, in 1822—did you make a voyage to the British Isles, Miss Johnstone?"

"Yes, I did. I sailed to Scotland."

"What was the purpose of that voyage, ma'am? Was it a pleasure tour? Was it for the sake of your health, or your nerves, perhaps?"

"Heavens, no! I've always enjoyed perfect health and the steadiest of nerves. No, it was a matter of duty. I went to fetch a friendless young orphan, a niece of Judge Grant's, so as to bring her back to Grantsboro Plantation to be brought up there in the bosom of her own relations."

"Ah! I see. . . . Now, Miss Johnstone, did any servant accompany you on your voyage to Scotland, your mission of mercy?"

"Yes, I took my maid Annie with me."

"Now, Miss Johnstone, when you speak of 'your' maid Annie, do you mean that Judge Grant had given her or sold her to you?"

"Oh, no. She belonged to Judge Grant, but it was her duty to wait upon me. That had always been her work, ever since she was old enough to do a woman's work."

"Ah; so the maid Annie Bad actually remained at this time the property of Judge Grant, not of yourself?"

"That's right; that's it."

"And this is the same Annie Bad who had recently given birth to a girl child; is that right?"

"That's right."

"How old was the infant, when you embarked on your voyage for Scotland?"

"Well, I think she might have been about six months old then. Yes, because she was only just weaned, I remember that."

"And did this infant accompany you, on this voyage to Scotland?"

"Certainly not! No, the baby was given to one of the mammies to take care of, and just my Annie sailed with me."

"And when you say 'my Annie,' Miss Johnstone, you refer to the girl Annie Bad, who actually belonged to Judge Grant—is that true?"

"Yes, Mr MacFarlane, I've already said so."

"So, Miss Johnstone, you sailed for Scotland in 1822, accompanied by the servant Annie Bad, while leaving the infant in Virginia. Is that correct?"

"Yes, that's right."

"Did you arrive safely in Scotland?"

"Yes."

"And did you succeed in *finding* the orphan niece, there in Scotland?"

"Yes, in Edinburgh."

"And did you succeed in bringing the orphan niece home with you, to be raised in the bosom of the Grantsboro family?"

"No," said Miss Johnstone.

"Why not?"

"She was unwilling to come; and it soon became apparent that she was—she was not—not the sort of child who could—who could deserve or appreciate such a favorable situation. And so I judged it was prudent not to pursue the matter any further."

"So you returned to Virginia without Judge Grant's orphaned niece?"

"Yes, Mr MacFarlane, I did."

"And your maid, Annie Bad; did she return to Virginia with you?"

"No, Mr MacFarlane, she ran away in Scotland, which I never thought so ill of her as to think she would, not with her little baby a-waiting for her at home."

"Ah! And did you return home, to Grantsboro, without the maid Annie Bad?"

"Yes."

"And what became of the little infant abandoned by this unnatural young slave mother?"

"I object, Your Honor!" said Mr Brown. "The form of the question—"

"I withdraw the question," said Mr MacFarlane smoothly. "What became of the baby called Diana, Miss Johnstone?"

"Well, she grew up at Grantsboro, along with the other little pickaninnies."

"Did you see her there, from time to time?"

"Oh, yes, all the time."

"Is she in this courtroom now?"

"Yes, that's her, there, in the grey dress," said Miss Johnstone, pointing. "That's Diana."

"Are you certain?" said Mr MacFarlane.

"Of course I am," said Miss Johnstone.

"Before today, when was the last time you saw her?"

"Well . . . let's see. It must have been at our revival meeting, and that was June tenth and eleventh. And after that, she went home with her mistress to Arrochar."

"When was that?"

"When she went home? I guess it must have been about the twelfth of June."

"Was that the last time you saw Diana, until today?"

"Yes."

"That was just about five weeks ago. Is there any doubt whatsoever in your mind, Miss Johnstone, that the girl at that table is the runaway slave Diana, whom you have known and often seen since her infancy, and last saw about five weeks ago?"

"Of course not. None whatsoever."

"Now, Miss Johnstone, do you know the other woman sitting at that table?" said Mr MacFarlane, with a jab of his stick.

"Yes, I do. That is my runaway maid, Annie."

"Also called Annie Bad?"

"Yes."

"The one who absconded in Scotland, in the year 1822?"

Mr Brown said, "I must object, Your Honor, on the grounds that no absconsion has been proven."

But Judge Lewis just waved his hand, as Miss Johnstone answered, "Yes."

"The mother who abandoned her infant daughter, Diana?" asked Mr MacFarlane.

"Yes."

"Now, Miss Johnstone, this is a very serious matter. Eighteen long years have passed since her absconsion; is that true?"

"Yes."

"And during those eighteen years, have you had even so much as a glimpse of this fugitive?"

"I must object, Your Honor," interrupted Mr Brown. "No proof has been presented that the respondent has ever been fugitive."

"Sustained," said Judge Lewis.

"During those eighteen years, have you had even so much as a glimpse of this girl Annie?" said Mr MacFarlane.

"Well, no, Mr MacFarlane, but—"

"And this girl Annie was—what, fifteen years old when she ran away? Is that right?"

"Rising sixteen."

"Well, Miss Johnstone, that would make her, ah, just about thirty-four years old now. How the years do pass! My esteemed colleague will no doubt make a great point of the changes that may be wrought by the passage of eighteen years; by the difference between our appearance at sixteen—hardly older than a child—and at thirty-four, in full adulthood. Perhaps we can spare him the trouble of making his point by asking you now if you are entirely, absolutely certain that the woman who sits before you at that table is indeed the girl who ran away from you in Scotland, all those years ago. Just what exactly is it about her that you recognise, ma'am?"

"Well—well. It is just her own self, her general favor, if you see what I mean."

"Her color? Her height? Her features?"

"Oh, well, all of those things, I guess. She was already tall at fifteen, remarkable tall for so young a girl—"

"Ah, remarkably tall, was she? It may perhaps please Your Honor to require the respondent to stand?"

Judge Lewis nodded; the bailiff gestured that Anibaddh was to rise. She did so. She was indeed tall.

"And her color?" prompted Mr MacFarlane.

"Well, her color is just the same as it was then. That don't change, you know, once they're past infancy. . . . She was very black then, and she still is. She was very thin in those days, a remarkable slim tall girl, but she's heavier-set now, as might naturally be expected with the passage of years, and childbearing."

"Her features, Miss Johnstone?"

"Well, her features are just exactly what I still know very well from all those years ago. And her bearing too; she always was very long-necked, up-chinned, don't you know."

"Any particular marks or scars?"

"She had none then, but I can't answer for what she might have gotten since."

"Now search your conscience and your memory well, Miss Johnstone, for this is a very serious and important matter. Is there any doubt in your mind, even the faintest whisper of a doubt, that the woman who stands there before you is indeed your runaway maid Annie Bad?"

"No doubt at all," said Miss Johnstone. "And I have an excellent memory for faces and figures."

"Thank you. That will do, I think; the respondent may sit down. Now, Miss Johnstone, do you know either of those two boys, sitting at that table with your old runaway maid Annie Bad, and her runaway daughter Diana?"

"No, I don't know them," said Miss Johnstone.

"Are those boys runaways from Grantsboro Plantation, or from Arrochar?"

"No," said Miss Johnstone. "No such boys as those two have ran away, and I'd have known it if they did."

"Now, Miss Johnstone, cast your mind back once again to the year 1822, if you will, and tell me: before you sailed from Virginia, in July of 1822, did Judge Grant write out a letter of permission for you, authorizing you to take the girl Annie Bad to Scotland with you?"

"Oh, well—well, no! Because, you see—"

"Perhaps he wrote out and gave you such a letter of permission, but you no longer have it?" rapped out Mr MacFarlane.

"Of course not, Mr MacFarlane, he never wrote out any such letter of permission, because—"

"Now, I want you to think back very carefully, Miss Johnstone," said Mr MacFarlane, interrupting her again. "Did he ever say to you any such words as: 'Miss Johnstone, I hereby grant you permission to take my slave called Annie out of Virginia, and into Scotland'? Did he actually utter any such formal words of permission to you, authorizing you to take his property out of this country?"

"Well, no! But it was always understood—"

"Was Judge Grant frequently required to be away from Grantsboro?"

"Well yes, sometimes he had to go away, when the circuit court—"

"And the circuit courts generally sit during the summer months, Miss Johnstone?"

"I believe they do, yes."

"So his business might have taken him away, for all or part of July 1822?"

"I guess it might have."

"Where was Judge Grant in July 1822, Miss Johnstone? Was he in residence, just then, at Grantsboro Plantation?"

"I—I guess he might have been, but I can't be sure, after all this time."

"Let me ask this, Miss Johnstone: can you testify with certainty that Judge Grant *was* indeed residing at Grantsboro for all of the month of July, in the year 1822?"

"No, Mr MacFarlane, not with certainty."

"He gave you no written authorization to take his property to Scotland; is that correct?"

"Yes, that is correct."

"And he gave you no explicit verbal authorization; is that correct?"

"Yes."

"And you cannot be certain that he was even present at Grantsboro at the time you embarked, in July of 1822; is that correct?"

"Well, yes, but it was always understood—"

"Thank you very much, Miss Johnstone," said Mr MacFarlane, cutting her short once again. "That is all; I have no further questions for you just now," he said, turning his back on her. Tap! tap!

Mr Brown rose. "I will not detain you much longer, Miss Johnstone," he said, bowing. "I have only a few very minor questions for you, merely to clarify a few of the points on which you have already testified, and in a very clear and straightforward manner, may I say, in response to the questions of the learned counsel upon the other side—who is, as it happens, I believe, some relation of yours?"

But Miss Johnstone had gotten rather lost in the maze, the twists and turns of this long query—and was not quite sure what the question was, when finally it was posed.

Mr Brown restated his question: "Is Mr MacFarlane a relation of yours?"

"Well, in a way," said Miss Johnstone. "He's married to my niece, Clara."

"Ah! I see . . . and your niece, Clara, is a daughter of the late Judge Grant?"

"Yes."

"Ah! Now, the negro girl known as Diana—when was it that she ran away, Miss Johnstone? Can you remember approximately the date for us, at all?"

"I know very well when it was, I can tell you exactly: it was the night of the twentieth of June, the very same night as Judge Grant went to his heavenly reward."

"And what were Diana's duties at Grantsboro, Miss Johnstone? What sort of work did she do? House? Field? Dairy?"

"Oh, house. For the last four or five years, she waited mostly on my niece Clara."

"Your niece, Clara Grant MacFarlane? Your niece, who is the wife of the learned counsel for the plaintiff?"

"Yes," said Miss Johnstone doubtfully.

"Ah! I see! And did your niece and her husband, and the servant Diana, all live at Grantsboro Plantation?"

"No, no. They live at Arrochar, nearby. That's Mr MacFarlane's place—his and his father's."

"Did the slave girl Diana live at Arrochar also, waiting upon her mistress there?"

"Well, of course she did."

"Ah! I see. Now, you told me a moment ago, Miss Johnstone, that Diana's duties at Grantsboro Plantation were in the house. But now you tell me that her duties were not at Grantsboro Plantation at all; that her duties were at the nearby farm called Arrochar. Now, which is it, Miss Johnstone? And do bear in mind, please, that you are upon your oath."

"At Arrochar," said Miss Johnstone sulkily.

"Ah! Well, that is quite a different matter, then. I beg you will take as much time as necessary in making your replies—I beg you will not be rushed or disconcerted—though I know that the witness box can be a frightening situation for those unaccustomed to it. Nevertheless, the accuracy of your replies is of the greatest importance, as we are all gathered here for the simple purpose of inquiring into the truth of the matter. Now . . . had Judge Grant *sold* the negro girl Diana to Mr Mac-Farlane or to Mrs MacFarlane? Or had he *given* her to them?"

"Oh, no, never sold, nor given; she was only leased to them. They don't own no hands of their own at Arrochar; they're all leased by the year, from other owners; and that's because old Mr MacFarlane objects to owning slaves."

"Oh, indeed! So let me ask if I understand the situation properly, then: the negro girl Diana was the chattel property of the late Judge Grant; and leased by the year to his son-in-law Mr MacFarlane, here, to work at Arrochar, waiting upon Mrs MacFarlane. Is that right?"

Yes," said Miss Johnstone.

"How much did a year's lease of the girl Diana cost Mr MacFarlane?"

"Well, I wouldn't have any idea about that, not as to say the actual dollars," admitted Miss Johnstone after thinking about it for a moment.

"Were any other slaves belonging to the late Judge Grant also leased to Arrochar?"

"Oh, yes," said Miss Johnstone.

"How many?" asked Mr Brown.

"Heavens, I don't know; lots of them."

"More than a hundred?"

"Oh, not so many as that."

"Fewer than ten?"

"Oh, more than ten, I'm sure."

"Sure, are you? *How* can you be sure?"

But Miss Johnstone could not quite say *how* she was sure; and Mr Brown said, "Never mind; I withdraw the question; let us go on. Certain slaves belonging to Grantsboro Plantation—numbering somewhere between ten and one hundred—were leased to Mr MacFarlane to work on his nearby farm called Arrochar. Is that correct?"

Miss Johnstone allowed that it was.

"And the girl Diana was one of these. Is that correct?"

"Yes."

"Now, Miss Johnstone, do you know whether Judge Grant included an indemnity clause in these slave leases?"

But Miss Johnstone had not the faintest idea what an indemnity clause was, nor whether any such clause was included in Judge Grant's slave leases.

"I beg your pardon," said Mr Brown. "Permit me to ask the question more clearly. Such leases sometimes include a clause indemnifying the slave owner from loss, whether by death, injury, or absconsion. In other words, Miss Johnstone, the lessee assumes the obligation to pay the owner the full market value—usually a stated multiple of the annual lease cost, four or five times would be usual—of any slave who may die, become incapacitated, or run away during the lease period. Do you know whether Mr MacFarlane—the esteemed counsel for the plaintiffs, here—was under any such obligation with respect to the alleged runaway slave, Diana?"

"I do not know, Mr Brown," said Miss Johnstone.

"Of course not. . . . No doubt the question would be better put to the interested party himself, perhaps later in these proceedings. . . . Thank you. Now . . . I hope you are not very fatigued, Miss Johnstone? Good; because there is another matter which I must ask you to elucidate for us. Cast your mind back once more, if you will be so good, to the year 1822. That was when, you have told us, you sailed for Scotland on a mission of mercy. I am going to ask you some questions about the journey itself. Now, first of all, Miss Johnstone, are you able to recall where you took ship?"

"Yes; at Alexandria," replied Miss Johnstone promptly.

"And at what season of the year, do you remember?"

"Well, it was summer, July as a matter of fact, I'm sure of that," said Miss Johnstone.

"How can you be sure?"

"I remember it was dreadful hot, and thirsty too, those two days in the wagon from Grantsboro to Alexandria, and we were dreadful crowded too, crammed in amongst the hogsheads and hessian sacks, heaped up all around us, and no shade to be had. I remember the bonnet I wore had a shallow brim, and did not shade my face so well as I would have liked, in such a blazing sun."

"When you say 'we,' Miss Johnstone—the 'we' who rode in the wagon to Alexandria—you refer to yourself and what other persons?"

"Me and my servant Annie."

"You and your servant Annie traveled in a farm wagon, then, from Grantsboro Plantation to the port of Alexandria?"

"Yes, it was three wagons altogether, with a cargo of tobacco and wheat consigned to Judge Grant's Glasgow agent. Virginia tobacco still fetched a very good price at Glasgow in those days, and Judge Grant's own breed in particular. And I remember envying Judge Grant, who rode alongside, a-horseback, in the breeze."

"Ah! Judge Grant accompanied you to Alexandria, then?"

"Well, I guess he did. And then he sailed down as far as Norfolk with us, as he had business there, and in Richmond too, on his way back up to Grantsboro. And that's why he had to take that horse along, which gave everyone a great deal of trouble; and I recall that he sold it soon after."

"Ah! So you are telling us that Judge Grant went aboard with you, at Alexandria, and sailed down as far as Norfolk in the same ship as you and your servant Annie?"

"Yes, he did," said Miss Johnstone.

"It was a long time ago, though, Miss Johnstone. Can you be quite certain that he did so?"

"Perfectly certain," said Miss Johnstone. "I remember it perfectly well; his horse gave quite a lot of trouble at Alexandria getting aboard;

it had to be blindfolded; and even then it took four stout men to get it up the ramp; and the same going off again, down at Norfolk. And I remember very well what he said to me, when he left the ship at last, to go ashore at Norfolk: he said, 'I envy you, Miss Johnstone, and I wish I was sailing for the bonnie hills and braes of Scotland myself,' he said."

"Ah! Well, that leaves little room for doubt, I suppose. Now, did you hide your maid Annie from him, during that passage to Alexandria, and down the Potomac, and all the way down to Norfolk?"

"Of course not! Why would I do any such thing?"

"At any time during that passage down to Norfolk, did Judge Grant forbid you to take his chattel property, the negro maid Annie, out of this country and into Scotland?"

"Well—I—he—well, no, sir, he did not."

"Did he instruct you to leave her in Virginia?"

"No."

"Now, Miss Johnstone, a few minutes ago, when my esteemed colleague asked you whether Judge Grant was in residence at Grantsboro during July of 1822 at the time of your departure, you testified that you could not remember. Yet you have just now testified, under oath, in response to my questions, that Judge Grant not only accompanied you from Grantsboro to Alexandria, but that he sailed with you down as far as Norfolk. How do you explain this discrepancy in your testimony? Which of your two accounts would you have us take as the truth?"

Miss Johnstone scowled and said, "Well, sir, you asked me in such a particular way that it came back to me, and I remembered more completely than I did earlier, when Mr MacFarlane was asking, and as for where Judge Grant might have been during the rest of that summer, I'm sure I couldn't say . . . and after all, it's a subject I hadn't thought about much in a very long time. . . ." She trailed off uncertainly; and Mr Brown let that note of uncertainty hang in the air for a painfully long moment, as though waiting for her to finish her sentence. When the silence became unbearably long, Miss Johnstone weakened and added, "And it was a long time ago."

"So it was, Miss Johnstone," agreed Mr Brown affably. "A very long time ago indeed. Now that you *have* remembered, however, under my more particular questioning—do you feel quite certain about your recall of that journey? Or could it have been some other journey that you are recalling by mistake, when Judge Grant accompanied you and your maid to Alexandria, and from there aboard ship down as far as Norfolk?"

"No, no, now that I've remembered, I'm perfectly sure about it; and I never went on no other trip with Judge Grant and my Annie to confuse it with."

Mr Brown turned away; had he gained his point or lost it? Grace could not be sure; his expression betrayed nothing.

"Now, Miss Johnstone, you have also testified that you are perfectly sure that the respondent seated at this table—this respectable matron—is in fact the same girl who saw her opportunity and seized it; the same girl who took her freedom in Scotland, all those years ago. And you have told us that you recognise her by her general favor, by her features, bearing, height, and color. Is that correct?"

"Yes," said Miss Johnstone.

"Ah," said Mr Brown. "And you last saw her in 1822, when she was fifteen or sixteen years old; is that correct?"

"Yes, until today."

"I see. Now, if you will bear with me a little longer, Miss Johnstone—I fear this is all a very tiresome business, and I will be as brief as possible—I have a few questions about Judge Grant's orphaned niece, the child whom you went to Scotland intending to fetch home to Grantsboro. Do you remember the child's name, after all these years?"

"Well, of course I do. Her name was Grace MacDonald."

"And how old was she then, in 1822?"

"She must have been seven or eight years old."

"Did you actually *see* her, there in Scotland?"

"Certainly I did."

"Did you see her on more than one occasion?"

"Yes, I did."

"And have you ever seen her since, Miss Johnstone?"

"Yes," said Miss Johnstone.

"When, and where, did you next see her?"

"Well, she was recently a visitor to Grantsboro Plantation," said Miss Johnstone.

"When did she come to Grantsboro?"

"In May," said Miss Johnstone.

"May of this year?"

"Yes."

"Had you ever laid eyes upon her from 1822 until May of this year?"

"Never," said Miss Johnstone.

"Ah! So the long-lost orphan niece came at last, after all, to the bosom of her Grantsboro uncle, and her cousins! What an affecting scene that must have been, Miss Johnstone! How would you character-ise her reception there, upon her first arrival? Would you characterise it as a scene of warm reconciliation? Of mutually rapturous greetings, Miss Johnstone?"

"No."

"No! Were her uncle and cousins not glad to receive her, after so many years?"

"Well, nobody knew who she was; she deceived us all, coming under another name, calling herself Mrs Pollocke—and lived there among us for weeks, never letting on who she was, the sly wicked creature!"

"How could that be possible, Miss Johnstone? Surely you yourself, with your excellent memory for face and figure, would have recog-nised her instantly! Do you mean to say that you did not recognise her?"

"I—well—no."

"No? Not by her general favor? By her features, her bearing? Her height and color?"

"No—she'd been just a girl, a child, all those years before. . . ."

"Yes, eighteen years before. And wasn't that just the same period of time which had passed since you last saw your fifteen-year-old maid Annie?"

"Well—yes—but—but I did think there was something just a little familiar-looking about Mrs Pollocke, when she first came!"

"At that time, did you tell her that she seemed familiar to you?"

"No."

"At that time, did you tell any of the family that she seemed familiar to you?"

"No."

"At that time, did you tell anyone at all that she seemed familiar to you?"

"No."

"Thank you, Miss Johnstone. I have no more questions of you, just at present."

"**I** DO SOLEMNLY SWEAR THAT I WILL TELL THE TRUTH BEFORE this court, and before my Almighty God," said Mr Boyce from the witness box; and sat down.

Under Mr MacFarlane's questioning, Mr Boyce testified that he was fifty years old; that he resided at Grantsboro Plantation in Loudoun County, Virginia, and had lived there for nigh thirty years; that he had been the Grantsboro farm manager for the past twenty-five years; and before that, had served as an overseer.

"Now, Mr Boyce," said Mr MacFarlane, "are you, as farm manager, required to know and recognise the hands belonging to the plantation?"

"Yes, sir, every single one of them," said Mr Boyce.

"To know them by sight, and by name?"

"Every one," repeated Mr Boyce.

"Now, those two boys sitting at the respondent's table—do you know those two boys? Are they from Grantsboro Plantation?"

"No, sir," said Mr Boyce. "I never saw those two boys before. They're not from Grantsboro."

"Ah. Very likely-looking boys, though, aren't they? You're certain that they were never at Grantsboro?"

"Perfectly certain, sir," said Mr Boyce.

"Well, well. Now the girl, sitting there, in the grey dress—do you recognise that girl, Mr Boyce?"

"Yes, sir. That's Diana, belonging to Grantsboro, that ran away a few weeks ago."

"Before today, when did you most recently see her?"

"I guess it must have been in June, at the revival, and that was just about a month ago."

"Did she look then just as she looks now?"

"Well, yes, except for that grey dress. That's her."

"Thank you, Mr Boyce. Now, sir: what about this other woman seated at the respondents' table, the one in green? Do you know her?"

"Yes, sir," said Mr Boyce. "I do. That's Annie, Annie Bad, the mother of Diana, that ran off a long time ago, when Miss Johnstone took her to England."

"Scotland?" prompted Mr MacFarlane.

"Objection, coaching the witness—" interrupted Mr Brown, just as Mr Boyce corrected himself: "Oh, yes, Scotland, I meant to say."

Judge Lewis said, "Counsel will refrain from coaching the witness."

"And how do you recognise this Annie?" asked Mr MacFarlane.

"Well, I guess I known her for a long while, for at least five years before she ran off. She was young then, but she has just the same features, and the same prideful look about her, and her carriage, don't you know, remarkably tall and narrow. She looks just the same, only older now, as anyone might expect after so long. And her daughter looks very like her too, mother and daughter."

"Had this Annie Bad any distinguishing marks about her? Distinctive scars, missing digits, a halting gait, any impediment of speech, that sort of thing?"

"No, sir, not then, when she run off, not that I recall."

"To you, Mr Brown," said Mr MacFarlane, and sat down. Mr James Grant leaned over to address some private remark to him, which induced a superficial smile.

Mr Brown rose, placed himself before Mr Boyce, and said, "Is it true that Grantsboro Plantation is one of the larger landholdings in your county of Loudoun, Mr Boyce?"

"Well, it's not the largest by any means," said Mr Boyce.

"How many acres, Mr Boyce?"

"All the land taken together comes to just about nine hundred acres, and about seven hundred and twenty acres of that is under cultivation," said Mr Boyce.

"Seven hundred and twenty acres under cultivation. I daresay that the cultivation of such a large holding requires quite a numerous labor force, Mr Boyce?"

"I guess that depends on what's meant by numerous," said Mr Boyce carefully.

"Is the slave labor force in excess of—well, oh, let us say, fifty persons, Mr Boyce?"

"Oh, yes."

"Is the slave labor force in excess of one hundred persons, Mr Boyce?"

"Yes . . . ," said Mr Boyce more slowly.

"Is it in excess of two hundred persons, Mr Boyce?"

"Oh, well, as for that, if I'm to count only actual tithable laborers on the land—and tithable persons following some other occupation about the place—and the children too young to work, or those discharged from labor on account of their old age or infirmity—and laborers leased out, or hiring out their own time . . . ?"

"Do you keep a written ledger, a roll, of all these various persons, Mr Boyce?"

"Oh, yes," said Mr Boyce.

"Why is that, sir?"

"Why, to keep track, of course, there being so many, and changing every week."

"Ah . . . so you prefer not to rely simply upon your memory, then, for such matters?"

"Record keeping is what paper and ink are for, sir—what roll books are for. I have more important matters to tax my memory with," said Mr Boyce.

"Yes, of course," said Mr Brown humbly. "Now, Mr Boyce, do you have your roll books with you, in this courtroom?"

"No."

"Did you bring them with you to Philadelphia?"

"No, certainly not, I—"

"That is unfortunate," said Mr Brown. "Apparently we are reduced after all, then, to a reliance upon your memory. Which, as you have said, is already taxed by more important matters than this. Well, we shall simply have to do the best we can, then. Now, sir: how does it happen that you are here in Philadelphia, to testify about this matter?

How did you learn that certain persons had been arrested, and that your presence was required here?"

"I—well, I was notified by Mr MacFarlane," said Mr Boyce.

"Notified in person?"

"No, by letter," said Mr Boyce.

"Did you bring that letter with you to court, sir?"

"I—no."

"Does that letter still exist, or has it been destroyed?"

"I—I can't be sure. I might have burned it, I guess."

"Burned it in Virginia, or here in Philadelphia?"

"In Virginia."

"Do you generally burn your correspondence?"

"Sometimes."

"What did the letter say? To the best of your memory?"

The judge sighed, and shifted his considerable weight.

"Well, it said they'd been found in Philadelphia, and I was to come and identify them."

" 'They' who? Who had been found?"

"Well, the fugitives, of course."

"Did Mr MacFarlane's letter refer to these fugitives by name, sir?"

"Yes, I believe it did. . . ."

"What names were named, in Mr MacFarlane's letter?"

"Diana. And Annie, her mother, Annie Bad, who'd ran away all those years ago; he wrote they both had been found."

"Did this letter make any reference to these two young men?"

"I believe it did," said Mr Boyce.

"Did it refer to them by name?"

"I don't think so. I'm not sure," said Mr Boyce after a moment's consideration.

"What *did* the letter say about them?"

"Well, it said there was two boys found also, Annie's boys born abroad after she ran away."

"Did the letter contain any suggestion or instruction that it was to be destroyed after reading?"

"I don't remember," said Mr Boyce promptly.

Mr Brown raised one eyebrow, and let this admission resonate for a moment.

"And since your coming to Philadelphia, Mr Boyce, have you taken advantage of any opportunity, before this morning, of seeing the respondents? Did you go to see them at the jail, for example?"

"No."

"Before you left Virginia, then, Mr Boyce, you had been instructed by Mr MacFarlane, by his letter, that the persons you would be required to identify at this hearing—and without seeing them beforehand—were Annie and Diana. Is that true?"

"I—well—yes, I guess that's true enough."

"Now, do you yourself direct each laborer at Grantsboro, Mr Boyce? Or have you overseers working under you?"

"I have two white overseers whose business it is to manage the slave crews; and they have negro drivers under them, to drive each crew," said Mr Boyce.

"And you yourself are responsible, answerable, to—to whom, Mr Boyce?"

"To Judge Grant himself," said Mr Boyce. "Until his passing, last month."

"Had you a contract with Judge Grant, or had he the right to turn you off at any time?"

"We never had no contract, and I guess he might have turned me off at his pleasure; but we always agreed very well."

"And to whom are you now responsible, Mr Boyce, since his passing?"

"Well, to—to his heirs, I guess. Or the executors."

"And who are his heirs, sir?"

"His children, of course; his sons and daughters."

"Please be so good as to identify them by name, Mr Boyce."

"Mr James Grant, Mr Charles Grant, Mrs Ambler, Mrs Pratt, Mrs MacFarlane, Mrs Grimshaw, Miss Julia Grant. . . ."

"Ah . . . are any of those heirs-at-law in this courtroom, Mr Boyce?"

"Yes."

"Will you point them out, please?

"That is Mr James Grant; Mr Charles Grant. There is Mrs Ambler, and Mrs MacFarlane. Miss Julia Grant. I don't see Mrs Pratt or Mrs Grimshaw."

"Thank you. Now, do the husbands of Judge Grant's daughters also stand to gain, if their wives gain, in this proceeding?"

"I guess they do."

"Those husbands are Mr Pratt, Mr Ambler, Mr MacFarlane, and Mr Grimshaw; is that correct?"

"Yes."

"Are any of those men in this room?"

"Yes."

"Will you point them out, please."

"I think that's Mr Ambler. And of course Mr MacFarlane. I don't see Mr Grimshaw here."

"You have a great many masters and mistresses here, Mr Boyce. By my count . . . seven of Judge Grant's heirs-at-law, or their spouses, all of whom stand to gain—or lose—by the outcome of this hearing, and any of whom may turn you off from your employment of thirty years, are in this courtroom and hearing your testimony at this moment. Now, Mr Boyce . . . are the house slaves belonging to Grantsboro under your direct supervision?"

"No, not the house slaves."

"How many house slaves are there, at Grantsboro?"

"Well . . . probably just about a dozen; it might be fourteen, or it might be ten . . . not counting the children."

"Are these dozen, or fourteen, or ten, house slaves under the supervision of either of your two white overseers?"

"No."

"Are they under the supervision of the negro drivers?"

"No."

"Under whose supervision are they?"

"Well, Miss Johnstone's, I would say, ever since Mrs Grant passed on."

"When was it that Mrs Grant passed on?"

"Oh, it was some years ago."

"What year, sir?"

Mr Boyce could not quite say with certainty what year it had been; but under further questioning he thought it was either 1828 or 1829; and finally settled for asserting that it was more than ten years before the present; and that he was certain of this because it was about the time that the Grantsboro stables had been rebuilt.

"More than ten years . . . thank you. Now, the slave Annie, who saw her opportunity, and took her freedom in Scotland in 1822, eighteen years ago—was she a field slave, or a house slave?"

"House."

"The slave Annie, then, was supervised not by you, nor by your white overseers, nor by your black drivers—but by Mrs Grant, now deceased?"

"Well—yes, in a manner of speaking. Her duty, though, was waiting on Mrs Grant's sister, Miss Johnstone."

"I see. Now, as for the slave Diana, who lived at Arrochar until some weeks ago—was she a field slave or a house slave?"

"House," said Mr Boyce.

"So she was not supervised by you, nor by your white overseers, nor by your black drivers. Is that correct?"

"Yes."

"She was one of some number—perhaps ten, or a dozen, or fourteen, you cannot be quite certain—some number of house slaves, under the supervision of Miss Johnstone, is that correct?"

"Well, no; she waited on Mrs MacFarlane, who lives at Arrochar mostly."

"Do you say, then, that she was not under Miss Johnstone's supervision after all, but under Mrs MacFarlane's?"

"Yes, I'd say so."

"And living not at Grantsboro, but some miles away at Arrochar?"

"That's right."

"How long had she been living at Arrochar?"

"Well, ever since Mrs MacFarlane married and went to live there."

"When was that?"

"I think it was about . . . about four or five years ago, or it might have been a little less, or a little more."

"As much as ten years ago?"

"No, not so long as that, I'm sure."

"How can you be sure?"

"Well, I—because it was about five years ago that Mr MacFarlane's new house was finished, about the same time that Mrs MacFarlane married him and went to live there."

"How old was the slave Diana at that time, when she went to Arrochar to wait on the newlywed Mrs MacFarlane?"

"I guess she must have been about—about thirteen or fourteen years of age."

"Thank you, Mr Boyce. I have no further questions of you at present."

MR BROWN SEEMED to be laying some grounds for challenging the witnesses' identification of the respondents. That might do for Anibaddh, Grace supposed; but it would be very difficult to save Diana on those grounds. And the question of Jeebon and Bajubon's identity, Grace noticed, had not been entered into at all. Would Mr MacFarlane undertake to prove that Jeebon and Bajubon were Anibaddh's sons? Or was it simply to be taken for granted, as the foal at the mare's side is supposed to be hers?

How does one recognise people? How instant recognition may be! Still, mistakes may be made. Who has not kindled at the sight of a known face and known figure—only to find oneself mistaken? The unknown stranger looks askance at our unwonted familiar greeting, and makes his escape as quickly as possible.

What of that sense that some new acquaintance seems familiar: Have we met before? Where, and when?

What of the changes that may be wrought by time? The boy of fifteen, with a shock of hair over his eyes, becomes by twenty-five quite bald; the signal feature now a shining dome, of a shape and a sheen never before seen or suspected. What of the plump dimpled smiling girl of fifteen, who is a gaunt mother of four by the time she is twenty-five? The shape of her mouth—indeed, her entire face—is transformed; for she has lost half her teeth, and hardly opens her lips to speak, much less to smile. The changes that may be wrought by the passage of a few years—especially during the passage from childhood to youth, from youth to adulthood—may be as thorough as the change from caterpillar to butterfly.

———

IT WAS ONE O'CLOCK. The judge announced a recess until half-past two, and swept out. Grace and Dan and his mother and Miss Babcock went to a hotel two blocks distant, where they sat in the presence of a chicken pie all but devoid of chicken, and wilted slaw. Grace was unable to eat—unable to chew, to swallow, or to tolerate even the thought of food in her stomach. She managed only to drink some tea.

They returned at the appointed time, but the judge himself was not punctual; and when he did come in, ten minutes late, Grace was dismayed to see how florid was his face.

Mr MacFarlane rose and declared that he had no more witnesses to call at present, but wished to reserve the right to call additional witnesses later, after hearing the testimony of Mr Brown's witnesses.

Mr Brown rose, bowed to his esteemed colleague, and addressed the judge: "May it please Your Honor, the testimony which I shall undertake to present for the defense of these respondents will be clear and conclusive: namely, I shall undertake to prove that Mrs Lyngdoh is not and never has been a fugitive from labor; but that she became irrevocably free in law, in the year 1822 when, with the knowledge and consent of her then-master Judge Grant, she was taken by Judge Grant's agent, his sister-in-law, to Scotland, and there, of her own free will and accord, and without coercion or influence or force from others, took her own freedom. It is the natural, legal, and inescapable conclusion that any and all of her children who have been born to her since her freedom—including her two sons who sit here before you— are as free in law as she is. I shall further undertake to prove that Mrs Lyngdoh's daughter Diana, born before her mother's freedom, is also free, and has been free since her eighteenth birthday, which occurred in January of the present year, having been manumitted at that term by Judge Grant. And, Your Honor, I will present documentary proof of that manumission."

As Grace heard these words, a terrible heat began to rise up in her. The blood rose up in her face and thrummed in her ears, so that she could hardly hear.

". . . and proceed now to call my first witness, Mrs Grace Pollocke," Mr Brown was saying.

Grace sat paralyzed. But no one noticed, because Mr MacFarlane leapt to his feet, saying, "I respectfully request, Your Honor, that you will require counsel to declare what this witness is to prove?"

The judge scowled and sighed, but he said, "Mr Brown, what is your witness to prove?"

"Your Honor, Mrs Pollocke was an eyewitness to Mrs Lyngdoh's taking of her freedom, all those years ago in Scotland. Her testimony will prove that when Mrs Lyngdoh took her freedom in Scotland, it was of her own accord and of her own free will; that she was neither captured nor coerced nor influenced by others. Mrs Pollocke will furthermore testify as to the circumstances surrounding the recovery of the deed of delayed manumission, by which the daughter Diana became free upon her eighteenth birthday in January of this year."

But Mr MacFarlane said, "May it please Your Honor, I must object to the hearing of this witness, on the ground that she is incompetent. I am prepared to prove that Mrs Pollocke is an atheist, an avowed infidel, who denies the truth of the Holy Bible—who denies a future state of rewards and punishments, and whose oath, therefore, is rendered meaningless, and her testimony inadmissible."

"May I ask how my esteemed colleague proposes to prove anything of the kind?" demanded an indignant Mr Brown.

"I have two witnesses who will testify as to her previous declarations on this subject," said Mr MacFarlane: Tap! Tap!

Mr Brown was caught short, for just a heartbeat. Then he said, "Who are my esteemed colleague's two witnesses, pray, Your Honor?"

The judge said, "Counsel will name his witnesses."

"Miss Arabella Johnstone and Miss Julia Grant," said Mr MacFarlane promptly.

"I must object, Your Honor, to the calling of Miss Julia Grant as a witness," said Mr Brown. "The statute of 1826 unequivocally provides 'that the oath of the owner or owners, or other person interested, shall in no case be received in evidence before the judge, on the hearing of the case.' And as Miss Julia Grant, being a descendant and an heir-at-law of the deceased Judge Andrew Grant, is an owner and interested person, her evidence therefore cannot be received in this hearing."

Mr MacFarlane said, "Your Honor, my esteemed colleague is in error on this point. While it is true that the testimony of the owner or owners or other interested persons cannot be received as to the *identity* of the fugitives, nor as to the *circumstances* surrounding their flight, they are not barred by the statute in question from testifying upon other matters such as this, the competence of a witness."

Judge Lewis considered for a moment, then said, "The objection is overruled. I will hear the testimony of the claimant's descendant, but only as to the competence of Mr Brown's proposed witness, not as to the identity of the respondents or the circumstances of their flight."

Mr Brown bowed and said, "Your Honor, I must confess that this development is quite unexpected—quite unforseen by me. But as the case cannot now be concluded today, I should like to request an adjournment of the matter until tomorrow morning."

But Judge Lewis was not amenable to an adjournment; a recess of half an hour was the most he would grant.

"MRS POLLOCKE, CAN THIS possibly be *true*?" breathed Mr Brown, as soon as he and Grace had retreated to a private room nearby. "Yourself an avowed atheist?"

"Oh, sir! Who will presume to interrogate another on such a subject? One's religious views, surely, are a matter in which one may decline to be examined by one's fellow mortals!"

"You do not deny it, then—but there I fall into the negative fallacy. Well; *have* you always declined, then, to discuss the subject? Have you never confessed yourself an unbeliever, within the hearing of Mr MacFarlane's two witnesses?"

Grace reflected. "I do not think I have made any definite avowals on the subject, even when questioned," she said at last. "But even if I had, sir, surely any confession of doubt—of skepticism—or even of frank atheism—cannot disqualify me as a witness?"

"Oh, but it can, and it does, Mrs Pollocke! But of course, madam! Is it not abundantly obvious, immediately obvious—indeed, self-evident!—that any individual who has convinced himself—or worse still, herself—that there is no hereafter to fear—no Almighty power to punish—living as a beast, and dying as a beast, looking to no hereafter—such a one cannot be suffered even to contaminate the sacred Book of Eternal Life, by swearing an oath with his unhallowed and sacrilegious lips!"

Living as a beast! Dying as a beast! With a great effort of forbearance, Grace set aside these insults and said, "Is the objection, then, to my swearing of an oath? In that case I shall affirm instead, Mr Brown—affirm, rather than swear, just as your Quakers are permitted to do."

"Worse still! It will not do, Mrs Pollocke, never. I should never have guessed you for an infidel. I wish I had known sooner. If our positions were reversed—if it were MacFarlane who attempted to present the testimony of a declared infidel—I myself should certainly impeach that witness instantly!"

"Oh, sir! But how can witnesses be subjected to any test of religion, since any such test is quite explicitly prohibited by your Constitution? Oh, yes, but so it is, Mr Brown; it is indeed. I believe it is the sixth article, which declares that 'no religious test shall ever be required as a qualification to any office or public trust under the United States.' Those may be the exact words, sir"—aye; quite exact, because she could see in her mind's eye the careless print, near the top right corner of the page, in the badly bound little edition she owned—"and if giving testimony is not a public trust, then nothing is."

"Oh, Mrs Pollocke, no; you have grievously misunderstood our founding charter. No, no; an avowed or admitted infidel is divested of all his franchises. Our Constitution tolerates all religions, but does not tolerate *no religion*—does not sanction blasphemy, or a blasphemer. No man can hold public office who is an infidel; from the President of the United States down to a tipstaff in this court, every officer is compelled to be sworn. No atheist can be sworn, and therefore no atheist can testify, or hold an office, however high or low. There is no unjustice in this—the man who denies his God should be prepared to be denied by his fellow man."

Grace fell silent, astounded. Had not words actual fixed meanings? How was one to argue with a man—a celebrated attorney—who earnestly believed that they were instead infinitely elastic? Who simply asserted that the words meant instead something precisely the opposite of what they said? There was no injustice in this, he asserted—but to her it seemed a very great injustice indeed; and once again she was convinced that Americans were subverting their Constitution in thought, word, and deed, with all the zeal they could muster. What a pity that Americans were so notoriously zealous!

Mr Brown was speaking, explaining, shaking his head. Grace tried to make herself listen. ". . . nor, worse still, the atheists among us who, despite every advantage of precept and example, persist nevertheless in sinful denial of their all-merciful Creator!" he was saying. "And who therefore, in their refusal to admit of a future state of reward and punishment—and acknowledging no obligation that binds them to the truth—cannot be permitted to bear witness!"

"But I do indeed acknowledge an obligation that binds me to the truth!" she cried. "Oh, Mr Brown, you must concede that others besides Christians may adhere to a moral code which binds them to respect and abide by all that is honorable in human institutions. Do you assume that all others besides Christians are adrift, without moral compass to guide them? That only Christians may live good and upright lives? What of the hundreds of millions of Taoists in China who meekly follow the blameless path of the Buddha—"

"Oh, their priests are veritable beggars, Mrs Pollocke; ignorant, groveling, lazy, and without influence; I have it on the best authority. And where the priests are worthless, ma'am, their followers cannot be deserving of any respect."

"Do you prefer that holy men be rich and powerful, then? Much attached to the good things of this world? Perhaps in that case you bear more esteem toward all those wise men of business who conscientiously adhere to the precepts of Confucius—"

"Certainly not; for they do not positively acknowledge any diety at all. While enjoying a full share of the gifts of the Great Giver, still they decline to positively assert even His existence—much less His mastery over us all. There is nothing at all of the devout in their system."

"Oh, devotion, is it? Then perhaps you do not entirely disapprove of the hundreds of millions of Hindus who so devoutly perform their sacred rites—"

"Oh, to their hundreds of thousands of painted idols! Theirs is darkest superstition, rampant idolatry, Mrs Pollocke! And no Christian could bear to apply such words as 'devoutly' and 'sacred rites' to such savage practices as they are known to perform, and since time immemorial! Widow-burning! Infanticide! Incest!"

"Jews? Mohammedans? Is their testimony inadmissible at the bar of American justice as well?"

"Ah; now, there is a different case, Mrs Pollocke; we do not class Jews—nor even Mohammedans, polygamists though the worst of them may be—among the heathen idolators, cannibals, polytheists, and atheists—for the very good reason that Jews and Mohammedans do acknowledge the One Almighty God—though they may persist in calling Him by some other name. And therefore even they, or at least certain enlightened individuals among them, may tread the path of righteousness. And therefore it is permissible, conceivable, that they too, in their reliance upon a future state of reward and punishment, an everlasting life hereafter, when virtue will be rewarded, and vice punished—they too may be trusted to bear honest and truthful witness."

"What is all this emphasis upon future reward and punishment? Is one to suppose that it is only the fear of future punishment which compels people to tell the truth? How debased, sir, how craven, how mean! I cannot think so ill of *all* the Christians of my acquaintance. Surely all of us may be trusted to recognise the value of speaking truth when truth is legitimately required of us? In justice to one another? In respect to our earthly institutions, set up by ourselves for the express purpose of determining the truth?"

But he only shook his head sadly.

Grace rushed on: "And do you mean to say that those who profess Christianity never do lie when they are upon their oath? Surely you, Mr Brown, do not actually believe anything so preposterous. Surely you have seen and heard professing Christians forswear themselves while upon their oath every day of your life."

A small wry smile played upon his lips while he considered. Presently he took out his watch and said, "Well . . . our half hour is nearly out. I am tempted to let MacFarlane make his attempt at impeaching you. He may fail. His witnesses may fail him. And I should indeed like to have you upon the stand."

———

WHEN COURT CONVENED again at half-past three, Mr Brown intimated that he would not withdraw his witness Mrs Pollocke; and so,
as foreseen, Mr MacFarlane recalled his witness Miss Johnstone to the
stand, for the purpose of impeaching his esteemed colleague's
witness.

"Miss Johnstone," said Mr MacFarlane, with a graver look than he
had used before. "During Mrs Pollocke's visit at Grantsboro, did you
have any opportunities of discussing matters of a religious nature
with her?"

"Well, I *attempted* to do so on several occasions, out of concern for
her eternal soul," said Miss Johnstone, through pursy lips.

"Why were you concerned about her eternal soul?"

"My nieces had informed me that they suspected her of being an
unbeliever. And that was one reason she was invited to Grantsboro,
was to attend our revival meeting, in hopes of saving her immortal
soul."

"You say you 'attempted' to discuss religious matters with her. Did
you not succeed?"

"She generally avoided any such discussion. She would change the
subject, in a most evasive way, which only aroused my suspicions all
the more. But on one occasion I did indeed charge her directly with
being an infidel."

"And what did she say to that?"

"Well, she did not deny it, so I took it to be true."

"Objection, Your Honor!" cried Mr Brown. "Speculative; and
fallacious."

"Overruled," said Judge Lewis after a moment, "but you may
attempt to demonstrate fallacy during your cross-examination, Mr
Brown."

Mr MacFarlane continued: "Did you observe any other occasions
when Mrs Pollocke's words or actions demonstrated a contempt for
Christian beliefs or principles?"

"Yes, I am sorry to say there was several such distressing occasions.
At the revival meeting, during the exhortation of the Most Reverend
Mr Stringfellow, a clergyman whose learning is widely respected, I

saw her rise and walk away, and refuse to hear his preaching or to join in the prayers or any part of the meeting. And afterwards, when he went to her privately to bring her sinning soul to prayer, she refused to pray with him, and he told me that again she walked away from him. And then on the next day, after hearing Mr Stringfellow's sermon— very learned too—in which he laid out the whole Christian doctrine as set forth in Holy Scripture, both old Testament and New, on the subject of slavery, she said . . . well! she said that the Bible was not binding on those who were not Christians. 'On those of *us* who are not Christians,' she said. And then she said—I remember it very well, it was so horribly shocking, to hear such a vile blasphemy, and over the dinner table, as though it were nothing at all—she said, if Christians had to submit to the authority of Holy Scripture, then she'd just as soon remain an infidel. We all heard her say it."

Grace could hear the collective horrified intake of breath in the courtroom. She felt her mother-in-law beside her fall still, too; and Daniel squeezed her hand. Grace did not recall uttering any such words on that occasion—though the elder Mr MacFarlane, she thought, had said something to that effect. Anibaddh, seated at Mr Brown's table, appeared unmoved. Had not this hearing been convened to decide the fate of Anibaddh and her family? How was it that Grace's religious convictions—or doubts—now engrossed this court?

Tap! Tap! "To you, Mr Brown," said Mr MacFarlane, and returned to his chair, where he slid down onto his spine, nearly recumbent in insolent nonchalance and triumph.

Mr Brown took his time. "Where shall I begin?" he said aloud, turning about, as though bewildered by a multitude of choices, all calling for his attention. "What mere mortal among us can presume to assess the state of another's eternal soul?" He bowed his head and closed his eyes for a moment, perhaps soliciting the aid of a Higher Power. Then he turned to the witness upon the stand, and addressed her thus: "Now, Miss Johnstone, you have testified that when you charged Mrs Pollocke with being an infidel, she did not deny it. And you have testified that you concluded therefore that your charge must have been true. I should like to know whether any other possible explanations for Mrs Pollocke's silence on this subject suggested themselves to you?"

"Well, surely any decent Christian would have hastened to dispel even the shadow of such a dreadful supposition," said Miss Johnstone.

"Surely, you say, surely. How are you so sure?"

"I—well—I—but . . . anyone would!"

"Did it occur to you, madam, that Mrs Pollocke might have maintained silence out of a perfectly justifiable resentment at your presumption in interrogating her upon so personal, so private, a matter?"

"Well, unless she had something to be ashamed of—"

"My question, Miss Johnstone, was whether that explanation for Mrs Pollocke's silence had occurred to you. Please answer yes or no."

"Well, I—"

"Yes, or no?"

". . . No."

"Did it occur to you that Mrs Pollocke might have maintained silence out of a wish to avoid any discussion with you about her private religious convictions?"

"No, but I—she—"

"Did it occur to you, madam, that Mrs Pollocke might wish to keep her own counsel on so personal a matter as her religious beliefs?"

"Well, if she had nothing to hide, why—"

"I ask you, Miss Johnstone, did this alternate explanation for her silence *occur to you*? Please answer yes or no."

"No."

"Now . . . has some person in a position of authority at Grantsboro—Judge Grant, the patriarch himself—charged you with the right, or the obligation, to conduct inquisitions as to the religious convictions of visitors who make their way to Grantsboro Plantation, Miss Johnstone?"

"No—but *most* folks—"

"We are not talking about 'most folks,' Miss Johnstone. We are talking about Mrs Pollocke, who quite properly declined to discuss her most private religious convictions with you, despite your impertinent queries. And she did so with remarkable forbearance and courtesy, under the circumstances. Now, let us move along to another question. You have testified that Mrs Pollocke declared that she would just as soon *remain* an infidel, than accept the preacher's teachings on slavery. I suggest to you, Miss Johnstone, that her actual words were, that she would rather *become* an infidel, than become a slaveholder, or embrace slavery, or adopt the view that the institution of slavery was endorsed or approved by the Almighty. Did she say 'become' or 'remain'?"

"Remain; she said she'd sooner 'remain' an infidel. I remember it very well. She said 'remain.' "

"Did she say 'sooner' or 'just as soon' or 'rather,' Miss Johnstone?"

Miss Johnstone was confused by this sudden shift of emphasis. "I beg your pardon?" she said after a moment.

"Did she say 'sooner' or 'just as soon' or 'rather'?" he repeated.

"She . . . ah . . . I guess she said 'rather' . . . 'rather remain an infidel.'"

"Alas, Miss Johnstone, your guesses and suppositions are of little use to any of us, by way of actual testimony. First off, you testified that she said 'just as soon.' Then you claimed that she said 'sooner.' Now you have changed your testimony again; now you claim to be sure that she said 'rather.' And yet you expect to be believed when you claim that she said would 'remain' an infidel, not 'become' one. It is incumbent upon witnesses to scrupulously speak truth, Miss Johnstone. Scrupulously. And if they cannot remember with perfect clarity and accuracy, they must not pretend that they can. Upon the witness stand, Miss Johnstone, error, no matter how well meaning, is not much better than malice. Thank you; I have no more questions for you."

MR MACFARLANE ROSE and called his witness Miss Julia Grant.

"Raise your right hand," said the bailiff to Miss Grant. "Do you solemnly swear that you will tell the truth, before this court, and before your Almighty God?"

But Miss Grant's hands remained at her sides. She said, "I do solemnly *promise* to tell the truth, but it would be useless for me to swear any oath—because—because, in short, I find, upon searching my conscience, that I—that I am not entirely convinced of the truth of the Bible—and I am not entirely convinced of—of any future state of reward or punishment, nor of any eternal life to come."

Silence fell.

"What?" cried Mr MacFarlane at last; Mrs Ambler threw up her hands, and Miss Johnstone gave an inarticulate shriek and then fell back, while Mrs MacFarlane ministered to her with smelling salts.

"May it please Your Honor, this witness impeaches herself," declared Mr Brown over the hubbub. "By her own statement, the witness renders herself incompetent to testify, and her testimony inadmissible."

Judge Lewis pounded his bench with his gavel until all fell silent. Miss Grant's cheek was pale, and the veil of her bonnet fluttered rhythmically—in time with her pounding heart, Grace supposed; or perhaps she might be trembling. Miss Grant looked up—her wild glance swept the courtroom—and for an instant, her one good eye met Grace's gaze. The other, the walleye, had gone to the wall indeed, on this terrifying occasion.

"I will not have this court made a travesty, a mockery!" declared Judge Lewis loudly. "I will not tolerate the getting up of stratagems and subterfuges expressly for the purpose of evading, of shirking, the obligation to testify. Do you understand me, miss?"

"Yes, Your Honor," said Miss Grant faintly.

"Do you understand, miss, the gravity—the enormity—of the declaration you have made before this entire court?"

"Yes, Your Honor," whispered Miss Grant.

"And before your Almighty Creator?" he thundered.

"Oh, but that's just the difficulty, Your Honor—" she started to say, but he interrupted her.

"Do you understand, miss, that by such a declaration, you place your immortal soul in danger of everlasting damnation, and your mortal body at risk of imprisonment upon a finding of contempt of court?"

"Your Honor, it is not my intent to defy your authority to compel me to testify. I will certainly comply if you order me to do so; and I will testify truthfully. But I feel myself bound in conscience to declare that I consider a future state of existence after death—a future state of reward or punishment—extremely unlikely. It is for you, Your Honor, to determine whether—possessed as I am of a profound skepticism on this subject—whether I am fit nevertheless to testify in Your Honor's court."

Oh, gallant Miss Grant! Cousin! thought Grace.

"With Your Honor's permission, I will withdraw this witness," said Mr MacFarlane suavely, "and will send instead for another, who, however, is unfortunately not in Philadelphia just at present. If Your Honor will grant a continuance in this matter for two weeks, I will undertake to bring forward the Reverend Mr Stringfellow to testify as to Mrs Pollocke's incompetence."

But Judge Lewis was now angry and suspicious. "Will you not withdraw *your* witness, Mr Brown, so that we can get on with this matter? Or do you persist in proposing her, despite opposing counsel's challenge to her competency?"

Mr Brown drew himself up and blazed forth: "I should be ashamed, Your Honor, ever to betray the sacred trust placed in me by the hapless beings I am called upon to defend, by waiving any rights which I might exercise in their defense, or by cravenly yielding in my attempt to produce the testimony which will secure to them their rights and their liberty. *My* witnesses, Your Honor, are present at this moment, and ready to testify. If my learned colleague now craves two weeks more to produce *his* witness, that is no fault of mine; nor is it the fault of my suffering clients, whose very liberty has been in placed in jeopardy by the claim lodged against them. I should deserve scorn and censure, or worse, Your Honor, in this life and in the next, if I were to acquiesce, merely for the sake of expediency and convenience, in any such arbitrary judicial encroachment upon their legal rights as to withdraw the witness whose testimony will secure to them forever their rights to life and liberty."

Judge Lewis sighed, and glowered at both attorneys for a long moment before pronouncing, "This matter is continued for two weeks. The respondents will remain in custody without bail during that period. Court is now adjourned."

Check! thought Grace, as a vision of a chessboard appeared unbidden before her mind's eye, complete with all its pieces disposed across its patchwork landscape, in their places from that long-ago chess game against her uncle, the game which she had won despite Mr MacFarlane's interference.

WHEN DANIEL HAD ROWED OUT TO THE MIDDLE OF THE river, clear of the traffic near the shore and the midstream islands, he raised the oars and rested. Water ran dripping off the blades, catching the late sun like prisms, and the little skiff *Wind Lass* sidled gently on the rising tide. The drips falling from the oars made rings, circles, spreading outward, overlapping.

Grace sat in the stern, facing him. The water rippling and slapping against the freeboard was dark green, opaque as jade, and it did not smell like the other rivers Grace had known: the Forth, the Hooghly, the Ganges, the Brahmaputra, the Pearl. Coal smoke from the steam ferry passing to windward drifted down upon them: a stink.

"Certainly that dreadful woman had no right to question you about your religious views," said Dan. "But as your lawfully wedded husband, I think I have; and even to expect an answer."

"How could we have failed to discuss this? Before we married?" said Grace in despair.

"I knew, even then, that I should have raised the question," said Dan. "I very nearly brought myself to it." He would not look at her; seemed entirely engrossed in scraping at a rough spot on the leather wrapping on the handle of the starboard oar.

The dread which had threatened to engulf Grace all day now came flooding back upon her. A vision of ruin welled up: their narrow brick Philadelphia house, roofless; curtains in shreds, blowing out the broken windows; desolate but still standing.

"But I didn't quite dare, for fear that you wouldn't have me," he said at last, looking up from the engrossing oar. "For fear that you'd break off our engagement, if you knew what I was. What I am. I couldn't bear the thought of losing you—losing you just when I'd found you—the woman I never expected to find, in this wide world."

The vision of ruin evaporated. This was *Daniel*, before her: Dan, her song, her fate. A boy, his mother's boy; as tender, as vulnerable, as Jamie. "What are you, then?" asked Grace.

"When I was small, seven or eight years old," said Daniel, twisting the oars in their locks; they had perhaps been greased, for they no longer squeaked; "I was often taken by my mother to church, where—like most small boys—I squirmed upon the hard pew, in agonies of boredom and restlessness, hearing little of the preacher's endless discourses, and understanding less. But I did gather from his exhortations that there existed on the surface of our earth such depraved individuals as . . . atheists! And infidels! This hint intrigued me deeply; what would it be like, I wondered, not to believe in God? And by way of investigation, during the preacher's eternal sermons, I ventured to experiment in my own mind—at first, for just a few terrifying seconds at a time, and afterwards, for longer moments. I ventured to try doubt, to experiment with doubt, to essay disbelief. To my astonishment, I was not struck down. My soul did not curdle within my breast. I was astounded to realise that no one could tell what I was thinking. I was relieved not to be transformed into a thief or a murderer—for I had no yearning after evil, you understand, but only an inquisitive nature, an investigative spirit drawn to independent experimentation. Between Sundays I was no wickeder than most boys; no wickeder than I'd ever been. My feet still walked reasonably near to the paths of righteousness; I still honored my father and my mother; remained diligent in my lessons and decent to my friends; continued to tolerate the existence of my enemies. But once having essayed to think what I'd been told was unthinkable—well, I'd discovered that it bore thinking upon, after all. And that was my first hint that preachers might conceivably be wrong—wrong even within this subject of their special expertise."

The little skiff *Wind Lass* had drifted around and now Grace, from her place in the stern, could see past Dan's shoulder the Christ Church steeple, white against the sky. In old pictures of Philadelphia, that steeple had dominated the city's skyline; but now it was only one spire among many, shoulder to shoulder with other towers, steeples, and belching chimneys.

"You are not to suppose, Gracie, that this weighty question figured at the forefront of my thoughts at all times. I didn't follow up this line of thought very diligently; I felt no urgent need to arrive at any conclusions. I was content to let the matter rest, and let time pass, while I continued in the outward business of my life. And then, after a while—I might have been fourteen or so . . . well, perhaps you too were warned by your mother not to cross your eyes, lest they should get stuck that way? Of course; but I guess you probably ventured to cross your eyes anyway—"

"Of course I did; so does every child of any spirit," said Grace. "I shall be very disappointed in Jamie if he fails to try it, merely because he has been warned against it."

"And no one's eyes ever get stuck," said Daniel. "But my mind, when I experimented with doubt—with skepticism—my mind did get stuck that way. Eventually I couldn't cross back with any ease to my previous state of unthinking belief. Yet I wasn't distraught in my new state of doubt, of skepticism."

"No . . . ," said Grace. "Not distraught. It is no more distressing than attempting to believe in something one cannot believe. But there is a considerable quantity of—of shame, of secrecy attached to it, I find. One looks about, wondering, is everyone else truly convinced? Am I the only doubter? Or do all these others, surrounding me, harbor secret unspeakable doubts too? Are they all so utterly convinced as they claim to be? And if they are—*why*? Is there some essential point—obvious to all but me—which have I failed to understand?"

"Ah, Gracie!" he said, and reached out to stroke her hair. "I should have known that you were to be trusted."

"But even if you had asked me my views then, before we married," said Grace, "I should have been at a loss how to reply. I have never yet truly arrived at any settled conclusion; and I have always avoided making any positive declarations on the subject. It seems to me, even now, a matter which defies positive declarations."

"It's a matter of temperament, I think," said Dan. "Some people can tolerate ambiguity; others can't. Whenever a pious person dismisses any of the mysteries of existence by asserting that God's inscrutable will would have it thus—why, then I can't help but notice that the name of God is invoked so as to avoid saying, 'I don't know.' If you'll just substitute 'I don't know' for 'God's will' in any sentence uttered by these pious people, it becomes quite clear that the two phrases mean just the same thing."

"Sometimes I have wondered," said Grace slowly, "if perhaps that is indeed just what is meant by 'God.' Might it actually mean 'All Which Cannot Be Known'? Or 'The Inexplicable'? Pious persons seem to derive great comfort from their conviction that there must exist a divine will, a divine design; while others of us do not suffer agonies from admitting that we do not know whether or not any such will or design exists."

"But I can't quite convince myself that those other fellows, no matter how vehement, actually *know* any more about it than I do—"

"And even those who are most vehement in their professions of faith must be concealing some tiny kernel of doubt—or why protest so much?" said Grace. They both fell silent, until presently Grace said, "But it is very hard to discern how much of our ignorance, about how and why things are, is simply that: ignorance—which may eventually be cleared away and replaced with knowledge, as we learn more about this world we inhabit. And it is equally hard to discern, on the other hand, how much of our ignorance, of what we do not know, is—is simply unknowable. Is beyond the reach of all ways of knowing. Now, *that* remaining mystery—if indeed there is any such residue, once our ways of knowing are complete, centuries from now—and if indeed they *can* ever be complete, if they are capable of completion—then—*that* remainder, if any, *that* might be the true size and shape of God—if there is indeed a God. And that residue of the unknowable—the divine—will perhaps prove to be a vast and glorious God; or possibly only a misshapen dwarfish god. But all this is speculation. Who is to say?"

"Come here, Gracie, darling; my jewel beyond price." He set a spare cushion on the boards of the boat's bottom, between his splayed legs, and she moved to him; sat leaning back against him, his arms around her. *Wind Lass* spiraled slowly in the eddying current; rudderless, unsteered. The steam ferry was crossing the river once more, thrashing, churning, smoking effortfully, gracelessly, back again toward the

Jersey shore; but its smoke did not blow down upon them now, for the wind had shifted, and meanwhile their little boat had been carried imperceptibly upriver upon the tidal surge. The sun had set over the city, and now the scattered clouds resting all around the rim of horizon seemed to glow lavender—peach—purple—gold, intensifying with each passing moment: just such a backdrop as might suit the apotheosis of a Wellington; a Washington; a Napoleon. To Grace, it was like hearing the *crunluath a mach* movement at the heart-bursting climax of a *piobaireachd*, that classical pipe music, the Great Music. Then, within a minute, the sublime brilliance began to fade, like a painting obscured behind its dark old varnish.

"And yet," said Grace, "when Dr Parker joined us together in holy matrimony on that day in Macao, my dear—when he pronounced us Man and Wife, in the Name of the Father, and of the Son, and of the Holy Ghost—you assented, I seem to recall; bowed your head and said amen."

"Oh, but it was not Dr Parker who joined us together in holy matrimony; it was we who joined ourselves together. 'I, Daniel, take thee, Grace, to my wedded wife, to have and to hold from this day forward, for better for worse, for richer for poorer, in sickness and in health, to love and to cherish, till death us do part.' "

"It goes on, 'according to God's holy ordinance; and thereto I plight thee my troth.' "

"Well, I did make a reservation in my mind, about God's holy ordinance."

"So did I, I suppose." The first star appeared—or perhaps it was the third? For now that she looked, she could see three glimmers in the dome of darkening sky, three points describing a vast triangle: Deneb, Vega, Altair. She thought of this as the Changing, when ways of seeing and knowing shifted; when the hidden vastnesses of the universe became visible—having existed all along, though invisible behind and beyond the small part which was visible in day's light. Now the other, larger part—the part which emitted its own faint light—became discernible. The Changing was not to be dreaded, not feared; but only marveled at, and delighted in. To think that it recurred every night! It was the nightly reminder of—well, what, exactly? What might be the meaning of this? If meaning it had?

Something leapt from the water, splashed; but she was an instant too late to quite see it. So much of understanding was like that: a flash, a quick movement at the corner of one's eye—at the periphery of one's understanding—one nearly apprehends—but then it is gone, again! And yet, there are the ripples, spreading outward; something really had been there; something really had emerged—ever so briefly—and then fell back again, sunk, submerged, leaving ripples, and the memory of the sound of the splash, and the memory in the mind's eye of the dark quick movement at the very edge of perception. One has never quite seen it; but one suspects that it does exist, and if only one were slightly quicker of apprehension! And of comprehension. . . .

Daniel was saying, "I do not pretend to *know* that the deity of my neighbors is merely a comforting fiction invented to explain the inexplicable. I only doubt the explanation which my neighbors embrace. I do not *know* them to be wrong; but neither do I share their passionate and furious conviction that they are right. I remain, comfortably enough, in doubt."

"Oh, aye, comfortable enough," said Grace, "so long as our neighbors do not suspect us, or try to elicit our sworn testimony. I do rather resent being told that I am only living and dying as a beast; that I deserve to be cast out from all human society; and that I cannot be trusted to distinguish truth from falsehood."

"Who said that?"

"Mr Brown."

"Rude of him—unless he was seeking to prepare you for the ordeal ahead. He may succeed in demolishing MacFarlane's witnesses. That dreadful Johnstone woman did not come off very well. It is quite possible that you will be permitted to take the stand after all, my dear."

"Ochone! I do not know what to hope. I hope that the world will come to an end. That some plague will descend upon the city, and bring all human affairs to a halt. I hope that—that something will happen to prevent my testifying."

"What! Why? Was that a shiver? We can go back, if you're cold."

"No, I am not cold, and I do not want to go back; not yet," said Grace. "But I am in trouble, my dear; I am very deeply troubled indeed, and I do not know where to turn, what I may do. If Mr Brown succeeds—if he does defeat Mr MacFarlane's attempt to impeach me, and

I am indeed called to testify—then I must either make for myself a very large mental reservation, and give false testimony; or else I may hew to the truth, and betray a suffering innocent. I do believe that bearing false testimony is wrong, morally wrong—in addition to being criminal. I should be very wrong to do it; but I think I should be equally wrong—no, far more wrong, in this particular case—to admit the truth."

"The truth about what?"

"About that deed of emancipation, by which Diana was apparently manumitted at the age of eighteen."

"What about it?" he said sharply. "Is something wrong with it?"

Grace trailed her fingers over the edge, in the black water, considering; and then, taking a deep breath, as though she were indeed about to dive into the water, she plunged—oh, that moment, still in air, before cleaving the water, but too late now to remain dry and safe!—saying, "It is a forgery. I made it myself." It was like plunging down into cold deep water, water that closes over one's head; one sinks into darkness, bubbles ascending.

"No!" cried Dan. "I can't believe it!"

Just a joke! thought Grace, for a panicked instant. Not too late to retract, after all. And if he does not believe me, I am perhaps still safe.

"But I saw it myself," he said, "at Mr Brown's office, when Miss Babcock presented it to him. It appeared perfectly genuine. I never entertained a moment's doubt of it."

"Thank you; aye, it is a good piece of work, and both the paper and the signature itself are indeed quite genuine. I am trained in the arts of verisimilitude, you know. And somehow all the necessary materials and knowledge came to hand, fell into my hands—and in so uncanny a manner that I felt actually obliged to make the attempt, at the least."

"How could you have done it?"

"I did anguish over it; and I intended, when I made it, only that it should serve to get Diana her passport. I never intended, never imagined, its coming to this—"

"No, no," he interrupted. "I mean, how, literally *how*, did you do it? Using what—what techniques? The paper, and the signature—where did you get those if, as you say, they are genuine? At Grantsboro, I guess?"

"Oh! No, I did not steal anything from Grantsboro. I may be an atheist, and a forger, and I shall perhaps commit perjury soon—but I am at least no thief. No, the paper and signature were on a letter written by my uncle and addressed to my stepmother, many years ago. It was the letter in which he proposed to take custody of me; to have me brought to Virginia to be reared there among my cousins. Somehow my stepmother had saved that letter all these years—and she sent it to me locked inside of that lacquered writing slope, her wedding gift— the writing slope you brought home from China in April. When I found that letter, I realised that I had a specimen of his handwriting; and his authentic signature; and even the very paper itself that he had used in those days, quite distinctive, and, fortunately for my purposes, of excellent quality; all linen, thick and smooth. Originally it had been well-sized, so it was not excessively absorbent. But the ink he'd used was decidedly not of the best; probably overthinned sepia to begin with. Sepia? Aye, that is cuttlefish ink, you know, squid—and it had faded considerably during the intervening years—eighteen years. Luckily it was not oak-gall ink, which is so acidic as often to etch the very paper itself; that would have been fatal, for my purposes—would have left the quite discernible palimpsest of his original writing etched onto the paper.

"And—well, my cousin Miss Julia Grant is an avid chemist, as it happens. Oh, aye, I suppose I have not mentioned that to you, but then we have had so little leisure, you and I! And she had told me of the bleaching action of her darling chlorine, and demonstrated it upon the linen sheets at Grantsboro. Their sheets *are* of an enviable whiteness— and she had sent me a packet of her bleaching powder, with instructions for mixing up the genuine Javelle water itself—and it burst upon me quite suddenly that a substance which bleaches stains from linen sheets might very well do the same for linen paper. . . .

"And then . . . let me see. I had learned from Rawley—aye, after you had retrieved her from those slave-catchers—I had learned from Rawley about free papers. And that the courthouse at Leonardstown in Maryland had burned down in 1831—with all its deedbooks . . . and I recognised the name of the town as one where my uncle the judge had gone ashore, when he had accompanied Miss Johnstone and Anibaddh—who was her maid then, you know, her slave—on that first downriver leg of their journey to Scotland. So I knew that he had indeed passed through Leonardstown, before its courthouse had burned, and all its records in it.

"And in just the same way that I had made that daguerreotype copy of Rawley's free paper for her, I then made a daguerreotype of my uncle's letter, so as to preserve for my own reference an extensive sample of his handwriting, as it had been in 1822. And once I had that—well, I took the plunge, assuring myself that I was only conducting an experiment, only trying what might be done; that I was under no obligation to take this experiment any further—no more than I am obliged to exhibit every painting I may attempt."

The continued existence of the daguerreotype she had made of her uncle's 1822 letter left Grace very uneasy. She intended to destroy it; to dispose of it, somehow—but how? It was not so easily done. If she had it with her, she could slip it into the river and watch it sink. But just now it was locked inside her lacquered writing slope, at home.

"And so one day," continued Grace, "when I was expecting no sitters nor callers, when Jamie was with your mother, and Rawley had her day out, and you were elsewhere upon your own business, I shut myself into my studio, and—and . . ." She trailed off.

"And made your forgery," Dan supplied. "I suppose you washed out the old ink and bleached the paper; but how did you preserve the genuine signature, while eradicating the rest of the writing?"

She told him just how she had done it: the judicious refolding and careful tearing; the bleaching, rinsing, drying, burnishing, and resizing of the paper; and then her painstaking creation of the new document, in her uncle's handwriting. "To my sorrow, it turned out rather well, much better than I had expected. Indeed, I thought it really might do; and so I subdued my conscience so far as to confide it to Miss Babcock, to be passed along to the Rani, with my compliments, so that she might use it—if she chose, if her conscience would permit!—to get the passport she needed to get Diana out of the country. Of course, *she* knew it for a forgery, and me for the forger! But what I had not known was that no document, no matter how authentic, could secure Diana a passport, now that your Pennsylvania legislature—"

"Not *my* legislature," said Daniel.

"—has revoked all rights of citizenship for black people. And so the Rani had directed Miss Babcock to return it to me as useless; or so she told me when I spoke with her at the jail, afterwards."

"Let me guess," said Dan. "Miss Babcock quite naturally assumed that the document was authentic. And when her dearest friends came under arrest, she realised that—useless though it was for obtaining Diana's passport—it might be essential to securing her freedom. And rather than return it to you as instructed, she presented it instead to Mr Brown."

"So it would seem."

"And—as neither you nor the Rani has told Mr Brown the bitter truth about that paper—he is relying upon it to secure Diana's freedom, and relying upon you to testify about 'finding' it among your stepmother's papers, preserved for all these years."

"Just so. Now I must find the resolve to add perjury to my list of sins. If instead I were to cleave righteously unto the truth, I should betray my lifelong friends, and condemn Diana, at least—if not all four of them—to a lifetime's bondage. Which shall I be: perjurer or traitor?"

"Perjurer, of course," said Daniel.

"So simple as that? So clear and obvious as that?"

"It is clear enough that you must commit one sin or another," said Daniel. "One crime or another. The only question is, which to commit?"

"I could refuse to testify."

"Unless MacFarlane succeeds in impeaching you, you are required to testify."

"And if I refuse?"

"You will be found in contempt of court."

"What care I for that?"

"Your refusal to testify cannot save Diana. It is still a betrayal, a condemnation of Diana. It is no solution to your dilemma. And cutting out your tongue, or fleeing the country, amounts to the same thing."

Grace was silent; for the last alternative—the one he had not quite named, the one she sometimes thought of in her despair—was unspeakable. In any case, she now saw that it too amounted to betrayal, condemnation.

Presently Dan said, "You need not choose whether to benefit yourself at the expense of another. You need not choose between two worthy parties. You need not choose between two unworthy parties. Your choice is whether to defend innocent virtue—or greedy cruelty. So that is clear enough. And as you stand to gain nothing, regardless of who prevails, you need not even try to set aside self-interest—except insofar as in committing perjury you *do* set aside self-interest; you do knowingly and willingly take up a burden of crime—or sin, if you will—in order to protect an innocent sufferer. And so it seems perfectly clear to me what your right course must be."

"A pious Christian would say that I must speak the truth, come what may; that the Almighty God will protect His innocents from harm."

"Oh, yes; and then, when the innocents *do* come to harm nevertheless—grievous harm, irremediable, as is so frequently the case!—that same pious Christian will sanctimoniously declare that God must have some higher design of His own, which is not revealed to us mere mortals. It won't do, Gracie."

Grace could not help it; leaning back against him, she silently wept.

He could not see her face, but must have felt the sobs that shook her. "I'm sorry, Gracie; I beg your pardon," he said, much more softly, bending over her. "The right course is perfectly obvious when it's someone else's duty to do it. Forgive me for my officiousness. The decision must be your own. And do not think for a moment that—that I will presume to disapprove, whatever you may do."

When Grace had regained her composure, she wiped her eyes and nose, saying, "How bitter it is that I—having always wished to prove that even unbelievers can be good and moral, trustworthy and scrupulous—having desired, in my pride, my vanity, to conduct myself in such a manner as to demonstrate this before the world—now find myself in a position where every avenue open to me is an odious one, to one degree or another!"

"They would be equally odious no matter what you believed," Dan pointed out. The moon had risen. Presently he said, "That cloud has blown up amazingly in the last ten minutes."

"If ever anyone has been calling down thunderbolts, we have. Hadn't we better get off the water?" said Grace.

"Oh, and the roof!" exclaimed Dan. "Dash it all! I was supposed to meet that slater at six o'clock, and I forgot about it completely!"

OF THE TWO WEEKS' continuance granted by Judge Lewis, a week elapsed. Daniel, though now much engrossed by negotations for the sale of *Rebecca Rolfe*, had instructed his lawyer to prepare the documents necessary to emancipate old Walter. Grace called upon Anibaddh and her family at the jail nearly every day, bringing books, newspapers, and good cheer (she hoped); she also engaged a caterer to deliver dinners to them. This was more expensive than she had expected; and one afternoon, when she had finished tinting another batch of daguerreotypes for Mr Cornelius, Grace wrapped them up and set off for his studio, hoping to be paid immediately. She was admitted by a boy about twelve years old, who thought that Mr Cornelius was engaged at just this moment with sitters; but if Madam liked to take a seat, he'd inquire when Mr Cornelius might be at liberty. From the reception room Grace could hear voices from the studio down the corridor: Mr Cornelius's voice, and that of another man, and a woman too. A couple, perhaps, were having their likenesses taken.

While Grace waited, another man came in from the street, a portly bald gentleman saying to the boy, "It was promised for three o'clock, and as it's nearly that now, and I happen to be passing near, I just thought I'd stop and see—"

"I'll find out, sir," said the boy, and went to tap at the door of the dark closet; the chamber of al-chymy, the Black Art, where, by the agency of mercury, the invisible was rendered visible—so Grace fancied it. Was Mr Cornelius doing so well as to have engaged an assistant? So it seemed; for Grace could see that the closet door opened a scant inch or two from inside—and then the boy returned, saying, "Your head's very nearly done, sir, and Mr Cornelius's assistant will bring it out in just a moment, if you don't mind waiting."

Grace rose to study the little gallery of finished daguerreotypes covering one wall of the reception room. There were some recognizable faces, those of Philadelphia's notable public men: Mr Sidney Fisher; Mr Thomas Cope; even Mrs Pierce Butler, formerly the celebrated Miss Fanny Kemble; and there, quite unexpectedly, was Judge Lewis. But there were plenty of unknown faces too. How fascinating they were, each one! For Grace it was a little feast, to study these eyes, noses, mouths, chins; and equally fascinating to study how each individual met the camera—whether with eagerness, distrust, amusement, gravity, resignation, shyness, self-conscious embarrassment, curiosity.

They were very like the miniatures on ivory which Grace painstakingly made—and yet profoundly different. Mr Gilbert Stuart's characteristic wet gleam inside the lower eyelid did not make an appearance in any of these images—but there was an elongated rectangular highlight across the top of each eyeball—reflected from the mirrors set outside the studio window, surely. What a pity, Grace thought, that the sitters' hands were not depicted, here, in this medium where they might be done so perfectly, so without effort!

There was a little display also of the various frames and cases from which sitters might choose. These were the same miniature cases available to Grace's sitters, ranging from small gilt ovals set around with dingy seed pearls suitable for young ladies, to sober unadorned rectangles suitable for deacons. Mr Cornelius—whose family business was metal fabrication—had contrived his own small brass mats for the likenesses he produced. They had an elliptical opening about three inches high and two inches across; and in majuscule letters along the lower right curve was stamped "PHILADA." Likewise, along the lower left curve was "R.CORNELIUS": the artist's signature. Behind this opening was a thin clear pane of glass; and behind the glass was the silver image itself. And this entire assembly was neatly enclosed in a small leather case, hinged at the left, like a book; with a little hook closure at the right. It made a neat sufficient whole, a bright gem.

Grace was studying the portrait of Judge Lewis for clues to his character when she heard the darkroom door open behind her. A whiff of barnyard stench billowed down the hallway. "It's turned out very handsome, sir," said a woman's voice—and Grace spun about, astonished—to see Mr Cornelius's assistant presenting the portly bald gentleman with his finished likeness.

"Ha!" he exclaimed. "Well! I guess I should feel grateful to all my friends and relations for putting up with the sight of that phys, day in and day out, for all these years! Might do for a jack-o'-lantern, to frighten naughty children with! And what's happened to my hair? Somehow there seems to be more of it, in my shaving mirror of a morning. Well; I guess that's why Mr Cornelius requires to be paid in advance, eh? I guess I can destroy it if I like—but what use is that, when I've got the original still perched here on top of my shoulders? So that's what my friends have been obliged to look at, all these years! Well, now I know what a debt of gratitude I owe them for their for-bearance. Ha! Must show this to Dickinson!" And off he went, tucking into his pocket the portrait in its neat case.

Mr Cornelius's assistant turned at last to Grace. Black hair; violet eyes; the right eye was, as usual, aiming off to the side, but it was steady, at least.

"Cousin Julia," said Grace.

"Cousin Grace," said Miss Julia Grant. "Do come into my parlor, won't you?" She led the way into the darkroom down the hall. "It's a bit dark, I'm afraid; and I must apologise for the curtains and rugs too—as being nonexistent." She turned up the lamp and raised its shade, so that they could see each other, perched on the two plain chairs against the wall. The little closet was stifling, reeking. "As for refreshment, I can offer you water ... or perhaps you would prefer— water? It is the purest, distilled."

Her hands were reddened, Grace noticed, but she looked happy and bright; nothing languid remained about her manner. "So *you* are Mr Cornelius's new assistant," said Grace. "In Philadelphia, after all—and doing chemistry! I congratulate you. And your—your family? What do they make of your new profession?"

"I don't know; I haven't seen or heard from them since—since a week ago, in court."

"You astounded me that day, cousin," said Grace.

"I astounded myself," said Miss Grant. "My own voice sounded so strange in my ears, ringing out there in that courtroom, before that glowering judge. He's only a judge, I told myself, just another frail old man like my father."

"You were very brave," said Grace.

"I was, wasn't I? I was terrified; but oh, cousin! How exhilarating it was, to speak up after all these years! Afterwards, I ran straight to my sister's house—where all of us had been staying, all crowded together. I snatched up all my belongings, and ran off as fast as I could, before anyone could catch up with me—and took a little room at a boardinghouse, in another part of the city. I didn't sleep a wink that night. I was too exhilarated—and too frightened, I admit. But my new life laid itself out before me, in my fancy. I'm just an impoverished old maid—oh, yes, I am, cousin, that's exactly what I am—but I won't become my Aunt Bella, a spinster officiously 'making myself useful'— making a nuisance of myself in the household of one of my sisters, whichever one could make her husband tolerate me. No one can disinherit me now, so I'm free to suit myself. Of course, I need the necessary; don't we all? But why shouldn't I work for it, as other old maids do? And why shouldn't I do the work I'm best suited for? I'd kept the book you lent me, cousin: Mr Daguerre's process. Oh, you noticed! Well, I'm sorry, but I couldn't part with it. I've studied it closely—very closely—and the next morning, before my resolve failed me, I came here, to Mr Cornelius's studio. Even if he hadn't written his address on the flyleaf, his advertisements in every newspaper would have directed me. And so—finding him here, overwhelmed by sitters and work—I presented myself to him. 'Good morning, Mr Cornelius,' I said. 'My name is Miss Grant, and I am your new assistant, sir; and which shall I commence, the polishing and sensitizing of the plates? Or do you prefer that I attend to the mercury fumer?' Of course, he only laughed at me for a fool; but then I dropped the secret password to him. 'Bromine,' I whispered. (I hadn't been quite sure before, but as soon as I came in I caught a whiff of that stench, and then I knew.) 'Bromine, Mr Cornelius, not chlorine. Your secret's safe with me. Try me today, sir, for just this one day. Don't pay me until you've seen what I'm worth.' And so—as six more sitters had come in just while we spoke—well, he had no choice but to take up my offer. And by the time he closed the doors that evening, the last of the sitters gone away satisfied—well, by then I'd made myself, if I may say it, entirely indispensable. Oh, cousin! Chemicals, from morning till night! I'm happy as a raccoon pulling crawdads out of the creek! And I'm paid for it!

Already I've suggested an improvement in the fourth process. And look; see what I've bought for myself: a pocket watch, with a seconds hand! Not very ladylike, is it? But I do love it so. And I calculate that I'll be able to lay by a little money each week; and when it's enough—well, what do you guess I'll do then, cousin?"

"Paris," said Grace. "Surely."

"Extraordinary," said Mr Ogden, when he had untied the string and removed the outer wrapper, revealing a stack of papers and a half-bound ledger book. "Will you only look at that! Some poor devil of a clerk has made a blunder, the ignoramus, and sent us the originals instead of the copies!"

Grace and Daniel had gone to Mr Ogden's office to sign the deed for enacting the manumission of old Walter. But Grace's signature, it emerged, was not required after all; and Mr Ogden's clerks had lost or failed to make the copy to be retained by Mr Pollocke. Mr Ogden had apologised for this oversight and had directed his head clerk Collins to put aside his other work and commence the copy instantly, promising to have it delivered before noon. But then Grace had offered to remain while the copy was made; offered to wait for it although Mr Pollocke had another engagement and could not wait.

So Daniel had gone, hastening to his appointment with the marine surveyor who, it was fervently hoped, would pronounce *Rebecca Rolfe* free of shipworm—and Grace had waited. Presently Grace had thought to inquire of Mr Ogden whether Judge Grant's executors had yet responded to his request for documentary evidence; for all such ledgers, letters, deeds, titles, conveyances, together with any and all other records whatsoever, as documented or had any bearing upon her trust.

"What's that, Mrs Pollocke? Oh, that other matter! Well—let me find out—Collins! Collins! Has anything come in from Leesburg, in that other matter of Mr Pollocke's? Oh, did it? Why wasn't I told? Apparently something has come, Mrs Pollocke, but I've had no opportunity yet to review the contents. Mm? Just now, do you mean? Well,

I suppose there's no positive reason that we cannot have it in, as you happen to be here. Collins! Just bring along the entire box, won't you?"

Collins had done so; Mr Ogden had laid out the documents—had exclaimed at the error by which the actual original ledgers and letters, not the copies made by clerks, had been sent to his office: "What a blunder, to have sent us the originals instead of the copies! Well, he'll lose his place for a certainty, as soon as his principals find out."

And now, in reply to Grace's proposal, he said, "Oh, no, Mrs Pollocke, I wouldn't recommend that you do anything of the sort. Very irregular—and I daresay that none of it will make any sense at all to you, ma'am, such a musty old pile of ciphers and papers! And as I've not yet had any opportunity to look it over for myself . . . Well—quite certain, are you, that your husband would have no objection? No, of course not; certainly I have no reason to object on my *own* account; certainly not—oh, very well, then, but you'll handle it all most carefully, Mrs Pollocke. Here, let us have it set out upon this desk, if you really think you want to look through all this dusty old business. I daresay it won't make any sense to you—accounts are dreadfully obscure to those not brought up to them—but if you have questions, I'll do my best to answer them."

THUS, DESPITE MR OGDEN'S disapproval, Grace now sat at a high desk in the corner of the room where Mr Ogden's clerks worked; and an old account book lay before her. Mr Ogden's clerks perched on their tall stools at the other high desks, copying. The room was silent except for the scratching of their pens against paper and the buzzing of a fly against the windowpanes.

This account book, Grace noted, had a red leather spine and marbled-paper covers, and it exactly resembled the other account books which she had examined without permission in her uncle's business room, that warm day.

If "patrimony" is an inheritance from one's father, she wondered as she laid open the book's cover, why is "matrimony" not an inheritance from one's mother?

This book dated from her uncle's optimistic and energetic youth, it seemed, when he had first set out to keep meticulous accounts. On the first page was written a title, with a box drawn around it:

THE TRUST FOR THE BENEFIT
OF MY NIECE
GRACE MACDONALD.

Here was her uncle's distinctive handwriting, so well known to her now in its every detail: the characteristic deep tails of his *y*'s; the peculiar shape of the *s*'s; the way the ink faded to almost nothing where the nib of the pen only grazed the paper at the top arc of his majuscule *G*'s and *D*'s; the break he left, failing to join the *o*'s and *a*'s to the letter that followed.

And here was the inaugural entry in the ledger, from the year 1818. She *had* been an heiress, in a very small way; worth then, at the age of four years, £503/6/6, the amount of a bill of exchange remitted from Glasgow. Her uncle had converted the sum to $2,276.13; and had then lent out most of this in small increments, at moderate rates of interest—6 or 6½ *per centum per annum*—for terms of two or three years, secured by small farms and building lots near Leesburg. In 1820, she saw, her uncle had made a loan which was secured not by real estate, but by three slaves belonging to the borrower. In the following year, the note was renewed—the amount increased—and the collateral for the loan increased as well, to include two more slaves.

As early as 1820, then, at the age of six years, she had been, without her knowledge or consent, not quite an owner but an investor in human chattel. This, Grace supposed, might be the nature of Original Sin: a sin committed by another, of which she'd had no knowledge and no hope of preventing. The stain of it besmirched her nonetheless.

In December of each year, her uncle had been in the habit of tallying the value of the trust's investments. Grace turned quickly from one year-end sum to the next, skipping for now the details. By 1825, the value of her trust had fallen below $2,000. Hadn't the world's financial markets suffered a painful contraction about that time? By 1826, her trust's assets were valued at just over $1,800. In August of that year, she noticed, her uncle had purchased for her trust three yearling colts, for a total of $135—three colts of his own breeding, if she was to judge by their names: Tressilian; Ivanhoe; Quentin Durward. How unlucky, then, that all three of these no doubt promising youngsters had died shortly—very shortly—thereafter, in September, in an outbreak of the glanders!

The year 1829 was the last for which her uncle had kept up his practice of tallying the trust's assets at year-end. After that, he had only struck a balance from time to time, at random. And yet the trust's dwindling dollars continued to be actively invested, not only in additional ill-fated and short-lived livestock, but also, by 1828, in slaves. Here was the toll of their names: Beck, Sal, Lewis, Frank, Jem, Ned, Eliza, Eston, Abram, Walter. And the knell of their fates: died of snakebite, of childbed, of hemorrhage, run off, run away, drownt, run over by the wagon, locked-jaw, ate hemlock. The very last entry of all was the purchase of old Walter, four years ago, for the last $25 remaining in the trust. In her mind's eye, her mind's ear, Grace saw and heard him amid his piles of bricks, in his old age slowly—*very* slowly— putting asunder what he had joined together in his youth—*tink! tink!*— the sole remainder of her mother's bequest.

That first little fraud, the matter of the colts, had garnered Judge Grant $135. But what had it cost him? She wondered if he had suffered agonies of conscience, lying awake of nights, the first time—the second time—the third time—he'd cheated her by transferring his losses to her account. Had he ever resolved to make up the losses, restore what he had stolen? Or had he assured himself that he was only making temporary loans to himself? Assured himself that he was only repaying himself for the trouble of administering the trust? Assured himself that he was entitled to deduct fees from time to time, as the money had come from his own sister, who surely would have been eager to help him through his times of financial need? Assured himself that the niece was unlikely ever to show up; was probably dead; certainly did not know of this trust, and unknowing, suffered no harm; and had no better claim to his sister's money than he had?

Had he suffered? Had his suffering increased with the magnitude of his fraud?

Or had it become easier, less troubling to him, as time passed— passed without repercussions, without adverse consequences, without shame of exposure or fear of penalty?

To think that she had loved him, a little!

Grace turned back again to the pages for the year 1822. She had at first skimmed rapidly over these early pages, but now she studied them closely. That year had ended at $2,126, very nearly where it had begun. Here were interest payments received, from two borrowers; here was a repayment of principal from another; and a new note issued, for $733.

And here, on November 15, was something else, quite different: *expenses reimbursed to A. Johnstone for her voyage to Scotland: <$171.54>*.

It was rather bitter, Grace thought, that her uncle had deducted from her trust the expenses incurred by Miss Johnstone in her attempt to kidnap Grace.

And what could be the meaning of the following entry? *November 15th: loss of trust property (absconded, & unrecov'ble): <$150.00>*

There was nothing on this page to indicate what property belonging to her trust might have been lost, absconded, unrecoverable. But Grace felt saliva flood her mouth, and her heart beat in her ears. She turned back to the previous page, for 1821.

He had made corrections at the bottom of this page. The original totals for the cash and assets columns had been crossed out—not just lined through but obliterated, under blots of dark ink—and revised totals were written just beneath.

And his last entry for the year, above the double underscores, looked as though it had been squeezed in, she thought. Usually he left four or five blank lines under his last entry and above the double underscores, but on this page there were only three blank lines now, under the last entry: *28th Decbr: purchase: slave wench Annie, age 15 years: $150.00. Bill/ sale & title transfer r'corded @ Leesburg.*

Quickly Grace checked the arithmetic, beginning with the balances at the bottom of the page from the previous year, 1820; and finishing with the year-end balances for 1821. Yes, he had indeed subtracted the sum of $150 from the cash column; and added it to the assets column; and his revised totals reflected that $150 transaction. In December 1821, according to this account book, he had sold Annie to his niece's trust.

By this arrangement, he had paid himself $150 out of Grace's trust, for the unrecoverable slave—and she herself (all unknowing) had lost a slave worth that sum. But why backdate the sale to December of the previous year? Did the fraud seem less obvious, less calculated, with a few more months under its belt? Why hadn't he entered the transaction in, say, March 1822—after Annie's baby had been born? It took only a moment for her to realise that it was because he didn't know, in March, that Annie was going to run away. And by October, when he received Miss Johnstone's letter (she could see in her mind's eye the entry in his 1822 daybook: *Letter from Miss J advising that Annie has run off in Scotland*)—there was no room to write the sale onto the 1822 page with a blameless preembarkation date—for it had been an active year, with several transactions each month. So he had squeezed it in at the bottom of the 1821 page instead.

PERHAPS HE'D CONSIDERED himself justified in this fraud. Had he convinced himself that the transaction was a legitimate and allowable expense connected with the attempt to fetch his niece home to Grantsboro? But no, Grace realised; if he had honestly believed that, he would have charged the loss of his slave directly to her account, just as he had charged Miss Johnstone's travel expenses. He had known very well that he was dishonest, or he would not have thought it necessary to backdate the transfer of title to the previous year.

Grace pored very closely through the entries for the following years, looking for similar anomalies. But he had apparently continued honestly—according to his lights, at least—for the following three or four years, for she found nothing more until she came to the one that had caught her eye earlier: the three colts, dead of glanders, in 1826. Perhaps until 1826 his conscience had troubled him sufficiently to deter any more raids, until he found himself in financial quicksand. But from 1826 onward, he had resorted to that particular technique of embezzlement with increasing frequency.

SHE LEANED BACK and closed her eyes, needing to think. The fly still buzzed against the windowpanes; the clerks' pens still scratched at their paper. Anyone might be wrong; was she wrong?

Judge Grant's executors in Leesburg had no way of knowing that one of the trust's slave assets—written off years ago as unrecoverable—had suddenly reappeared in America, within reach. And though they had informed Mr MacFarlane of the embezzled trust—informed him in sufficient detail for him to report it to the heirs—Mr MacFarlane could not have studied the accounts for himself. He could not have seen this account book—this proof that Anibaddh was not now, and had not been since December 1821, the property of Judge Grant or his heirs.

This account book proved furthermore that Anibaddh's infant Diana, born the following month, had never belonged to them either.

There was no legal basis for the claim which they had brought to court before Judge Lewis.

"HERE IS THE COMPLETE and correct copy of the deed your husband has signed, ma'am—" said the head clerk Mr Collins.

But Grace interrupted him: "I must speak with Mr Ogden, immediately, please—oh, aye, it is exceedingly important. Of supreme importance and urgency."

And when Mr Ogden grudgingly emerged from his private office, Grace said, "Oh, Mr Ogden! One must not leap to conclusions—and indeed, I do not think I have leapt to any unwarranted conclusions—but look at this, sir, pray, and tell me whether I am not justified in desiring to send instantly—instantly, sir, to Mr Brown!"

. . .

GRACE WAS USING NOT WATERCOLORS BUT OILS FOR THIS miniature; and she was painting not upon an ivory disk, but upon a small rectangle of silver-plated copper. Two days earlier, she had taken up a broad brush and laid down her ground—mostly yellow ochre, dirtied with a little raw umber, and paled with lead white. What a tide of relief, of ease, had washed over her then, as she had lapped paint over that silvery surface! Now that the ground had dried for two days, she saw that a faint palimpsest of the underlying image—the mirror image of her uncle's handwriting—was perhaps still just discernible, though far from intelligible. Or was it only her imagination? In any case, Grace intended to apply more paint.

She studied her sitter; laid out tiny gouts of lead white, raw umber, and ivory black in addition to her yellow ochre upon her tiny palette; and began the sketch *en grisaille*.

"Noisy, aren't they?" remarked the Rani; for the two men repairing the roof over the back half of the house sounded like half a dozen at least.

"Very. And it costs me a vast deal of mental effort to keep them from falling off," said Grace. "They might tie themselves to the chimney, of course—but being men, they won't. They disdain to take any such precaution."

"They cannot help it, the poor dears," said Anibaddh. "Keeping safe is women's work."

"Catching them when they fall—throwing ourselves under them, to soften their fall—holding them up in thin air by the sheer force of our will, or of our virtue—*that* is women's work," said Grace.

"Davy fallen off of the roof one time, at Grantsboro, when he was fourteen," volunteered Diana, the sitter, from her chair on the raised platform. "He was a-cleaning of the chimneys. But he only fallen in a bush, and got hardly a scratch. He fallen off of those horses too, plenty of times, until he learn how to stick onto them."

For Diana, every subject led to Davy. This was forgivable, as she and Davy were to be married in New York within a fortnight. From there, she was to return with Davy to Montreal, where he had secured a place as undercoachman for an opulent family of that city. Canada suited Davy very well—far better than did America, where he was a fugitive in law, and thus liable to re-enslavement if caught. But his betrothed Diana was now indubitably free.

Diana had a great deal to say about Davy's feats of strength, Davy's cleverness, Davy's mastery of horses, and Davy's superlative prospects in Canada, a place she evidently pictured as a northerly Eden. Her mother drew her out, though scant encouragement was needed. Diana was eager, as she sat for her likeness, to recount the details of their courtship: the difficulties they had suffered when separated, at first by only the few miles between Grantsboro and Arrochar; and then by the much greater—the perhaps insuperable—distance between Virginia and Canada, after he had run away. Grace once let herself meet the Rani's eyes, and saw there some well-concealed amusement behind the tender maternal indulgence.

It seemed marvelous to Grace that although she had always felt very near to Anibaddh—had always trusted and loved her—it was only now that she knew that they were indeed kin, joined in the person of Diana. The Rani patiently listened as her daughter—Grace's cousin—rejoiced in her bright plans; and Grace marveled privately: We *are* kin. We always were.

WHEN GRACE HAD proceeded as far as she could at one sitting (for oils dried far more slowly than did watercolors, even in this heat), Diana went away, full of the urgent necessity of completing her trousseau before embarking with her mother and half-brothers aboard *Rebecca Rolfe*, which had been sold to new owners in New York and was due to sail some five or six days hence.

Anibaddh remained behind. From the studio window she watched her daughter walk along the street below, around the corner, out of sight. Only then did she turn to Grace and ruefully admit, "I still cannot quite slake my thirst for the sight of her. My daughter, a free woman! I think she is a little less angry with me now than she was at first. But she has not forgiven me."

"That may require some time," said Grace.

"Eighteen years of abandonment! She may never forgive me that. But she has some petty grievances too. Just now, she cannot forgive me for not being Davy, come back to lead her north. She'd been warned to expect someone, that night—and had made up her mind it would be Davy! Quite *expected* Davy."

"I hope she'll forgive *him* promptly, as she's so determined to marry him."

"Poor Davy! It is a wonder that I did not have to ransom—or somehow spirit away—numerous grandchildren too; for she has given me to understand that she is a thorough-grown woman, and not to be mistaken for some innocent maiden. I hope nothing is wrong there, as regards this lack of babies, I mean. But I will suppose that the miles separating them—he at Grantsboro, and she at Arrochar—might account for that. It is clear that no maternal hints are wanted as to the performance of conjugal rights and duties. She is quite sure that she knows a great deal more about the matter than I ever have."

Grace thought of the old woman whose cabin across the creek at Arrochar was surrounded by a thicket of Barbados flower: Krishna Chura. Had that malignant old alchemist, cultivating her potent beans, anything to do with the absence of children at Arrochar? But some things were outside the scope of what could positively be known—by herself, at least; and this was one of them. Grace must content herself with ignorance. "Had Diana indeed been told to expect you, that night?" she asked.

"Told only to be ready—told that someone was likely to come, if not that night, then the next, or the next, to bring her north to freedom. The who, the how, and the wherefore of it all are forever to remain deep secrets, though; and I know only a little of it myself. Several people helped us, guided us—people whose names I'll never know. There are many deep and well-kept secrets there, secrets not shared even between father and son."

Grace thought of old Mr MacFarlane playing his pipes, that night on the dam at Arrochar; thought of the tune he had played, and its various names: "Too Long in This Condition." "The MacFarlanes' Gathering." *Thogail nam Bo theid sinn.* "To Lift the Cows We Shall Go." She suspected that the elder Mr MacFarlane kept certain secrets from his son—and from most of his neighbors. But that too lay beyond what she could know. Grace said, "It must be difficult to contemplate giving her up again, so soon after finding her."

"Oh—perhaps not so very hard! Not so hard as it would be if she were well brought up, or even civil! I daresay that Mrs Pollocke is sorrier to give up Miss Babcock—whom I *did* bring up, I will point out— than I am to relinquish my uncivil daughter. In any case, I shall have her miniature to gaze fondly upon, by way of consoling myself. May I see? Ah! Just as handsome as herself, but quieter; and far more respectful. I do hope she and Davy will learn to read and write. She told me yesterday that I was the onliest negro she ever hear talk like a white missus, and it give her a start every time I open my mouth."

"Ah! And what said you to that?"

"I informed her that her conversation had startled me from time to time too. But enough of my furious lusty daughter. Look; Mr Brown has returned to me a certain invaluable paper, and I have discreetly brought it along to return it to you, in private."

Grace knew it instantly, from its outer folds. Nevertheless, she opened it, to look once more upon this artifact, this artifice, her own artful forgery. Might it indeed have stood up in court? Might it indeed have convinced that peevish judge? She really thought it might. "One ought not to boast of one's own accomplishments," she remarked, "but I do believe that my version of my uncle's handwriting is as good as his own. Do you wish to see it burnt? The only fire in the house is down in the kitchen."

"Do with it as you please. It is yours. I don't need to see it destroyed."

"I do, though," said Grace. "It has been like an unruly child, a prodigal son; not at all what I, its mother, had intended or hoped. What distress its existence has caused me!"

"I can imagine," said Anibaddh. "I owe you a great debt."

"No, Rani, you owe me nothing; but I do think that I have succeeded at last in retiring that old debt which I have owed you since I was eight years old."

THE SLATER AND HIS assistant had begun by removing a score of slates. Then it had become apparent that the flashings around the chimney and in the valleys behind the dormers needed replacing too. And when the old corroded flashings were peeled back, it was revealed that a great many of the roof boards were suffering from rot as well, and ought by rights to be replaced. Within days, most of the back half of the roof, the part over Grace's bedroom, had been dismantled. The slates had been stacked for reuse, and the unsound boards torn off and thrown down, a pile of wreckage in the backyard—to the detriment of the cucumber vines growing there.

As dusk drew in, the slater and his assistant had once more descended their ladders and gone home, promising to return in the morning. Luckily the weather had continued clear and dry, though each day now was hotter than the one before; and the nights brought little relief.

DANIEL HAD SAID that he might be late again. After Grace had put Jamie to bed, she ventured to enter the spare bedroom, where she and Dan had been sleeping while the roof underwent repairs. It was on the south side of the house, and it was stifling. It would be like sleeping in a tandoor. The windows were open, and mosquitoes cruised along the wall over the bed.

Grace climbed the winding narrow stair to the top of the house once more. As she opened the door to her unroofed bedroom, a gust of hot air entered with her, having—like herself—spiraled up the winding central stair, to gush upward—outward—skyward. Only the ridge beam and rafters remained overhead; the walls rose up to meet darkening sky.

WARM MIDNIGHT AIR STIRS, lifts, bringing the tidal-mud smell of the river, from two streets away. The gauze canopy which Grace has hung from the roof beam overhead sways, rocks, lifts. Grace has made a room of gauze; ceiling and walls of transparent *baft-hana* muslin draped from roof beam and rafters: a scrim, a screen, a transparent tent. The gauze spills onto the floor around the mattress which she has dragged up the stairs.

It is near midnight when Daniel finds her here. Lying on her back, she can hear baffled mosquitoes just outside the muslin mesh—but here, inside it, her pale uncovered starlit skin is protected; his too. Just above her lips is poised Daniel's collarbone; his collarbone in which she rejoices, as she rejoices in every part of him. She closes her eyes to taste the salt on his skin; the shape of the collarbone; the particular texture: *his* skin. Opens her eyes again, to see beyond this cherished shoulder (oh, his chest; his strong arms!) through the loose translucent weave wafting, rippling, breathing; up into the dome of black sky filled by the Shining Ones, the approving ones.

Ravishing, those brightest three: Deneb, Vega, Altair—that vast triangle embossed upon summer's night sky—so delightful to the eye, so reassuring—for here is pattern, here is geometry; here, therefore, must not there be design? Meaning? Intent? But no; they are only constellations: Cygnus, Lyra, Aquila; swan, harp, eagle; gorgeous accidents, whose tales, meanings, names are only fictions devised by other humans not much wiser than oneself, fictions devised to explain the inexplicable; to dispel fear. How exquisite nevertheless! How lovely they are, straddling the broad gorgeous splash, that celestial river, that Milky Way!

She has swathed herself too; has wrapped herself around and around—seven proverbial layers deep, as courtesans do—with the precious *baft-hana* cotton Daniel brought from Bengal. She has wound the ends together in a loose knot, so that it scarcely stays on her hips.

Now the knot comes untied by itself; and that is the last thing they know.

On AUGUST 19, 1839, LOUIS-JACQUES-MANDÉ DAGUERRE'S stunning invention known as the daguerreotype—the first practical photographic process—was announced to the world. His ownership of the process had been purchased from him by the French government, and the details were published immediately as a "free gift to the world"—*offert à l'humanité, libre de droits*—free except in England and Wales, where a patent had been already secured. Within days, the seventy-nine-page pamphlet had been translated and published in English.

The new process was promptly taken up in America by various practitioners, notably in Philadelphia by the resourceful and ingenious Robert Cornelius. His self-portrait, reproduced in this novel, is one of the earliest photographic portraits ever made, probably in October 1839. The other two arresting portraits reprinted in this novel were indeed made at the studio Mr Cornelius established in the spring of 1840 at the corner of South Eighth Street and Lodge Alley in Philadelphia. As the true identities of those two sitters have been lost, I have taken the liberty of attributing their fascinating faces to the fictional characters Grace MacDonald Pollocke and her husband Daniel Pollocke.

We are at a loss, from our twenty-first-century perspective, to understand how eighteenth- and nineteenth-century American slaveholders (among them four of the first five Presidents of the United States) justified their "ownership" of other human beings. Those justifications are worth examining not only for the light thus shed upon our national past, but also because they illuminate the methods by which individuals and polities continue to attempt to maintain even their least tenable positions. The sermon delivered by Thornton String-fellow in Chapter 14 of this novel is drawn literally from his influential essay *A Brief Examination of Scripture Testimony on the Institution of Slavery*, first published in 1841. (There is, however, no factual reason to suppose that he was personally as perverse as I have drawn him here.) I have referred also to Thomas Roderick Dew's economic and social arguments set forth in his 1832 essay *Abolition of Negro Slavery*. The invaluable book *The Ideology of Slavery* (edited by Drew Gilpin Faust, Louisiana State University Press, 1981) offers a survey of these and other constantly shifting justifications central to nineteenth-century American discourse about slavery.

David Paul Brown, whose forensic eloquence I have enlisted in defense of my fictional characters, was the great eminence of nineteenth-century Philadelphia courtrooms. In setting forth his views upon the admissibility of atheist witnesses, I have used his own words from his 1856 autobiography *The Forum; or, Forty Years Full Practice at the Philadelphia Bar*. Mr Brown also figures repeatedly, and heroically, in William Still's powerful (but disgracefully seldom-read) classic account *The Underground Railroad* first published in 1872.

All of the other characters in this novel are entirely fictional.

Peg Kingman
Potter Valley, 2009

ACKNOWLEDGMENTS

Many people have generously shared with me their time, resources and expertise during the making of this book. In particular, I must thank Walt Barr, Valerie Kelly, Gerry Teasley, Roger Turner, and Cynda Vallee. I owe thanks also to Bruce Laverty at The Athenaeum of Philadelphia; Phil Lapsansky at The Library Company of Philadelphia; and Karen Hughes-White and her staff at the Afro-American Historical Association of Fauquier County.

I must also acknowledge my debt to those who are no longer living. I have made use of works authored by David Paul Brown and Thornton Stringfellow, attributing their published words to fictional versions of themselves. I have also drawn from many other contemporary observers, travelers, writers, journalists, and diarists; and have put their very phrases - in some instances word for word - into the mouths and minds of my fictional characters. I have mined the writings of Fanny Kemble, Sidney George Fisher, Harriet Martineau, Fanny Parks, Isaac Mickle, William Still, Mary Chesnut, Frances Trollope, George Chinnery and many others, appropriating their insights and their authentic language.

I am grateful to my editor Starling Lawrence, and all the people at W. W. Norton who have applied their patient, courteous and diligent expertise to the making of this book.

Finally, I must express my thanks to my husband David Turner, for his unflagging support and kind encouragement.